THE SONS OF BRUNOS

P. C. MULRONEY

The Sons of Brunos

Copyright ©2024 by P. C. Mulroney

First Printing, 2024

ISBN: 979-8-9915876-0-0 – Hardcover
ISBN: 979-8-9915876-1-7 – Softcover
ISBN: 979-8-9915876-2-4 – Ebook
ISBN: 979-8-9915876-3-1 – Audio book

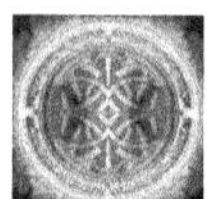

Published by P. C. Mulroney
www.sonsofbrunos.com

Cover design by: - **Leraynne S.** @leraynne
Map design by: - P. C. Mulroney & Chaim Holtjer
Book Interior and E-book Design by Amit Dey (amitdey2528@gmail.com)

This book is dedicated to my family who have always encouraged my imagination. A special thanks to PM, MH, and WM for their advice, patience and support.

CONTENTS

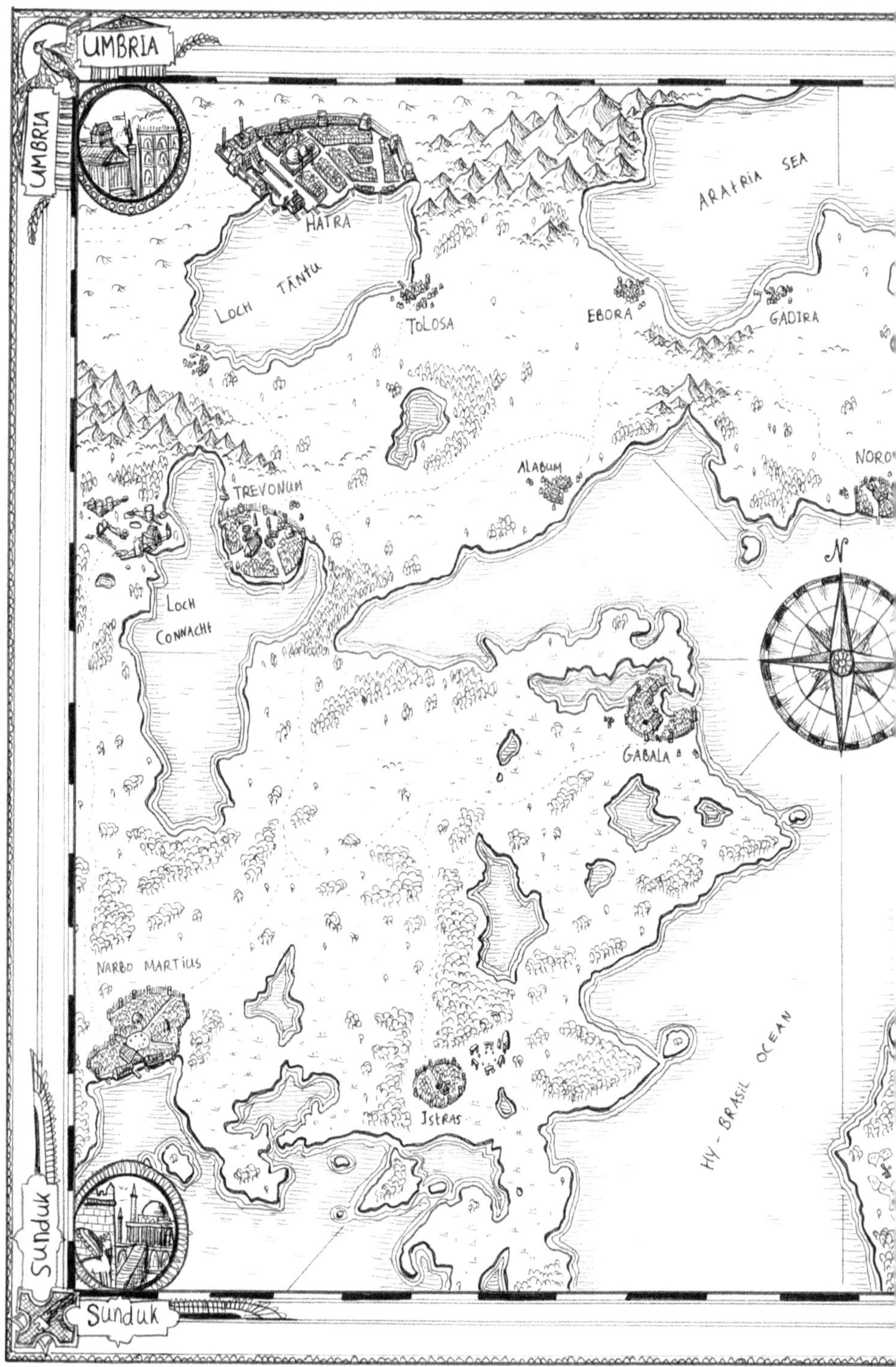

UMBRIA
UMBRIA
UMBRIA
Sunduk
Sunduk
HATRA
LOCH TANTU
TOLOSA
ARATRIA SEA
EBORA
GADIRA
ALABUM
NORO
TREVONUM
LOCH CONNACHT
GABALA
N
NARBO MARTIUS
ISTRAS
HY-BRASIL OCEAN

TALAMH
GALICIA
GALICIA
GALICIA
BALIF
BALIF
KUNDUZ
SANGUIS SEA
SUSA
TARSUS
GENUA
SINOPE
DUEA
PATAVIUM
LAKE DULCIS
MYOS
TEOS
OPPIDUM
IASC SEA
NEAPOLIS
EDESSA
MEDBIAN
APOLINA
KARALIS

CHAPTER 1

THE JOURNEY BEGINS

Valerik entered the senate chamber with head held high and an exaggerated sway in his step. The young general made his way to the heart of the senate floor and looked above at the second-floor balcony to see all the Republic's leaders staring down on him. Each senator sat along the benches that wrapped around the marble mezzanine. A grandiose podium stood tall in the center of the pews, directly overlooking the senate floor below. Behind the podium was a small staircase, which led to the private council chambers reserved only for the members of Umbria's elite government officials.

Valerik looked down upon his superiors who sat on the council. *What have any of these men done?* Valerik thought to himself. *I am a self-made man. An orphan from Apolina, I climbed my way to this point on my own. I studied our people's greatest philosophers. I mastered the techniques of our bravest warriors and yet these sumptuous men sit and decide what is best for Umbria, with no knowledge of the people's hardships. It is a complete disgrace. It needs to change.*

Valerik did not wait for the council master to address him. He took off his helmet and proclaimed, 'I hope this meeting is to give me my reward. I did your job with the Balifates. Their only remaining settlement is Teos and laying siege to that is a fool's errand; one that not even I could accomplish.'

The Senate dressed in the standard royal garb, a luxurious white toga with purple accents, looked down upon Valerik with contempt. The portrayal of arrogance and disrespect from the general had disgusted Umbria's senators and council members. After an uncomfortable silence, Pravus, the council master, begrudgingly spoke. 'Your efforts with the Balifates are not only noted but greatly appreciated Valerik, however there is a new enemy.'

Valerik looked up at the Pravus with disgust. Pravus was a pale, skinny and conniving man, no more than fifty-five in age. For years he had gained wealth and power at the expense of the common citizens. It was clear he valued his own agenda above the Republic. 'I tire of your constant warmongering Pravus. I finish one war, and you start another!' he exclaimed in an outburst.

Frustrated, Valerik closed his eyes before taking a step back from the council floor. He turned towards the massive chamber exit. After a moment, he opened his eyes and looked at the light shining through the door cracks that led to the city plaza. He heard the clicking of wooden carts being pulled by horse, and the chatter of the people outside in the city's forum. His anger subsided after remembering who he was truly fighting for. He turned back around to face the Senate and asked, 'Where am I going this time?'

Pravus smiled, showing his decrepit yellow stained teeth. He was pleased to see Valerik's benign compliance. Pravus relished the moment. He loved the authority that he held over Umbria's top general. He grinned ear to ear, and slowly replied, 'To the north. To the eastern tribes of the Galicians, a town called Norova.'

'And what is the crime?' Valerik asked, questioning his orders in an almost defiant tone, upset that yet again he was being dispatched to deal with another war started by the Senate. Valerik had not forgiven the council for their actions in instigating the conflict with the Balifates.

Pravus responded brazenly in a voice devoid of all empathy. 'The chieftain of that tribe, a man named Brunos, attacked and raided two of our settlements east of Norova. The town militias stood no chance against the barbarians. Few survived, even those who did not resist met the same fate.'

Valerik took his worn, battle-scarred helmet, which he held at his side, and placed it on his head. 'To those who shed Umbrian blood, I will show no mercy. I will arrange my men and depart immediately!' Valerik replied. Despite his grievances with the Senate, he would see that justice was brought to anyone that harmed his people. He then bowed to the council before turning back to the large doors from whence he came.

The royal senate guard opened the doors to the grand hall for Valerik. The general examined the Senate's security while leaving the senate building. *These fools truly believe two swordsmen and two spearmen are enough to protect them from danger. Perhaps it was fine a few hundred years ago when Apolina was an independent city state, but now it is just reckless. They should not value tradition above common sense. But maybe I could use their arrogance to my advantage.*

Valerik put aside his thoughts and stepped out of the entranceway to the capitol building. He stood in the center pathway formed by eighteen symmetrical hundred-foot Ionic columns on either side. He took a deep breath and looked out at the capital city of Apolina. The white marble of the government buildings and the stone and brick of the commoners' homes had never looked so appealing. Valerik wanted nothing more than a peaceful life within these walls and thus lamented leaving once again for battle.

He slowly approached the staircase that led down to the city forum. When walking past the last column, he spotted his second in command, Dara, who was waiting for him outside the senate building. Despite the metallic clicking of Valerik's war boots, she had not noticed him leave the chamber. Her dark emerald eyes stared out at the beautiful city below. Her bright red hair flowing in the wind almost matched the silver and burgundy on her battle scarred armor.

Valerik took the first step on the staircase and called out to Dara, 'Are you coming along or are you just going to stand there all day?'

Dara quickly snapped out of her thoughts and rushed to her general's side.

'So, did you get the reward you were expecting?' Dara asked Valerik, hoping the Senate would give her general the recognition and honor he truly deserved.

'No,' Valerik replied with a hint of disgust. 'We did get tasked with another fight, though. The eastern tribes of Galicia. We are meant to go and lay siege to the city of Norova and then report back to the Senate upon our success.'

Dara looked at her general with excitement. She was almost too eager to return to battle, especially after just resolving their four-year conflict with the Balifates only days prior. 'Shall I prepare the men?' she asked impatiently.

'Yes,' Valerik replied sternly. 'With any hope, they will be as eager as you are about this.' The pair then descended the stairs, entering the square where their horses stood waiting tied to a city watering trough. Valerik mounted his black Andalusian steed, Genitor, whose strength and stature mirrored that of his owner.

'Go on ahead,' Valerik commanded, 'I will see you and the men soon at the city limits.'

Dara obeyed her general's orders and rode ahead to go prepare the men while Valerik himself turned towards his home in Apolina. The army would depart at nightfall, which gave the general a few hours of relaxation in his home.

Valerik opened the wooden door to his humble home in the heart of Apolina. The sun gleamed through the front facing windows of Valerik's residence, which overlooked a city courtyard. The pale red mortar walls and dark brown wooden floor complemented the decor Valerik had collected over his many years in Umbria's army. *It is good to be back home,* he thought as he made his way to the bedroom. He unlocked a chest found at the foot of his bed and reached out, grasping an orange tinted blade in his hand. *Looks like I will need your help once again, my old friend,* Valerik thought, staring at the sword in his hand.

Some considered the sword Valerik wielded to be an ancient artifact, perhaps one with even mystical power. Before joining the

Umbrian army, Valerik studied ancient texts which described a warrior clan that lived secretly in ruins along the coast of the Iasc Sea. His unrelenting drive to be the best made him travel to the ruins and there he encountered the ancient warrior tribe. Their people referred to the land as Praeterita and they offered to train Valerik if he could prove himself worthy by passing their people's trials. The trials nearly killed him, but Valerik persevered and proved his worth as a warrior. The sword which Valerik held in his hand was a gift given to him by the grandmaster of the clan. Ever since then, Valerik only used this ancient sword in battle.

The Umbrian general sat in his chair and stared out at the courtyard, polishing his sword. *There truly is no better place than Apolina. If only all the world could share in this beauty.* He knew it was almost time to reconvene with his troops, but he waited as long as possible before leaving, just sitting and enjoying the city that he called home.

When the time for departure came Valerik made his way to the city limits where Dara had gathered the men. From there, they all embarked on their new conquest. The journey to Norova was simple, but long. It took Valerik and his army nearly twenty days to march through the flat plains of the Umbrian countryside, which were full of grain fields and orchards, only being interrupted by the occasional small forest and bustling brook. During the journey, Valerik amassed an even larger army by recruiting men in the towns he passed. Soldiers from Karalis, Neapolis and Oppidum all wanted an opportunity to serve under the legendary command of Umbria's greatest phenom. These new enlistees brought his total men to a respectable forty-two hundred, all ready to fight and die for their general. This army dwarfed the militia of Norova, which stood at only fourteen hundred soldiers led by their chieftain Brunos.

As the Umbrian army marched, the unsuspecting people of Norova continued about their daily lives. Norova was a modest settlement built upon a small hill overlooking the Hy-brasil Ocean on the south side. A wooden palisade surrounded the town, enclosing all the dirt roads and wooden homes with thatched roofs within. At the heart of the town, there was a large cobblestone meeting hall with a wooden roof. This building was luxury by Norovan standards and it is where all major gatherings took place in the town. Besides functioning as a political gathering place, it was also the home of the chieftain, Brunos.

Brunos was a tall and powerfully built man. His hair was dirty blonde with a raggedy beard to boot. A good father and fair leader, the citizens of Norova adored him. Even though he was a ferocious warrior on the battlefield, he and his fourteen hundred men were woefully unprepared for the impending threat, which was fast approaching.

Brunos and his sons were having dinner in the town hall when they heard the war horns blaring from the wooden palisade. Immediately, Brunos jumped to his feet, with his son Vindex following closely behind. They rushed out of their dwelling in the center of the village and found Norova under attack. Valerik had attacked immediately as he believed it would be a quick battle.

'I want that ballista ready now!' Valerik exclaimed, pointing his men towards Norova's northern gate.

Four legionaries quickly rushed to push the large wooden crossbow within range of the wooden wall. They then loaded a bolt into the track and fired at the Norova gate. The iron gateway buckled under the force of the ballista shot. Before the Galicians had time to fortify their defenses, a second crash roared through the barbarian town. The Umbrians were not waiting for their adversary to deploy a defensive position.

Brunos looked around at the calamity that enveloped him. Galician soldiers were running to the northern gate, some with nothing but a sword in hand. The unexpected sneak attack from the Umbrians gave the Norova natives little time to react. Dust scattered the air from all the soldiers pounding over the dirt road. Brunos knew what was about to happen. He turned to his oldest son and said, 'Vindex, get you and your brother out of the town. Use the western gate on the south shore. Take one of the caravan horses stationed there and make sure no one sees you. Do you understand?'

'No! I won't leave you. I want to fight with you. I am a man now. Stop treating me like a boy,' Vindex firmly retorted, disobeying his father's wishes for the first time.

Brunos lost his temper and yelled, 'You are sixteen! You are not an adult, much less a man! Now get your younger brother and leave this place at once and do not come back until I send for you. Is that understood?'

Vindex looked at his father. Sweat was building on his forehead. His eyes were darting back and forth, and his jaw was twitching. Vindex would contest no more. He had never seen his father like this, and he quickly agreed to the plan. Vindex turned around and ran back inside the hall to retrieve his brother. Before entering the hall, Vindex heard one last thunderous crack. The city gate had fallen. Vindex looked over to see his father sprinting to join the Galicians at the opened gateway.

Brunos ran quickly through the empty streets, arriving at the gates just when the dust began settling. He stared out at the open gateway and saw a tall, brawny man standing in front of the battle line. Each soldier tightened the grip on their blades, sensing the battle was about to begin. The Umbrians, awaiting their orders, looked to Valerik, who stood in front of the battle line only twenty paces from the Galician gateway.

The general took off his helmet and clearly announced, 'Brunos, come out and attest to your crimes and we shall occupy this town peacefully. Stay back in the crowd and I will show the same mercy you displayed to my people.'

The Galician soldiers, most of whom were shirtless only with a spear or sword in hand, were steadfastly awaiting Brunos' response. Brunos, tactfully buying more time for his soldiers to don their leather and metal tunics, replied, 'What crime do you speak of?'

Valerik knew what Brunos was planning. He idly watched the Galician soldiers gather their tunics and kilts and equip their shields. His distrust of the Senate made him want to hear the barbarian's side of the story. He stared Brunos in the eyes and spoke, 'You have made an act of war against our Republic. You and your forces raided, pillaged, and murdered the citizens of Patavium and Genua. I offer a simple deal. Accept an honorable death at my blade and we occupy Norova peacefully integrating it into our Republic. Resist and you will all perish.'

Brunos looked behind him to see that his troops had equipped most of their gear. He then replied, 'The Galician people do not wander west of Norova. I ordered no attack. I have no ill will for the Etruscan people. Perhaps your information is incorrect.'

'The Etruscans …' Valerik mumbled before elevating his voice so all the Galicians would hear. 'The Etruscans have not existed for many decades and I believe you know this, Brunos. Stop stalling for time. Do you accept my deal or not?'

Brunos looked out at the daunting number of Umbrian soldiers standing behind Valerik. He felt a pit in his stomach forming. He spoke. 'I offer a new deal. I will go with you. If that means my end, so be it, but you have to leave my home. Let my people remain free and I will go with you.'

Valerik paused for a moment, considering the offer. 'No,' he said. 'Norova will be occupied or destroyed. That is my offer. Sacrifice yourself and let your people join our Republic's prosperity or be a coward and let your people perish.'

Brunos turned his head to his fellow countrymen. A single tear fell from his eye as he thought about his children. With a heavy sigh, Brunos sheathed his blade and stepped forward towards the Umbrian army. Just before crossing the threshold of the gate, Brunos felt a hand on his shoulder. One of his citizens had grabbed him, preventing him from leaving the town. Brunos turned his head to see all the Galician soldiers take a step forward, signifying they would not let their leader go.

'Please,' Brunos whimpered. 'This is the only way. We don't have the forces to fight them.'

The man holding Brunos' shoulder looked his chieftain in the eyes and spoke. 'Live by the sword, die by the sword. Whether I live or die, I want to be free. I will not be made a slave.'

Brunos saw the rest of his people salute over their chest, signifying they were ready for battle. He then wiped his tears from his face and stood tall. He took out his blade once more and pointed at Valerik, speaking, 'No deal. For my people, I will fight.'

'Ironic,' Valerik replied. 'If you truly cared about your people, you would have surrendered. And now you and your village will pay the ultimate price.' He turned to his men, pointed at Brunos, and spoke, 'Soldiers, do what we came here to do, but leave that one alive for me.' He then stepped back as his proud legionaries, led by Dara, charged into the open gateway. The Galician warriors gallantly challenged the legionaries refusing to back down.

Vindex and Viridox heard the Umbrian legionaries' long shields clashing with the Galician battle line all the way on the opposite side of the city. The brothers were almost at the west gate when Viridox asked his brother, 'What is going on? Who is invading us? Where are we going?'

Viridox was three years younger than Vindex and was far less mature. He held onto his older brother's hand as they ran through the city streets. Vindex replied, while guiding his brother, 'The city is not safe. Father told us to run and take one of the caravan horses until the invasion is over. We will wait on the coastline away from the city until he sends for us.'

Viridox nodded his head, understanding their orders. When they arrived at the gate, they saw only one horse tied next to the entrance. Vindex quickly ran over and helped his younger brother mount the beast and then ran to the wall. He quietly peered through the cracks of the palisade in order to see if the coast was clear. With no attackers in sight, Vindex unlocked the gate and guided the horse and his brother outside. He then mounted the steed and rode west, fleeing from the battle. After some time, the pair stopped along the coastline and looked out at their town, hoping that the fight would soon be over and that they could return to their home.

The battle inside the city walls raged on as the sun set over the horizon. Brunos and his men were slowly faltering. The Galicians could only look on in horror as the number of Umbrian soldiers seemed to increase with each advance they made. Galician soldiers lay dead or wounded everywhere one looked on the battlefield, but this did not waver Brunos. The chieftain remained on the front line, encouraging his troops with his exhibits of strength.

His powerful frame and warrior training made him the best of any Galician soldier. Brunos swung his sword, slicing an Umbrian legionary while stunning another with a ferocious shield bash to the invader's face. With the legionary fallen on the street, Brunos stepped on the Umbrian soldier and screamed, 'For Norova!'

The Galician fighters let out a bombastic chant in their native tongue, 'Troid! Troid! Troid!'

Brunos continued on the offensive, devastating the Umbrian front line, slaying or crippling two dozen Umbrian legionaries by himself. 'We will retake the gate!' Brunos exclaimed. 'Push them back and make a chokehold! We can still win!'

Another ferocious roar overcame the Galician soldiers, who now pushed back the Umbrian advances. Galician morale was at an all-time high and the soldiers from Norova believed they could defeat the Umbrian army. Brunos led the soldiers from the center, pushing the legionaries in the street back to the gateway, when he suddenly heard the chanting stop from his army's right wing.

Umbria's second strongest warrior had cut through the Galician lines and was now devastating the right flank of the army. This destructive force was no other than Valerik's second in command, Dara. She silenced dozens of brave Norova citizens in mere moments, smiling as their lifeless bodies fell onto the dirt road. She looked up to see the surrounding Galicians had stopped chanting. They looked on in fear, shaking at the power they had witnessed.

'It's always funny to see how quickly hope dies when faced with bleak reality,' Dara spoke, staring at her opponents. 'So now, who's next?'

By the time Brunos had even noticed her on the battlefield, she had already decimated his right wing. He saw countless Galicians laying in the dirt, their blood pooling around one woman who had a horrifying genial smile upon her face. He turned to his soldiers and said, 'Hold the line here. Stop the advance. I will deal with her.'

He then left the center line, dodging and blocking swings of iron and steel that blocked his path to Dara. She noticed her new challenger approaching and took her battle stance, waiting for what she hoped to be a worthy opponent. Brunos knew this opponent wouldn't be like the rest of Valerik's soldiers. He carefully took a stance of his own and the pair inched towards each other as soldiers on either side continued to fight around them in a pocket.

'I've been looking forward to this,' Dara said with a sinister grin as she pointed her blade at Brunos' throat. 'You're just lucky my general wants you alive.'

Brunos, not finding the situation as amusing as his dueling counterpart, retorted, 'I wonder if your blade is as sharp as your tongue, you wench.'

Dara's brow frowned as she raised her sword. With a loud scream, she took the first swing, slashing her blade against Brunos' shield. Brunos retaliated, driving his shield into her shoulder, overpowering the Umbrian warrior. Dara quickly had to disengage and step sideways to avoid being thrown into the crowd of fighting soldiers behind her. After regaining her balance, she attempted to stab Brunos' side, which he parried with the side of his own blade. The two then circled each other, awaiting their next opportunity to strike. After a few prods back and forth, Brunos saw an opening to strike.

Dara stood too close to the hoard of men surrounding her on her left side. Brunos used this opportunity and charged shield first and sword drawn to push her into the crowd. Dara immediately realized what Brunos was trying to do, and she quickly dropped to the ground. She raised her shield overhead and rolled past Brunos. With one quick thrust of her sword, Dara sliced open Brunos' leg while rolling past her enemy. Dara watched her adversary fall to one knee in pain as she proudly raised herself from the dusty street. Brunos could now see that the hoard of soldiers surrounding him were almost entirely Umbrian. He knew he had lost.

No, Brunos thought to himself. *I will not die here. I will not let this be the end of Norova. For my sons, for my people, I will fight!*

Brunos gripped his sword tighter than ever before and screamed a heroic roar. He powered through his pain and attempted to stand once more. Dara grew annoyed with this display of defiance. She stood behind his back as she watched him hobble up to his two feet.

'Don't you know when you are beaten?' Dara exclaimed over Brunos' belligerent screaming.

Suddenly, the screaming stopped. Brunos' eyes widened, and the air was stripped from his lungs as he felt a cold iron blade pierce the calf of his uninjured leg. There truly was nothing Brunos could do now. With two injured legs, he fell down once more on the dirt road.

'Pathetic,' Dara scoffed as she put her sword back into her sheath. 'And here I was, hoping for an actual challenge.'

Brunos rolled in the dirt to look up at the battlefield. He did not see a single Galician soldier remaining on the street. The Umbrian legionaries quickly made their way to the city center, where the routed Galicians made their last stand. After a brief skirmish, the battle was over. Brunos lay listening to the victory screams of the Umbrian army. He stared up at the star filled sky and muttered under his breath, 'I'll be seeing you soon, Áine.'

Brunos let out a loud, involuntary cough. His body was going into shock. As his heartbeat slowed and his fatigue increased, Brunos closed his eyes and imagined his two sons far away from the city, safe in the home of a neighboring Galician village. A small smile appeared upon his face as he thought to himself, *At least not all of Norova will perish tonight.*

After seeing her opponent completely defeated, Dara exclaimed, 'Bring in the general!'

The Umbrian legionaries aligned into rows as they made a path for their leader. Shields to their chests, they all stared forward as Valerik slowly made his way into the barbarian town. Brunos saw the opposing leader entering through the gates and, with his remaining strength, he sat up. Brunos felt nothing but a fiery rage as he looked at the man who destroyed his home.

'As you requested, he is still alive,' Dara spoke diligently, standing next to the side of the defeated barbarian leader.

Valerik did not answer his second in command. His eyes were glued to Brunos, and the pair continued to share a hate filled gaze. Before Valerik could interrogate the barbarian about his crimes, Brunos broke the silence. With eyes still locked and in a voice showing no fear, Brunos challenged Valerik and said, 'Why don't you just finish me? Or do you not have the stomach to do the dirty work yourself?'

'Oh, I do, and I will,' responded Valerik methodically. 'Just not yet.' He dragged Brunos through the dirt to the town center outside of the home where the chieftain had lived his entire life. Valerik turned to his men and screamed, 'Burn it down! Burn it all to ash!' He then looked back at Brunos and continued, 'After you see your town destroyed and your people slaughtered, only then will I let you die. Just remember Brunos, you chose this.'

Brunos' face of anger and defiance turned to fear as he helplessly looked on. Tears flowed from his pale blue eyes as the town that he governed his whole life went up in flames. The fire was so bright and the smoke so dark; it shined like a beacon in the night sky. Vindex saw the flames all the way from the coastline and knew something dire had happened.

'Viridox, stay here!' Vindex instructed his brother with an imposing voice, 'I will be back. Promise me that you will not move from this spot.'

'I promise,' Viridox replied, scared and frightened, not knowing what would happen to him or his brother.

'Good. Everything will be okay,' Vindex responded before turning back and running towards the town, which was now overwhelmed with fire. Upon arriving at the west gate, Vindex had to push in past the flames that had spread to the walls. A stench of blood filled the air as Vindex entered the town. He ran down the alleys, narrowly making his way through the fire. He looked in the windows of some homes to find the bodies of dead Galician women and children who had tried to hide from the Umbrian invaders. Vindex felt like vomiting but pressed on, hoping that his dad was alive.

If he is alive, I can find him, we can run. Father knows the chieftain in Trevonum, he can take us there. We can escape. I just need to find him, Vindex thought as he pressed on through the town's streets, narrowly evading Umbrian legionaries patrolling the area. *I need to get home. If father is alive, he will be at the hall. I know it.*

Vindex hurried to the town square, where he heard the calamity of the Umbrian soldiers. He hid behind a crate of animal hides that was not ablaze. He crouched down, hiding behind the crate, and felt a cold liquid soak his dark green pants. Vindex looked down and almost threw up to see he was squatting in a sea of blood. *Who are these monsters?* Vindex thought.

He listened to the crowd and heard some legionaries screaming, 'Ha ha, kill him already! Show the barbarian trash what they deserve!'

Vindex peered over the animal hides to see his father on both knees in the center of the town square. A towering figure which Vindex did not recognize stood over Brunos, humiliating his father.

Valerik paced around the collapsed man and said, 'I hope you enjoyed your last moments – watching everything you have ever loved burn.' He then drew his blade and pointed it at Brunos' throat and calmly said, 'Goodbye, scum.'

'No!' Vindex screamed, revealing himself from behind the crate. He pushed his way through Umbrian soldiers to get to his father's side. He reached into Brunos's belt and pulled out his father's blade. Vindex's eyes were watery as he pointed the sword at Valerik, who stood unnerved above the child.

'Vindex, what are you still doing here?' Brunos screamed with tears flowing from his eyes.

'Ah, it appears we missed one,' Valerik stated as he slowly approached Vindex. 'Are you planning on striking me down, boy?'

Vindex was trembling. Too frightened and nervous, he could muster no reply. Despite all his fears, though, he did not lower his father's blade. He stood there shaking, but would not step away.

'Vindex run!' Brunos screamed in fear. He could not lose anymore to these Umbrians.

'It would be best for you to listen to your chieftain boy,' Valerik spoke.

'I won't let you murder my father,' Vindex said with a weak voice.

Valerik's eyes opened a little. 'Brunos, you didn't tell me you were a father. And yet you still did not take my deal. How selfish are you, Brunos? Why make the children suffer?'

Brunos ignored Valerik and pleaded with his son. 'Vindex, you must flee! Now!'

Valerik took a few steps closer to Brunos and Vindex. 'Why flee? I think we could use this as a good learning moment for the boy, Brunos. Don't you agree?'

Brunos and Vindex did not respond. They remained steadfast, waiting for what the Umbrian would propose next.

'I have always said the younger generations are the future,' Valerik continued. 'Without them, who would carry on the knowledge we discover? Hopefully, this demonstration will teach you Galicians some common sense. Boy, pay close attention! This is what happens to those who do not accept reasonable peaceful propositions. Your father could have avoided everything here tonight if it was not for his pride. I hope in the future you remember that.' He drew his blade and pushed into Brunos' chest in one quick blow.

Vindex watched as the blade pierced his father's chest and protruded several inches through his back. Vindex screamed, 'Father!' He lunged with his father's sword at Valerik, who had no weapon to defend himself, as his sword was stuck in his father's rib cage.

Valerik easily grabbed Vindex's hand with one arm and stopped the blade from swinging further. He released his hand from the sword impaled in Brunos, who now fell lifeless, and turned both arms on Vindex. Valerik twisted Vindex's blade until it fell out of his hands. After he had disarmed Vindex, Valerik slapped the boy with his backhand, causing the Galician to fall at his feet next to his deceased father. 'I hope you understood this lesson. Do not forget my words.'

Vindex was shaking and crying, but could still make out the tyrant of a figure standing above him. He would never forget what this monster looked like. A tall, powerfully built, wide jawed man with deep brown eyes. His deep voice echoed in Vindex's mind.

Valerik stepped backward and proclaimed for all to hear. 'Take what you learned and share it with the rest of the Galicians. Leave here before I change my mind.' Filled with fear, Vindex complied with Valerik's command. He picked up his father's blade and ran out of the still burning city as fast as he could.

Dara approached Valerik, who was watching the child run away. 'Why did you let one live? I thought we were enacting justice and revenge for the actions that this savage did,' she stated while gesturing at Brunos' corpse.

Valerik looked at his second in command and replied, 'To be truthful, Dara, I do not know if Brunos raided our cities.'

'What do you mean?'

'Before the battle, he mentioned the Etruscans. They have been gone for a long time. Why would he assume we were Etruscans if he had raided an Umbrian settlement?'

'We had our orders, and you offered them a peaceful option to join the Republic. You did all that you could do.'

'Perhaps, but I feel something else is at play,' Valerik said, looking out to the distance. 'On our way back to the capital, I want to stop and see Genua and Patavium myself. Something is amiss.'

'Very well. I will inform the soldiers. I still do not understand why you let the boy live though, Valerik. Whether or not Brunos was guilty, we massacred these savages. What is one more barbarian?'

Valerik turned his head and said, 'If Brunos was telling the truth, he did not know of Umbria's existence. There needs to be a living survivor to tell the tale so the rest of Galicia knows we are not a people to be taken lightly.'

'Understood,' Dara replied. 'Shall we go before we burn with the rest of this awful town?'

'Yes. Mount your horse. We are heading for Patavium,' Valerik replied, gesturing to his men to leave the city.

The Umbrians rode off into the night, triumphant in their victory. On the journey to Patavium, Valerik's mind had already forgotten about the boy he let live from Norova. His mind was focusing on the truth of Patavium and Genua.

If my suspicions are true, the Senate has gone too far. If I am right, they will pay dearly, Valerik thought as he rode his horse Genitor through the beautiful countryside.

While this invasion was nothing more than a footnote in Valerik's conquests, it was utterly life changing for Vindex. The young boy ran as fast as he could from the burning town until he reunited with his brother on the coastline. Viridox had kept his promise. He had not moved from the spot where Vindex left him.

'Brother!' Viridox cried out, rushing over to Vindex to hug him, 'What happened, what is going on?'

Vindex looked at his brother with no life in his pale blue eyes, the image of his father's corpse still flashing through his mind. Vindex only snapped out of this trance after seeing his younger brother shaking in fear. Even though Viridox had not seen the atrocities committed by the Umbrians, he still heard the sounds of the battle and the screams of the inhabitants from the coastline.

Vindex knew he must bear a brave face for his brother to lead him to safety. He grabbed Viridox, embracing him in his arms and said, 'I will explain it all later, Viridox. Right now, we just need to get out of here, some place safe where we won't be able to be followed.'

'What about Gadira?' Viridox asked quickly. 'It is a town just north of us. We should be able to make it there in less than a day.'

Vindex immediately rejected the idea. He knew that if they could travel that distance in a day, so could the Umbrian army. There was nowhere else to go besides west. They needed to cross The Withered Peaks of Galdesha. Vindex pointed at the Galdeshan mountains that were in plain view behind Viridox's head and said, 'There. We cross the mountains and run to the Western Galician tribes. Hopefully, they will be able to help us.'

Viridox looked at his brother with deep concern. 'You can't be serious. We'll be eaten by wolves before we pass that mountain.'

Vindex took his brother and placed him back on the horse. Before mounting himself, he told his brother, 'There is no other way. I will gladly face wolves over those Umbrian soldiers.' The two brothers took one last look at their burning home before riding off towards The Withered Peaks of Galdesha.

Just as quickly as it began, the siege had ended and the sons of Brunos were fleeing to the west, hoping to find an asylum with the neighboring tribes. Viridox and Vindex traveled in the dark, relying on the moon for light, uncertain of what would come next.

CHAPTER 2

A CURIOUS SENEX

Vindex and Viridox traveled west through long abandoned and overgrown trading trails. The pair only made stops to rest their horse before continuing their journey. They avoided the main roads and small farms on their travels, fearing the possibility of nearby Umbrians. After many hours, Vindex and his brother were at the pathway to the Withered Peaks of Galdesha. The horse slowly climbed up a short stone and gravel road leading into the mountain valley before descending into the lush landscape. The path was brightened by the moon and Vindex could see beautiful surroundings all around him. Two towering mountain ranges stood tall on either side of the green valley below. Some peaks had jagged and sharp terrain, while others were flat and round. The valley in between was full of life. Wild horses and deer roamed freely over the grassy fields. A lake reflected the moonlight illuminating the only way forward. The narrow stone and gravel path extended the length of the valley to the other side, where it connected to the western Galician tribe's road network.

We are almost there, Vindex thought, leading his horse into the valley.

Viridox looked around his surroundings and asked, 'Vindex, can we rest now? We have reached the mountains and have seen no Umbrians on our travels. I am tired and miserable. I need a break brother … we need a break.'

'Just hold on a little longer,' Vindex answered. 'We will get through this valley and then find a place to shelter.'

Viridox nodded his head after hearing his brother's words. As the horse continued to travel deeper into the valley, Viridox's blue eyes closed. Vindex turned around to see his brother had fallen asleep on the horse. He thought, *It's okay brother. I will protect you.*

Vindex pressed onward, determined to make it to a settlement before morning. Just as he was coming up on the end of the valley's trail, he saw a faint light coming from just under the peak of the last mountain in the northern range. Vindex stopped his horse and examined the mountain. He saw a small, rocky path leading up the side of the mountain slope to where the light was coming from.

'Brother, wake up,' Vindex spoke, gently shaking Viridox. 'Do you see that light? There must be a fire up there.'

Viridox opened his eyes and looked up at the mountain's peaks. 'What light? I don't see anything.'

Vindex did not reply, and watched as his brother closed his eyes once more. Viridox's fatigue was too great, and he was quickly asleep once more. Vindex then turned back to the light. He could not look away. Something unearthly was calling to him. *I have to investigate,* Vindex thought as he rode off the valley path and headed for the mountain trail.

Vindex carefully steered his horse up the mountain, going slowly to ensure that Viridox would not fall off when taking a turn. After a long hard journey up the mountain, Vindex was finally at the last bend. He turned around the corner and saw the light that he was seeking. A bright campsite awaited him two-thousand feet in the sky. The camp was on flat land where a large plateau stretched out from the face of the mountain peak.

Vindex hopped off his horse and grabbed his sleeping brother, carrying him over his shoulder. *Poor brother,* Vindex thought. *He has completely shut down after what he saw today. To be honest, I don't blame him. I would too if I didn't have to keep him safe.*

He walked over to the fire and softly placed Viridox next to the flames. *That should keep you warm,* Vindex thought. He took a moment to watch as his little brother slept. His green long-sleeved tunic and brown trousers were dirty and ripped from the long, hard journey. The outfit hung loosely over the thin angular body. His face was young and capped by short, unruly blonde hair. Vindex thought, *I will keep you safe. I promise.* He then turned around to face the mountain's slope. The fire was still burning strongly, so Vindex knew he was not alone. He needed to find whoever lit the flame.

Vindex grasped his father's blade and walked away from the fire. He looked around his surroundings and noticed the path up the mountain slope had ended at the plateau. There appeared to be no path to the summit, as the peak was too steep to climb. He then noticed structures carved into the mountainside. He stepped closer and saw four doorways and eight windows. Someone had quarried homes on the face of the granite summit. The entrances appeared to be barren of all life. There was no melted wax from candles in the windows, no wood or cloth on the exterior, just pure clean carved granite. It appeared as if no one had lived here for generations.

I've got you now, Vindex thought as he cautiously approached the rocky homes embedded in the mountain slope. Before entering the first structure, he looked once more at the campsite and pathway leading up the mountain to make sure that no one was within sight. He saw no one aside from his horse and brother. He took a deep breath and moved quickly into the open doorway.

'Argh my head!' Vindex angrily grunted, covering his face in his hands. 'Who builds a home only two feet wide?'

He ignored his throbbing head and continued his search. He put his arm out to lead by touch, as the moonlight was not enough to illuminate the inside. After carefully feeling the entire area, Vindex found the inside of the structure was no more than two feet wide. *Is this an unfinished building?* Vindex thought. I suppose *it does not matter. All I need is to find who or what is living here. I can worry about its history when my brother is safe.*

Vindex stepped out of the first small stone home and looked over at the fire. His brother was still there, sleeping unharmed.

Three more to go, he thought, clenching the fist that held his father's blade. He slowly approached the second entrance, unsure of what awaited him. Vindex extended his arm before creeping inside the stone building.

The inside was empty. It was identical to the first structure, only a few feet from the doorway to the back wall. *Blast it,* Vindex thought after canvassing the entire area. Only two more now. He inspected the third structure, only to find the same interior again. Vindex was now certain that he would find the person who lit the fire in the last building.

Sword at the ready, he looked over to Viridox once more, ensuring his safety. Viridox remained alone, sleeping at the fire, not another soul in sight. Vindex inhaled deeply, gathering the courage to enter the last structure. He stood outside the doorway, slowly inching his way forward. All Vindex could see was darkness. He could not tell if someone was inside. Just before crossing the threshold to the home, he heard an unfamiliar voice speak behind him coming from the campsite where he left his brother. Vindex's heart dropped.

'Should I assume you're looking for me in there?' a mysterious man spoke, directing his comment at Vindex.

Vindex spun around as fast as he could and saw a figure in a dark brown cloak sitting down next to his brother at the campfire. He pointed his sword at the mysterious man and sternly said, 'Stay away from my brother.'

'Well, that's no way to treat a host,' the man replied, refusing to move away. 'You're in my home, after all.'

Vindex stepped closer to the man, pointing the blade towards him and spoke, 'So you're the one who lit the fire. What is this place?'

The man paused for a moment, not answering the boy's question. After taking a minute to think, he removed his cloak, revealing himself to Vindex. The old man was pale and withered, with a medium length curly white beard. 'I can tell you, Vindex,' he spoke, 'but I will first need you to put your sword away.'

Stunned, Vindex slowly put his sword back into his sheath. 'How do you know my name?' he asked the old man, who was now brewing something in the campfire.

'I know a lot of things,' the old man deftly replied, as he focused more on his potion than on Vindex, who was now sitting down by the fire next to his brother.

Vindex, growing weary of the man's mystery, asked, 'And who are you exactly? I'd say a proper introduction is in order.'

'You want to know my name?' the man responded, seemingly shocked.

'Why is that a surprise?' Vindex questioned, keeping a careful eye on the liquid brewing and his brother, who was still sleeping.

The old man quickly responded, 'It's not a surprise, no, it's just been a long time since I've had anyone ask me. My name is Sophos Cato. I'm the last of the Galdeshans.'

Vindex leaned in closer, staring at the man through the crackling flames. He inspected Cato carefully before replying, 'You lie. The Galdeshans are just myth. Legends told from father to son, nothing more.'

Cato spread his arms out and waggishly replied, 'Do I not look like the embodiment of a myth?' Vindex's face stayed stern, unamused by the old man. Cato continued in a serious tone, 'We are real, well, we were, I suppose. It's only me now.' He put the black tin brewing pot down beside him and somberly looked into the flames. 'I've probably been the only one since, even long before the birth of your father's grandfather.'

Vindex examined Cato. He noted he could not be past his seventies in age. This made him skeptical of the old man's words, so he replied, 'That's impossible. Unless ...'

'Unless the legends were true,' Cato interjected, now making eye contact with the boy. His dark blue eyes stared across the flames into Vindex's pale blue eyes. 'I have been here for generations, guided by the spirits of these hills.' To prove to Vindex that he was the last of the

Galdeshans, Cato raised his hand over the campfire, instantly putting out the flames.

Vindex was stunned. Never had he seen any act so magical or enthralling. 'How did you put out the fire?' he asked, curious to know if that power could be learned.

Cato looked at Vindex and responded, 'You will know all in good time. Now I suggest you rest like your brother.'

Vindex looked at his brother, who was still asleep, and agreed. He placed his head next to his brother's and looked at the night sky. Vindex felt safe and after a few minutes fell asleep.

Cato left the campfire and made his way to the edge of the precipice. He sat with arms and legs crossed in meditation and called to the spirits, asking them for guidance. He wanted to know how to help the two boys, and to answer a question that he himself did not know. Cato opened his eyes, not fixating on anything in the real world, and asked the spirits of old, 'How did Vindex see the fire?'

CHAPTER 3

THE TEACHINGS BEGIN

The following day the sky was clear, not a single cloud to dampen the rising sun. When the light from the dawn sun crept over Viridox's face, it was enough to awake him from his sound slumber.

'I slept like a rock last night,' Viridox muttered, opening his eyes. He looked around and saw that he was on a rock and dirt covered plateau, high among the peaks of the mountains. He picked up a small stone and spoke, 'or among them, rather. It is a good thing I don't roll in my sleep.' He threw the small stone off the mountain and watched it fall to the valley.

Viridox stood up and saw his brother sleeping on the opposite side of the campsite. He began walking over to Vindex when he was suddenly startled by an unfamiliar voice.

'Let him sleep. He needs his rest,' Cato said calmly.

Viridox turned around to see the old sage sitting next to the smoldering fire on a large stone. Viridox examined the man for a moment and, seeing no immediate threat, introduced himself. 'I'm Viridox,' he spoke politely. 'And who may you be?'

'Sophus Cato,' the Galdeshan replied. 'Now come, I have breakfast for you. I will tell you about what you missed last night as you slept.'

Viridox happily accepted the invitation and cordially listened to the old man's story. He feasted on freshly cooked mutton, which Cato had prepared for the brothers.

'So, our home is really gone. My father, my friends, everyone … all gone,' Viridox said, walking over to the edge of the cliff.

'I'm so sorry,' Cato replied, 'but as long as I am here, you and your brother are welcome to stay as long as you wish.'

'Thank you,' Viridox replied, his empty eyes staring out at the land he once called home.

Viridox could feel the muscles in his neck twitch as one tear after another fell from his eyes. Everyone he had ever known was now gone. In an attempt to subdue his grief, Viridox quickly scarfed down the remaining food that Cato had prepared.

Cato attempted to change the subject, trying to distract the boy from his pain. 'It looks like you were hungrier than I thought,' he spoke, looking at Viridox, who was quietly wiping away his tears. 'Come now, let us find some more food for your brother so that he does not go hungry.'

Viridox stood up and said, 'I will gladly carry back whatever you kill.'

Cato looked at Viridox and said, 'I am far too old for hunting. You will be going for me.' He handed a bow to Viridox and equipped him with arrows. 'There you are. All ready for the hunt.'

Viridox looked at the old man who had now headed back toward the mountain dwelling and said, 'I do not know how to fire a bow, much less hunt. No one ever taught me.'

Cato stopped in his tracks and turned around to face Viridox. He walked over and took the bow from Viridox's hands. He smiled and spoke, 'I would be happy to teach you. Come along with me.'

Cato took the horse and walked Viridox down the path that led from the valley. Three marksman posts designed for practicing one's archery skills greeted them at the trail's end. Viridox had not noticed these the night before. They were as old as the huts on the mountain. Green moss covered the wood from each post. It was clear they were abandoned a long time ago.

There Cato trained the boy on how to properly hold, aim, and shoot his arrows. Viridox took his stance and pulled the string back with his hand. He held and aimed toward the target before letting go. A faint twang rang as Viridox watched the arrow fly until landing on the lowest point of the target.

'Impressive,' Cato spoke. 'Your first shot hit the target. I don't think I was so lucky when I first learned to shoot.'

Viridox smiled and grabbed for another arrow. He quickly fired it, only to miss the target.

'Patience Viridox. Archery cannot be rushed. You need to focus on each shot.'

Viridox nodded his head and took aim with a new arrow. He exhaled and let go of the string. The arrow flew twenty-five yards and nearly hit the center target. 'Much better. This is rather fun.'

'I can see a future bowman in you. Keep practicing. It takes a lot of time to master.'

Viridox continued to practice on the targets for about an hour while Cato watched and critiqued his technique. When Viridox felt comfortable with the bow, he asked Cato, 'So how do I hunt?'

'Sneak up on your prey and don't let them see you. For large animals, aim for the broadside above the front shoulder and for small ones, just try to hit it. I think I should go check on your brother now, so I wish you luck in your hunt. With any beginners' luck, we'll all have a good dinner tonight.'

'I will do my best.'

'That's all we can do,' Cato replied, headed back to the mountain trail.

Cato walked slowly up the old mountain trail. He stared down with each step, reflecting on how his home came to be so decrepit. *How could I have let this happen? This was once a beautiful place. Maybe one day it will be again.*

Upon reaching the campsite, he found Vindex still asleep. Cato was very curious about the young man's background. He sat next to Vindex and brewed the drink he had left next to the fire the night before.

After a brief while, Vindex's eyes opened sharply, and he shot up from his slumber yelling 'Father!' Vindex's heart was racing. Sweat stained his forest green tunic and trousers and his arms were shaking out of control. After taking a few heavy breaths and looking around his surroundings, he gained control of himself.

'Calm yourself, Vindex. It was only a dream,' Cato said soothingly.

Vindex faced the old man and replied, 'I wish it were only a dream. The sad truth is that it is real.'

Vindex turned away from the Galdeshan to face the cliff's edge. From this height, it was very easy to see where the town of Norova once stood. Vindex sat there a moment, staring at the smoldering ruins of what was home.

Cato sat next to the boy and, too, stared out at the burnt remains of Vindex's home. Eventually, he spoke. 'We all live with haunting memories of the past. Moving past them is what makes life for the living possible.' He reached down to his side and picked up a tin can filled with the concoction he had been brewing since Vindex's arrival. 'Here, take this,' he said, handing the drink over to the boy.

The drink was a strange lime toned liquid. Vindex asked, 'What is this?'

'It is a drink I made to bolster your strength. Your brother ate all the mutton I prepared, so I figured I better give something to you as well.'

Now that Cato mentioned his brother, Vindex frantically looked around for Viridox. 'Where is my brother?'

'He is out hunting. He wanted to get you something to eat. I taught him how to use a bow and if my instincts are correct, he should be returning very shortly with a nice meal for you. Now drink up. It is very important that you do.'

Vindex drank the lime-tinged drink, trusting that the old man was not trying to do him harm. Cato smiled, seeing Vindex finish the potion he had made. The two then sat for a few moments alone when they heard Viridox coming around the bend of the road.

'I hope you two are hungry!' Viridox proclaimed, coming into view as he proudly pointed to a deer he had shot which was dragging behind the horse. 'I brought dinner!'

'Viridox!' Vindex exclaimed. 'Where did you learn how to hunt like this?'

'Cato taught me this morning.' Viridox cheekily replied, dismounting the horse. 'Now, will you help me carry this deer to the fire so we can eat? Hunting makes me hungry.'

'Hunting makes you hungry. Nothing else?' Vindex sarcastically replied.

'If you don't want any, Cato and I can split the meat. All up to you.' Viridox retorted.

Not wanting to call his brother's bluff, Vindex helped his brother carry the deer to the fire, where they then prepared, roasted, and ate the beast.

As the night fell, Viridox grew tired once more and made his way to a newly established tent that Cato had prepared outside one of the stone shelters. Vindex wished his brother goodnight before heading over to Cato, who was meditating on the mountain's edge.

'Are all the legends about the Galdeshans true Cato?' Vindex asked, interrupting the old man's meditation.

Cato stood and faced Vindex. He paused for a moment, unsure of what to say. Eventually he replied, 'I guess it depends on what you have heard. We existed a long time ago. I am sure some things have been altered over time.'

'I grew up hearing stories of ancient scholars and warriors who had endless knowledge and wisdom. They say there was nothing on earth that a Galdeshan could not master.'

Cato scoffed silently. 'There is a big difference between knowledge and wisdom, Vindex. For all we mastered, we somehow forgot that.' There was a silent pause before Cato asked, 'Why do you ask?'

Vindex took his father's blade draped in its sheath off his belt and placed it in his hands. He looked up at the old man and asked, 'What do you know about the art of the sword?'

'I see. Why do you want to be trained?' Cato asked.

Vindex, with a fiery spark in his eyes, stared at Cato and answered, 'I lost everything except for my brother. I have to fight back.'

Cato reached out and took the sword from Vindex's hands. He walked the young man back to the campfire and sat him next to the flames. 'Rage is like a fire, Vindex. When we are in control, we can use it as a powerful tool, but when we lose control, it can destroy everything, even those we love. I can see the pain and anger in your eyes and I understand how you feel, but you must keep a level head. This is the first lesson in swordsmanship. Never let your anger guide you.'

Vindex nodded his head and asked, 'So, will you train me?'

'Swordsmanship isn't as familiar to me as, say, alchemy, but yes, I will teach you. I warn you though, it will take years to master,' Cato replied with a smile.

'One of the very few things I have left in this world besides my brother is time. If you train me, I will do whatever it takes to flourish.'

'I am glad to hear it. Now get some rest. We will start practicing in the morning.'

Vindex took Cato's advice and returned to where his brother lay and rested beside him. Horrid dreams would plague Vindex's mind yet again as the campfire gleamed a bright light over the sleeping boy. Despite all this, he would be ready for training in the morning.

CHAPTER 4

VALERIK'S GAMBIT

The flames from the torches on the pale red mortar wall illuminated the room where Valerik sat meticulously working at his desk. He had maps and papers thrown about in a fashion only a true strategist could understand. Valerik heard a sharp knock on his heavy oak door. 'Enter!' he proclaimed.

Dara swiftly entered Valerik's chamber. She took off her helmet and heavy chest plate. 'I see you have already made yourself at home,' she said, noting how quickly he returned to planning future conquests.

Valerik kept his eyes lowered, looking at his maps and documents. He shuffled between a few papers and thought, *Is this really what I want?*

Dara sat down at the corner of Valerik's table and watched as he frantically scribbled down notes. She asked, 'Are you ready for the senate meeting tomorrow?'

Valerik looked up now and leaned back in his chair. He let out an elongated sigh and replied, 'Do you remember what we found when we traveled to Patavium and Genua?'

'Sure. Both towns were destroyed. There was hardly any sign of any invasion at all. We didn't find any barbarian remains or arms,' Dara answered pragmatically.

'But what did we find?' Valerik emphatically interjected. 'Two different legionary shields in each town. Each with an eagle engraving. That is the marking of the Senate's personal legion, -- a legion that I do not command. What were they doing there?'

'Perhaps they were citizens who retired back to their farms when their service ended,' Dara replied.

'Maybe, but with no evidence or remains of the barbarian invaders, it just makes little sense,' Valerik replied, looking away from Dara to stare out at the bustling city street below.

'You really think the Senate did this?'

Valerik looked at the innocent citizens of Apolina going about their daily lives. He dreaded the thought the Senate could have committed such atrocities on its own people. 'I do,' he softly spoke.

'Why would they do such a thing?' Dara asked. 'They have nothing to gain.'

'Because they needed an excuse to keep expanding. The public will only support an aggressive war for so long. After a while, they lose conviction. If we were the victims, however, they would support all the Senate's actions implicitly. They sacrificed two Umbrian towns to justify a Galician invasion. Those warmongers will pay,' Valerik spoke, clenching his fist.

Dara's eyes widened, seeing her general's anger. She smiled and said, 'I take it you have a plan.'

Valerik turned around from the window and faced Dara. He stared and sternly asked, 'Do you have my back, Dara?'

Dara returned her general's gaze and answered, 'Of course. No matter the fight, we fight it together. Just like we always have.'

'Good!' replied Valerik, shaking his head with reassurance, 'Because tomorrow, we start the fight of our lives. All our other battles will seem trivial in comparison.'

'You're planning on taking down the Senate, aren't you?'

'I will do what I must to protect the Umbrian people,' Valerik replied, grabbing hold of Dara's shoulders. 'Do me a favor and find a list of soldiers whom you know we can trust. I need loyalty and I need numbers.'

'It will be done, General,' Dara responded before quickly taking her armor and leaving the room.

Valerik walked past his table and into an adjacent room where he lay in bed, contemplating what the next day would bring. He thought, *I am not sure if I am right, but I know the safest hands for this nation are my own. The Senate must fall if Umbria is to flourish. Tomorrow either I or the Senate dies.*

The sun shined brightly the day the Republic's fate would be decided. Valerik viewed this as a positive omen, believing it was nature's way of showing support for his plan to end the tyranny of the Senate. Dara met him at the front door as he left to meet the Senate. She had organized a group of the twelve strongest and most trustworthy soldiers at her disposal. Among the twelve were six of her finest shield maidens, as well as some low-ranking captains and infantry men who supported Valerik in past conquests.

Valerik recognized most of the troops, but to inspire the ones he had not yet met, he proclaimed, 'Some of you soldiers I know and some of you I don't, but that doesn't matter. If you stay and fight with me, I promise you nothing but the highest of ranks and honors in the new free society we will create. This is no time for introductions, only a time to listen and follow orders. Am I understood?'

The group, including Dara, responded in unison with a resounding, 'Sir, yes, sir!'

'Very well. Follow me,' Valerik commanded as he mounted his horse. He led his troops in single file as they calmly walked through the Umbrian capital. Bystanders looked on in awe as they watched Valerik and Dara, the two most respected soldiers in Umbria's army, marching through the streets. By the time Valerik and his party reached the senate building, the sun was already half noon. Valerik looked over at his troops who were hitching their horses and said, 'It starts now.'

They quickly climbed the staircase from the forum and attempted to enter the senate building but were stopped by two senate guards.

'Hold on Valerik,' the first guard spoke. 'You know the rules. Only those who are summoned can enter and the Senate has only summoned you.'

Valerik, thinking on his feet, replied, 'Gentlemen, these brave soldiers were instrumental in my conquest of the Galician village. They deserve recognition from the Senate.'

The second senate guard now spoke. 'I thought Dara left her personal guard here after the war with the Balifates ended. How did they help you in Norova if they were stationed in the capital?' he asked, staring at Dara's shield maidens, who were dressed in their standard attire; iron plated tunics, kilts and shin guards with their spears and round shields covered by their burgundy colored capes.

Before Valerik could respond, Dara interjected, 'You are correct that I did station my bodyguard here in Apolina, but these six brave soldiers behind me would not sit idle with the rest of my maidens. They insisted upon returning to the frontline and now you deny them their praises from the Senate. How dare you!'

Valerik looked at Dara with proud eyes. He smiled and nodded while they awaited the guard's response.

'Very well,' the second guard spoke. 'We will allow you to enter. Follow us.'

The two guards opened up the large door that led to the senate chamber. Two additional guards were inside. When all of Valerik's party had entered, all four guards closed the door, locking the party inside. The four guards then took Valerik and escorted him to the senate floor while leaving his companions at the now sealed exit.

Valerik looked behind him before staring up at the senators who were seated on the balcony. He saw the four senate guardsman standing directly behind him, blocking his exit. He then turned his attention to the senators. Valerik looked up and stared at Pravus, who already had an annoyed look on his face.

Pravus looked around the room and sensed something was wrong. He raised himself off his seat and proclaimed, 'What is the meaning of this assembly? You were supposed to report to me alone, Valerik.'

Valerik stared intently into Pravus' angry eyes and spoke. 'What happened in Genua and Patavium Pravus? I demand answers.'

Pravus masked a guilty expression with anger. He yelled, 'You demand nothing from me, you insolent brute. Have you forgotten to whom you are speaking? You are nothing but discarded trash from the city gutter. I made you who you are today. Without my support, you would still be a footsoldier marching on the frontline. I think it is best you check your tone when speaking to me!'

Valerik held his composure and addressed the rest of the Senate. 'How many of you knew that your Senate's legion was responsible for the raid on Genua and Patavium?'

Pravus quickly interjected. 'That is preposterous!' he exclaimed, 'Why would we attack our own people?'

'I have my theories, but that is why I am demanding answers, Pravus. Why would you do this?'

Pravus' hands gripped around the balcony rail. He shouted, 'I told you the Galicians were responsible. A barbarian chieftain led the raid on our towns.'

'See, I would believe that, and I did until I spoke with that chieftain. Before killing him and his people, he told me he did not mettle in Etruscan affairs and he dared not travel east. This struck me as odd, so I traveled to Patavium and Genua myself before returning to Apolina. Do you want to know what I found? Show them, Dara,' Valerik spoke, holding his gaze on the balcony members.

Dara lifted one of her shield maiden's cape, revealing a legionary shield with an engraved eagle. She took the shield off her soldier's back and threw it on the senate floor. A loud metallic clang was heard throughout the building.

'And what does this prove?' Pravus scoffed. 'That one of our first legion soldiers lived in Genua? This is hardly evidence, Valerik.'

'There were no signs of a barbarian force in either town. No clothing, shields, weapons, nothing. The only things we could find among the rubble were a few of your private legions' shields. I think that is more than just a coincidence,' Valerik replied.

Pravus lowered his brow and said in a slow deep voice, 'Why did you really come here today, Valerik?'

'You know why I am here, Pravus. The Senate has committed treason against the Umbrian people. Pravus, I am here to expel you from your position. Don't worry though, I will keep your dream alive of an ever expanding Umbria. But I will not do it at the expense of our own people's lives.'

Pravus interjected, 'You are the one committing treason, Valerik, but I am a reasonable man. You say you share my vision for an Umbrian world. If that is true, I want you to march north past Genua to the land of the Sunduk and lay siege to the city of Susa. If you do that, I can forgive this treasonous transgression.'

'You still don't understand. Your time is over. Your seat is forfeit. I did not come here today to negotiate. Gentleman of the Senate, may I have your attention, please. I do not know how many of you knew of Pravus' deception, but I know that now you have a choice to make. Today marks the end of the Umbrian Republic and the birth of the glorious Umbrian Empire. I will lead you and our people to a golden age. The likes of which no one has ever seen before. With my guidance and help, Umbria can expand across the globe of Talamh. We will peacefully annex and welcome new factions to our Empire, and we will only fight as a last resort. I will prioritize Umbrian lives above all else, something this Republic has forgotten to do. The arrogance of this Senate has led to countless Umbrian deaths. None of you have seen the horrors of Pravus' orders. Had I not been the one in control of the war with the Balifates, they would still be a threat knocking at our doors. And with that, I leave you fine senators a choice. For those who support Pravus, stand tall with him and for those who will support me, stay seated. For my supporters, I promise a life still filled with power so long as you support my rule and defend our people.'

Out of the nineteen remaining council members, excluding Pravus, thirteen stood with their Senate leader. Six remained seated in support of Valerik.

'I see you have made your decision,' Valerik spoke quietly. He turned to Dara and his soldiers looking past the senate guard that stood between them and said, 'Arrest the standing council members. We will deal with them later.' Dara and her company quickly made their way into the senate balcony that stood above the senate floor where Valerik stood, alone with the senate guard.

'This is treason!' Pravus exclaimed in a shrieking voice. 'Kill him! Gut his pathetic body and litter the streets with his blood!' he yelled while gesturing for his guards to attack Valerik.

The four elite senate guards, dressed in black cloth and shiny bronze armor, closed in on their target. Valerik drew his sword and stared down at his opponents, who he once would have considered allies. 'Think for yourselves! You don't have to do this,' he proclaimed. Valerik's cry made no impression on the guards who continued to move towards him.

The two spearmen were in the middle, pikes aimed at Valerik's chest, while the two swordsmen encroached around him. The Umbrian general was encircled. Valerik recognized his predicament. He quickly closed with the spearman closest to him. Valerik dodged the guard's spear thrust, and instead of parrying with his own blade, he spun to the side of the guard, took his sword and slashed down on the spear, breaking it in half. He grabbed the falling spear tip with his left arm and hurled it into the face of the swordsman that was the closest to him. In an instant, the body of the guard hit the floor, dead. This death did not stop the guardsman as they were still set on killing Valerik per Pravus' order. Valerik took the wooden pole which the spearman was still holding and pulled the guard close to him. He pushed his blade deep into the spearman's abdomen, causing the guard to fall to the senate floor.

Valerik now had the advantage. The remaining two guards tried to catch the general by surprise and both rushed Valerik at the same time. With no shield in hand, Valerik needed to act quickly to defend himself. Valerik focused on the swordsman and rushed into the guard, grappling with him and overpowering the man. Valerik then turned the body of the swordsman towards the oncoming attack from the spearman. The last guard panicked when he saw he had killed his comrade. He dropped his spear and with a loud scream; he attempted to attack Valerik with nothing but his fists. In an instant, the scream was silenced. His body dropped along the marble floor. Valerik slowly sheathed his bloody sword.

It didn't have to be this way, Valerik thought to himself as he stared at the lifeless Umbrian bodies.

Valerik then stared at Pravus, who was in absolute shock at how quickly his elite guard was dismantled and said, 'Your time is over, Pravus. Accept the binds we place on you or accept your place on the floor with your men. The choice is yours.'

Pravus realized he had no options. He put his arms behind his back, waiting to be held prisoner. Dara bound him with rope, securing him and the rest of his allies. Dara and her men brought Pravus and his supporters down to the senate floor while leaving the loyal senators in their seats.

Valerik stood amongst the bodies, living and dead. He spoke, 'For those of you who showed faith in me today, I will reward you for your efforts. I will grant you powerful and lucrative positions in the administration of my new Empire. Make sure you earn them.'

Pravus scoffed, looking up at Valerik from his knees. 'Your new Empire? Do you not know my support in this land extends past the depths of this chamber? You will fight half the Republic before they allow you to turn it into an empire run by your tyranny.'

Dara quickly kicked Pravus in the face, knocking him to the ground. Blood trickled from his nose and from the corner of his mouth. She looked down and taunted Pravus. 'Far better than a Republic run by scum like you!'

'Leave him be, Dara,' Valerik spoke. 'He is not wrong. This battle is far from over.' He looked over at the man standing next to Dara and said, 'Soldier. What is your name?'

'Thrün, sir,' replied the soldier, saluting the general.

'And your rank?'

'I am an infantry officer sir,' Thrün replied, still saluting the general.

Valerik spoke. 'Take these prisoners and half of our troops in this room to the barracks. Seize the building and make it safe. Lock these senators in the soldier's quarters. Tell the men stationed at the barracks you are under my direct command and that you have been promoted to centurion in the Umbrian army.'

'Sir, yes sir!' Thrün replied. He gathered the soldiers and led the bound senators out of the Senate.

After half the troops had left, Valerik turned to Dara and said, 'You go to the governor's villa in the heart of the city and see if you can convince him to join our cause.'

'And if he isn't persuaded?' Dara asked menacingly.

'Use your charm. There will be enough bloodshed in the coming months. Do not injure him unless he attacks you. That is an order. Is that clear?' Valerik said firmly.

Dara looked at her general with a hint of disappointment. 'Understood,' she replied before rushing out of the chamber. She mounted her horse and headed for the governor's villa.

Valerik, now standing in front of six soldiers, said, 'The rest of you, ride with me.' The troops made their way down the steps of the council chamber into the city forum. They mounted their horses and made haste for the city walls. Valerik was meeting back up with his legion, which had been stationed outside the city limits. Although he hoped for a peaceful transfer of power, he was prepared for a city occupation. The time to lay siege was now.

By the time Valerik had reconvened with his men, the governor had already invited Dara inside his villa. Governor Brutus Heriax was a short, muscular man with black hair and a big bushy beard. Heriax had been Apolina's beloved governor for nearly a decade, despite his quick temper and bold nature.

'So why did you call this audience Dara?' he asked as he made his way to the dining table.

'Well,' Dara spoke, 'I am here with a proposition of sorts.'

'Of sorts? What deal do you bring me?' he replied testily, thinking that Dara was wasting his time.

'I have it on very good authority that a coup might be forming. I am trying to find allies,' Dara responded, leaning forward on the dining table, 'I was hoping I could count on you.'

'Who is it that is threatening our mighty Republic? We must tell the senators at once!' Heriax replied in rage, shooting out of his seat.

Dara subtly removed her hands from the table and slowly made her way to her sword. Before she could take out her blade, however, a servant rushed into the room.

'Governor!' the servant spoke. 'Valerik has gone mad! He is marching his men through the city gates. Our forces have already engaged, but we need you to lead the men.'

Heriax yelled at the servant, 'Grab your sword and go join the fray! I will meet you there shortly.' He then ran to his chamber to put on his armor and grab his weapon. Dara followed. 'Is this the coup you were trying to warn me about? Valerik? What has overcome him?'

Dara, blocking the doorway, replied, 'He has mentioned to me during campaigns before that he was not happy with the way the Republic ran itself. Perhaps he has hit a breaking point.'

'Apparently so,' Heriax replied while gathering his armor. 'It pains me to say this, but I will need your help, Dara. I cannot fight a man like Valerik alone. It would be the death of me.'

'Don't you worry. He won't be the death of you,' Dara replied. She stepped close to the governor, whose back was still turned. She drew her blade and stabbed him in the back. Her blade entered between his ribs next to the spine. Before he even realized what had happened, he was on the ground, drifting into his last sleep.

Well, that was fun, Dara thought as she emerged from the governor's villa. She presumed Valerik would need her to fight, so she got on her horse and raced to join Valerik who was fighting in the city streets. Apolina had a considerable city militia, but despite its size, the militia was no match for the combined efforts of Valerik and Dara. The two warriors led from the front, decimating the militiamen that dared oppose them. By the time the afternoon sky had fallen, and the light had left, the city was under their command. Valerik was in complete control of the capital.

Valerik remained in his own quarters that night, not wishing to sleep in the governor's building or the senate chamber. Instead, he returned to his modest abode, which he had called home since joining the army. The Emperor entered his bedroom and laid down, content with his first steps towards an Umbrian Empire. He was not naïve enough to believe that taking the capital meant the rest of the Republic would happily transition into his new Empire. He knew that turmoil was about to ensue, but he slept peacefully knowing that the hardest part, the decision to challenge the Republican leaders, was over. His peaceful slumber would be disrupted just before the break of dawn when Thrün pounded on his door.

'Pravus escaped sir,' Thrün said with a sense of shame. 'I entrusted two of my men to watch him overnight and when I awoke this morning, the three of them were gone, not to be accounted for.'

Valerik looked at Thrün, and replied, 'It is of little difference whether or not he escaped. The rest of Umbria will soon know of my intentions. And in all my time on campaign, I know for certain that most of the small towns will join us. The only real threat is if Pravus makes his way to Tarsus and creates a stronghold there, but even so, I never expected this to be an easy battle.'

Thrün, surprised he wasn't being berated or demoted in rank, profusely apologized. 'I am so sorry, Valerik. If my poor judgment creates a problem for the Empire, I will be the one to fix it.'

Valerik measured the man. 'I'll see to it that you have the opportunity. Now, if there is nothing else, I would greatly appreciate you leaving my chamber. I intend to get a few more hours of sleep before my duties call upon me,' Valerik stated. Thrün turned and closed the chamber door while Valerik closed his eyes once more to continue his much-needed rest.

CHAPTER 5

THE LAST OF THE GALDESHANS

Vindex woke from a peaceful sleep. The sun was high above the horizon and he could feel the warm welcome rays on his face. He sat up from his cot, opened his tent and saw his brother and Cato sitting around the fire, making breakfast.

'How was your sleep? No nightmares?' Viridox asked.

'Not last night thankfully,' Vindex replied.

Vindex sat at the fire and joined Cato and Viridox for breakfast. He waited patiently until the meal was over and then asked, 'Do we finally start my training today Cato?'

Cato looked into Vindex's eyes. He could see the emotions that Vindex was trying so hard to suppress. 'Very well,' he said. 'I think for today I want you to spar with Viridox. I have these for you.' He handed the pair two wooden swords that he had crafted the night before. 'It is time that you test your skills on each other.'

Viridox took the training weapon. The sword was perfectly balanced and seemed a perfect extension of Viridox's self. He pointed the blunt top at his brother and said, 'Well then, let us begin.'

With the same joy, Vindex took his matching sword and replied, 'You are on.'

The two chased one another around the mountain edge, blocking and dodging each other's incoming swings. This was no training. Cato knew this would be the case. However, he wanted to see what the latent abilities of each of the boys were. He sat at the fire and keenly watched each boy's movement. It was clear Vindex was the more gifted of the duelists. It was not because of his larger physical stature. Rather, Vindex displayed an innate prowess.

I have seen those motions before, Cato thought while watching Vindex swing. *But it can't be. It must be a coincidence.*

Vindex was already showing the promise of an incredible swordsman striking the areas of weak defense over and over. The only reason Viridox hadn't immediately lost at the start of the duel was because Vindex was having too much fun fighting his brother. It had been weeks since Norova had burned, and this was the first time that Vindex truly felt normal again. These practices would go on for many months. Cato would let the boys fight amongst themselves, studying each's innate strengths and weaknesses.

Cato would not teach the pair sophisticated techniques until the boys grew into men. In fact, it was not until Vindex came of age at eighteen, nearly two years after they had arrived on the mountain, that Cato began formally training the young man.

The two years passed rather quickly as Vindex and Viridox went about their daily routines. They hunted in the morning, before being taught by Cato in the afternoon. Just before sunset, they would each practice their archery and swordsmanship. During these years, Cato watched Vindex and Viridox closely. He could not forget about the fire and the skills Vindex had displayed. There was immense strength hidden within Vindex who could be both fierce and magnanimous. However there was an ever present shadow deep in Vindex's core which troubled Cato. Viridox, on the other hand, was an open book. He freely shared his emotions, and he was extremely loyal.

On the evening before Vindex's eighteenth birthday, Cato decided it was time to teach Vindex the secrets he alone possessed. The midnight moon shined particularly bright as Cato rubbed on his arm, waking him up. Cato said, 'Hello there, Vindex. Happy birthday.'

'Cato?' Vindex questioned, rubbing his eyes. 'Why are you waking me up in the middle of the night? How do you know this is the day I was born?' He sat up from his cot and faced the old man, who had yet to respond. 'And when am I going to learn not to bother asking those questions because I will never get an answer?'

Cato smiled and said, 'Well, perhaps today you will. Follow me.' He walked to one of the three stone structures that were built into the mountainside.

Excited at the prospect of learning more about his mentor's seemingly endless knowledge, Vindex shot up and followed him to the building. 'Is this another one of your games, or are you finally going to reveal your secrets?'

'When have I ever been one to play games? I am and have always been a serious hermit,' Cato replied emphatically, evading Vindex's question.

'Very serious,' Vindex replied sarcastically. 'Now, why have you brought me here? I have seen this building many times. There's nothing inside.' Vindex emphasized his point by kicking the rock wall on the inside of the doorway.

'For now,' said Cato as he stuck out his hand to the granite wall. Almost immediately after placing his hand on the rock wall, a light lime light appeared, and the wall vanished. Vindex could now see a doorway leading to another room.

Vindex looked in awe. It had been sometime since Cato had used any mystic power. Stumbling over his words, he spoke. 'You really are a Galdeshan.'

'I see you're a fast learner. It only took two years for you to figure that out,' Cato replied sarcastically, crossing his arms at the young man.

'Well, you hadn't exactly turned rock to air before Cato, so no, I didn't believe you,' Vindex replied, still flustered as to what he just saw.

'Oh, but I didn't turn it to air.'

'There is a hole here the size of a doorway now.'

'I know.'

'And it wasn't like that before you placed your hand upon it.'

'Most certainly not,' Cato said, still playing with his pupil.

'So, you turned the rock into air?' Vindex said in a way that suggested that he wanted answers.

'I did no such thing,' Cato replied with a broad smile.

'Then what did you do?'

'I turned granite into argon.'

Vindex stood there in silence, watching the old man amuse himself with his own foolishness. After he had settled, he said to Cato, 'Fine. You changed granite into what was it, argon? How did you do that?'

'Well, it is a long story, Vindex. In short, I use what the Galdeshans called the Maith,' Cato replied.

'The Maith?' Vindex asked, puzzled.

'Yes,' Cato responded, 'It isn't a creation or something we made. It is something that, as far as we know, has always existed. In our studies of alchemy, we came across a way to change the matter of inorganic molecules by using the Maith. My people called what gave us our power fairies, but they act mostly as spirits.'

'Spirits?' Vindex asked, trying to keep up with the information that he was being told.

'Yes. After death, your consciousness joins a collection of other spirits and shares its knowledge in one collective intelligence that possesses almost limitless information.'

Vindex quickly asked, 'Can you see my father, then? Can you speak with him?'

'Sadly, no,' Cato responded, hesitating to continue upon seeing the dismay on Vindex's face. 'After death, only a select few keep their consciousness. The rest join together in a collective of all the shared information from their lives. You could think of it as the largest library of knowledge ever created.'

Vindex chuckled softly before letting out a long and sincere sigh. He knew he was foolish, but Cato had sparked his deepest desire. All he could do was stand in silence.

'I'm really sorry for you, son,' Cato spoke as he put his arm on Vindex's shoulder. 'I wish I could help.'

Vindex looked at Cato and replied with a heavy heart, 'No, it's fine.' He then brushed off Cato's arm and looked into the dark room the sage had opened for him. Before asking more about the challenge he was ultimately going to endure, he wanted to know more about what Cato meant by a retained consciousness after death. 'Do you know how to maintain your being after death, Cato?' he asked bluntly.

'Yes,' Cato replied straightforwardly, no longer playing games with his pupil. 'It is a practice the fairies taught us during the Galdeshans' most troubling times.'

'I see. Can you teach me?'

'Well, that depends on this trial,' Cato replied as he pointed into the dim cave that stood in front of them. 'My people used this building to test each of our adolescents when coming of age to see their connections to the Maith. That way, we would know if they had the strength necessary to access and use the surrounding spirits.'

Vindex looked confused. 'What does this have to do with me?'

'I believe you are a descendant of the Galdeshans Vindex,' Cato replied in a very strict and serious manner. 'When you first came here a few years ago, you told me that you saw a fire from below. The fire that was lit that night had no regular flame. It was Galdeshan fire, a flame so faint that regular eyes cannot see it. It exists outside of the visible light spectrum of those who do not have any Galdeshan genes.'

Vindex thought back to that night he initially met Cato. He instinctively mumbled, 'But Viridox never saw the light.'

'I know. Which is why I especially need you to go in here, Vindex. I need to know how it is possible that there is another remaining Galdeshan. It has been a mystery to me since you arrived.'

Vindex nodded. He understood the task at hand, while not yet realizing the greater implication of this discovery. If he succeeded in Cato's trial, it would show that he and Viridox may not be full-blooded brothers. The cave was enormous. A small staircase led to the room's center. A few candles were lit on a small altar against one of the cave's walls. Light beamed in from a man made opening in the ceiling that symmetrically matched a circular carving in the ground. On the other end of the cave, Vindex saw a hawthorn tree growing out from under the rock. He also noticed that the sides of the cave were covered with thick nettle plants. As Vindex went down the stairs, he approached the circle carved in the ground. He stood on the markings, staring at the scripture, trying to decipher what the symbols meant when he heard Cato's voice.

'Kneel at the center of the circle, Vindex, and close your eyes. Only open them when you have cleared your mind of all worldly things. You need to reach a state of inner peace to pass this trial,' Cato spoke calmly. 'This is your trial. I will not abandon you, but I must wait outside with the door sealed. Good luck my friend.'

'Thank you Cato. I will try my best,' Vindex spoke before kneeling down in the center of the floor carving. Cato resealed the doorway, leaving him alone in this mystical room. Vindex then began his trial.

The young man had great difficulty clearing his mind. Despite knowing Cato could reopen the doorway, he felt trapped in the cave. He imagined the walls closing in on him and his anxiety grew. Instead of peacefully clearing his mind, Vindex had thought back to the last day he saw his father. He relived the memory of his father's death, feeling the heat from the burning buildings and the pain from Valerik's blow. Suddenly, Vindex felt another presence in the cave with him. This unnerved the young man greatly, as he believed Cato had left him alone. Vindex still had his eyes closed when suddenly his memories became more vivid and detailed. His face grimaced and his body hunched over in pain. *This is no dream,* Vindex thought. *I have never experienced a nightmare so graphic before.*

Unable to take the pain anymore, he collapsed on his hands and opened his eyes to see that the floor had changed. He no longer stood on mountainous rock, but instead on a white marble floor with red and green accents. He looked up and saw what appeared to be a throne.

Seated on the chair was a very familiar man. As Vindex rose to his feet, two men walked through him as if he did not take up space in the room. One a soldier, the other appearing to be some kind of prisoner.

'Ah Captain Agis, I see you have found our most infamous traitor to the Empire,' Vindex heard a recognizable voice boast.

'Yes, I did, Valerik,' The soldier replied, pushing the prisoner down in front of him.

That voice, that name. I know this man. If only I could see his face, Vindex thought, staring at the figure who sat upon the throne just far enough away to obscure his identity.

'So how does it feel to finally lose Pravus?' Valerik asked, looking down on the man in chains upon what used to be the senate floor.

'Just make this quick,' Pravus responded, refusing to look Valerik in the eyes.

Not taking kindly to Pravus' continued defiance, Valerik stood and walked down the stairs. With each step, Vindex saw a clearer and clearer picture of the man. This was, in fact, the monster who killed his father, the same one who had haunted his dreams for two years, and who would continue to haunt them for many more.

'I will not make this quick,' Valerik said, standing in front of the former Senate elder. 'Look at me!' Pravus slowly lifted his head to look Valerik in the eye. He had no fight left to give. Valerik saw the broken man and spoke to Agis, 'Bring him to the newly constructed prison and leave him under constant surveillance. He will spend the rest of his days alive in his cell. There will be no escaping this time. I will not be putting down another rebellion. We need to focus our efforts on reconstruction now.'

'You don't wish to hang him, sir?' Agis asked.

'No. I will not make him a martyr. I want his supporters to quietly die off. No need to give them something to fight for,' Valerik replied. 'Now take him to his cell.'

'Yes, sir!' Agis exclaimed, grabbing Pravus by the back of his cloth garment and dragging him out of the Emperor's hall.

Vindex stood up in anger seeing the man who he despised the most right in front of him. *If they can't see me, this would be a perfect time to strike. I don't care if I get captured or killed. He falls now,* Vindex thought while reaching for his father's blade. He unsheathed the sword and charged Valerik, screaming, 'I'll kill you, you bastard!'

With a running start in hand, Vindex swung his blade on a horizontal angle directed at Valerik's abdomen. This blow would surely gut the man if successful, but to Vindex's surprise, he went right through the Umbrian General. Not being able to catch his feet from the attack, Vindex fell on the ground and dropped his sword. The fall forced his eyes closed and when they reopened; he found himself back in the rock room in the Galdeshan Mountains. Vindex picked himself up and looked around, trying to find his father's blade, which was now broken in half, shattered by a collision with the cave wall.

Cato heard the commotion from outside the room and quickly used the Maith to remove the seal on the chamber. He entered to find Vindex on his knees, bent over his father's broken weapon. Vindex turned around in response to seeing the light from the doorway.

'What just happened Cato?' he asked, sweating, panting, and disoriented.

'My son, what did you see?' Cato asked, rushing to Vindex's side.

'I saw the man who killed my father. He was right in front of me in this grand hall. What does it mean?' Vindex asked, looking up at Cato in need of answers.

'Were you able to clear your mind before opening your eyes?' Cato asked urgently.

'No,' Vindex replied. 'I couldn't help it. After you left, I was swarmed with the memories of my home's destruction and my father's death. I tried to clear my mind, but the images only grew stronger until eventually I saw the man who butchered my dad right in front of me. His name is Valerik. Is what I saw a premonition?'

'Not a premonition, no,' Cato replied, looking down at his pupil nervously. 'What you saw was what is happening as we speak. Your consciousness was transported into the Maith, and you could see a fraction of what the spirits witness daily. While this isn't the expected outcome of the trial, it does secure my suspicion about your lineage. It appears as if your unresolved tension with this Valerik altered your trial and brought you to him.'

'So, I am a Galdeshan,' Vindex replied after taking a deep breath. He then stared somberly at his father's broken sword, which lay on the floor in front of him.

'It appears as if you are,' Cato responded. He knelt beside his pupil and looked at the broken sword. 'Why don't we fix this?' he said.

Vindex looked over at the old man and asked, 'How? I broke it in two.'

Cato smiled and replied, 'Have you not been paying attention to anything that has happened tonight? Here, take out your hand.' He took Vindex's hands in such a way that he was holding the two pieces of the sword, only separated by less than an inch of air. 'Now I want you to concentrate, Vindex. Sense the feeling of the spirits around you and use their power to fix the sword.'

Vindex closed his eyes and focused with all his might. He sat in silence, trying to embrace the feelings of the Galdeshan fairies, and despite his best efforts, he could not fix his father's blade. Cato decided it would be best to intervene. Without saying a word Cato raised his hand behind the boy and soon after a bright lime colored light filled the room. When Vindex opened his eyes, the sword was repaired. The small gap had been filled with the same steel that comprised the rest of the blade. Vindex was shocked by the repair. He ran his fingers over the side of the blade. The sword felt as strong as the first day it was smelted.

Vindex turned back to Cato and exclaimed jubilantly, 'I did it!'

'I am so proud of you!' Cato replied, knowing that Vindex had not fixed the blade on his own. He then opened his arms to give the young man an embrace.

'I can't believe this! I'm part Galdeshan!' Vindex yelled, hugging the old man back.

'Neither can I. And that's saying something because I know almost everything,' Cato retorted, finishing the embrace with the young man.

The pair exited the chamber and when outside, Cato resealed the entrance. A glow came from the doorway as stone consumed the entrance once more.

'Goodnight Vindex,' Cato spoke as he walked over to his dwelling. 'It brings me so much joy to no longer be the last Galdeshan.'

Before letting the old man get too far away, Vindex interjected, 'What about Viridox? He never saw the fire that night we came, but he is my brother. Shouldn't he be part Galdeshan as well?'

Cato stopped in his tracks. His forehead wrinkled as he went deep into thought. After a moment, he turned around and replied, 'It wouldn't be impossible, but I think it is unlikely. I have been watching you both for some time and he has aroused little suspicion of what may be his true lineage. As for you, Vindex, I knew your heritage was not purely Galician, which is why I needed you to take this test.'

Vindex only now realized that Viridox was his half-sibling. Despite this revelation, nothing would change between the two. He loved Viridox and that would never change because of his Galdeshan roots. He looked at Cato and asked, 'So who is Viridox's real father? We were born from the same mother, so it must be from the father's side.'

'You are right, Vindex. This gift you have is inherited from the father, but the question is not who Viridox's father is, it is who yours is? Brunos is the undeniable father to Viridox, but the spirits tell me something different regarding you.'

Vindex paused for a moment before affirming in his own mind that he did not want to know who his father was. Brunos had raised him, and because of that, he would be the only person Vindex would ever call father. To distract him from his paternal lineage, Vindex entertained himself with all the possibilities of the Maith. Excited to learn more about this magic, Vindex asked Cato, 'Now that I am a Galdeshan, will you teach me how to retain my consciousness in the Maith after death?'

Cato smiled, seeing his pupil so keen to learn the arts of his ancestors. 'When you are at the end of your days, Vindex, come back to this mountain and only then will you be granted the secrets to a retained consciousness after death.'

'Well, hopefully I do not need to learn that art for a long time then!' Vindex retorted.

The two engaged in conversation before realizing it was time to rest once more. Vindex returned to his cot, where he would drift back into another peaceful sleep.

NEW FRIENDS

Time passed quickly on the mountain. Vindex and Viridox continued to hone their skills with blades and bows. Viridox's swordsmanship could not approach the skill level of his brother, so he focused on the bow. His skills with a bow were not only comparable, but surpassed those of Vindex. Vindex supported his brother's training. He encouraged him to continue practicing with a bow and blade until his trial in the Maith came. Viridox hoped he too would share in the magical powers that his brother and Cato possessed. Vindex spent many hours convincing Cato to allow Viridox to test his powers as Vindex had done so many months before.

When the night finally came to test his connection to the Maith, Vindex and Cato brought Viridox to the chamber. Vindex watched as Cato instructed his brother on how to perform the ritual. Viridox listened and acknowledged what they expected of him. Cato and Vindex stepped out of the chamber into the open mountain air.

'You really think he can do it, don't you?' Cato asked Vindex calmly as he stared out at the valley beneath them.

Vindex turned his head to face Cato and replied, 'I do. There is nothing special about me, Cato. Nothing that my brother does not also possess. Perhaps the spirits will come to him even if he is not of Galdeshan blood. Have you ever tried the ritual on someone other than a Galdeshan?'

Cato heard the young man's question but did not answer. He let out a loud sigh.

'You'll see,' Vindex continued softly, 'The spirits will come to him. They have to. He is my brother. We are the same.'

An hour passed. Cato broke the silence and spoke. 'I think we should let him out. He hasn't connected to the Maith.'

Vindex quickly protested. 'Give him more time,' he pleaded. ' I know he can do it. Just have faith.'

Cato turned to Vindex with soft, sympathetic eyes. 'You can have faith in the absence of truth, Vindex, but here, now, we know Viridox can't reach the Maith. Why leave him to suffer alone in a cold, damp, dark room?'

Vindex could not argue against Cato's assessment. He somberly nodded and allowed Cato to open the seal to the chamber. After the seal opened, Viridox knew he had failed. He quickly stood up and rushed out of the chamber embarrassed.

'I am going to bed. Please don't stop me.'

Vindex and Cato left the young man alone for the night and agreed that it would be best for them to turn in as well. Vindex stared at the sky from his cot and thought about his brother's disappointment. *I know,* Vindex thought to himself. *I'll plan a brief excursion tomorrow to cheer him up. He is going to love it.*

The sun had barely crested over the horizon the next day when Vindex went to wake up his brother. The rest of the mountain slept as Vindex approached his brother with a smile.

'Wake up,' Vindex spoke loudly, trying to awaken Viridox.

'Brother, if the birds are not up yet, then I shouldn't be either,' Viridox responded irritably, rolling back over onto his side.

'Well then, cock-a-doodle-do!' Vindex exclaimed as he threw his brother's leather boots at him. 'Come on, let's go. I have a great day planned.'

After getting hit with his own boots, Viridox sat up, rubbing his eyes. 'You know if I could beat you in a sword fight, I might just kill you,' he said as he put his shoes on.

'I love you too, brother. Now come let us go,' Vindex replied, mounting the old horse that had led the two out of Norova all those years ago.

The pair traveled together on horseback, making the long journey down the mountain. After a few hours, they made their way to the lush green valley below. The grass was covered with dew that glimmered in the morning light and the valley was full of animal life. Wild bucks and horses roamed free as they grazed on the pastures and drank from the small lake that jutted out from the southern mountains.

'So now that we are here, will you tell me what's going on?' Viridox asked, getting off the horse alongside his brother.

'Well, Viridox, I think it's time you and I tame some new horses. We've gotten old, and our friend has gotten older,' Vindex replied as he ran his hand over the horse's mane that brought the pair down the mountain. He then led his brother into the tall grass, looking for strong steeds for their future adventures.

'I also think it will be fun,' Vindex said, smiling at his brother.

Viridox smirked in return and replied, 'It will be fun for whoever gets the faster steed.'

'Right you are. And I intend to have the most fun here today,' Vindex responded as he calmly walked forward, guiding the old horse by his leads into the wide green landscape in between the tall, mountainous rock.

After some brief searching, they stumbled across a herd of wild horses ripe for the breaking. In it stood a tall, white, muscular thoroughbred. Vindex looked at his brother and pointed at the horse which his eyes were desperately keen on. 'That's the one for me, Viridox.'

'He is a beauty, but the question is, how do you plan to catch it?'

'Watch me and follow suit when your turn comes,' Vindex replied as he hopped on the saddle of the old nag. He then began to slowly approach the area where the herd was grazing.

Just before being in earshot of the herd, Vindex bared down on his steed, causing the nag to run as fast as it could. He knew the grazing stallion could outrun his horse, so he needed the element of surprise. Fortunately, Vindex took the herd by surprise and was able to ride right next to the white stallion he had his eye on. Vindex now had to act quickly. The nag could not keep up with the thoroughbred for long. He took his left foot out of his stirrup and closed the distance between the two as he prepared to jump onto the wild colt. With one powerful push off his right leg, he successfully landed on the back of his future obedient companion. The wild beast bucked as soon as Vindex landed on his back.

'Woah, woah, easy there. Calm down, boy,' Vindex hushed while struggling to hold on to the horse. He stroked the horse's mane and whispered to the horse. After a short time, the stallion stopped bucking and allowed Vindex to guide him through the valley. Vindex slowly led the horse back to his brother, with the old nag following closely behind.

'That was impressive,' Viridox said with genuine amazement that his brother was able to successfully pull off such a task.

'Don't be too impressed. You'll be doing it next,' Vindex replied from aloft on his steed, looking at his brother, who was sitting in the grass. 'Just find one you like and give it a go.'

Viridox smiled as he pushed his arm off the ground, getting up eagerly. 'Sounds like a plan.' He mounted the old nag and slowly crept to a different part of the valley where the horses now grazed.

After some inspection, Viridox found what he thought to be a true steed. A beautiful buckskin colored horse with a long black mane. He listened to his brother's advice and tried to imitate his impressive feat. He slowly approached the pack before accelerating into it. Viridox directed himself to the buckskin prize which he had set his sights on. As he approached the horse, he removed his right foot from the stirrup and prepared a jump to the left. He pulled the nag in closer and leaped out left hoping to land on the horse, however at the last moment the wild horse veered leftward making the gap too far to jump. Viridox, now in the air, had no options but to crash land.

He smashed into the horse's rear. He spun in the air before landing with momentum on the ground, causing his body to roll over four times before stopping.

Vindex immediately rushed over to help his brother, but before he could get there, Viridox could feel something breathing over his forehead. He slowly opened his eyes and saw a grey mare looking down on him. Startled by the sight, Viridox shot up and sprawled backwards away from the horse on his hands and knees. However, the wild horse followed and by the time Vindex had gotten to his brother, the horse was licking Viridox in the face as if he was a sugar cube.

'I think she likes you,' Vindex said playfully, watching his brother struggle to stand up, fighting the affection of the grey mare.

'Oh, really?' Viridox said, trying to cover his mouth from the horse's tongue, 'Whatever gave you that impression?'

'Probably the licking,' Vindex replied bluntly.

Viridox tried to stand but was knocked over by the mare who was not done licking the now grown man. 'Any time you want to help, brother, by all means, come in.'

'Oh, no. You're doing a great job. I believe in you,' Vindex replied coyly, watching his brother struggle.

Eventually, when the horse grew tired of licking, Viridox stood once more. His hair was a mess, covered in dirt, grass, and drool. He stood next to his new horse and smiled at the affection he had received. His mind had forgotten about the disappointment of the previous night and instead his full thought was on befriending his new companion. He hopped on the horse's back and patted the mare lovingly.

'What are you going to name her?' Vindex asked curiously, seeing the intense bond the two already shared.

'I think I'll call her Alesia. And you?'

'I think I'll call my steed Bucephalus. Now you know that was only part one of this adventure, Viridox.'

'What was part two?'

'Simple … a race!'

With no warning, Vindex had already taken off, headed for the path to the summit.

'You know that's cheating, Vindex!' Viridox exclaimed as he chased after him up the same path only a few meters behind, despite not being ready for the start.

By the time they reached the halfway point, the brothers were neck and neck. The stampeding hooves knocked off the stones along the narrow trail that led up the mountain's edge. As they continued up the path, the trail grew narrower, leading to Viridox and Alesia being pushed to the edge. Despite the danger, the two brothers were exhilarated.

'I think this may be one time I beat you at something!' Viridox exclaimed, taking the lead by just a head. As they came around the last edge before the final stretch to the camp, Viridox and Alesia proved too much for Vindex as he finished an entire horse's length behind, despite having the head start.

'Well played brother,' Vindex said as he got off Bucephalus now at their camp. 'Its best two out of three though, so don't take too much pride in victory just yet.'

'I can race you one more time,' Viridox responded cheekily. 'It won't take too long.'

Vindex walked up to his brother and put his arm around his neck before squeezing him playfully and said, 'Next time I won't go easy on you is all.'

Viridox, still with his head in Vindex's arms, refused to humor his older brother and replied, 'I'm sorry, I'm a bit confused. Is that what the Galdeshans call cheating? You started well ahead of me, mister.'

The pair walked back to the fire where Cato was residing. He was happy to see the two men again. He was especially joyous to see Viridox in better spirits. Cato looked at the two new horses they brought with them and said, 'I think you forgot one.'

Vindex and Viridox looked at each other and then over the cliff's edge.

'The nag!' they both exclaimed simultaneously.

'He will be alright. He knows how to get back up without your guidance,' Cato replied sincerely. 'I hope you two had fun today.'

Vindex slapped his brother on the back and replied, 'Yes it was a fun little trip.'

Viridox continued, 'It was the best. I even bested him in a horse race where he cheated at the start.'

Vindex said grumpily, 'Of course you bring it up to Cato.'

'Cheaters never prosper,' Cato said with a smile.

Vindex grumbled, now sitting down at the fire, dissatisfied with his inability to be the best at every task he put his mind to.

Cato and Viridox stopped the teasing when they saw Vindex genuinely upset from their jokes. After relieving the tension, the three ate dinner over the open flames before night set. As the moon showed itself, illuminating the mountain, Cato asked Vindex to come with him to the chamber to continue his training with the fairies. Eager to improve his connection to the Maith, Vindex happily agreed. He wished his brother goodnight, then set off with Cato. As the pair entered the chamber, Cato sealed themselves off from the outside world.

With his brother and mentor gone, Viridox stood up and walked to his dwelling to pick up his bow. Not wanting to seem less motivated in improving his skills than his brother, he would practice his archery until Vindex was done with his training. He closed his eyes and pulled back the bow and took the shot at the target post he had built. Viridox only opened his eyes after hearing the stone arrow hit the wooden post. A perfect bullseye. Viridox smiled to himself as he drew his bow once more.

VALERIK'S VISION

Vindex stared blankly at the rock wall. Aggravated and tired, he yelled. 'I can't do it!' Three times he had failed the task Cato had proposed.

'Concentrate Vindex,' Cato replied calmly, 'You can do it. You just need to clear your mind.'

Vindex stood up and turned to Cato, who was standing at the closed entrance to the chamber. 'Cato, I can't. Every time I rest, or my mind becomes too peaceful, I am brought back to relive that day all those years ago when my father died. It isn't a choice. If it was, I promise I would be doing more.'

Cato's face paled. He felt a pit in his stomach, a feeling which time had not healed. He slowly opened his mouth and said, 'I know all too well what it's like to be plagued by memories of the past, Vindex. But I assure you, despite this, you can still transcend into the Maith like I have shown you.'

Vindex took a deep breath and sat back down. He was determined to try it once more before quitting for the night. He crossed his legs and tried to vacate his mind of all thought, only focusing on the spirits that surrounded him. Just like the first three trials, Vindex again struggled to clear his mind. Too many thoughts raced through his head and he could not connect to the Maith.

I am nothing but a failure, Vindex thought to himself sitting in the cold stone meditation room. *I failed today in the race with my brother.*

I can't connect to the Maith. And most of all, I failed at saving my father. I was weak and stupid. I should have done more. I could have done more. I vow to never be that weak again. I will connect with the Maith. I will perfect this craft. And I will avenge my father!

Vindex's thoughts spiraled as he focused more and more on his past failures. As he concentrated on the night his father died, Vindex could vividly picture the flames of his burning home. Amidst all the chaos, Vindex could clearly see one thing through the flames. That image, which was burned into his memory, was Valerik. The Umbrian general stood before him in all his strength and power. Vindex knew he had not cleared his mind. He opened his eyes to tell Cato he had failed, but as his eyes widened, he was no longer in the meditation chamber. He had been transported yet again to Umbria.

Vindex quickly looked around and saw what appeared to be a meeting of Umbria's top generals and captains. Valerik stood in the center of the hall with his allies seated on either side.

'Umbrians,' Valerik spoke, 'You have all worked hard with me. It has not been an easy few years, but we have finally brought about a golden age for our people. Our harvests are boundless, and our cities are bustling. I think it is about time we share these good fortunes with the rest of the world.'

The group cheered in agreement with Valerik's proposal. One who looked exceedingly eager was his second in command, Dara. She could not contain her own excitement and desperately asked, 'Where will we go first?'

Valerik looked at his most trusted companion and replied, 'You and I will be going nowhere. We have not only a city, but an entire Empire to run. Leadership is not always on the battlefield.'

The joy in Dara's eyes shattered when she heard she would not be in the front line, but true to her character and because of her admiration for Valerik, she held her tongue and remained silent.

Valerik looked at Dara seeing her dismay and replied, 'You won't miss much anyway, Dara. I doubt many nations would willingly oppose the fruitful bounty I am offering to their people.'

This enraged Vindex as he stood there watching. 'Your fruitful bounty is grown through blood,' Vindex said sternly, hoping someone in the meeting could hear him.

Just as Vindex finished his sentence, Valerik looked away from the circle of generals. He moved his eyes from his friends and colleagues and stared at the other end of the palace hall where Vindex stood. Vindex's heart dropped. He shook in fear, thinking the Umbrian Emperor could see him. He reached for his waist and grabbed onto the hilt of his father's blade. Just as Vindex was about to pull the blade from his sheath, Dara softly elbowed Valerik, bringing his attention back into the circle.

'So, who will go?' Dara asked.

Vindex, seeing Valerik return to his conversation, sighed in relief. He sat on the ground, his heart still beating quickly. *I am going to need to better prepare, if I hope to avenge my father,* Vindex thought to himself as he continued eavesdropping on the Umbrian leaders.

Valerik weighed his options carefully. He looked around the circle of commanders and thought of everything they had done during the civil war. He contemplated on who would be the best at expanding the Umbrian sphere of influence. Eventually, he settled on two men. Captain Thrün and Commander Agis. Thrün was cold and calculating. Valerik knew he would get the job done efficiently, with as minimal casualties as possible. Agis, however, was more brash and hotheaded, but always came through in difficult situations. During the civil war, Agis had even saved Valerik's life – something the Emperor had not forgotten.

Valerik spoke, 'Captain Thrün, Commander Agis, you two will be charged with leading the expansion efforts.'

'Sir, yes, sir,' the two replied in unison, saluting their Emperor and general.

'Thrün,' Valerik continued, 'I want you to go to the northern society of the Sunduk. You will need at least three thousand men. Hopefully, you can use your diplomacy to prevent any bloodshed. Show them our prosperity and use your numbers as a threat. They are practical people, and I am sure they want to avoid war if they can. As for you, Agis, I want you to march west to the remaining tribes of Galicia. Take fifteen hundred men with you and stop at Trevonum. If the Sunduk do not comply, Trevonum will be a critical staging point for an invasion. The strategic value in maintaining that settlement is greater than advancing south to the rest of Galica.'

Vindex was irate hearing the man he so despised declare that he was launching a campaign to take control of Galician land. *Diplomacy! What a joke,* Vindex thought to himself, thinking back to the methods Valerik used in Norova. Vindex used his hatred to focus. He closed his eyes once again and concentrated until he felt his presence return to the chamber in the mountains.

Vindex opened his eyes and was overjoyed to see himself back inside the cave. Still on his knees from the meditation, he looked over at Cato, who stood at the chamber's door and said, 'They're coming.'

'You saw him again?' Cato asked, increasingly worried about his pupil's inability to connect fully to the Maith.

'Yes,' Vindex said standing up, 'I saw him, and his army is coming.' His demeanor was frightened, but somehow joyous.

Cato walked over and placed his arm on the shoulder of the young man. He said, 'Vindex, focus! You can do this. You just need to concentrate.'

Vindex looked at his mentor and brushed him off his shoulder, pushing past him on his way to the door, which was still sealed. 'Cato, as long as that man breathes, I will never have the peace of mind needed to connect to the Maith,' he said while placing his hand upon the door, attempting to unseal the entrance.

'Only a foolish man seeks revenge,' Cato replied as he walked to the door. He reached out his hand and conjured the Maith to reopen the gateway.

Vindex looked across at Cato standing next to him. He spoke not with anger, but with a broken spirit. 'You wouldn't understand Cato. This is not a choice. I lost everything.'

Cato looked down at his own feet before taking a deep inhale. 'Vindex,' he replied, 'Look around you. Where have you been these past few years? This is the home of my people. My race, my family and my home are all gone. With time, everything goes, including your wounds. Please stay and finish your training.'

Vindex paused for a moment. He never truly grasped the plight of Cato, who, before finding Vindex, was the last remaining Galdeshan. Vindex then spoke softly, 'That may be so Cato, but these wounds are still fresh. If I do not try to heal them myself, I will never learn the Maith and I will never find peace. You know I am right. I have to do this.'

'I suppose I understand. A younger version of myself may have even wanted to join you, but I know with age that this is not the right choice, my son. Stay here, train with me, I beg of you. There are greater forces at work than what you realize,' Cato replied sensitively, trying to remain as unassertive as possible, not wanting Vindex to feel forced into staying.

'What bigger forces are at work Cato?' Vindex asked. 'Valerik wishes nothing more than to see the destruction of my people, and you wish me to sit here and do nothing. Even without my personal goals in mind, this man is a bloodthirsty tyrant who must be stopped!'

'Tyrants come and go,' Cato quickly said under his breath instinctively. His eyes quivered, rethinking the past horrors that he once bore witness.

'Well, what stays forever, then? You on this rock doing nothing? Surely with all your endless knowledge you must know there are more important things than this?' Vindex replied, cutting Cato off from speaking. He reached out, placing his hand in front of Cato's and said, 'Join me, please. I still need you. We can do this together and then complete my training.'

Cato took Vindex's hand with both of his own and gently lowered it. Vindex had a look of disappointment and betrayal in his eyes. 'I can't come with you, Vindex,' Cato spoke somberly, 'And one day you will understand why.'

Vindex, confused and hurt, lashed out, 'What is so important that you must stay on this mountain? As you said, your family is gone. Your home is abandoned and forgotten. Why stay here?'

Vindex did not mean to attack Cato with these questions. They came from a genuine curiosity regarding why Cato was so adamant about not leaving the mountain. Vindex got his answer. 'It is not a choice that I stay here, Vindex,' Cato spoke, 'I have a duty to uphold. I have told you about the Maith and how it binds us and how we can call upon it for aid. My people discovered it thousands of years ago, and with that discovery, we found something else. Something much worse. We called the other, the Olc. It is a force so great that it nearly destroyed the entire world, and it would have, if not for the sacrifices of my people. I stand watch as guardian forever for something buried deep in this mountain. So long as I stand guard, it is powerless to escape.'

Vindex was perplexed. Never had Cato mentioned such a threat or a story to the young man. 'And the Olc is bound as long as you are here, which is why you can never leave. Is this why you wanted me to finish my training? To take over the mantle from you?' Vindex asked.

'Eventually, yes,' Cato replied honestly. The mountain had trapped him for more than a lifetime and, while not willing to abandon his post, he was elated at the prospect of finally resting. 'I have been here for so long, Vindex. I am tired. I just hoped one day, if you chose to, you would take my place.'

Vindex questioned no further. He understood Cato's mindset on why he should stay. However, he also knew that it was impossible as he could never master the Maith until his demons were slain. 'I will come back,' Vindex said confidently. 'I promise you; I will come back. And when I do, I will have the peace of mind needed to finish my training.'

Cato saw the determination in the young man's eyes. He nodded his head and gestured towards the opening of the cave. The two stepped out together, knowing that it would be the last time for a while that they would share each other's company.

Vindex turned to Cato as they walked back to the campfire where Viridox was now resting. 'Thank you,' he said.

Cato smiled and nodded his head before shaking Vindex's hand. The young man then ran to his brother, waking him from his slumber. 'It is time to go, brother,' Vindex said eagerly.

'You know, Vindex, I can't remember the last time I woke you up while you're sleeping,' Viridox said groggily. 'Where are we going?'

'To the western tribes of Galicia. Valerik's army is coming and we need to warn them,' Vindex responded grimly.

Viridox looked perplexed. 'Shouldn't you be staying here with Cato to finish your training?' Viridox looked over at Cato, who gave an exacerbated shrug. He empathized with Viridox's mindset but did not interject, knowing that Vindex would not be swayed.

Vindex looked at Viridox and simply said, 'Do you trust me?'

'Of course, Vindex.'

'Then ride with me. I know what we need to do. We shall come back here after we are done,' Vindex said, placing his arm on his brother's shoulder. 'We will come back here, and we will be champions,' he continued muttering, mostly to himself.

The two brothers quickly packed what little belongings they had amassed during their tenure on the mountain. Each loaded their provisions on their horses, Bucephalus and Alesia. They then mounted their steeds and started down the mountain. 'Wait!' Cato called.

The pair turned around and dismounted their horses. Vindex thought maybe he had found a way to join them. They looked on as the old man ran towards them on the rocky path.

'If you plan to do this,' Cato said, 'You will need proper equipment.' He lifted both his hands and closed his eyes, concentrating on the Maith. Conjuring the spirits for aid, a bright lime glow fell over the path. Vindex and Viridox looked away, shielding their eyes until the light died down. As quickly as it appeared, the light had dissipated into the air. They opened their eyes and found two pairs of armor, a shield and a blade for each. The helmet, chest plates, tunics, shin guards, and small circular shield were colored silver. The armor shined brightly, even in the moonlight. 'Think of this as a going away gift,' Cato said with a smile.

Vindex lifted the chest plate as Viridox inspected his new blade. 'This is so light. What is it made of?'

'It's an old Galdeshan secret, I'm afraid,' Cato replied, 'Just know it is the strongest metal you will come across in your travels. Only a blade from the fires of Medila can penetrate its shell.'

The pair donned their new armor and thanked the sage once again. Before they could mount their horses, Cato interrupted once more. 'One more thing. Take this.'

He handed Vindex a bag full of gold. 'Not every man can be swayed with just words,' he said before letting the two ride off down the mountainside.

As the two approached the valley below, Viridox looked to his brother who was on his right and asked, 'Where to first?'

Vindex looked back at his brother and replied, 'To Ebora first. We shall see after that what is the best course to take.'

The two rode off into the night sky, beginning what would be a day's journey traveling to the Galician village of Ebora. Vindex was nervous. He had seen none of his former countrymen in years. He worried about whether he could convince the people there to join his cause before it was too late.

As for Viridox, he had full faith in his brother's command and was feeling safe and secure following his direction. He would help Vindex in any way he could, so long that it brought him inner peace. Bucephalus and Alesia rode hard through the night, following the lead of the sons of Brunos.

C H A P T E R   8

CITY STREETS

The sun was shining brightly the next morning as Agis and Thrün began their journey out of Apolina. As the two armies marched from the city walls, Valerik watched from the capitol building's balcony. Valerik leaned against the limestone railing. He was at the highest point in all of Apolina. He was content and smiling when he heard the door leading to the terrace open. It was Dara.

Valerik did not have to look to see who was there. He had spent years with Dara at his side. He could tell it was her from the sound of her footsteps. 'How are you, Dara?' he said without turning his attention from his marching legions as they exited through the city walls.

Dara approached her general and stood next to him, looking out at the army flowing out of the city. 'I would be better if I were down there,' she said.

'I know you are not thrilled with my decision, Dara, but I need you here. I need you with me,' Valerik responded, turning to address Dara directly.

'Valerik,' Dara hesitated, not knowing what her general meant, 'What is there left for us to do here? I do not understand.'

Valerik pulled away from her and walked to the other side of the terrace. 'We have created the perfect society, Dara. No one is starving. The people are being taught how to read. Opportunity is nearly endless. And none of this could have been done without you. I am very grateful for your loyalty during this reconstruction. And because of your hard work, I think it is time for us to take a break.'

'Sir,' Dara spoke, 'The job is not complete until every nation has what we have accomplished here.' She walked back to be at his side, looking out at the beautiful city beneath them. They saw narrow alleys, clamoring markets, and countless red terracotta roofs.

'I know,' Valerik replied, 'Don't forget I am the one who taught you that. And besides, we aren't giving up; merely just giving others a moment to shine. After the bravery Agis and Thrün showed during the civil war, I say it's only fair to allow them this chance to spread our influence. Additionally, our people all over the Empire need us. They need us to make the right decisions and to continue to protect this new way of life. We fought during the civil war so that we could govern. Not for the sake of battle.'

'I suppose,' Dara said begrudgingly. 'We both know that I prefer the risks of the battlefield, but I'll try to enjoy the society we have built.'

'Perhaps we can enjoy it together. I wish to walk around the city today. What do you say?' Valerik asked his pupil, hoping she would accept the proposal to enjoy the fruitful city in which they resided.

'Sure,' replied Dara enthusiastically with her arm extended, pointing towards the rooftop door signaling Valerik to take the lead.

The two exited the capitol building, which was once the proud home of the corrupt Umbrian Senate. Valerik and Dara made their way down the steps to the plaza. Despite the recent civil war, business was booming. People were hustling in every direction to buy and sell their goods at the markets. Wooden market stalls stood tall all over the slate city square. Buildings constructed of concrete walls surrounded the square. Some walls were white, some red, others purple, orange, or grey. During the reconstruction Valerik instituted change, which allowed citizens to paint their homes whatever color they wished. Sometimes the colors clashed with the terracotta rooftops and the cobblestone roads, but Valerik did not care for outward vanity. He only wanted his people to be prosperous.

Valerik and Dara had to push their way through the packed crowd. As they marched through, Valerik admired the marketplace. The citizens wore tunics of fine silks which they could not afford when the Senate was in authority. They had more money to buy goods and a wider variety of stocks for purchasing. Fish native only to Teos and dyes from Hatra could all be found within Apolina's great market. Finally, the pair made their way to a side street and could step away from bustling the marketplace.

'I have never seen the streets so packed before,' Dara said in shock as the two made their way down the cobblestone lane.

Valerik grinned ear to ear. 'Before the Empire, these poor people barely had enough to fill their bellies. Now they have so much excess they can freely spend on their heart's desire,' he said as the pair stopped outside a shop next to an alleyway.

'Unless the thing they wish to purchase is freedom,' a stranger spoke, emerging from inside the shop.

Dara rushed over to the man and pulled him into the alley. She pushed him against the building's wall. 'Do you have any idea who you're speaking to?' Dara asked as she tightened her grip around the man's tunic.

'Aye, I do,' said the man calmly. 'That brute standing behind you is none other than the mighty Valerik.'

'How dare you say such things to your Emperor? A brute! I should have your tongue for saying that!' Dara exclaimed menacingly with rage in her eyes.

'Dara enough. Let him go,' Valerik interjected, trying to intercede and end the conflict.

The stranger turned his comments to the Emperor, now scoffing, 'There he goes again, imposing his will onto others. What if she wanted to have my tongue? Why should your authority stop her? Who proclaimed you the Emperor of all Umbrians? Last I checked, it was a self-appointed title, given to and by a man only interested in himself.'

Dara's green eyes widened, and in a rage, she attacked. She pushed her forearm against his throat, pinning him to the building while raising him a few inches off the ground. He gasped for air as she ferociously choked him with a demented grin on her face.

'Dara! Release him! Now!' Valerik asserted.

Dara looked over at her general with disgust. She did not want to obey his order this time. She stared the stranger in the eyes and continued to put pressure against the man's throat. As the man squirmed, his face became red and his lips slowly turned blue.

'Enough!' Valerik exclaimed with a ferocious scream. He grabbed Dara by the arm and pushed her behind him. His stare at her said more than words ever could. He then turned back to the stranger, who was now on the ground, holding his neck and breathing heavily.

'Why do you say such things?' Valerik asked the stranger. 'Don't you see how much better life is here?'

The stranger looked up and slowly regained his composure. 'A better life born from the blood of our own people. We may not have been as prosperous before your Empire, but at least we had the freedom to govern ourselves. You spoke about the corruption of our own Senate, but at least the people had the power to vote them out. What happens when you become corrupt, your highness?'

Valerik looked at the man with an audacious look. 'I have made this city, no, this entire nation, a better place. You should thank me for appointing myself ruler! You have more freedoms under my rule than with the Senate.'

'Yes. I suppose we do,' The strange man replied with contempt in his voice, 'But what happens when you decide you no longer want us to be free? What if you decide we can't own our homes or sell our goods or plant our crops without your approval? Before, we may have had corrupt leaders, I will admit it, but we still had the power to choose our own destiny. We could elect who we wanted. Who elected you?'

Valerik's face wrinkled. He was angry with this stranger and was at a loss for words. Before he could muster any reply, the man spoke once more.

'I would rather die a destitute free man than a rich servant to someone else's bidding,' the stranger said, staring Valerik in the eye.

'Then let us grant you that request,' Dara replied quickly as she drew her blade on the outspoken critic.

'Dara no,' Valerik said sternly, maintaining eye contact with the stranger. 'He has a right to believe this, so long as he does not create any insubordination among the populace.'

Dara put her sword back and gave an evil glare at the man, who was now visibly trembling.

'Have a good day,' Valerik said as he turned around with Dara to continue their walk throughout the city.

This was not the first time Valerik was reviled for his actions. Despite all the criticism and bloodshed, he knew his actions were necessary for the greater good of the Umbrian people. *That man knows nothing. Only I know what is best for the Umbrian people,* Valerik thought to himself as he continued to walk the city streets with Dara.

The sun was now at its midday peak, and Dara and Valerik continued their walk of the capital city. At approximately the same time, many miles away from Umbria, Vindex and Viridox were approaching Ebora. Ebora was a modest farming community. The small circular village had no wall. It consisted of several dozen wooden buildings spread sporadically through the fields.

Exhausted and grumpy, Viridox turned to his brother and asked, 'Is this it?' in disgust.

Vindex stayed silent. He had also been hoping for more. They knew little beyond the walls of their home in Norova. They had hoped that this village would be comparable in size or population. To their dismay, it was nothing more than a farming village. 'We will make do with what we are given. No one said this was going to be easy,' Vindex said after a long pause.

As they entered the village, they saw children laughing and playing in the streets. Men and women were tending the fields, and cattle were being moved around the dirt square. Wooden homes had crooked doorways and thatched roofs, with large spaces of green grass between each building. Dirt roads connected the town's buildings to the main street. It was the first time in years where Vindex and Viridox truly felt back at home.

They made their way down the main road and saw an old man seated outside of the mead hall in the center of the town. Covered in nothing but a raggedy brown tunic with no sleeves, he looked older than Cato and was terribly skinny. His long white and grey beard had not been cut in many years.

Viridox turned to his brother and said, 'I bet that's the village elder. Best we go and introduce ourselves. Don't you think?'

'Just what I was about to suggest,' Vindex replied as the pair dismounted from their horses and walked the remaining distance on foot.

'Welcome to Ebora,' The village elder spoke. 'My name is Kastis. How can I help you fine gentlemen?'

Vindex stepped in front of his brother, taking the lead in the conversation. 'I am Vindex. First son of Brunos, and one of two survivors of the massacre of Norova. Beside me is the only other survivor, my younger brother, Viridox.'

Kastis stood up. He was in disbelief. 'You say you are from Norova? Impossible. That settlement was destroyed nearly five years ago.'

'I know,' Vindex replied solemnly, 'I was there.'

Kastis became zealous. 'What happened? There has been nothing but speculation about what occurred there since our traders found it burnt completely to ash all those years ago.'

'The Umbrians happened,' Viridox chimed in, stepping forward to take over the conversation from his brother. He did not want his brother to relive that night yet again, explaining the history to Kastis. 'The Umbrians came and decimated our home. If it was not for my brother Vindex, I would not be here today.'

Kastis looked in disbelief. His eyes softened as he sat back down and said, 'I am sorry for you, boys. You must have been very young when it occurred. That is just awful.'

Viridox continued to speak on his brother's behalf, replying, 'What's worse is that they are back, and on their way here now.'

'Oh dear,' Kastis said alarmingly, 'How can I help?'

Vindex jumping back into the conversation asked, 'How many people live in this village, Kastis?'

'Maybe seven or eight hundred?'

'And how many men and women are of fighting age?'

'Women?' Kastis scoffed. 'Surely you do not mean to send the daughters of Galicia to the front lines of war?'

'When the Umbrians came to my home, they killed every man, woman, and child indiscriminately. I'd rather have them die valiantly on the battlefield protecting their homeland than in their dwellings victims of brutal savages,' Vindex replied forcefully, making his desperation clear that he, in fact, needed as much help as possible.

Kastis, while not agreeing with Vindex, understood the severity of the matter. He replied, 'I will see what I can arrange for you two. In the meantime, please rest. You seem tired from your travels.'

Vindex and Viridox looked at each other and nodded in agreement. Rest sounded good and they followed Kastis into the mead hall where there were some cots prepared in the back. After Kastis left, Viridox turned over to look at his brother, who was in a cot only a few feet from him. He asked, 'Do you think we have a chance? Honestly?'

Vindex shifted his gaze to his younger brother and replied, 'So long as we stay together, we will always have a chance. Now let's get some rest.'

Viridox took comfort in his brother's assurance and smiled before laying his head back on his cot. After only a few minutes, Vindex could hear snores coming from his brother. Viridox was sleeping comfortably, something Vindex slightly envied. Vindex closed his eyes and tried to drift off to sleep. His attempt was in vain, however, as his mind wandered. Vindex raised himself from his cot and walked to an isolated portion of the hall where he knelt down and closed his eyes, trying to conjure the Maith. After a while with no success, he had an idea.

He would redraw the symbol from the mountain. With his finger he pressed into the dirt floor and drew from memory the symbol in Cato's cave. Vindex stepped back to admire his work. He saw the circles with a small diamond in the center surrounded by jagged lines on all sides. *Perfect,* he thought.

He knelt down and attempted to clear his mind to conjure the surrounding spirits. Eventually, he could feel the Maith around him. He opened his eyes and found himself kneeling in the same cave where he originally learned how to conjure the Maith. He stood up and walked through the sealed door and came out to the campfire, where he saw Cato cooking a very early dinner. 'Well, hello there!' Cato said with joy, looking toward Vindex.

Vindex looked around, presuming he was speaking to someone else, but after finding no one, he asked, 'You can see me?'

'Well, of course I can,' Cato replied. 'I am a master of the Maith, after all.'

'Interesting,' Vindex spoke as he approached the camp. 'But those who have not been trained can't. So, when I had my visions of Valerik in Apolina, he could not see me.'

'Correct. Now I'd offer you food, but you're not really here to enjoy it,' Cato said, as he dined on the meat that had just come off the fire.

Vindex smiled and replied, 'Well, I am not really hungry, but I could use some advice.'

'What kind of senex would I be if I didn't help you? Come, take a seat,' Cato replied, gesturing to Vindex to sit beside him.

'A bad one I suppose,' Vindex replied as he sat across the fire staring at Cato. 'Now I need more guidance on how to connect to the Maith. I could only come here because I drew the symbol from the cave in the dirt where I was meditating. Otherwise, I would not have been able to bring myself here.'

Cato looked disappointed. 'You are focusing on the wrong thing, Vindex,' he said sharply. 'This ability you use is only a fraction of the power the spirits can give to you, but you refuse to fully connect with the Maith. You don't need any symbol to meditate on. You just need to embrace what is always surrounding you.'

'I know Cato, I know. I can't fully connect unless I have a completely clear head. The problem is, I am not as level-headed as you,' Vindex replied quickly. 'Now please help me learn how to conjure the Maith so I can see what others are doing, as I did on the mountain. I will need it if I am to succeed on my journey.'

Cato sighed. It disappointed him that Vindex's personal interests were greater than learning for the sake of knowledge. Eventually, he disclosed some information about why Vindex was being transmitted to certain people and places. 'It appears that whatever your subconscious is thinking of is where you appear. Usually it is Valerik, but today you drew the symbol from the cave in the ground. Despite your best efforts to clear your thoughts, you could not and poof, here you are.'

Vindex took a moment to think about how he could use this to his advantage. 'I think I can make that work,' he said, more talking to himself than to Cato.

Cato looked across at him and said, 'I hope it does. So that you can return here to finish your training properly.'

Vindex reaffirmed he would return after his journey ended. He was not disinterested in learning the ways of the Maith. He just cared more about avenging his father. The two talked a while longer before Vindex thought it was best that he return to his body in Ebora.

Taking a deep breath, Vindex closed his eyes on Cato and waited a moment. He reopened them and was next to the village elder, who was watching him intently. 'Kastis,' Vindex said, startled. 'Have you talked to your village? Do you know who will join me?'

'I have,' Kastis replied, not looking at Vindex, but at the symbol under him. He walked around the circle to analyze the symbol on all sides.

Vindex got up and stood between Kastis and the symbol he had drawn. 'What did your town have to say? Will anyone join me?'

'For the right price,' Kastis quickly replied, looking now at Vindex instead of the ground.

'Well, the price shouldn't be a problem,' Vindex retorted, taking out the bag of gold given to him by Cato.

Kastis stared at the bag filled to the brim with gold coins and then looked over Vindex's shoulder to look at the symbol once again. He then faced Vindex in the eyes and asked, 'Who are you really?'

Vindex pretended to be confused at what the man was asking. 'What do you mean?' he asked.

'That symbol. I know it. I may not be as old as that society, but I have heard the stories. You are a Galdeshan,' Kastis replied in shock and fear.

'I do not know what you are talking about. The Galdeshans are just a myth told from father to son,' Vindex confidently replied.

'And yet you sat meditating on the symbol of their people that you constructed,' Kastis replied. 'I may be old, but I am far from senile.'

Vindex insisted yet again that he was not in any way a Galdeshan and that he would much rather return to the business at hand which was drafting the men and women of Ebora to fight against the impending invasion.

Kastis agreed to Vindex's request and went to the exit of the room. He informed Vindex that he would collect his brother and wait for him outside the hall in the town center. Before leaving the room, he looked over his shoulder, pointed at the circle and said, 'Be wary, Vindex. Magic of that nature was never intended for mortals like us. It is easy for the power to consume us. Make sure that you keep yours in check, if not for your sake, but for the men you lead.' He then exited the room, leaving Vindex alone with his thoughts.

Vindex looked down at the symbol in the dirt and quickly erased it with his foot covering up what he had drawn. He reached for his helmet, which he had removed while meditating, and left the hall. He walked to the town center to meet up with his brother, who stood in front of a large assembly. Vindex looked out at the crowd and asked Viridox, 'What is the good word?'

Viridox looked at his brother and replied, 'About two hundred men and women combined.'

Vindex replied desperately, 'That can't be. That's not nearly enough. Are we sure there are no more?'

Viridox looked at his brother and said, 'You can count them yourself if you wish. This is all we have, Vindex. What are we up against?'

Vindex glanced at Viridox's eyes before looking back at the crowd in front of him. 'Fifteen hundred,' he mumbled.

Viridox was stunned. 'Fifteen hundred!' he spoke. 'Those odds are insurmountable. We'll be killed for sure.'

Vindex avoided his brother's glare while he thought of a solution. After a moment, he looked back at Viridox and replied, 'Not if I go to the tribe of Alabum in the south. I can recruit more men there and make it back to the mountain valley to combine the forces before the Umbrians arrive.'

'Who will train these men and women, then?' Viridox protested. 'You are the better fighter between us two. They will need your instruction.'

'I may be better with a blade,' Vindex replied, 'but your skills with a bow are unmatched. Teach these men and women how to shoot and I will teach the people of Alabum how to fight while I march back to you.'

'How much time do we have?' Viridox asked curiously, hoping they had at least enough time to properly train for battle.

'Only a few weeks,' Vindex replied, 'Which is why we must hurry.' He put out his hand to shake his brother's. 'Meet me at the end of the mountain of Galdesha with your unit. We will win, yet, brother.'

After the pair shook hands, Vindex ran past the crowd to his horse, Bucephalus. He quickly unhitched him and rode out fast toward the next Galician tribe.

'I sure hope we do,' Viridox whispered to himself as he watched his brother gallop through the dirt road, heading south toward Alabum.

'Where is he going?' Kastis asked, walking up to Viridox, who was still standing in front of the crowd.

Viridox responded, 'There has been a slight change of plans. We need more soldiers than you can provide, so Vindex is traveling to

Alabum to garnish further support. I will stay here and train your people in the meantime.'

Kastis nodded and went back to the crowd and explained this situation to his people, who did not mind the change. They were still going to be paid for defending their own homeland. Viridox rounded up the group and began drilling them immediately by teaching them the same lessons Cato had taught him on the mountain. Viridox hoped it would be enough to overcome the Umbrian invader. All hope was now with Vindex and his ability to get more fighters from Alabum.

C H A P T E R 9

WAR

Vindex rode swiftly through the night on Bucephalus. The pair only rested for two or three hours before riding once again. Vindex knew the clock was ticking, and he needed to reach Alabum and recruit more soldiers to their cause before it was too late. It took just over one day for Vindex to arrive at Alabum. *I can't waste anymore time*, Vindex thought to himself as he rode into the town square.

The village, in a lot of ways, reminded Vindex of Ebora. Alabum consisted of small wooden homes built around vast farmland. There were no fortifications protecting the settlement. The population mirrored Ebora, only having about eight hundred occupants. When Vindex arrived in the center square outside the main hall, he could not locate the town elder.

'Excuse me,' Vindex spoke, addressing a young girl who was carrying water from a well. 'Where is your town elder?'

'He is away on some trading business, I think,' the young girl replied. 'He won't be back for another fortnight.'

'Damn,' Vindex mumbled to himself. He then replied to the girl with a forced smile, 'Thank you for your help.'

The girl then walked off, continuing with her daily chores while Vindex planned on what to do next. *I can't wait here for two weeks,* Vindex thought. *The Umbrians will be nearly through the mountains by then. I guess I need to recruit these people myself.*

Vindex then hopped on top of Bucephalus and exclaimed with all his might. 'Ladies and gentlemen of Alabum. My name is Vindex. You probably do not know me, but you may know my father, Brunos of Norova. Several years ago, my homeland was destroyed and now the same invaders who wiped out my tribe have returned. This time they have their eyes set on all of Galicia. I am trying to amass an army to stop the oncoming threat. Brave men and women have already enlisted from Ebora and are undergoing training with my brother Viridox. Our hope is that we can double our forces with the strength and courage of your village. So please, if you are willing to fight for your land, families and homes, meet me at the outskirts of town in two hours. The Umbrian enemy is fast approaching and I will need to return to my brother's force soon. I will pay you with the finest coin for your efforts. Do not do this for me, but for all of Galicia!'

After Vindex finished his speech, he heard some murmuring amongst the people, but after a few moments, everyone returned to their daily lives. With no new allies, Vindex went to the edge of town, hoping someone would come to join his cause. *Perhaps someone will come,* he thought to himself as he settled in, waiting for the two hours to pass.

Little did Vindex know that his speech was being spread all over town by those who heard it firsthand in the town square. After each villager had heard the situation, nearly three hundred volunteers approached Vindex at the edge of town ready for battle. Each recruit brought the best weapons they could find, which were mostly composed of wooden shields or rusty farming equipment. Despite this, Vindex was overjoyed. These new soldiers would increase the Galician's ranks to five-hundred. Not enough to directly combat Umbria's fifteen hundred trained legionaries in open battle, but now there was a hint of hope.

Vindex moved out right away, but without horses and with added numbers, it took him two full days to meet his brother at the entrance to the Galdeshan peaks. Now, with the forces reunited, the two brothers only had about two and a half weeks before the Umbrians would arrive. The enlisted men and women were not soldiers. They were ill-equipped, most did not have shields, hardly any had bows, and most only had rusty farming tools as weapons. Each day, Vindex drilled his recruits. He divided them into two units. The first unit was infantry and they would train with Vindex daily for twelve hours each day, improving their skills in hand to hand combat. The second unit belonged to Viridox and much the same as his brother, he practiced their archery skills for twelve hours each day. In the absence of bows, many members of Viridox's unit became slingers, equipping themselves with slings and stones that they practiced hurling at targets under Viridox's instructions. Many in Viridox's unit adapted naturally to this task, as it was like the stone throwing they had learned to hunt rabbits as children. Through this intense training, many of the men and women from Ebora and Alabum became capable fighters.

The night before the battle, Viridox entered his brother's tent in the soldier's camp and found him meditating. He tapped on his shoulder, waking him up from wherever his mind was and brought him back to the soon to be battlefield. 'Vindex, I was wondering, can you create weapons for the men? Give them the equipment they need to fight in this battle. You know, like Cato did for us before we left the mountain.'

Vindex stood up from his meditation and sat on a small wooden stool. 'I would if I could Viridox. I have been talking and training with Cato for weeks now while I meditate, but I just can't do it. For whatever reason, I can't alter matter without Cato's direct help.'

Viridox just stared at his brother, wishing he had completed his training before going on this desperate endeavor. He calmly asked, 'Then what are we to do, Vindex? As of now, the soldiers only have rusted tools and wooden shields. We will be lambs for the slaughter!'

Vindex looked at his brother reassuringly. 'I have a plan,' he said confidently, 'And if everyone does what I say, most of us should be able to make it out alive.'

Viridox nodded. 'I will do what you ask of me, Vindex. I just don't want to become a martyr.'

'And you won't,' Vindex replied. 'Have faith. I have never steered you wrong. Now go get the men and women ready for instruction. By the morning, the enemy will be here, and we need to be ready when they come.'

'Of course,' Viridox replied, leaving the tent to organize the troops.

Vindex remained in his tent for some time until the sun had finished setting. He was trying to create the so-called plan he claimed to have. By the time he heard all his soldiers gather outside of his tent, Vindex knew he had a working strategy for the incoming threat. He stood up and pushed aside the tent's cloth, stepping out in front of the five hundred total soldiers he had amassed from both villages.

'Eyes front, soldiers, and quiet your mouths. The commander is present,' Viridox exclaimed, quieting the troops for Vindex, who had just stepped into their view.

'Thank you Viridox,' Vindex said, looking at his brother. He turned to his troops and exclaimed with the confidence of a tenured general, 'Brave men and women of Galicia! You stand here today with me and my brother to fight not only for your future prosperity, but for the freedom of you, your families, and your homes! Our goal today is not to defeat the enemy, but to send a message to the Umbrians that we will not give up our sacred lands so easily. That being said, I have no intention of sacrificing any of you. We need to stay alive in order to fight another day. I have come up with a plan that should protect us.'

Vindex paused and looked over to the mountains. 'There is a natural chokepoint at the valley's entrance. I will lead our infantry and fortify this area. It will mitigate the enemy's numerical advantage since they won't have the space to engage all their soldiers at once. While we stand firm at the chokepoint, our archers and slingers led by my brother will climb a back trail up the mountainside. The cliffs are too steep to climb from inside the valley, so as long as our frontline holds, they will have complete protection from the enemy. When the Umbrians arrive, our slingers and archers will pepper the enemy, leaving them weakened before they reach our soldiers on the ground. Hopefully, this will wear the enemy down enough so that they cannot push through our infantry. In the event we lose ground, wait for my retreat signal. If even one person abandons their post before my order, it will put all of Galicia at risk. When I call the retreat, stay together. Break off in pairs. This will make you harder targets for the enemy to cut down. Run to the forest for protection. If you lose the group, make your way to Trevonum on your own. If all goes well, we will regroup outside the city's walls. Lastly, do not forget what you are fighting for. This is our land, our homes! We will not let anyone take that from us! Do I make myself clear?'

The soldiers chanted in unison, 'Sir, yes, sir!'

'Good! Now rest for the rising sun. For with it brings the death of our enemies!' Vindex exclaimed, raising his sword into the air.

His army reciprocated, raising their arms before disbursing back to their encampments. Viridox walked over to Vindex's side and said, 'You almost made me believe we have a fighting chance.'

'That's because we do, brother,' Vindex replied. 'Just make sure that when the time comes tomorrow, you have Alesia at the ready to escape down the mountain's back, so you can make your way to Trevonum. We may not be able to go together.'

'I will Vindex,' Viridox responded, patting his brother on the back. 'Now I am off to bed. I suggest you do the same. As you said, we will be in the fight of our lives tomorrow.'

Vindex smiled as his brother walked to his tent. He looked at the whole campsite before walking back inside his dwelling. He went to the bed, despite knowing he could not sleep. After several hours, he decided it would be in his best interest to conjure the Maith to bring him to Agis and his oncoming army.

Vindex knelt down and focused on the enemy commander. The Maith quickly transported him to the Umbrian's camp at the other side of the Galdeshan Mountains. When Vindex looked around, he found Agis and his men sleeping with no watchman on duty. *Sloppy,* Vindex thought to himself as he walked through the camp. *This would have been a great time to attack.* Vindex, now seeing his opposition firsthand, opened his eyes once more, and the Maith transported him back to the Galician camp. He believed in his people and his plan. He believed they could win. After returning, he closed his eyes once more, not in meditation, but in rest. He needed his sleep if he was going to push back the invaders.

The night passed quickly, and Vindex had only been asleep for about two hours before Viridox rushed into his tent. Vindex was having a nightmare when Viridox shook him awake. Viridox exclaimed, 'Brother, the time is here. We need to move!'

Vindex opened his eyes and saw his brother. 'Oh, you're alive!' he shot out of bed to hug Viridox.

Viridox hugged him back while sarcastically replying, 'For now anyway. The Umbrians are almost here. We have to move.'

Vindex shook his head, waking himself up. Now reoriented, he finished the embrace and said, 'Of course. It is time we go.'

The two brothers stepped out of the tent to see the men and women scrambling to get their gear ready for the battle. Nearly half the infantry men and women had wooden shields and worn leather armor. The other half had no shields and only had tunics covering their bodies. Despite their lack of armor and weaponry, each person stood ready to fight for the land they held dear.

Vindex, in a commanding voice, exclaimed, 'Men and women of Galicia! The day of glory is upon us! Do your motherland proud and follow my design. Archers and slingers go with Viridox now. He will take you up the mountain trail to a point where you can effectively ambush our enemy. The rest of you stay strong and stay with me!'

Viridox rushed off, taking his men and women up the mountainside. He stationed his soldiers behind some jagged rocks on the cliff, out of view of anyone in the valley below. As for Vindex, he donned the gear gifted to him from Cato. He placed the shield on his back and held his father's blade in his right hand and Cato's in his left. He grouped together with the infantry unit three hundred strong and formed a bottleneck at the narrow valley entrance, positioning himself in the middle of the front line.

The steadfast Galicians did not wait long before they could see the Umbrian army. They could hear the echoes of soldiers marching in unison well before they could make out the force itself. The echoes and rumbling unnerved some of the Galician troops until they looked at their leader. Vindex stood tall, eyes fixated on the terrain in front of him. His stoic nature rejuvenated his soldiers as they waited for the enemy. The Umbrian army consisted mostly of battle hardened legionaries, with one cavalry unit that protected Commander Agis in the rear.

When the Umbrian forces saw Vindex and his men, they stopped to send word back to Agis. Soon after, Agis joined his soldiers in the front line to assess the situation. The Umbrian army advanced to within earshot and then stopped. Vindex's heart was racing with excitement. The oncoming battle was the beginning of his revenge plan. He just needed to lure out Valerik. The same was not true for his soldiers, however. They were terrified of the overwhelming numbers of the enemy army, and despite seeing Vindex's swordsmanship and Viridox's archery skill during their training, they wondered if their leaders could defeat such a force.

Umbria's army remained motionless, ready to advance on their leader's order. The soldiers were eager for battle. The force in front of them were mere peasants armed with pitchforks. Umbria's elite would slaughter them if it came to blows. Commander Agis spoke for his entire army when he announced, 'Who dares to stand before the soldiers of Umbria with arms in hand?'

'Someone who doesn't want you to enter,' Vindex yelled back at the opposing general.

Agis lowered his brow and stepped a few feet closer in order to hear the Galician better, but not so close that a conflict could break out just yet. 'And why do you stand between me and my destination?'

'Well, what is your destination?' Vindex asked despite already knowing the truth. He wanted to get Agis talking to lower his people's guard.

'Trevonum,' replied Agis with his head held high and his brow now leveled. 'I am on urgent business directed by the Emperor of the Umbrian people himself.'

'And I suppose the thousand men you have behind you dressed like soldiers are your security escort for an ambassador such as yourself,' Vindex retorted.

Agis' face reddened as he yelled out, 'And who do you think you are to question the authority of Umbria?'

'My name is Vindex. I am the son of Brunos of Norova. I am joined by the bravest Galician men and women from Ebora and Alabum to send a message to your great Emperor. We do not want Umbrians in Galician lands. So, turn back now!'

The soldiers behind Vindex cheered, and those that had shields banged their weapons against them. Agis was none too happy with this defiance. He screamed back, 'If you do not stand aside now, you will perish! This is your last warning. We can still do this peacefully. There is no way you can fight all of us.'

'You're right,' Vindex replied, 'I could never fight all of your men. But I am not surrendering.'

Agis tilted his head and widened his jaw. He could not understand such defiance from a band of peasants. Only eighty feet separated his legionaries with Vindex's force. If he would not surrender, he would die. 'Very well,' Agis spoke, 'In accordance with new Umbrian law, you and your people have denied a peaceful transition and as such …'

Vindex refused to listen to Agis' lecture about Umbrian law and instead used Agis' speech to his advantage. He cut the Umbrian commander off in mid-sentence, raised his head to the sky and let out a roaring scream, 'Viridox!' This was the signal Viridox and his men were waiting for and with little to no hesitation, fifty archers and one hundred and fifty slingers took aim at the Umbrian forces.

The first volley had already hit the Umbrian legion before Agis had his wits about him. After nearly a hundred of his own men fell dead or injured because of the raining arrows and stones, he ordered his men to charge the ground troops. 'Push through the line!' he shouted, 'And make your way up the mountainside to deal with those missiles!' His men charged Vindex and his small villager army. The time to fight was finally upon them.

With shields raised protecting their sides, the Umbrian troops ran to the Galician's position. The volleys became less and less effective as the legionaries advanced, but the missiles still cut down some Umbrian soldiers before the fray began. It was quickly apparent that Vindex's men and women were hopelessly outclassed. Even with the bottleneck of the valley, Vindex's soldiers found it very hard to fight off even one legionary. Their rusty farm tools and weapons hardly impacted their opponents' armor. Their wooden shields and leather armor offered little protection against the Umbrians' weapons.

Vindex found himself in the front line, battling three or four men at a time. With two blades in hand, he was an unstoppable force that cut the Umbrian soldiers down one by one as they challenged him. Despite Vindex's heroics, the battle would have been over in minutes, but for the natural terrain. The valley funneled them to a narrow pass which the Galicians defended well, mitigating the Umbrians' numerical advantage. As Vindex continued to make his way through the Umbrian soldiers, he caught the attention of Agis, who was still towards the middle of his men. Agis saw the devastation which one Galician was causing and rode back to his cavalry to create a plan. Vindex did not notice this. He was too busy dodging incoming blades and spears to the best of his ability while cutting down as many soldiers as he could. Sweat poured down Vindex's face, blurring his vision as it ran into his eyes. With each passing moment that Agis took to regroup with his unit, Vindex and his forces chopped away at the trained Umbrians in the bottleneck they had created.

When Agis finally reached his cavalry unit, he implemented a plan that he believed would win the day. He ordered his men into a loose formation and told his calvary to charge the side covering the path to the mountain ridge where the archers and slingers stood. He planned to break through this militia and take out the missile support before wrapping around trapping the Galicians in a pocket.

After Agis finished explaining the plan, a member of his calvary asked, 'And what of the Galician with the two blades? He has killed nearly twenty of our men single-handedly.'

'Leave him to me,' Agis said confidently as he dismounted his horse. He rejoined the infantry and shouted, 'I want a loose formation!'

'Yes, sir!' the Umbrian soldiers replied as they widened the gaps between one another so that the calvary would have space to run through to the Galicians without trampling Umbrian soldiers.

As the Umbrian army spread out, it became increasingly difficult for Viridox and his men to be accurate in their volleys, but they still continued to fire, hoping to lend any aid to Vindex and the frontline. Vindex saw the Umbrians spread out and was confused. This made it easier for the Galicians to strike down the legionaries who were in the bottleneck at the end of the valley. *Why would Agis do this?* Vindex thought to himself while parrying an incoming slash with his blade. He then heard his challenger approach.

'Barbarian!' Agis hollered across the battlefield. Agis straightened his posture, his blade and shield at the ready.

'So, what was it, Captain Agis?' Vindex asked as he advanced from the front line to face Agis one on one.

The Umbrian legionaries spread out to give their leader space as they furthered their attacks on the Galician frontline. The battle continued between the forces, but it was apparent that the fight between the commanders was grabbing the attention of all participants.

'Commander Agis,' replied the Umbrian with a hint of disdain. Vindex had unknowingly hit a nerve with the Umbrian commander as he felt his own people had yet to recognize the new title that Valerik had given to him at the end of their Civil War.

'It matters little,' Vindex replied as he put away his father's sword into his sheath and took the shield off his back in its place. 'Whatever legacy you have for yourself ends today.'

'You barbarians are all the same. Arrogant filth that needs to be cleansed. This land will be Umbrian and your sorry way of life will be forgotten. Now prepare to die, you insolent dog!' Agis replied as he charged Vindex, who stood ready with his shield raised.

The battlefield took notice as the two collided. Even with all eyes on the pair, the fighting did not stop on the frontline. Viridox saw the battle below and gave new orders to his troops. 'Fire at the enemy's flank! We do not want a stray arrow or stone to hit Vindex. Do not fire near the frontline,' Viridox exclaimed. His soldiers obeyed and Viridox put down his bow to watch his brother duel.

The two leaders were the best either force had to offer, but even as Umbria's best, it was apparent that Agis was the lesser of the two men. Agis swung at Vindex, who blocked the blow with his shield and kicked him back, creating a space between the two warriors. They circled each other, looking for an opening, and when Vindex believed he found one; he swung his blade at Agis' side, causing him to block it with his shield. Vindex expected him to block the attack and had already begun swinging his left arm, holding his shield, not giving Agis time to counterattack. Before he knew it, Agis was on the ground after receiving the blunt force of Vindex's shield on the side of his head. Blood trickling down his face, Agis took off his helmet, bleeding from above his right eyebrow. He wiped off the blood and looked at Vindex with a face of hate. Never had Agis been this tested in battle before, and now he felt fear as he questioned whether he could beat the Galician. He gritted his teeth, stood back up, and gripped his blade tightly. He charged Vindex with a stabbing motion. Vindex quickly evaded spinning around him, using the brunt of his elbow to hit the Umbrian in the forehead. This staggered Agis and in that moment, Vindex followed through with an overhead blow that connected, slicing the bottom of Agis' chin down to the left side of his chest.

Vindex had beaten Agis, surrounded by his legionaries. Agis lay on the battlefield, holding onto his bleeding chest. He stared up at Vindex, who stood above him and said, 'Please have mercy. I beg of you.'

Vindex looked down at Agis, watching the blood cover his body. His eyes widened and teeth gritted as he lost sight of the battle around him and thought back to the night Norova fell. Vindex remembered hiding behind crates, knees drenched in blood while he watched Valerik torture his father. *These people know no mercy. They are the savages,* Vindex thought while still in a trance. He blinked quickly, snapping himself out of his trance. Vindex did not reply to Agis. He took his sword and raised it up, ready to strike down on the Umbrian Commander.

But just before he landed the final blow, an Umbrian cavalry soldier ran over Vindex. The force from the horse threw the Galdeshan into the air, knocking both the sword out of his hand and the helmet from his head. Face down on the ground, he caught his breath before attempting to stand back up. Agis now slowly rose to his feet and looked at his opponent, who was face down in the dirt. Agis then nodded at the horseman, who stood above Vindex. The horseman took his spear and drove it into Vindex's back with his full force.

Viridox was watching and screamed, 'Vindex!' as he pushed his way through his troops, who continued to rain arrows and rocks down upon the enemy soldiers. As Viridox was running down the mountain path, he saw his brother move. The spear had not pierced through the armor given to him by Cato and instead had snapped the shaft. The cavalryman opened his jaw in disbelief. He stood upon his steed as he saw Vindex rise from the dirt. Vindex wasted no time and pulled out his father's blade, slashing the horseman, causing him to fall off his stallion. He walked over and delivered the finishing blow. Vindex then scanned the battlefield, looking for Agis. The Umbrian commander had not gone far. Vindex saw Agis at the same place where they had dueled, slouched over, holding on to the left side of his chest. Vindex, angered by the calvary's interruption, marched over to Agis who had not the strength to flee.

Agis looked up at his enemy, who stood above him and asked, 'Who the hell are you?' not believing that this man was truly just a mortal after surviving a spear to the back. Vindex cared not to answer and instead impaled his father's sword through Agis' stomach, leaving him to suffer a slow painful death on the battlefield.

As he took the blade out of Agis, Vindex turned to the rest of the battlefield. The Umbrian cavalry had nearly broken through the bottleneck the Galicians were holding. Vindex knew now was the time for a retreat. The enemy commander was dead, and the Umbrians had lost far more men than his own forces. With one confident yell, Vindex screamed, 'Retreat as one! Group up and fall back!'

The Galicians followed their leader's command and slowly disengaged from the enemy. Viridox ordered his men to stay to offer some cover fire before they withdrew from the battle as well. While the men were retreating, Vindex found himself too far into enemy ground and he quickly realized that he was surrounded by Umbrian legionaries. A large portion of Umbria's infantry broke off from the Galician frontline when they heard the barbarian retreat. They were more focused on defeating the barbarian who slayed Agis instead of chasing routed peasants. Vindex was now desperate. With all the strength and energy he had left, he fought his way through the hoard, attempting to flee west with his army. Despite his best efforts, he found himself alone, surrounded at the end of the valley. Vindex looked for his brother, but found his archers had already retreated from their position on the mountain. He then looked to his right and saw his militia running in pairs, headed to the forest on the way to Trevonum.

He glanced around at the enemy soldiers that remained from the Umbrian army and thought to himself, *This is no place to die. We have achieved a great victory, but my fight is far from over.* Vindex backed up to the cliff to protect his back and then took his stance, waiting for a battle as the Umbrians slowly encroached upon him.

Vindex felt the cold mountain on the back of his neck. He looked up and saw a low-hanging branch from a hawthorn tree growing out of the rock. *I know I can reach that,* Vindex thought, *But I will need some type of distraction. I don't want to be cut down while trying to climb up to the trail above me.*

Suddenly an arrow whizzed by Vindex's head, striking an Umbrian on his left side. He looked to the right and saw his brother on Alesia riding toward them. This attack surprised the Umbrians as they believed the army to have routed, so when they turned their attention to Viridox, Vindex knew the time to run was now. He jumped with all of his might and grabbed hold of the tree branch, slowly climbing higher and higher.

'Stop him!' an Umbrian legionary screamed as he rushed to grab Vindex down by the legs.

Just as the Umbrian soldier was about to grab hold of Vindex's foot, another arrow whistled through the air. Viridox had shot the legionary in the side of his exposed neck, causing the Umbrian to fall immediately. Vindex continued to climb and made it safely to the trail above, which led down the backside of the mountain.

'After him!' the Umbrians screamed as their cavalry units ran through the valley exit and headed to the backside of the mountain.

Vindex wasted no time. He sprinted down the trail to his brother, who was waiting for him. Viridox looked behind his shoulder to see two dozen Umbrian cavalrymen quickly approaching.

'Hurry brother!' Viridox shouted.

With almost no time to spare, Vindex reached his brother. Viridox extended his arm as he grabbed Vindex, whose cut and bloody arm was reaching back to his brother. Viridox used all his might to throw his battle-scarred brother up onto his horse. The two then rode west, headed for Trevonum. The Umbrian cavalry initially tried to pursue, but Alesia's speed was too great for the other horses and the two brothers quickly lost the Umbrian forces, who now turned their attention to counting the dead and aiding their wounded.

Vindex, who was now sitting behind Viridox on the horse, smiled through his pain and said, 'Thank you, brother.'

Viridox replied sincerely as the adrenaline faded from his body, 'I'll always have you back.'

'How are the men and women?' Vindex asked quickly, hoping that his people survived.

'Most paired up on horseback and rode together to Trevonum. We should be catching up to some of them soon. We took heavy losses.'

Vindex did not answer his brother. He thought about all the men and women he had lost today, but soon realized that it was a needed sacrifice. Somehow, a ragtag team of peasant farmers had managed to kill an Umbrian commander and severely damage the effectiveness of the invading army.

Vindex was silent for a long time as the pair rode on the path to Trevonum. After what felt like over an hour, he spoke to his brother, changing from their previous topic, 'Where's Bucephalus?' he asked worriedly, looking around his surroundings for his friend.

'He is okay,' Viridox replied. 'I had one of my men take him when we retreated. He should be at Trevonum when we arrive. How long do you think it will take to get to Trevonum?'

'Possibly a few weeks.'

After hearing the word weeks, Viridox responded, 'Well, if it's all the same to you then, would you mind us resting for a bit? I know I was not in the front line, but after all that, I just need a break.'

'Of course. Let's set up camp here,' Vindex replied, understanding what that battle had done to his brother. He had never seen or experienced the horrors of war before. 'It will give me a chance to meditate as well.'

Viridox nodded in approval as he stopped Alesia on the road to Trevonum. The two walked into the thick forest and set up a tent in the dark green grass under a large oak tree. The shade from the forest gave adequate relief from the blazing sun. Vindex and Viridox then looked around, admiring the beauty of their land. The uneven, hilly terrain of the forest was lush with ramsons and trout lilies. The two brothers felt at home.

'You rest, brother. I will keep the first watch. I doubt the Umbrians followed us this far, but I want to err on the side of caution,' Vindex said.

'I understand. Wake me when you need your turn.'

Viridox then closed his eyes. He had earned his rest. Vindex stayed vigilant, never letting his guard down. He would not let the Umbrians surprise them as they regained their strength.

UNWELCOME GATES

A week had passed since the battle of the Galdeshan Valley. Vindex and his brother were slowly approaching the city of Trevonum. For the last week they had marched through the forested hills of Galicia determined to reach Trevonum as soon as possible. They were tired and haunted by the memories of the battle, but their aches were not enough to destroy the resolve they shared to regroup with their militia outside the city limits. The pair only hoped that the recruits from Ebora and Alabum were waiting at Trevonum, ready to continue the fight.

The brothers did not have to wait long to find out, as in the near distance, the two saw the large wooden walls of Trevonum standing tall over the horizon. The cut oak logs stood high, one placed meticulously after the other, creating a twenty-five foot impenetrable wall. Even from afar, the brothers could see lookouts guarding the palisade. Viridox smiled and turned to his brother on the back of his horse and said, 'We made it!'

Vindex, looking over his right shoulder and saw the walls for himself, and he, too, smiled joyously. 'This is it, brother,' he spoke as he hopped off the horse, to walk beside Viridox. 'Inside that city, there should be an army larger than even an Umbrian legion.'

'What is your plan when you get inside the town?' Viridox asked, 'I doubt they will just hand over their army to you.'

Vindex looked up at his brother as they continued their way down the path. 'Trust me. I will figure it out.'

'If you say so, Vindex.'

The two continued down the dirt path toward the town gate. Vindex and his brother saw many tents on either side of the roadway. The heavy iron gate was closed and the town watch stood on the palisade overlooking the road. When walking by the tents, the brothers realized the camp was full of their militia.

'You're late,' One of Vindex's men said with a smile as the rest of the force gathered around.

Vindex was in shock. He said cheerily, 'I did not expect to see all of you here. How many of us are there?'

The soldier quickly replied, 'Everyone from your brother's missile unit is here and accounted for. Those who were on the front lines, however …' the soldier paused, 'Well, we're missing a little over half of the troops.'

Vindex held his head in shame. 'I am sorry,' he spoke. 'I should have called the retreat earlier.'

The soldier interrupted his general, 'Don't apologize, sir. We all thought you were dead. When you called the retreat, we were all able to slip away because you distracted the rest of the Umbrians. Without that, we surely all would have perished. What happened back there? There were over a hundred men focused only on you. How did you survive?'

Vindex looked up at his brother, who was next to him on horseback, and said, 'I had a little help from my brother.'

Just as Vindex finished his sentence, Alesia neighed loudly and smacked Vindex's side with her head.

'Okay, okay,' Vindex said, reaching out and petting the loyal steed, 'And a lot of help from you. Good girl.' He paused for a moment to pet Alesia, and suddenly asked, 'Where is Bucephalus?'

'Right around the tent hitched to a post we set up,' the soldier replied. 'We didn't want him running off on you.'

Vindex eagerly jolted around the side of the tent to see his horse. 'Bucephalus!' he exclaimed as he went over to pet him. 'I was worried about you. Next time we will fight together.'

Bucephalus neighed in approval and before Vindex could even take his belongings out of the bag on his horse's back, the town watchman on the wall rudely interrupted him. 'You there by the horse!' he exclaimed loudly. 'Do you lead these people?'

Vindex looked up. He saw the man standing in the center above the archway. 'And what if I do?' he asked, seeing what the man would say as he continued to rummage through his belongings.

'Then we would need to escort you inside the city walls,' replied the watchman bluntly.

The soldier that greeted Vindex upon his return quickly ran over beside the general to inform him of what was happening. 'Sir,' he spoke, 'I should have mentioned this earlier, but we haven't been let into the city. That is why we are camped outside. Their chieftain said he would not let us in until he spoke to our leader.'

'Is that so?' Vindex replied joyously, seeing the advantage in a meeting with the Trevonum chieftain. This would be the best possible way to gain access to the city's army. 'I suppose I will have to pay him a visit then.'

He walked to the now open gates where the town watch was waiting dressed in bronze armor with long flowing dark orange capes. Vindex turned to his brother and gestured Viridox to follow him inside, but the town watch spoke out, 'Our chieftain requests to see you alone.'

Vindex protested, 'This is my brother. He leads the men with me. He must come!'

Before the watchman had time to answer, Viridox interjected, 'It is fine, brother. You take care of the negotiations. It is probably best that we do not ruffle any feathers.'

Vindex looked at his brother and it was clear he was not happy with the watchman, but he followed the soldier inside the city limits. After the gates closed behind him, Vindex got to look at the city of Trevonum. The sheer scale shocked him as he glanced down every road and alleyway. The wooden homes and trading shops outnumbered his hometown of Norova, and yet, despite the appearance of prosperity, Vindex felt as if something was missing.

The two were walking down the main road for sometime when Vindex asked, 'Any chance you can tell me where we are going?'

The town watchman sternly replied, 'You'll see soon enough. Now be quiet until we get there.'

Vindex remained quiet as instructed. He continued to follow the rude man until they reached the meeting hall which towered above the adjacent stores and homes. The watchman opened the grand mahogany door and gestured Vindex inside without a word. He looked around at the interior of the building. The wooden walls complemented the cobblestone floor. Stone pillars on the walls arched into the ceiling, holding up large wooden beams. Decorative swords, axes and shields hung on the walls with name plates underneath them. Vindex read the list of names as he passed through the chamber. *Kramm the Conqueror, Bluvuk the Untamed, Islak the Great.*

Vindex continued to walk through the chamber until he found a door at the end of the hall on his left. Vindex opened the door to another large room. He found the chieftain sitting on a wooden throne, which was draped in deer hides and surrounded by gold coins stacked high above the chieftain's head. He was taking a drink from his golden chalice when Vindex entered, but upon realizing he had a visitor, he placed the cup down and spoke in an almost angered tone, 'Who are you that dare enter my chamber without warning? Introduce yourself now.'

The chieftain had only said one sentence and with this first impression, Vindex became irritated. The chieftain was a slob. He was short and stout, with wine stains covering most of his robes. A dirty ginger beard with curly ginger hair covered a harsh, ugly face. Vindex gathered his thoughts and replied, 'Your honor, I apologize for not letting you know I was coming. In truth, I didn't know either. Your town watchman escorted me here from the walls and ...'

Before Vindex could finish his statement, the chieftain stood up off the throne and approached him while hollering, 'So you are the one who has his people squatting outside my city walls! Have you no shame! Coming to your superior and asking him to care for your people. Is that what your goal is, sonny?'

Vindex clenched his hand into a fist. The man was now testing his patience, but Vindex knew he had to maintain his poise. He needed Trevonum's support to battle Valerik. He politely replied, 'That is not the case, sir. I merely ...'

Again, before Vindex could finish his statement, the chieftain interrupted again. 'You know nothing is free here in Trevonum, boy. Not even squatting outside the city walls.' He looked down at Vindex's belt and noticed the pouch of Cato's gold. The chieftain reached out and grabbed the bag off of Vindex's body and opened it to inspect its contents. 'This is impressive,' he said. 'How could you have gotten this much money, I wonder? Theft? Murder? Blackmail? I suppose it makes no difference, considering it is mine now.'

The chieftain took his seat once more and dumped the bag of gold onto the coin pile beside him. Vindex was irate at this point and screamed out at the man, 'That is theft! My men and women have done nothing but take shelter after a battle in which we protected your town! That gold is my payment to them for their service, which, may I remind you, protected your people!'

'Protected my people!' the chieftain scoffed. 'Ha! You jest. My people do not need your protection. We are the strongest men and women in all of Galicia. No one has dared defy us since Islak the Great defeated the Sunduk invaders right after the separation of the Galician tribes. If there was a new enemy, I would know about it.'

'What is your name?' Vindex replied angrily, tired of this diplomatic meeting.

'My name is Megorath,' the chieftain replied. 'Why do you want to know?'

'Because I can no longer give you the respect to call you sir or your honor when you are clearly a drunk, bumbling buffoon,' Vindex said sternly. 'My men and women fought an army of over one thousand Umbrian soldiers at the Galdeshan mountains. A man named Commander Agis led that army. He was under the direct order of a ruthless Umbrian general, named Valerik, with orders to conquer this settlement. Agis is dead. I saw to that myself. But a larger Umbrian army will come and try to take these lands. I promise you that.'

Megorath could tell that Vindex was telling the truth just by the passion in his voice. Still, he did not want to admit he needed any protection, nor did he want to relinquish his newly gained gold. He replied, 'Very well. Let us suppose that you did, in fact, defeat this army. Why should I believe they will send another? If a pathetic force like yours could stop an invasion, I doubt they would want to test the strength of Galicia's finest.'

'You do not know who Valerik is, do you?' Vindex replied, interrogating the Trevonum chieftain.

'I may have heard the name before,' Megorath bluffed before turning the pressure back onto his guest. 'And who are you? How am I to know any of this is real?'

Vindex looked straight at Megorath and confidently said, 'My name is Vindex, son of Brunos.'

Megorath looked like he had seen a ghost. 'Brunos?' he asked. 'That is impossible. I was told that there were no survivors from Norova.'

'Aside from my brother and I, there weren't,' Vindex spoke somberly. 'We barely made it out alive all those years ago, and now the man who destroyed my village is back. He is now the Emperor of Umbria and he ordered an attack on your town. I suspect that when he hears of what happened in the mountains, he will come here himself to see that the job is completed. And if that happens, Megorath, I do not have a force strong enough to protect you.'

'If he does, it will be to his own demise. I need not your protection. My forces shall suffice,' Megorath replied bluntly, turning his head away from Vindex to count his newly acquired gold.

'You underestimate him. He is the most brutal warrior I have ever seen. If you wish to beat him, you will need my help. Let me command your army and allow my militia to train with them.'

Megorath laughed from his belly after hearing Vindex's demand. He spun around and looked at Vindex in the eye. 'You ask too much outsider!' he said through his laughter. 'I will be generous though, because it seems as if you may have done a service for my people. I will take your gold not only as payment for your squatting, but as an entry into my town for your forces. When you enter, though, you and your forces may not leave the city until your so-called Umbrian invasion arrives. I still do not know if I can fully trust you, so you will be watched during your stay here. However long that may be.'

'You cannot possibly expect me to agree with those conditions.'

'Take it or leave it, Vindex. No alterations. No compromises,' Megorath said proudly.

After mulling it over for a bit, Vindex asked, 'Where would we stay?'

'Your men can stay in one of our many garrison buildings. As for you and your brother, you can stay at the inn across from the tavern,' Megorath replied, feeling more generous than usual.

'I suppose I really don't have a better option.'

'I'll presume that is a deal then,' Megorath said as he showed Vindex to the door. Before letting him leave, he leaned in close and said, 'My men and I will be watching you. So, no funny business.'

As Vindex left the meetinghouse, he noted that there were watchmen all over the city. At every other building, there would be a soldier stationed. Vindex walked back to the gates unsupervised and could feel their eyes on him. It was an uneasy feeling. Never had he been to a place quite like this. It was a large town with hundreds of wooden buildings built on stone foundations, and yet there was little life. *Strange. There are more soldiers on the street than citizens,* Vindex thought to himself as he walked down the stone and dirt road.

Within a few minutes, he reached the gates and informed the town watch of the arrangement that he struck with Megorath. This prompted the men to open the large wooden and iron gates. Vindex walked out to his men to inform them of the news.

The first to question him on his way back was his brother Viridox. 'How did it go?'

Vindex frowned and replied through a clenched jaw. 'Swimmingly.'

Viridox looked at his brother and knew something was wrong. He moved closer and whispered, 'What happened in there?'

Vindex took Viridox aside to speak in private. 'What happened, brother, was an oaf robbed me. The leader of these people is a glutton and a fool. He took all our gold for passage into the city. I am going to tell the troops. You and I will stay in the inn. The rest of the men will sleep in the barracks,' Vindex replied, vividly unhappy about the entire arrangement.

'I see,' Viridox said. 'Will they provide the troops proper armament and weapons inside?'

'Based on their leader, I wouldn't hold my breath,' Vindex said agitated. 'Now come help me tell the rest of the troops. We may as well settle into our new home.'

The two brothers helped pack the belongings of the men and women and went into Trevonum together. As the brothers and soldiers walked through the city streets, the only faces they saw were that of armed guards. No pedestrians or citizens were in sight. Vindex felt uneasy about the situation, but with no other choice, he continued to the city barracks, where he helped his men unload their gear. After his soldiers were situated, he and his brother walked to the inn alone.

'Does this place give you the creeps?' Viridox asked his brother.

Vindex had been looking at the soldiers who were watching them. He turned his gaze back to his brother after hearing his question. He replied, 'Yes, it does. There is something not right about this town, or at the very least, its leader.'

Viridox nodded in agreement as they made their way into the inn. Upon opening the wooden door, the owner and manager of the establishment greeted them. Unlike everyone else they had met so far in this city; the owner was kind and thoughtful. She was a middle-aged woman whose hair was just beginning to grey. She was sweet and hospitable, and offered the two men a meal before showing them to a room they could share.

'If I had more space, boys, I would give you each a room. Sadly, this is all I can offer,' the innkeeper said.

'This is plenty, honestly,' Vindex said graciously as he and his brother went into the room and closed the door.

The room was small but comfortable. A tiny window in the center of the room stood as the dividing line between the two beds that were placed in either corner. Each had a small wooden trunk placed at the foot of the bed for their belongings. Vindex took the bed on the left while Viridox got the right.

'Home sweet home, I suppose,' Viridox said as he placed his armor in his small trunk.

'At least we have a place to call home while we make our next plan,' Vindex responded seriously.

'I agree brother, but before we do any planning, I think it is time for us to get some rest. We have traveled a long way,' Viridox responded as he got into bed and pulled a cloth sheet over him.

Vindex nodded and followed his brother's lead. He, too, got into bed and relaxed. His body and mind had taken a beating this past week and while the cuts from the battle were healing, the mental trauma was far from mended.

RETURNING TO THE EMPEROR

The remains of the Umbrian army were demoralized and leaderless. Weary and hungry, they quickly retraced their steps to the capital of Umbria. Not a single soldier could understand how the Galicians defeated them, nor could they rationalize how their mighty commander was slain by a mere barbarian. Each soldier felt a strong sense of shame. Their defeat was a calamity.

In a week's time, they arrived at the capital's front gates and were met with thunderous applause from the citizens, who all assumed they were victorious in securing more land for the Empire. The applause quickly died down when the Umbrian citizens saw how haggard each legionary looked. The gates closed behind the soldiers, who heard whispers in the crowd.

'Is that all of them?' asked an Umbrian baker.

'Where is Commander Agis?' another citizen remarked.

The legionaries all felt pits in their stomach. They kept their heads down and rushed back to their garrison building. It had been some time since Umbria had such an embarrassing defeat. When back in their barracks, the cohort removed their armor, put away their shields, and gathered together.

'Who is going to tell Valerik what happened?' one soldier asked nervously, hoping that his peers would not nominate him.

'I thought we agreed on the way here that Quintus would speak with the Emperor,' another legionary replied.

The crowd of men looked at Quintus.

Quintus, being the centurion under Agis, understood it was his responsibility. He reluctantly took up the task, knowing it may be the last time he saw his comrades. He looked around the room of his brothers in arms and spoke in a quiet, shaky voice, 'See you at the mess hall later.'

There was an eerie silence after Quintus' remark. The soldiers understood Valerik did not tolerate failure lightly. They sat quietly on wooden benches, kicking the dirt floor, averting their eyes from Quintus. After only a moment, Quintus left the barracks without speaking another word. He quickly proceeded on foot to the Emperor's Chamber, where the imperial guards on duty greeted him.

'I am here to give a report to the Emperor,' Quintus said with a shake in his voice. 'We are back from our expedition into Galicia.'

The two imperial guards looked at each other before turning to Quintius. One guard spoke. 'Good luck. You are going to need it.'

They then opened the chamber door and let Quintus inside the building. Quintus walked inside, thinking to himself, *Why would I need good luck? Has word already spread of our failure to defeat the barbarians?* When he reached the imperial floor, he understood. The Emperor was nowhere to be seen. *Oh, no*, Quintus thought in fear as he saw Dara sitting at Valerik's station. Quintus took a nervous gulp before walking over to his commandant. He thought once more. *I already didn't want to tell Valerik about our loss, but at least he is reasonable. The worst I would probably get from him is a dishonorable discharge from the military. With her though … Gods have mercy on me.*

Dara did not take the same approach to leadership as Valerik. On the rare occasions in which Valerik killed, it was always well thought out and necessary. With Dara, however, it was random, cruel, and merciless. A woman of few scruples, she had no remorse for the deaths of those who upset her. Quintus had heard the reports of Dara's cruelty.

One story told in every barrack in Umbria was from a campaign during the civil war. On route to Tarsus, Dara and her legion established a camp in the woods. In the middle of the night, one watchman fell asleep on duty. When Dara heard of this misconduct, she broke both of the soldier's legs and chained raw meat to his body. When the legion dismantled the camp, Dara left the crippled man in the woods to fend for himself against the wolves.

Quintus felt his heart racing as he approached Dara. Sweat poured from his face and his breaths grew quicker until he stood right in front of Dara's desk.

Dara noticed this disheveled, sweaty man and took a break from the papers and maps to ask condescendingly, 'What do you need, soldier?'

'Commander Dara,' Quintus replied nervously, 'I um … I don't need anything, I just …'

Dara's brow lowered, annoyed that she was being distracted from her duties by this quivering legionary. She stood from her desk and walked around to meet the soldier face to face and asked once more, 'What do you need?'

'Is Valerik here by any chance?' Quintus blurted out in panic.

'No, he is not,' Dara replied impatiently. 'He is taking care of something in the city. Why do you ask?'

Quintus took a deep breath in and replied quickly. 'It is an update on the Galician invasion. I would greatly appreciate an assembly with our leader.'

Dara paced around him, breaking down what little resolve Quintus had left. 'Why do you need him? Surely you can leave your successful report with me,' she spoke. 'Where is Agis? He should be the one reporting back to us, not you.'

'Agis is dead,' Quintus said somberly, looking down. 'And the invasion was a failure.'

Dara stopped her pacing behind Quintus when he relayed this news. She grabbed the trooper by the shoulder and spun him around. She was irate that some filthy barbarians killed one of her friends and comrades – a comrade that helped win the Umbrian Civil War. 'Explain what happened immediately, soldier. That is an order!' she exclaimed.

'Yes Ma'am. We made it as far as the Galdeshan mountains, but when we reached the other side, there was a Galician force waiting for us,' Quintus quickly replied.

'I know Commander Agis very well,' Dara said, 'His tact and skill were huge parts of why we won our civil war. How is it that barbarians destroyed him and the rest of your legion? Were you outnumbered?'

'No general, we were not outnumbered,' Quintus replied, answering Dara's last question first.

'Then what happened?' Dara interjected through her gritting teeth.

Quintus shook, now completely intimidated by the Umbrian leader. 'I do not know. We had them outnumbered, but they had archers in the mountains and … and …' he said, fumbling over his own words.

'Archers?' Dara asked rhetorically. 'Archers. You lost one of our greatest commanders because of archers? And yet somehow you lived to tell the tale where he didn't. Maybe it was not the element of surprise that led to your defeat. Maybe it was the cowardice of you and your men.'

Dara said these things in a calm but threatening way. She slowly took her blade from her side and lifted it at eye level for Quintus to see. She then continued, 'And you know what we do to cowards. Don't you?'

Quintus panicked. His heart raced faster than ever before and, hoping to save his own life, he continued to speak about the battle. 'That's not all,' he cried. 'There was this man. The other forces' commander. He was like nothing I have ever seen. He made quick work of Agis in combat, and I can't be certain when I say this, but he probably killed nearly a hundred of our men on his own.'

Dara lowered her blade and tied it back to her belt. Her curiosity peaked. 'He made quick work of Agis?' she asked calmly, trying to probe for more information.

'Yes. He was truly like nothing I have ever seen before. As you may know, I have fought with the likes of Valerik and yourself during the civil war. I truly believe this man could be even greater than our leader,' Quintus said, trying to inform Dara of how serious that matter was.

Dara looked Quintus in the eyes and said, 'Impossible. No one is as strong of a warrior as Valerik. Not even I hold a candle to him.'

'I know, general, but trust me, he was devastating on the battlefield,' Quintus said, regaining his composure.

'What do you know about him?' Dara asked, walking back to her desk to collect some paper so she could write this information down in ink.

'He created his army by drafting men and women from the town of Ebora. I remember him saying that. He may have mentioned another village, but I can't remember. It is all a blur now,' Quintus said as he tried to recall the rest of the details.

Dara wrote Ebora down on her paper before pressing for more information. 'And what about a name? Did he say his name?'

'Yes, he did,' Quintus replied. 'He introduced himself as Vindex, son of Brunos of Norova. Whatever that means. Not like we would know of a filthy barbarian's lineage.'

Dara's quill, fresh with ink, dropped from her hand after hearing where the man was from. 'Are you sure he said that?' she asked, back still turned to the soldier as she hunched over her desk.

'Yes, I am certain,' Quintus replied confidently.

Dara turned around, stared Quintus in the eyes, and said in a menacing tone, 'Tell me everything that happened during the battle.'

The two then talked for a brief while about the specifics of the battle. Everything from the numbers of the enemy to the number of soldiers Umbria lost was all charted down by Dara. Most importantly, however, Quintus told Dara exactly how Agis was defeated in combat and how Vindex appeared to survive a mortal strike to the back from a spear. After all was said and done, Dara dismissed Quintus back to the barracks. Quintus, feeling as if he had a closer brush with death in this meeting than on the battlefield, ran back to his post, adrenaline still rushing through his body. Shortly after Quintus' departure, Dara left the hall herself. She had an imperial guard collect her horse for her while she waited on the capitol building's steps. When the steed arrived, she hopped on her horse and rode through the city, hoping that she could find Valerik in one of his usual spots.

A HELPING HAND

'**D**o you think these will suffice?' Valerik asked, holding a bowl full of herbs and flowers.

'These should work nicely. I'll be able to make several tonics with these ingredients you have brought me. Thank you, Emperor,' replied an Umbrian doctor, as he took the bowl from Valerik's hands.

The doctor walked with the ingredients over to a mixing bowl when Dara opened the white ash door and rushed inside the clinic. It was a standard two-story Umbrian domicile which the herbalist had converted into a home for the sick. The clay walls were red with white stripes. She could see several patient cots on the cobblestone floor in the back room on the first floor. The doctor was at his workbench up against a side wall with his back turned, mixing an assortment of herbs and flowers. Right behind the doctor, Dara saw Valerik kneeling over a cot, applying a cold compress to a patient's head.

'Valerik!' Dara shouted while walking toward the Umbrian Emperor.

Valerik turned around happy to see his second in command. 'Dara!' he exclaimed. 'How are you?'

Dara did not answer the question and instead replied in a serious tone, 'We need to talk.'

'I'm sure it can wait, Dara,' Valerik replied, dismissing his subordinate.

'It is urgent,' Dara spoke through the grits of her teeth. 'We need to talk.'

Valerik saw the expression on Dara's face and knew something was wrong. Before agreeing to leave with Dara, he quickly asked the doctor, 'Is there anything else you need?'

'No, my liege. Thank you for all you have done already,' the doctor replied as he continued to make the elixir for his patients.

'Very well,' Valerik spoke. He then followed Dara outside to a nearby alley which was void of any pedestrian onlookers.

Before Valerik could even ask what was so important that Dara had to drag him off into a back alley, she began talking, 'Before I say what is so urgent, I just have to ask, what has become of you?'

'What has become of me?' Valerik questioned, confused and defensive to Dara's criticism.

'Yes, what has become of the mighty Emperor? Running errands for doctors and traders, I don't even recognize you,' Dara replied in an exasperated tone.

'I became Emperor to help my people,' Valerik replied. 'I make all the decisions for Umbria because I know what is best. That does not mean, however, that I am not above offering my aide to those who need it, especially the sick and weary.'

Her general's caring demeanor disgruntled the Umbrian warrior. She couldn't even muster an answer. Dara rolled her eyes, dumbfounded by what she perceived as a shift in his character.

Valerik reacted with obvious annoyance. He snapped, 'Are you going to tell me why you dragged me out here?'

'We have a new enemy,' Dara replied quickly, crossing her arms over her chest. By the tone of her voice and her body language, Valerik knew she was holding a grudge.

'Who is it?' Valerik asked, not worried but curious who this new adversary could be.

'He is a man named Vindex,' Dara said. 'You have already met him.'

'If I had already met an enemy of ours, he would surely be dead,' Valerik scoffed, full of self-assurance.

'Not this time,' Dara quipped. 'He is the son of Brunos from Norova. You know, the kid you let run away so that he could warn the rest of the Galicians not to quarrel with us. What a horrible decision that has turned out to be.'

'I see,' Valerik responded. 'I do remember that child. Surely that must have been nearly a decade ago. Although I must say it matters little. Even if he were to reunite the West and Southern Galician tribes, he would still be no match for our Umbrian steel.'

Dara stared intensely into Valerik's self-assured eyes. She opened her mouth and said bluntly, 'He killed Agis and decimated his legion. We sent an army of over a thousand men, and he defeated it with a group of peasant farmers from the town of Ebora.'

Valerik's expression quickly changed. His eyes lost confidence and widened in sorrow. He took a step back and turned away from his companion. He placed his hand to his temple and stared into the bustling street, alive with horses and citizens. Valerik softly replied, 'Agis is dead? Are you absolutely sure?'

Dara, still emotional about the loss to Umbria, replied, 'Yes, I am sure. I'm sorry, but his death is partly on you. Had you killed the child all those years ago, our fellow leader, our friend, would still be here with us.'

Valerik took a deep breath. He did not like what Dara had to say, but he knew she was right. He lamented the loss of not only one of his top generals, but of his friend, who he had grown to know so well over the transition period of the Umbrian Empire. 'That is a hefty loss,' he mumbled, dismayed, still refusing to look at Dara. A few moments of silence went by before Valerik pulled himself together. He turned around to face Dara with new resolve and courage in his eyes and he said, 'Thank you for bringing it to my attention.'

'That's it?' Dara exclaimed in a rage. 'A filthy barbarian murders our friend, and you feel nothing for revenge. We must send more legions there immediately and hunt this man down! I will not rest until he pays for what he has done, and neither should you!'

Valerik quickly replied, 'Dara, I agree, but we cannot right now. I have just sent five more legions from here and three from Tarsus to help Thrün defeat the Sunduk at Susa. I cannot afford to lead our remaining men to Galicia. It would leave Apolina completely defenseless. We must wait until Thrün returns.'

Dara was characteristically impatient. She asked with a hint of aggression, 'What if I go to help Thrün defeat the Sunduk? Surely you can spare me and my shield maidens while you continue to run the city.'

Valerik thought for a moment. Although he would miss the company of Dara for what would be an extended period, he agreed it was in their best interest for her to go. 'Very well,' he said, 'You go and capture the city of Susa. When you do, leave four legions to defend it from the remaining Sunduk Empire, then come back to the capital. After that we will avenge Agis.'

Dara smiled. 'It will be done, my lord,' she said as she left Valerik's side. She ran from the alley to her horse and rode back to her home to gather a cohort of shield maidens and supplies for the journey ahead. Valerik too returned home, but instead of prepping for a new adventure, he sat in his chamber alone, totally isolated from the outside world. He stared blankly at the wall facing him, silently grieving the loss of his friend. He vowed he would avenge his fallen comrade. His goal was no longer just to simply conquer the Galician tribes, but to find the man named Vindex and reunite him with his father.

TAVERN TALES

After a long nap Vindex and Viridox woke in their new quarters in the city of Trevonum. The two were in their shared room relaxing in their separate beds when Viridox sat up and asked, 'Why don't we go to the tavern, brother? I think after all we've been through; we deserve a drink or two, or more.'

'I agree with the sentiment,' Vindex replied, sitting up on his own so that he was facing his brother, 'But with what money? It seems you have forgotten the oaf running this place stripped me of all our gold.'

'Perhaps you could make some gold like Cato did on the mountain,' Viridox replied optimistically.

'No Viridox, I can't,' Vindex replied disappointed with himself. 'At least not yet, anyway.'

'In that case,' Viridox responded cheekily, 'we may as well use these.' He took out a small pouch with silver denars and flicked one at his brother, using the end of his thumb.

Vindex caught the coin in midair. He held it in front of his face and realized the silver pieces were authentic. 'Where did you get these?' he asked his brother, not understanding how he had a bag of money considering he was by his side most of the day.

'I found it,' Viridox replied with a twinkle in his eye.

'Found it where?' Vindex pressed impatiently.

'I may have misappropriated it from one of the watchmen when we were moving in. What difference does it make, though? After what

Megorath did to you, it only seems fair,' Viridox replied in defense of his actions.

'That isn't how we do things, brother. You need to give that money back,' Vindex said, trying to be a positive influence.

'Tell me if you feel that way after a few mugs of ale,' Viridox replied standing up gesturing to the door. 'Come on then. Let's go.'

Vindex begrudgingly agreed. He stood up and followed his brother. They went down the wooden stairs of the inn and walked out the main entrance to the crisp night sky of the barbarian town. The town seemed almost deserted. An occasional passerby would walk in silence as the town militia stood on every corner watching the two brothers. The dirt and stone road they traveled was lit by torches placed on posts one every fifteen feet, providing just enough light to show that the town watch was monitoring them.

The atmosphere dampened the spirits of the young men. Viridox tried to remain upbeat. He looked at his brother and said, 'You know it's funny. I haven't had mead since the days in Norova, where we would go to the tavern with Dad.'

Vindex smiled, replying, 'And Mom would insist we were too young to go. In a weird way, I am almost happy that she passed before what happened the night the Umbrians came. It was better the way she went.' There was a slight pause as the two continued to walk on the crisp fall night.

'Do you remember when Mom brought us to the Morrígan Cairn?' Vindex asked. 'She was the first person to teach us what it meant to be strong.'

Viridox replied with a smile, 'I do. I also remember her telling us our greatest strength would be our bond.'

'She was a smart woman,' Vindex replied, looking out at the night sky. 'I miss them a lot, you know.'

'I do too,' Viridox said quickly. He reached his arm out and pulled his brother in close as they approached the front door of the tavern. 'But you still have me. And we still have ale. Let's get a drink!'

Vindex smiled, joining his brother's embrace. 'Yes, we do,' he said as they entered the tavern together.

Once inside, the two looked around and saw the happy citizens of Trevonum singing and dancing and a small few playfully wrestling. The air was thick with the scent of ale and the wooden floor soaked with spilt beer. The tavern was a large semioval building with stone walls and a wooden roof. Vindex looked past the crowd to examine the back wall, which was flat with two closed oak doors on either end. In the center of the building stood a large stone support column, with a wooden bar built around it on all sides. Vindex and Viridox pushed through the smiling crowd trying to find a place to sit.

'At least this place appears to be normal,' Vindex said to his brother as he sat down in an unoccupied booth.

'You can say that again,' Viridox replied, also elated to be out of the brisk fall cold. 'Now, let me grab us some drinks.'

Vindex smiled and nodded his head as Viridox went to get the first round. He eyed the room while his little brother was at the counter. *There doesn't seem to be any militia inside this tavern. How strange,* Vindex thought to himself. *If the citizens of this town are truly this jovial and happy, why is there such order and hostility in the streets?* Before Vindex could get too deep into thought, his brother returned to the table with mugs of ale.

'Well,' Viridox said to his brother, sitting down, 'I'm sure this will take the edge off. And then who knows, maybe you'll be able to connect to the Maith after.'

Vindex replied with his eyebrows raised. 'Are you suggesting that my inability to connect with this ancient spiritual power could somehow be resolved by alcohol?'

'I don't know, maybe,' Viridox stuttered slightly, not knowing if his brother was playing along with the joke.

'Well, if it's a theory, we better test it!' Vindex said with a smile.

The two drank several rounds over the course of a few hours at the tavern. They attracted the attention of the locals and impressed them with their tales of heroism and bravery by recounting the battle of the Galdeshan Mountains, while also scaring them by telling them the truth of what happened to the town of Norova. As the night went on and the crowd slowly died, most patrons went home, leaving only the tavern regulars to accompany the sons of Brunos.

With fewer people in the crowd, Viridox spotted what he could only describe as the most beautiful woman he had ever seen staring at him on the other side of the tavern. 'Do you see that?' he asked his brother, 'I think I might have an admirer.'

Vindex laughed. 'You could hardly get a horse's affection, let alone a woman's!' he said in a lighthearted tone.

Viridox confidently replied, 'First of all, Alesia and I have a great relationship. She loves me and you know it. Secondly, you'll see brother. Just watch.' He stood up and walked over to introduce himself to the woman on the other side of the tavern.

Vindex stayed put in his seat, eager to watch what he thought would be his younger brother making a fool of himself. To Vindex's shock, his younger brother somehow struck up a conversation with the young beauty. As the two talked on the opposite side of the tavern, Vindex watched as his brother followed the stranger into a back room. *I can't believe that worked,* Vindex thought. *No, there has to be something else going on. Perhaps I should go make sure he is safe.* Before Vindex could get up from his seat to check in on his younger brother, two men came and trapped him in his booth.

'Is this seat taken?' one man asked Vindex as he was already sitting down across from him.

The other man sat at Vindex's side, trapping him at the table. Vindex looked at the two men and replied, 'You can actually have the booth. I was just getting up.'

Vindex gestured towards the two burly men, asking one of them to move away so he could pursue his brother, however neither man moved. Instead, the man on his right placed his sword onto the table while the man across placed his elbow on the table, pivoting his body to tower over Vindex.

Vindex quickly realized that his brother's departure and the two giants joining him were not isolated events. He looked at the men sitting in front of him and asked forcefully, 'Where is my brother?'

Viridox was too enamored by the beautiful woman he followed to pay attention to details that may otherwise have tipped him off that something was wrong. They passed through a hallway before entering a private room at the back end of the building. After Viridox walked in, the door was quickly closed behind him. Viridox turned his head to see two armed guards at the door. It was at this moment that Viridox stopped fixating on the lush brown hair that he followed and instead scanned his surroundings. The soldiers at the door differed from the ones on the road. They had the same equipment, but their colors under their armor were blue, not orange. What was additionally odd was that in front of the woman, there was a singular wooden chair sitting in the middle of the room.

The woman turned around to face Viridox. 'Please have a seat,' she said politely.

Viridox, seeing no other course of action, walked over to the seat which faced the doorway. He sat down while the mysterious woman positioned herself in front of him, cutting off his path to the door. Viridox knew that even if he got around the woman, he would still have to deal with two armed guards. He was good with a bow, but his hand to hand skills were not strong. With no weapon and without the combat skills to defeat the two men, Viridox sat ready to play the woman's game.

After Viridox sat down, the woman turned to the two guards and said, 'You can leave us now. Just be sure you are on the other side of the door.'

This surprised Viridox. He asked the woman, 'What do you want from me?'

The woman quickly responded in an uplifting, perky tone, 'My apologies. I can only imagine what this looks like. I suppose proper introductions are in order. My name is Orla. I am a daughter of the tavern owner and the leader of the dissenter movement here in Trevonum. I'm hoping that you can assist me.'

Viridox's face scrunched up. Hoping to get more information, he spoke, 'Dissenter movement? I just got here, ma'am. I don't know how I could help you. What exactly do you need?'

Orla promptly replied. 'I understand you are confused, so I will try to explain. I am sure that you have seen in your short time here that our movements are constantly watched. The streets are empty aside from soldiers and yet our tavern bustles with life.'

'I have. Your entire city makes me uneasy if I am being truthful.'

'As it should,' Orla replied bluntly. She walked to the corner of the room and grabbed a second chair and placed it in front of Viridox. She sat and looked him in the eyes. There was a pause for a moment before Orla spoke again. 'Our leader is a tyrant. He gives no voice to the people. Our tavern only stays open because it makes people happy and lessens the civil unrest. He hosts monthly competitions in archery, swordsmanship and more to find the strongest of our city. When he does, he indoctrinates them into the army. Pays them well and gives them freedom while the rest of our city is left destitute and oppressed. He leads the military and decides everything from what shop owners may sell to when people can go on walks and travel the streets. Each citizen has their own individual curfew set by our town watch. The more in favor you are with the chieftain, the more freedoms you have. Sadly, only those who can fill his coffers earn his favor. The taxation on our goods kills our economy only to make his wealth greater. The man sits upon a literal gold throne while the people who have made him rich have nothing.'

Viridox had heard a similar account from his brother about this leader. He empathized with Orla and her people and replied, 'My brother talked to him on behalf of us when we first arrived. From how that meeting went, we could tell he was an oaf, but I didn't imagine he was a downright totalitarian.'

Orla smiled, seeing how Viridox agreed with her position. 'Does this mean you will help me?'

'That depends on what you want me to do.'

'When the time is right, will you lead your militia against Megorath with my men? We can take back our city from the town watch and have freedom once again!' Orla responded as her eyes flashed with enthusiasm.

Viridox's gaze wandered from Orla's as he became hesitant to reply. Eventually he gently spoke 'If it were up to me, I would, of course, but I am not the commander of the troops. That is my brother.'

Orla's face crinkled as she leaned back in her chair, confused. 'Are you not the hero of the Galdeshan Mountains? You spoke all night of your triumphs. All my men who listened to your stories told me it was you.'

'Well, of course I am the hero,' Viridox replied, 'I just leave the commanding to my brother.'

'I see,' Orla said, relaxing her demeanor. 'I suppose I should have known. The strategists are never the cute ones.'

'So, you are saying I'm cute?' Viridox quickly replied.

Orla rolled her eyes and spoke as she got up. 'I am getting your brother. Try to stay focused.' She then walked to the door to inform one guard to bring Vindex to them.

Viridox perked up in his seat as he waited for his brother. He was completely focused, knowing this was his chance to impress Orla. The two waited only for a minute before Vindex entered with two guards escorting him.

'Get your hands off me!' Vindex exclaimed while pushing the guard's hand off his shoulder. The tactics Orla employed in order to communicate with the two brothers had disgruntled and overtly annoyed Vindex as he huffed into the room.

'Brother!' Viridox spoke, 'What have you learned since I last saw you? Orla was telling me all about the town's workings.'

Vindex, still irritated, snapped, 'What I have learned is to never leave home without my blade.' He looked over his shoulder and leered at the guards, who stood at the door next to the two burly men who cornered Vindex at the booth.

Orla quickly replied, 'I apologize for my tactics, but not everyone at the tavern is a dissenter and I needed discretion when trying to recruit you. If Megorath found out, he would have my head.'

Vindex stood next to his brother and stared down Orla in an intimidating fashion. 'Alright,' he spoke bombastically. 'You have me here. What is it you want?'

'I need you and your forces to overthrow Megorath and subdue his town watch. The oppression of my people has …' Orla replied before Vindex cut her off.

'Absolutely not.'

'Brother!' Viridox exclaimed. 'Won't you at least hear her out?'

'Viridox, I can empathize with their plight on some level, but we have much more pressing and dangerous issues than Megorath's incompetence.'

Orla interjected, trying to find a compromise that would help both parties. 'It's not incompetence, it is oppression. Besides, I can assist you with your enemy after we overthrow Megorath,' she said, hoping to reach an arrangement.

Viridox looked at his brother. 'Vindex, I implore you please.'

Orla spoke once more. 'Megorath has made this town his own personal prison, Vindex. The rich are able to buy their freedom and the strong earn theirs only to oppress the weak. Our people are so heavily taxed and our trade so regulated that many of us go hungry each night. The tavern only runs because Megorath fears a rebellion if the people were denied their ale. The people of this town have cried out. They need a hero, but I am in no position to answer their pleas, so please think about it. Help us, and we can help you.'

Vindex stayed quiet for a while. After calming his temper and exploring all the potential outcomes of such an alliance, he came to his decision. 'Fine, I will help you,' he said. 'But only after the threat of Valerik and the Umbrians are gone. Their rule would be worse than

Megorath's. Infighting now would do us no good. Until the Umbrians arrive, I must forge an alliance with Megorath to bolster my own forces. The Umbrian threat will take all of us working together. If we live through that, I will try to help your dissenters reinstate a new chieftain in this city. That is my only offer.'

Orla stood next to her men, who were looking at her in query, not knowing if the two brothers would be enough to overthrow Megorath. Eventually, she spoke. 'It is a deal. We have stayed idle for this long. We can survive a while longer. Just promise you will liberate my people when your enemy is defeated.'

'I never break a promise,' Vindex said as the two grasped each other's forearm formalizing their arrangement.

'Well, it seems we are all in agreement. Men, you are dismissed,' Orla spoke.

Vindex followed the guards who had left the room. He turned around over his shoulder and said, 'Let's go home, Viridox.'

Viridox did not follow. He looked over at Orla and said, 'I was hoping I could get to know you a little more without the armed guards this time.'

Orla smiled and replied, 'I'd like that.'

Vindex stared at Viridox with irked eyes and a vacant expression. After a moment of silence, he sarcastically spoke. 'Very well. You two enjoy yourselves. I will be back at the inn when you're done.' He then closed the door behind him and walked out of the tavern.

'So,' Viridox said, 'Do you know a good place to get a drink around here?'

'Shut up,' Orla replied, chuckling. She pushed Viridox towards the door and they both made their way to the bar.

While Orla and Viridox shared each other's company, Vindex traveled the streets of Trevonum alone. Vindex scanned his surroundings and noticed only two types of people were out at this hour, patrons walking home from the tavern and the town watch who stood at every street corner with spear and shield in hand. Orla's claims about curfews appeared to be true. The town watch stopped the tavern patrons one by one. They asked for each citizen's papers, which showed the person's designated curfew times. The soldiers came upon one old man, who sadly had no permit papers, and kicked him onto the street, binding his hands with rope before escorting him to a local jail cell.

Disgusting, Vindex thought to himself. *My father would never have treated his people this way. Megorath should be ashamed of himself. I could not imagine living this way. I suppose that is why Megorath gave my brother and me unlimited access to the city. He knew we wouldn't be quiet.*

Despite his inward rage, Vindex remained calm and quietly walked down the muddy road back to the inn. There was no way for him to help, not now, anyway. *After Valerik is defeated, I will help free these people,* Vindex thought as he turned down a different street on his way back home. Something was different about this street. There were no guards posted watching from the shadows. Vindex looked to his right and found a small circular stone temple. *Maybe they do not guard their holy sights,* Vindex thought to himself. Vindex did not care why. He was grateful for the freedom. He opened the doors and was pleased to find an empty room. *Finally, some peace and quiet.*

Vindex felt overwhelmed after allying with Orla and her dissenters. 'I need help,' he mumbled in the center of the shrine. 'If I am going to stop Valerik and help Orla, I need to be stronger. I need the Maith.'

Carvings of the Galician gods were plastered in a ring on the stone floor. Vindex stood in the center of all the carvings and knelt. He closed his eyes and imagined the mountains where Cato trained him. He reached out his hand and touched the rock floor, which reminded him of the chamber atop Cato's lookout. With no other thoughts clouding his head, Vindex took a deep breath and hoped that when he opened his eyes, he would see his mentor on the Galdeshan Peaks.

Vindex could feel the Maith around him. Although he could not speak with the spirits, he could tell they were guiding him. He opened up his eyes and smiled, seeing that Cato stood in front of him.

'Do you have any idea what time it is?' Cato asked while stretching his arms back, yawning to exaggerate the late hour.

'How did you know I was coming?' Vindex asked, still with a wide grin on his face.

'Let's just say I had a hunch,' Cato replied. 'I sense your connection to the Maith has grown significantly.'

'I believe it has. It hardly took me any time at all for me to come here. Before I would meditate for hours before I saw results.'

'Yes, yes. I am very proud of your progress. I still have much to teach you, though. Is that why you came here tonight?'

'I figured you would already know why I am here,' Vindex said, testing his mentor's infinite knowledge.

'Let's see, you hope I can solve all your life's burdens for you,' Cato replied with a smirk.

'I see your connection to the Maith is still strong.'

'Oh no my young friend,' Cato said sarcastically. 'That was not the spirits telling me. It was just my regular intuition.'

Vindex rolled his eyes at his mentor, who was now beginning to take the visit more seriously.

'You know I can't fix your problems, Vindex,' Cato said earnestly.

'I know,' Vindex replied, 'It's just that when you have all the knowledge in the world at your disposal, I would assume you have all the answers.'

'One day, you will share this knowledge, Vindex. And when you do, you will see that even with all the information in the world, there are still things that you simply must solve on your own,' Cato replied candidly, not wanting to give the young man false hopes. Vindex took a moment to ponder over what Cato had told him.

'I suppose since you're here,' Cato continued, 'we may as well do some actual training.'

'I would like that very much,' Vindex replied, taking a seat in front of the old man, who began teaching the lesson.

Vindex had never been more motivated to strengthen his connection to the Maith. He realized no spirits would help him unless he conquered his own personal issues. With small goals in mind, he decided it was best to focus on learning to talk to the spirits through the Maith, as he believed having almost endless knowledge would turn the tide on the battlefields. Vindex believed only after Valerik's defeat could he focus on mastering the rest of the Maith.

With his new outlook, Vindex jumped right back into training with Cato and immediately felt his connection to the Maith grow. He was unsuccessful when attempting to speak with the spirits, but found comfort knowing his connection was getting stronger. Cato and Vindex continued their mediations and drills for a couple of hours before Cato ended the session.

'I think that's enough for today,' Cato spoke. 'I am, in fact, an old man. I don't have the same stamina that I used to.'

'Oh, please,' Vindex retorted. 'You don't look a day over a hundred.'

'Let's see how you look when you get to be my age,' Cato scoffed back. 'I bet you won't be smiling then!'

'Probably not,' Vindex quipped. 'But that's because rigor mortis would've set in by then.'

Cato smiled and looked at his pupil. 'I think it is time you go home, my friend. We will do this again tomorrow. I want you here everyday so we can practice your connection to the Maith. You have great potential, Vindex. I hope we can unlock it together.'

Vindex humbly smiled and replied, ' Goodnight Cato. I will see you tomorrow.'

'I won't be going anywhere,' Cato replied with a wink. Then he stared out at the valley below and somberly said, 'After all, I can't.'

Vindex then closed his eyes and thought back to the temple in Trevonum, where he was meditating. When opening back up, Vindex saw the shrine altar sticking out from the stone floor. He was back and decided it was time to go home.

The cool fall breeze caused goosebumps on Vindex's arms as he traveled in the dark down the road to the inn. The only people on the streets now were the town watch. *How many troops does that oaf have to staff an entire city like this?* Vindex thought to himself as he looked out at the soldiers standing guard. He quickly put that thought to rest, though, as he wanted one night without worrying about what future problems he would need to endure. He quickly picked up his pace back to the inn so he could rest.

All was quiet at the inn when he arrived. He walked up the creaking wooden stairs and opened the door without knocking. When the door opened, he found his brother already asleep. *I hope his date went well.* Vindex thought as he quietly got into his bed.

When in bed, Vindex stared up at the dark ceiling. His mind was racing about all the things to come. The Umbrians, the dissenters, and returning to Cato on the mountain when everything was completed. A great weight was building on top of Vindex, but he was able to drift off to a sound safe slumber. He would have no nightmares or interruptions tonight. Just a rare but blissful, peaceful rest.

CHAPTER 14

THE CALM BEFORE
THE STORM

Viridox awoke to a soft knock on the door in the morning. He lifted the fur blanket off his body and quietly got out of bed. He creaked open the door and saw Orla on the other side.

Viridox smiled with delight and asked, 'Orla? What are you doing here? Please come in.'

'Why thank you,' Orla replied. 'I really enjoyed our time together last night, and I wanted to see you briefly before my daily duties keep me away.'

'I am glad you did. Come sit,' Viridox whispered as he sat on his bed. 'Let us be quiet so we do not wake my brother. When I arrived at the inn last night, he was still not back. I do not know where he went, but I am sure he needs his rest.'

Orla nodded her head. The pair whispered with each other for sometime, telling jokes and talking about the future until they heard a loud grumpy groan from Vindex. The pair had woken him up with their incessant babbling.

'I see you're up, brother,' Viridox said cheerily.

Vindex rubbed his eyes and rolled back over, saying, 'Sure, I'm awake. How could you tell?'

'Your disgruntled groan gave it away,' Viridox replied with a smile.

'Looks like you two hit it off after our interrogation last night,' Vindex said, slowly sitting up in his cot.

'It was not an interrogation,' Orla answered. 'Just a simple civil discourse between two parties.'

'Oh, is that what you call it here?' Vindex countered. 'And here I am, silly old me, thinking holding a man prisoner in a booth at blade's point against his will was not civil. I clearly have much to learn about politics and alliances.'

'You're just grumpy because we woke you up. It really wasn't that bad,' Viridox replied.

Orla then added, 'Well, had I not done that, I never would have met Viridox. You are very lucky to have him as a brother.'

'Oh, really? Do tell,' Vindex smirked, looking directly at Viridox's face, which was losing its color.

'Oh yes. He went into great detail about your past last night. I think my favorite story is the one where he protected you when you were younger from the invading Umbrians. Such a caring and brave soul,' Orla replied, putting her arm around Viridox's side.

Vindex looked back at Orla and smiled, 'Either incredibly brave or incredibly delusional. I'll let you figure that out on your own.'

Viridox quickly redirected the conversation, saying, 'Well, I am glad we could all share this beautiful morning together, but I am sure your father needs your help in the tavern, my dear. Plus, your loyalists can't operate without their leader.'

'You shush about that Viridox! Are you trying to get me killed?' Orla snapped, 'You are right, though. Also, don't forget we have plans for tonight. I will see you later.'

'Of course I won't forget. I am looking forward to it,' Viridox replied as Orla left the room, leaving the brothers alone.

Vindex chuckled to himself. 'Tell me brother, is one brave if he fabricates the past to impress a girl?' he rhetorically asked.

'I suppose it can be,' Viridox replied. 'Especially when you know there is another person who could refute the story if he so chooses. Which bears the question, will you?'

'I have no interest in your love affair,' Vindex said bluntly. 'However, I believe you should be telling her the truth. Lies are no foundation for a relationship.'

Viridox sighed. 'You are right, but my story is far less exciting than yours.'

'Well, not entirely true,' Vindex replied through a cheeky grin, 'You did save me at the end of the Galdeshan Mountains. No wait, that was mostly Alesia. The fine horse that she is. So, I guess you are right, your story is much less exciting.'

Viridox stared at his brother with a blank expression.

'I'm only kidding,' Vindex replied, still chuckling. 'Mostly that is.'

Viridox rolled his eyes, 'Next time I find you in a tight spot, I think I'll just watch.'

'You better not,' Vindex protested, pointing his index finger at his brother's face. 'I'll kill you if you do.'

'How would you kill me? You'd already be dead,' Viridox jokingly replied, getting up out of bed.

Vindex smiled and pushed his brother towards the door. 'Get out of here and be productive today. Make some allies, find who we can trust among Megorath ranks, or just make some money. I need to meditate,' he told Viridox.

'Meditate or sleep,' Viridox replied as he was exiting the door.

'Goodbye Viridox,' Vindex responded, evading the question, watching as his brother closed the door behind him. *I will meditate after a quick nap,* he thought, while closing his eyes once more on his bed.

As his older brother slept, Viridox made his way around the town. He had not yet seen everything the city offered. Today was a commerce day, so the streets were bustling with life as shopkeepers sold their goods. Viridox walked out of an alley and was nearly struck by a horse and wagon. Behind the wagon were many farmers bringing their livestock and produce to market. Viridox pushed through the farmers, sheep and cattle and observed just how different Trevonum was to Norova. After some time walking, Viridox stumbled upon a missile range where he believed soldiers were practicing their archery. He leaned over the fence and looked in at what he presumed to be a regular scheduled training.

As he watched, he overheard one instructor say, 'The contest will begin shortly. Pick your bow and take your place. Quickly now!'

Contest? Viridox thought. *This could be fun.* Viridox did not hesitate. He hopped over the small wooden wall and walked to the shooting section of the missile range.

'Hello there,' Viridox said in a friendly tone. 'I hear you have a contest going on.'

The instructor turned around and replied, 'We do. And who may you be? Do you want to enter?'

'My name is Viridox. And I would love to enter the contest. Is there any reward for winning?' Viridox asked, hoping to get some compensation for his inevitable victory.

'Well, you seem mighty sure of yourself,' the man replied. 'You will need ten denars to enter, but if you somehow win, you will get one hundred back. In addition to the monetary gain, you will be given the choice to join the archery unit in our city's military. A very prestigious role.'

'I'm only after the money,' Viridox replied, reaching in and taking ten denars from the pouch of money he had stolen from the watchman the day before.

'Very well Viridox. Grab a bow and take a station. You will be given three shots. Whoever's arrows are closest to the center of the archery post at the end wins the prize,' the man responded, both speaking to Viridox and the rest of the competitors.

Viridox hurriedly grabbed his equipment and then hustled back to the only open station. There were nine other men taking part in the competition, all standing in a row preparing to release their arrows. Each contestant possessed a smug look of self appreciation. As the instructor called for the archers to ready their bows, they all drew their stances and stared at their targets. When the man yelled fire, all nine of the other participants quickly fired their arrows, one after another. Viridox was waiting to see what the competition looked like before beginning himself. It did not surprise him to see that most of the men fell far from the bullseye. One man, however, who was nearly double Viridox's age, hit within the yellow bullseye on all three shots.

'Yes!' the archer gloated. 'I will take my prize money now.'

'The competition is not over. That young man to the right has not fired his arrows yet,' the instructor replied.

The aged archer walked over to Viridox, who had still not taken a single shot. 'What are you, scared? I wouldn't blame you. There is no way you can best my score.'

Viridox paid no attention to the older man. Instead, he turned to the target and fired an arrow. Everyone watched as it flew over a hundred feet to hit the target directly in the center dot within the yellow bullseye.

The fellow competitors gasped at seeing such a precise shot, but it did not impress the old archer who scoffed. 'Just luck. Let's see him do it twice.'

Viridox ignored the old man and looked at the instructor. 'Move the target another three meters.'

The instructor replied, 'Viridox, you will not be allotted any extra points for distance. Are you sure you want to move the target?'

Viridox looked at the old archer and replied, 'I do.'

'Very well,' the instructor replied. 'Move it back!'

Two soldiers ran to the post and quickly carried it back three meters. Viridox prepared his next shot. He took a deep breath, feeling the string of his bow tighten around his fingers.

'You're going to miss you cocky brat,' the aged archer scoffed.

Viridox stared at the target and released his bow. The crowd watched in awe as the arrow soared through the air. Even before reaching the target, the contestants knew this too would be a bullseye shot. When it hit the target, the second tip split the first arrow in two. The crowd was in shock, including the archer who was previously ridiculing the young man.

Viridox had one shot left. He quickly took his arrow, cast his bow, and fired. The arrow followed the same path as his last shot and came into contact with the second arrow on the board, splitting that in two as well. Viridox's target had three arrows, all exactly on the bullseye, two splitting the previous arrows in half.

'Just luck?' Viridox asked with a smirk. He turned to put his bow away and walked past the middle-aged archer who had been so confident of victory.

He took the reward money from the manager and thanked the contestants for a friendly competition. He then fastened his winnings in a pouch around his waist and left the missile range. The men who competed had hardly moved. They were in shock at the tremendous feat that they had just witnessed.

Viridox was happy as he went back onto the city street, counting the denars he had won. *This sure beats the fifteen I stole from the guard yesterday*, he thought to himself. And with that thought, Viridox remembered what his brother told him before going to the tavern. Viridox stopped for a moment, contemplating on what to do before ultimately choosing to go to the post where he had stolen the pouch.

Viridox made his way to the training post where he saw Trevonum soldiers sparring with each other. He quietly made his way to the backside of the training grounds and stealthily returned twenty denars to one of the communal chests. *Well, that's my good deed of the day done,* Viridox thought as he left.

Viridox decided it would be best to return to his brother. The archery contest, while good to keep his skills with a bow sharp, was not exactly training. What he wanted was to work on his swordsmanship, and he knew there was no one better to train with than Vindex. He had not trained with Vindex since before the battle against Commander Agis and despite being confident in his abilities with a bow; he felt he needed to improve his skills with a blade greatly before entering another battle.

When he arrived back at the inn, he found his brother sitting on the ground in meditation. Viridox knew he was communicating with Cato through the Maith so he decided not to disturb his training and instead opted to wait patiently for Vindex to be done. After a few long and boring hours, Vindex's eyes opened. He slowly stood up after hours in the same position and saw his brother watching him from the bed.

'How was it?' Viridox asked, hoping his brother was getting closer to mastering the secrets of this ancient magic.

'It went well,' Vindex replied, 'Although I am still not strong enough to even talk with the spirits, as Cato does.'

'So, does that mean we are still in dire financial trouble?' Viridox asked, hoping to coax Vindex to say yes.

'I am afraid so.'

'Well, not anymore,' Viridox replied, throwing the bag of money he had won from the missile range into Vindex's hands. 'And the best thing is, this is all legitimately earned. And yes, before you ask, I returned the watchman's money. Even if I didn't really want to.'

'I am proud of you, brother. How did you make this much? It is an impressive sum for one day's work,' Vindex responded, counting through the denars one by one.

'I won it in an archery contest.'

'So legitimate is a stretch, as I am sure the other men you faced had no chance of beating you.' Vindex retorted jokingly.

'That would be a correct assessment,' Viridox said cockily. 'But now that I have solved our money issue temporarily, I need a favor from you.'

'And what is that?' Vindex asked cautiously, afraid of what his younger brother may ask.

'I want to train with you daily with a sword. My skills with a blade are sloppy at best, and you are the best swordsman I know. If we are to beat Valerik, I will need to hold more than my own on the front lines. I can't hide behind you forever,' Viridox responded seriously.

Vindex's eyebrows raised, and he chuckled a bit before replying, 'Who am I to deny a request like that?' He got up and said, 'Let us go now then.'

The two brothers made their way to the barracks, where each took up wooden spears with blunt ends to begin their practice. After taking ten paces back from each other, the brothers turned and took their respective battle stances. The barracks circled a mud filled training ground which was cut off from the main road by a small wooden fence. Without a word spoken, Vindex went in for his first attack. Not expecting such a prompt start, Viridox had no time to dodge, and the blow landed him on his rear.

'Just like old times,' Vindex said with a smile.

'Too much like old times,' Viridox replied, being helped to his feet by his brother's hand. 'Okay, let's try that again.'

The two retook their stances, but instead of allowing Vindex to press the attack this time, Viridox took the lead. With several fast strikes from either end of his spear, he pushed Vindex back into the corner of the barracks' training grounds. A small grin of satisfaction grew on Viridox's face as he believed he was in control. He quickly learned, however, that he was not. Viridox attacked with an overhead strike of the spear, which Vindex blocked. Vindex then spun his spear at an angle, striking Viridox spear hard, which flipped Viridox's weapon from his hand. After he was disarmed, Vindex swiped his spear under one of his brother's legs, causing him to fall into the mud. Just when Viridox thought things couldn't get worse, Orla walked by the garrison.

'Viridox?' she questioned as she walked past the barrack fence, wondering if the man in the mud was truly him.

'Yep. That's me,' he said quickly, getting to his feet and leaning on the fence post, looking across from her. 'I'm just having a friendly sparring session here with my brother.'

'Then why are you the one in the mud?' she asked, confused how Vindex could have beaten him.

'Oh yes,' Vindex interjected, who stood only a few feet back leaning against his spear, 'Do tell why you are the one covered in dirt and grime.'

'I was just going easy on you, of course,' Viridox replied.

Both Orla and Vindex looked at Viridox with an expression that clearly showed they had not believed his last claim.

'Okay,' Viridox said, turning to Orla. 'Everything I told you may have been slightly exaggerated.'

'How slightly?' Orla questioned, while crossing her arms.

'Well,' Viridox began, 'maybe exaggerated isn't the right word. Everything I told you was true, just I was not the one accomplishing the fantastic feats. It was my brother. I did not simply let him be commander because I did not want to deal with the logistics of leadership. He is the actual warrior. I'm nothing more than a lackey.'

'Well, it's about time you owned up to it!' Orla exclaimed, reaching out and lightly smacking Viridox across the face. 'You know, lying is not a good foundation for a relationship!'

'That's what I told him!' Vindex exclaimed, loving every second of Viridox's shame.

'How did you know?' Viridox questioned quietly.

'Do you mistake me for a fool?' Orla exclaimed. 'You do not get to where I am in life without having some intuition and basic common sense. I've just been waiting for you to come clean. The moment I met your brother last night, I could tell he was the warrior and not you.'

'Thank you!' Vindex shouted jovially from behind Viridox.

Orla looked over Viridox's shoulder to look Vindex in the eye. 'Shush,' she spoke, aiming to keep Vindex quiet.

'But I thought you only liked me because of my heroic feats,' Viridox replied nervously.

'By the gods, you know nothing about women, do you Viridox? Were you raised under a rock?' Orla asked rhetorically.

Before Orla could continue, Viridox quietly interjected, 'It wasn't under a rock, it was on top of a mountain.'

'Just shut it,' Orla quickly replied with a smile. 'Last night I did not go out with you because of your tales of heroism, but because I actually liked you.' She took her finger and pushed into Viridox's chest playfully.

'Really?' Viridox asked.

'Really?' Vindex exclaimed.

'Yes, really. And don't make me come over there, Vindex!' Orla replied confidently. 'Just no more lying from here on out.'

'I wouldn't dream of it,' Viridox replied with a huge smile.

'Good. Then I will see you when you two boys are done,' Orla replied before walking away.

'Yes, you will!' Viridox exclaimed as she was walking away. Turning back to his brother, he said with the same silly smile on his face, 'I'm gonna kill you.'

Vindex smiled in return, saying, 'Try it.' Vindex took his battle stance, ready for whatever attack his brother would make.

Predictably, Viridox was no match for his brother, and he ended up with his face down in the mud only moments after taking his first swing. After that, Vindex decided it was enough sparring for the day. Vindex extended his hand to his brother, who was still in the mud. The two went home together, and Viridox washed up to prepare for his date with Orla. This schedule became routine for the two men. Each day, Vindex would train with Cato to enhance his connection to the Maith. In the afternoon he would practice spar with Viridox, training him to become a better swordsman.

Then in the evenings, Viridox would continue to court Orla when she was not preoccupied with her rebel movement. As time passed, Viridox found himself content and secure. He adapted well to a comfortable city life, something he had not experienced since he was a child.

Vindex did not share the same feelings as his brother. Unable to move on from his past, he was in constant fear of the oncoming Umbrians. Vindex never allowed himself to find peace in this new life. Instead, he kept his mind occupied solely on training for the ever-present threat of Valerik and the Umbrians.

A TRIUMPHANT RETURN

Vindex and his brother were not the only ones working hard preparing for a fight. Dara's words had not struck fear into Valerik, but they ensured he trained more while Dara was off assisting Thrün. His standard training practice was to spar with the five best men from his personal unit, Legio X. He trained in mock combat with these men armed with only a wooden sword that was laden with a lead core so that it weighed twice as much as his regular blade.

'Again!' Valerik exclaimed, shouting at the five men from his legion who were now groaning prostrate on the sand arena in the center of the city barracks.

'With all due respect, sir,' one soldier responded, 'Why have we been doing this? Every day for months on end, you have beaten us to a pulp. Rarely do we stand a chance. I just don't see the point.'

'As I've said before, soldier, the battle before us will be like nothing we have faced. We are hunting down a man by the name of Vindex, who according to testimony made short work of Commander Agis,' Valerik replied. 'Now again!'

The five men stood up, short of breath and panting. They had been battling for hours in their full legionary gear. Sweat stains covered their tunics and their breastplates were dented and covered in sand. This did not bother Valerik, however, as he wanted to maximize his endurance for the upcoming conquest.

The five men quickly got into formation and encircled Valerik. Three soldiers led the charge, one from the center and two from Valerik's sides. They wanted to push Valerik into the other two legionaries, who were waiting to strike from behind.

Valerik, however, realized his contestants were setting a trap. He quickly pushed forward, closing the gap with the three men who were charging him. The two legionaries on the side stabbed their spears towards Valerik, but he was too quick. He ducked under the thrusts and slammed into the middle soldier's chest with his shield. The blow flew the legionary like a rag doll and he hit the ground unconscious.

With one eliminated, it was a simple task of defeating the final four who were now standing in a straight line facing their Emperor. Valerik took a moment to analyze his opponents, trying to find the perfect opportunity to strike. When the moment was right, Valerik swung his wooden blade with all his might against the soldier on the far left. The blow staggered the legionary, knocking him off balance. With this opportunity, Valerik forcefully kicked the soldier who let out a soft wheeze before falling down into the sand square. The other three, too tired to think of a proper formation, rushed Valerik together, who dodged, countered and struck until each had fallen on top of each other in the arena sand.

'I don't care how good this Vindex is,' one soldier groaned, 'There is no way he is a match for you.'

'I would hope not,' Valerik replied, 'But I will be damned if my confidence becomes my undoing. I have fought for too much in this world to let hubris stop me now.'

Just as Valerik was about to shout at his men to ready their weapons again, a clerk from the capitol building ran in and exclaimed, 'Emperor Valerik! Dara has returned. She is waiting for you in the throne room.'

Valerik smiled. He turned to his soldiers and said, 'Men. You are dismissed for the day.'

Valerik exited the barracks and mounted Genitor. He pushed his horse to a fast trot and arrived at Apolina's grand plaza within thirty minutes. He dismounted Genitor and tied his steed to a nearby post before running up the steps to the capitol building. Two imperial guards pushed the entryway open for their leader. He saw Thrün and Dara waiting at the end of the large entrance hall amidst the bureaucrats of the Empire, who were hard at work managing Umbria's day-to-day operations.

'Dara!' he exclaimed, happy to see his pupil and closest friend. 'I am so happy you are back. It is good to see you as well, Thrün. I take it you have good news for me?'

'Yes, my lord, we do,' Thrün said, stepping forward. 'The city of Susa has fallen to Umbrian control. We left the legions from Tarsus to defend it in our absence.'

'Excellent,' Valerik replied. 'To be honest, I had expected you to be back sooner, Dara. I sent you nearly a year ago.'

'We ran into some complications,' Dara replied, crossing her arms and glaring at Thrün, 'But we are back with a victory for Umbria.'

'Well, what is important is that you won. I hope you are ready to go on a new conquest,' Valerik replied, looking directly into Dara's eyes.

'And what of me, sir?' Thrün interjected, awaiting new orders.

'You, my friend, will be tasked with guarding the city. This new conquest requires my direct supervision. Dara and I will head out immediately.'

Thrün seemed shocked. He had not seen Valerik leave the capital since the days of the civil war. 'Understood sir,' he replied, making his way out of the hall.

Valerik watched as Thrün left and then turned back to Dara and said intently, 'So are you ready to get revenge for Agis?'

'Absolutely,' Dara replied with a sinister grin.

'As am I,' Valerik said confidently, 'Go. Prep Legio X. Then meet me in my chambers after it is done. We will be leaving soon.'

'Of course,' Dara replied obediently before rushing out to mobilize the legionaries for the campaign.

Shortly after Dara's departure, Valerik left the capitol building to head back to his home. From there, he packed his gear for the journey. It would be some time before Dara could mobilize the forces for departure, so Valerik stayed patient. He studied his maps, previous campaigns, and any historical documents he had about the Galician tribes. After nearly two weeks, he heard a knock on his door. It was Dara. The time he had been waiting for had finally come.

'All the men are ready,' she said as she entered through the chamber door.

'Excellent,' Valerik spoke. 'I should probably get ready myself then.' He stood up from his desk and got changed into his armor, placing the metal plates on top of the burgundy cloth covering he was wearing. After suiting up, he grabbed his blade that he kept in a chest at the foot of his bed.

Dara noticed Valerik's blade. It was the same sword he had used since Dara first started working with the Emperor. She asked, 'Don't you think it's time you got a new weapon? You could get a more suitable sword from the blacksmith before we go.'

'I shall not.'

'Any reason why?'

Valerik looked Dara strongly in the eye. 'This blade was a gift from my master in Praeterita. It has been a sword passed down through the generations to only the strongest of warriors. Earning this blade nearly cost me my life.'

'You know, Praeterita is just a myth, right? If it was real, that blade would have broken a long time ago.'

Valerik replied, 'I assure you, my friend, Praeterita is very real. Perhaps after we settle this Galician business, I will bring you there to train. I warn you, though, you may not be strong enough for the trials.'

Dara glared, 'I can assure you if Praeterita is real, I can pass any trial they throw at me.'

'You truly have the spirit of a warrior.'

'I do. Which is why I want to leave and get our revenge for Agis. Can we go?' Dara asked, pointing to the door.

'In a moment, I have not yet told you why I wanted you to join me back here.'

'And what did you want to tell me?'

'This is going to be a dangerous campaign. I am not worried about the other barbarian troops, but this Vindex that you told me about, I want you to stay away from him. Is that clear?' Valerik said sternly.

'Valerik!' Dara exclaimed as if she was a child having a temper tantrum. 'That is simply not fair! Agis was as close to me as he was to you. I have an equal right to reunite this man with his father!'

'That is not the point, Dara,' Valerik replied in a powerful voice. 'You are the second most capable warrior I know, behind only myself. However, we do not know what this man is capable of. I do not, no, cannot, afford to lose you. You mean too much to me to have some barbarian filth end your journey prematurely.'

Dara was shocked. Never had she felt such genuine affection from her commander. The only thing she could muster in response was a simple 'Okay.'

'I'm glad we are clear on that. Now let's go find this bastard,' Valerik said confidently as he put on his helmet and walked out his chamber door. Dara was left speechless. She gazed at her leader as his crimson cape flew in the air with his steady gait. Quickly snapping out of her trance, she rushed to catch up to her general, who was now outside mounting his horse.

The two rode together until they reached Legio X, outside the city walls. Eight thousand men stood ready to march outside the city. The men comprised the best fighters in the Umbrian army. Valerik wanted revenge for the murder of his friend and he was taking no chances. Umbria was ready for war and without another word Valerik signaled for the march to begin.

UMBRIA MARCHES

Life in Trevonum became routine for the two brothers. Each day, the brothers followed a strict regimen. Vindex would meditate in the mornings trying to enhance his connection to the Maith while Viridox would maintain his archery skills at the city firing range. In the afternoon, the pair would train with wooden swords and spears, strengthening their hand to hand combat abilities. At night, Vindex would usually return to meditating with Cato or he would visit his soldiers in the barracks while Viridox spent his nights courting Orla.

Then one day, a louder than usual rooster, awoke them early in the morning just before sunrise. The two brothers yawned and stretched as they slowly got out of their warm beds.

'Are you ready to train again today?' Vindex asked his brother, while opening the trunk at the foot of his bed.

'Actually, no,' Viridox replied quickly. He did not get up to open his chest, which held his armor and bow. Instead, he sat at the side of his bed and stared out at the town's farms, imagining the life he could have with Orla as local cattle farmers.

'No?' Vindex questioned. 'What else do you have planned?'

Viridox smiled peacefully before joyously saying. 'I think I am going to ask Orla to marry me.'

Vindex opened his mouth, shocked by what Viridox had said. 'Are you sure? You have only been together about a year?' Vindex asked, worried that his brother may make an impulsive mistake.

'Yes, I am sure,' Viridox replied. 'I know it may seem foolish, but when you meet the right person, brother, you just know. I want to share my life with her. Why not start now?'

'Well, I am happy for you. Let's call off training for the day so you can go out around town and see if you can find a proper engagement gift for Orla when you ask her the big question.'

'A good idea. It is a merchant's day after all. I doubt the shops will be open just yet, but I can go out and get an early start.'

'Have fun,' Vindex told his brother as he left, closing the inn door behind him.

Perhaps a little foolish, but he sure seems happy, Vindex thought to himself. *I wish there was something I could get for them. Perhaps I could even make something!*

With that realization, Vindex knelt down on the wooden floor and meditated. With each breath, Vindex pushed aside all other thoughts besides Cato and, in only a few moments, Vindex opened his eyes and saw his mentor standing before him.

'Cato!' Vindex exclaimed cheerfully. 'I have news to tell you.'

'As do I,' Cato replied softly but seriously, not making direct eye contact with Vindex.

Vindex knew that something was amiss, but he wanted to start off on a positive tone and thus he replied, 'You can tell me about your news after. My big announcement is that Viridox is going to ask Orla to be his wife.'

'That sure is news,' Cato said happily. 'I hope she says yes. Not even the spirits can foretell that.'

'I believe she will,' Vindex replied confidently. 'I've seen those two for the past year. They are inseparable, which at times has been very annoying, but I am happy for them. That brings me to why I am here so early. I want to get a gift for them.'

Cato looked a bit puzzled. 'Surely you have the money to buy one? Why do you need me?'

'I want to make one,' Vindex replied. 'I want to use the Maith to make a meaningful gift for my brother and Orla.'

'Not to discourage you, Vindex, but are you sure you can? We have been trying for many months to change matter with little progress.'

'Well, no, I am not sure if I can, but I do know I want to try. It would mean a lot to Viridox if I could make something for him and Orla,' Vindex replied, taking a seat in front of his mentor.

'Very well,' Cato replied, sitting down next to his pupil. 'The first thing we must do is decide what you wish to create.'

'I don't know what to do. What would you do for a marriage proposal?'

Cato looked outward into the valley below and smiled. 'Back in my day,' he said, 'we had wedding bands. Rings of gold or silver that you gave to your love.' He then looked down at his old withered hands and stroked his empty ring finger gently. 'Is that something you would be interested in?'

Vindex thought for a moment before undoubtedly replying, 'Yes. That sounds perfect.'

'Then let us begin. Cross your knees and kneel. Eventually you will alter matter easily, like me, but for the first time your technique matters. Extend your hand and imagine the ring in your mind.'

Vindex agreed and adhered to Cato's teachings, hoping that their lesson today would yield a different result from all their previous attempts. While the two Galdeshans were in meditation, Viridox was in the bustling streets of Trevonum. The market day had brought all the citizens out to do their weekly shopping. So many people made navigating the streets difficult for Viridox. He went shop to shop and yet could not find a suitable gift for his future bride. After spending many hours walking around the streets and the market square, he had thought there was no hope.

How in this entire city is there not a suitable gift for a bride? Viridox thought to himself angrily as he walked back towards the inn. On the journey back home, Viridox passed by the city's metalworker. *I doubt they will have anything, but I may as well try,* Viridox thought before opening the door to the blacksmith's shop.

After entering, the metalworker greeted him and asked, 'Good afternoon, sir. What can I get for you?'

'I am looking for a wedding gift,' Viridox replied, perusing over the man's stock.

'Ah,' the metalworker replied, 'I have little outside of weapons and tools, but I may have something satisfactory.'

He went into the back room and, after a moment, returned with a silver chalice in his hands. Across the bowl were two hands holding a heart in the middle. 'What do you think?' the metalworker asked.

'Wow!' Viridox spoke as he took the chalice from the blacksmith. 'This truly is incredible.' Viridox rotated the artwork in his hands. He imagined a future where this chalice would hang over a fireplace mantle, in a small home that he and Orla would share. 'I love it,' Viridox said, immediately handing his coin to the blacksmith.

'I am glad you like it,' the blacksmith spoke. 'A pleasure doing business with you.'

'Thank you,' Viridox replied quickly before leaving the shop. When outside, Viridox held the chalice up to the light. *I can't wait to show Orla later tonight,* he thought. *But first I should show Vindex. I am sure he will be impressed, too.*

Viridox quickly ran back to the inn to show his brother the present he had found. Upon entering the lodge, he climbed up the stairs and saw something unusual. Viridox looked at the door to his room and noticed a bright lime green colored light shining through under the door. After the green light faded, he heard his brother grunt as if he was in pain.

Viridox hastily pushed open the door, afraid for his brother's safety, and exclaimed, 'Vindex, are you okay?'

Vindex stood up and turned around. 'I am more than okay,' he extended his arm and opened the palm of his hand to his brother.

Inside his hand was a beautiful silver ring, with a crystal that Viridox had never seen before.

'What is this?' Viridox asked in amazement.

'A gift from me to the happy couple. It's a wedding band for Orla.'

'I have never seen this gem before. It is stunning. Where did you find it?' Viridox asked, taking the ring from his brother.

'It is a Galdeshan crystal,' Vindex said with a smile.

That was the last clue needed for Viridox to piece together what had happened. 'You made that with the Maith, didn't you?' he said with a shocked grin.

'I did!' Vindex replied joyously.

Viridox hugged his brother. He was so proud of him that after years of practice, he could finally conjure the Maith to alter elements. 'Cato must be thrilled,' he said, letting go of the embrace.

'He is and he is for you as well. It's getting late. Orla will be expecting you soon on your daily date. So go hurry up and ask her.'

'Of course. Meet me in the tavern. If she says yes, we shall have our celebration there tonight.'

'I will meet you there,' Vindex replied, shoving his brother to the door.

Viridox left the inn with his heart pounding and his legs feeling like jelly. He had never been more delighted before. Not even the night that he and Orla first met had Viridox felt such excitement. He hurried along to the usual date spot and waited for Orla to arrive. He could not wait to ask her the question.

Vindex remained in his room, not wanting to get to the tavern too early. He laid in bed staring at the ceiling, just thinking to himself. *I cannot believe I used the Maith to change matter. I created that ring from nothing. Imagine the possibilities. I could provide arms for my men. Extra coin to pay them. If I get stronger, I might be able to use this as a weapon against Valerik, too.*

He was deep in thought for sometime before realizing the hour had gotten late. *I am sure Viridox and Orla are at the tavern already. Probably best for me to join them.* He stood up out of his bed and headed to the lodge door when suddenly Cato appeared in front of him.

'Cato?' Vindex questioned. It was very odd for his mentor to visit him.

'In all of our excitement earlier,' the old sage spoke, 'I forgot what I was going to tell you.'

'What is it?' Vindex asked, feeling a serious undertone in Cato's speech.

'Valerik is coming,' Cato said bluntly. 'He has an army of eight thousand. As we speak, they are passing through my mountains.'

Vindex's face became pale and devoid of color. His stomach turned and his throat tightened. Valerik was not even at Trevonum, and yet his presence was already being felt. 'How long will it take an army of that size to reach here?' he asked, nervous at the impending threat.

'Only a little over a week.'

Vindex took a deep breath and said, 'Okay. Thank you for telling me.' He pushed through Cato's projection and opened up the door to the inn.

'Don't do anything brash,' Cato yelled, watching his pupil walk down the stairs to the inn. 'You still have to come back to the mountain to realize your true destiny.'

'I don't intend to do anything that will get anyone killed besides Valerik,' Vindex replied, still on the staircase.

Cato nodded and faded back to his post on the mountain. He walked over to a ridge where he had lit a Galdeshan flame to give him light, as the moon was now rising. The eight thousand men walking in unison created a marching sound that could be heard on the peaks of the mountains with utter clarity. Their fearless Emperor joining the ranks only enhanced the threat of this invading force. Valerik rode Genitor at the back of the army, with Dara at his side.

As they traveled through the valley, Valerik stared at Cato's lookout fixated specifically on the peak.

'Hello? Are you even listening to me?' Dara exclaimed, snapping her commander out of his inattentiveness.

'My apologies, Dara,' Valerik spoke. 'I was just a little distracted. What were you saying?'

'Distracted with what? What were you staring at?' Dara questioned, annoyed that her commander was not listening to her.

Valerik looked back up at the mountain peak. After a moment of examining the ridge, he spoke. 'Nothing, I suppose. You are right. There is nothing up there.'

'Very well. In that case, may we continue with what I was discussing?' Dara asked impatiently.

'Yes, of course. What did you ask me?' Valerik asked, giving his full attention to Dara.

'I asked what our plan is for this farming settlement of Ebora. It isn't directly on the way to Trevonum, but Quintus said that is where Vindex recruited his soldiers.'

'My plans have not changed. We will go to town and speak with their leader. If he disobeys or is found to have aided Vindex, we will take him hostage. If not, we will welcome them and the people to our new Empire. We'll take any necessary provisions for our journey and continue on.'

'Understood. I will ride ahead and inform the leading centurion that we will continue north outside of the valley,' Dara replied, before riding off ahead to inform the soldiers that the plan remained the same.

Valerik nodded and watched Dara ride off. He was now alone at the back of the army, with no one to accompany him. As the soldiers marched through the night sky, Valerik looked back one last time at Cato's peak. *I could have sworn I saw something there,* Valerik thought to himself. *But there is no time to investigate. I have to stay the course. I will avenge Agis.*

With the army slowly approaching, Vindex was now on edge. Pushing his way through the streets, he made his way to Megorath's hall. When outside, two guards tried to stop him from entering.

'Halt!' one guard spoke. 'Megorath has not summoned you. You can not enter.'

Vindex had no time for games. He exclaimed, 'Let me in this is a matter of life and death!'

The guard put his hand out, gesturing to Vindex that he could not proceed. 'I am sorry sir, but no one …'

Vindex cut the soldier off mid-sentence with a quick jab from his right hand. After a brief skirmish, Vindex opened the door to Megorath's hall, stepping over two unconscious town watchmen. He walked through the long corridor until he reached the door at the end, which led to Megorath's personal chamber. He pushed it open and looked up at the oaf on his throne of gold. Vindex sternly spoke. 'We need to talk. Now.'

At the same time Vindex was talking to Megorath, Viridox was walking back to the tavern with Orla. 'My dear, I have something to ask,' Viridox said while holding Orla's hand.

'What is it Viridox? Is everything alright?' Orla asked, concerned as she had not seen Viridox so flustered before

Viridox's face blushed. Nervous and scared, he let go of Orla's hand before quickly pulling out the ring. He looked her in the eyes and knew he was making the right choice. The spark that was there on the first night they met was still there over a year later. 'Will you marry me?' he asked nervously, hoping that his love would say yes.

Orla was shocked. She had not expected a proposal so soon. 'Yes!' she exclaimed, overjoyed, hugging him. She put on the ring and admired it in the winter moonlight. 'It's beautiful. I have never seen anything like this before.'

'The rarest jewel, for the rarest gem. You make me feel complete,' Viridox replied, ecstatic that Orla accepted his proposal. 'Now let's go to the tavern to celebrate. My brother will be waiting for us there.'

'I would love to, but I can't Viridox. I have a dissenter meeting. My people are growing restless waiting for this Umbrian threat you and your brother have spoken of. I need to keep them in line,' Orla replied sincerely.

'I understand,' Viridox responded. 'I am sure Vindex can wait a few more hours, anyway. I'll join your meeting and then we shall celebrate. After all, I am part of the movement as well.'

Orla smiled at her fiancé and the two made their way to the location of the dissenter movement. Meanwhile, Vindex was still in Megorath's chamber, desperately pleading with the man who was not taking him seriously.

'Sir, I implore you to listen to me!'

'I will hear nothing of it. You and your militia have been here for over a year and no threat has ever come to our gates. Why should I believe you now that an Umbrian army is on the way?' Megorath scoffed back at Vindex, not even having the decency to step off his throne while talking about a potential invasion.

'Are you truly the fool that you appear? I am telling you with absolute certainty that there will be an invasion from the strongest force this world has ever seen at your doorsteps in a week and a half, and you will do nothing to prepare?'

'Why would I?' Megorath protested. 'You have the best warrior in the land right here. I can handle whatever threat comes my people's way. If an army comes, I will deal with it then.'

Vindex was in a horrified state after hearing Megorath claim he was the best warrior in all the land. 'If you won't act, then I will,' Vindex proclaimed with a demanding tone. 'I will lead your men for you while you sit amongst your riches.'

This angered Megorath. He stood from his throne and, despite being several inches shorter than Vindex, walked up to him, attempting to be threatening. 'You will do no such thing. I will be out on the front line, as any good leader would do. These are my men. You are in my home.'

'And your home is going to be destroyed if we don't create a plan!' Vindex yelled, interrupting Megorath.

'Do not interrupt me again, boy, or you will be driven out from my dwelling, do you understand?' Megorath replied, irate at Vindex's insolence.

Vindex cracked his knuckles and looked down on the stout man and menacingly said, 'Thrown out by who? All your guards are taking a nice nap outside, so as I see things, it is just you and me.'

When Megorath realized he had no outside protection, he took some steps back. In a more calm and cooperative voice he said, 'Maybe we could make a plan for this potential invasion.'

Vindex, after seeing Megorath's change in demeanor, calmed down as well. He replied, 'I am glad we agree. Now let us begin.' He gestured over to the chieftain's war table and sat down with him, extrapolating potential defense strategies to use against Valerik and his forces.

As the night went on, Vindex and the chieftain remained hard at work, deducing a means to combat the incoming invasion. Meanwhile, Orla was speaking and gathering support for the dissenter movement. Since the time Viridox and Vindex had joined, the movement had grown four times over, reaching almost a third of the city's population. Orla was finding it difficult to appease such a large group, but had faith in Viridox that there was a greater threat looming. After the meeting was over, it was late at night and the two decided they were too tired to celebrate. Instead, they opted to go back to the inn.

'You know I love you,' Viridox said to Orla, who was walking right beside him.

'I do too,' Orla replied as they continued walking.

Viridox held her hand and continued to express his emotions. 'You know I have little in the way of family. It's just been me and my brother for as long as I can remember. But despite all that, when I'm with you, I feel normal. I feel at home, like you are my family.'

Orla understood all Viridox had gone through and understandingly replied, 'You are family to me, too,' she then squeezed his hand as they continued to walk back to the inn together.

The pair had a silent night, just enjoying each other's company. Hours passed, and the two fell asleep while Vindex was still arguing with Megorath about the Umbrian invasion. When Vindex was finally about to leave Megorath's hall, he turned around and asked, 'So, we start the plan tomorrow?'

'Yes,' Megorath replied reluctantly. 'We shall train until the threat arrives.'

'Very good. I shall see you in the morning,' Vindex replied civilly as he left the chamber.

It is too late for a drink now, Vindex thought to himself as he walked back to the inn. *I am sure Viridox will understand. Should I tell him why I did not come, though? It would surely ruin the joy of his engagement night. No, he has to know. Delaying it would be worse. When I see him at the inn, I will tell him about Valerik's arrival.*

When Vindex arrived back at the inn, the hour was very late and Orla and Viridox were already asleep sharing a bed. Vindex smiled, happy that his brother had found someone who brought him love in this world. Hopping into bed on his side of the room, Vindex rolled over and went to sleep. It was going to be an early morning for everyone in the town the following day, and he wanted to be well rested.

The bright morning sun illuminated the room the brothers shared and a beam of light on Viridox's face woke him. 'That was a great night,' he spoke, directing his comments to his future bride.

Orla shared his feelings. 'I never thought I would be so happy.'

'I don't want to dampen the cheerful tone, but I have some bad news,' Vindex chimed in. He had been up for some time.

'Good morning, brother. You seem very serious. Is everything okay?' Viridox replied quickly, concerned by Vindex's expression.

Vindex had made some morning tea for the two to help them wake up. He gave Orla and Viridox a cup each before answering Viridox's question.

Viridox quickly started drinking his tea and asked, 'What do you need to talk about, Vindex?'

'Valerik is here,' Vindex said with conviction.

Viridox spit out the drink in his mouth back into the cup. 'Here? Now?' he exclaimed.

'Not this second, but he will be here soon. Within the week, I would imagine.'

'How do we fight him?' Orla asked, knowing the gravity of the situation all too well. 'Have you spoken to Megorath about enlisting his forces?'

Vindex replied. 'I have already talked to Megorath. He and I will lead the army. Hopefully, it will be enough against the Umbrian onslaught.'

'What exactly are we up against?' Viridox asked, taking another sip of tea.

'Eight thousand men. The best that Umbria has to offer.'

Viridox choked on his drink, coughing some of it up. 'That's enough of that,' he said as he put the tea on the nightstand next to the bed. He turned to his brother and asked, 'Eight thousand? Are you sure?'

'Unfortunately, I am. Cato said it himself, and this morning while you were sleeping, I used the Maith to transport myself there and it is an army the likes of which I have never seen before.' Vindex replied, 'I am going to the barracks now to begin defensive drill training if you want to come.'

Viridox looked over at his partner and looked back at his brother. 'I will,' he replied, standing up. He turned back to Orla and said, 'I will still see you tonight, my love.'

'Of course you will Viridox,' Orla replied to her fiancé before addressing Vindex. 'My dissenters may be of some use to you as well. I don't want to show my hand to Megorath so soon, but we can enlist them if we are in dire need.'

'That is much appreciated, Orla,' Vindex replied. 'It may indeed come to that. I will keep you updated on the situation.'

Orla then quickly departed to go rally her followers in case of the worst. Shortly after her departure, the two brothers made their way to the barracks.

As they made their way out of the inn and into the streets, Viridox asked his brother, 'What are our chances?'

Vindex had no reply. 'I don't know,' he spoke. 'Not good, that's for sure.'

'When are they ever?' Viridox asked rhetorically, shrugging his arms as the two made their way to the barracks.

For the next week, sunrise to sunset, the men of Trevonum and the men and women of Vindex's militia trained together in defensive strategies. The only way they could seize the day is if everyone listened to Vindex's explicit command. As the week ended and the next began, everyone knew the invasion was almost upon them. The battle was soon to begin.

THE BATTLE FOR TREVONUM

Almost two weeks had passed since Vindex, and his forces began preparing for Valerik's invasion. The uncertainty of when Valerik would appear was putting a lot of stress on Vindex, and as a result, his ability to use the Maith diminished. He could no longer track the enemy with the aid of the Maith.

It was a cold and cloudy day. A slight snow fell from the sky while Vindex and Viridox were training in the street near the city's main gate. Megorath was angry. He did not like training in the cold weather and went to find the two brothers.

'Vindex!' he shouted as he got closer to the siblings, 'You have completely wasted my time. It has been two weeks now and there has been no news of your promised threat. I'm shutting this training down right now!'

'You can't do that!' Vindex exclaimed as Megorath pushed past him on his way to the men who were practicing their drills.

'Yes, I can,' Megorath said defiantly, looking back at Vindex. 'Don't forget who is in control of this city. My people are freezing, preparing for something that only exists within your own imagination. I have had enough!'

He headed toward the training post, but just as he was about to speak to the men who were in the middle of their drills, a watchman from the gate shouted, 'Megorath! You might want to see this.'

Megorath followed by Vindex and Viridox climbed up the ladder leading to the upper platform of the city wall. After all three had reached the platform, they looked out to see two men walking towards them, leaving a faint trail behind them in the quarter inch of snow that had fallen.

'What the hell is his?' Megorath asked, concerned when he realized that one of the two men walking towards them had his arms bound and sack over his head.

Viridox looked at his brother and asked, 'Is this him?'

Vindex was speechless, partly because the man was too far away to tell for sure, but also because of the lingering fear that had been instilled in him since Norova.

Viridox saw the troubled look on his brother's face. He turned back to the two men approaching in the snow and took out his bow, clenching it in his left hand. He was the only one on the wall that had any arrows, so he felt a responsibility to be ready.

The two men continued to walk until they stood one-hundred feet back from the gate. With this little distance between the two, Vindex knew for sure the man in the back was Valerik, but he could not tell the identity of the man with the sack over his head.

'Gentlemen!' Valerik exclaimed, greeting the men on the wall that looked down at him. 'I have come to make a deal!'

'Who are you?' Megorath replied, taking the lead in the conversation.

'Oh, my apologies. I forgot to introduce myself. My name is Valerik, Emperor of Umbria. I came searching for something, or rather someone. Perhaps you could help me with my quest,' Valerik replied in a charismatic tone.

So Vindex was telling the truth. I don't see any army though. What could he be planning? Megorath thought before tactfully replying, 'Perhaps. What is it you are searching for?'

'I appreciate your hospitality,' Valerik replied. 'I am looking for a particular Galician, whom I am led to believe may reside within your city walls.'

'And who may that be?' Megorath asked.

Vindex and Viridox looked at each other nervously in fear that this buffoon would turn them over to Valerik to save his own skin.

'He goes by the name of Vindex, I believe. I knew his father Brunos,' Valerik replied cordially.

'Oh, really?' Megorath replied, 'I think I know who you are talking about.'

'Wonderful,' Valerik replied with joy. 'Now if you could just bring him out here to me. I would greatly appreciate it.'

Vindex and Viridox both looked at Megorath, wondering what he was going to do. The man was clearly a coward, and it filled the two brothers with worry as Megorath opened his mouth again.

'I don't think he'd like that,' Megorath said confidently.

Vindex and Viridox were shocked. They had not expected such defiance from a man of such few scruples.

'And why is that?' Valerik replied, losing his charm and showing an angry expression.

'I may not be a good man,' Megorath said. 'But I am not so bad that I would entrust a fellow Galician's life with someone who reeks from the bloodshed of my people.'

Valerik became enraged. 'You speak of bloodshed!' he exclaimed. He kicked the bound man in front of him onto his knees and removed the sack from his head.

'Kastis …' Vindex said quietly, seeing the old man's face as the sack came off.

'This man here, and the one you are protecting inside, organized an army that decimated nearly a thousand Umbrian lives!' Valerik yelled, angered by Megorath's lack of cooperation.

'And had they not, how many of my people would your army have senselessly slaughtered?' Megorath quickly retorted.

'Only the ones who fight back,' Valerik replied calmly, regaining his composure. 'Which brings me to a new deal. I don't want to kill any of you. Only Vindex. Besides that, the rest of you can go about your daily life under my new Empire. You will keep your land, your jobs, I will take nothing from you. I promise only prosperity and security.'

'At the cost of our freedom,' Megorath said defiantly.

'There are worse things to lose. First thing that comes to mind is your life,' Valerik said, elevating his voice to ensure that those behind the walls could hear him as well. 'I see where your leader stands, but to those who do not agree with his dated ideals, stay inside your homes, and lock your doors. No harm will come to you. I am here for two reasons, Vindex, and to spread with you the prosperity of my people. My men are under strict orders to not enter or destroy any of your homes or places of livelihood. So long as you give me Vindex and do not resist my offer of protection, you will be safe.'

Valerik paused. He slowly unsheathed his blade before continuing, 'If you do not agree to these terms, and you do fight back against my men …' He pushed his blade through Kastis' back, causing him to fall forward, bleeding in the snow. 'I won't be responsible for what happens to you.'

'Kastis!' Vindex shouted, drawing Valerik's attention to him.

Before Valerik could get a word in to question the man who seemed enraged by Kastis' death, Viridox, who had his bow already pulled back, asked his brother, 'Do I take the shot?'

'Shoot him now!' Vindex replied angrily. Kastis was another death on a long list that Vindex considered himself to be responsible.

Viridox fired the bow just as Valerik was about to speak. Seeing the arrow coming at him, Valerik leaned his torso to the left and extended his left arm over his right shoulder, catching the arrow in mid-flight just as it was passing his ear.

'Who is this guy?' Megorath asked to himself, amazed at Valerik's speed and confidence.

Valerik took the arrow and spun it around to point it at Viridox. He said menacingly, 'For your sake archer, I hope you heed my warning and stay inside when the battle begins. Otherwise, I'll be looking for you on the battlefield.'

'Looks like I've made a friend,' Viridox scoffed, with a bit of false bravado.

Not a fool to give Viridox a second chance, Valerik slowly walked backwards until out of range of the bow, making close note of the archer's face as well as the man who mourned for Kastis. Before leaving, though, he shouted, 'I will be back with my forces tonight. I give you five hours until the siege begins. Plan accordingly. All of you.'

The three leaders stood in silence for some time on the wooden palisade, each processing what had just happened. After some time had passed, Vindex looked at a town watchman and said, 'Open the gate and get the body. Please give him a proper burial.'

The watchman obliged, not because he was under command of Vindex, but because of the basic decency and respect for a fellow Galician now fallen.

Megorath turned around and spoke to another soldier who was on the ground, a lieutenant in the army, and said, 'Get the men together. I want everyone guarding this gate.'

'Yes, sir,' The soldier replied before quickly running to prepare the troops.

Vindex rapidly looked over at Megorath, who had his back turned and was walking towards the ladder. Vindex reached out and grabbed the chieftain's arm, spinning him around. 'That was not our plan!' Vindex said aggressively. 'What about the west gate? You are leaving it completely defenseless.'

Megorath looked at Vindex with eyes of fear and said, 'We are outnumbered, and clearly out skilled as well. We need to hope the enemy comes directly through the center gate, otherwise we won't stand a chance. And as long as you are here, you are under my command, so you will obey that order. Is that clear?'

Vindex just stared blankly as Megorath turned back around and went down the ladder to the city streets. When back on the ground, Vindex shouted, 'I beg you to listen to me. That plan is suicide.'

Megorath shouted back, 'This is the only way. Do not disobey my orders.' He then walked down the road, leaving Vindex and his brother alone on the wall with the town watch.

Vindex took a deep breath and looked over at Viridox. He knew this battle was going to end in defeat and he needed to formulate a new plan for their survival. Before he began postulating scenarios, he turned to his brother and said, 'Viridox, this is a losing battle. I don't want to drag you into this because of me. Take Orla and stay inside and …'

Viridox cut his brother off. 'I will not hear of it. I know I wasn't there, but he was my father, too. I'd like nothing more than to see that Umbrian slime fall.'

'Are you sure?' Vindex asked. 'I do not mind if you choose to stay inside.'

Viridox placed his arm around his brother and earnestly replied, 'I have made up my mind, brother. You will not sway me. I am going to be by your side. I want to see Valerik perish.'

'As do I,' Vindex responded, looking out at the trail Valerik made through the snow as he departed from the gate. 'The only problem is how to kill him without dying in the process.'

'You have a plan, don't you?' Viridox asked nervously, afraid of the consequences if he didn't.

'Not yet, but I will,' Vindex replied reassuring his brother, 'In the meantime go tell our men and women to stay inside with Orla and her followers. Barricade the tavern and order them to stay inside no matter what. I will not let them die because of a man who is clearly operating out of fear.'

'Of course,' Viridox replied as he made his way to the ladder. 'I hope you have a plan by the time I return.'

Vindex said to himself after Viridox had already left, 'As do I.'

Vindex did not want to waste any time and immediately began thinking of ways to escape the city if the battle turned in the favor of Valerik. He got off the wall and walked around the perimeter of the town, trying to find an ideal place to regroup with his brother if the front-line fell. At the end of the wall, he looked out onto the lake where Trevonum sat and saw a small boat on the pier. This gave him an idea. He took the boat and paddled it to the southeastern shoreline of the city. He took it out of the water and carried it from the shore to a barn that was located nearby. He then hid the boat under some hay for safe keeping. After the boat was hidden, he looked out across the lake and saw the road to Narbo Martius. The road was really nothing more than a rough dirt track, but it was on the opposite side of the lake from Trevonum and cut through dense forest. It would make the perfect escape route in the midst of battle if needed. Immediately, he ran back to the inn and hopped on Bucephalus, and guided Alesia behind him. He traveled as fast as the horses would allow to the thick, forested path and tied the steeds to a tree branch, leaving them ready for a quick escape. All that he had to do now was return to Trevonum, which was a long journey without a horse. After an hour or more of jogging, he arrived back where he started just as the sun was setting.

Viridox saw his brother outside the wall and instructed the watchmen to open the gates. He climbed off the wall onto the street below and embraced his brother. He frightenedly asked, 'Where the hell have you been? Megorath has been looking for you for hours.'

'I'm sorry, brother, but I was getting our plan together,' Vindex replied, nodding his head to the right, indicating he wanted his brother to follow him. The two walked to a more secluded area against the wall so that they could speak freely.

Viridox took off his helmet so that he could better hear Vindex's whispers.

'There's a boat hidden under some hay behind a barn on the southeast side of the city. If things start to sour here, we are going to take that boat and paddle across the lake into the forest that leads to Narbo Martius. Hopefully, we won't need it, but it is there if we do,' Vindex whispered to his brother.

'And we walk from there all the way to Narbo Martius? That will take weeks on foot,' Viridox questioned, unsure about the logistics of his brother's plan.

'I brought Bucephalus and Alesia to the forest already. I have loaded them with some provisions and they are waiting for us there in the event we need to retreat.'

Viridox smiled as he put his helmet back on. 'I never doubted you for a minute,' he said as the two walked back to their post on top of the city walls.

When on top of the wooden palisade, Vindex attached Cato's shield and polished his father's blade. He looked over at his brother, who was wearing the same armor except that he still had the helmet and sword that Vindex had lost in the battle with Agis at the Galdeshan Mountains.

Vindex quipped, 'It's a good thing you still have the full set. You'll need the extra protection.'

Viridox looked at his brother with fear in his eyes. He became more flustered and nervous with each passing hour. He replied, 'Vindex, people are about to die, and I might be one of them. I've never been on the front line before.'

'Brother, you have been training with me every day for a year. You don't give yourself enough credit. I promise you will hold your own, and besides, I am with you, always,' Vindex said as he put his arm over his brother's shoulder. As the brothers talked, the sun slowly set and the cold set in. The entire town of Trevonum stood watch, waiting for the Umbrians.

The snow was still falling in the night sky as the Galicians looked into the distance. Trevonum stood illuminated by torches placed all over the city walls and at the front gates shining bright like a star in the night sky. This made it an easy target for the Umbrian army as all the surrounding farmland and woodland was pitch dark, concealed by the cloudy snowy night. Valerik saw this strategic advantage and purposefully waited until sunset before deploying his soldiers.

The Umbrians approached the city walls slowly, using the darkness to their advantage. Valerik took six thousand men with him to invade the northern gate while instructing Dara to take the remaining two thousand to the western wall. Dara was under strict instruction not to attack until Valerik's men had made contact with the enemy at the main gates.

Valerik continued his slow approach until he was about five hundred yards outside the city. Covered by the night sky and the falling snow, the Galicians had not spotted him, his men, or the ballista which Valerik would use to smash open the city's gates. After cranking the track back, the Umbrian men loaded the ninety-pound wooden log into the ballista's track. Valerik looked at the gates and back at his men and commanded, 'Fire!'

There was a quick popping sound as the Umbrian soldiers pulled the rope that launched the projectile at the gate. Before the Galicians even had time to question whether they heard a pop in the distance, the large wooden rod came crashing at the gate. The force from the blast was enough to knock a few soldiers who were not ready off the wall back onto the street below. Trevonum's gates already showed signs of breaking just after one shot. The gate had been bent and pushed in on its hinges. The gate could only survive a few more hits before collapsing onto the interior city street.

'Get down!' Vindex exclaimed after feeling the blast on the wall. He, his brother, and the fellow Galician soldiers ducked under the small cover offered by the wooden palisade.

'Do you see anything?' Viridox questioned anxiously.

Vindex peered his head over the wooden spike at the top of the wall. He quickly exclaimed, 'Brace yourselves!' as he saw another incoming blast from the ballista flying into view.

After the blast hit, Vindex looked back at his brother and replied, 'No, they are hiding in the shadows. It is too far to see.'

'What are we supposed to do?' Viridox asked, losing his nerve. 'Wait here until they burst the gate down?'

Vindex did not reply. He saw no other option but to play Valerik's game. He did not know what lay ahead of them in the fields, so rushing the enemy was not an option, and even if it were, he did not have the authority to command such an attack. So, there they sat, waiting until the barrage from the ballista ended. Valerik took this opportunity to be as thorough as possible. He wanted the gates to be opened before sending in his men. And finally, with one last ferocious bang, Vindex, Megorath and Viridox watched the gates collapse. Their first line of defense was gone.

The sound of the iron gates falling on the dirt road rang through each Umbrians' ears as they watched the Galician's defense fall. Valerik looked back at his men who were stationed behind the ballista and yelled, 'All units, march!'

The Galicians looked on in horror as they saw the six thousand men Valerik commanded come out from the shadows and into the torchlight. Megorath took command over his own troops, seeing the legionaries approaching. 'I want my swords and axe-men ready in front of the gate. Fight them back. Do not let them enter the city. Bowmen, I want you firing down at them from the walls. We need to take as many of them down as we can before they reach us.'

For once Megorath was correct, they truly needed to limit the numbers getting into the city walls. Trevonum had a respectable militia, three thousand strong, composed of axe-men, swordsmen, and bowmen. This impressive force was only a third of Valerik's legionaries though, and if the Galicians were to win, they needed to maximize the city's fortifications.

As the legions made their way to the walls, Vindex noticed that some units were carrying ladders. Valerik had not planned on flooding into one opening in hopes of victory. He intended to take the walls and ensnare the settlement. Vindex shouted with a hint of fear at the archers alongside him, 'Men! Fire on the troops with ladders. We cannot let them take the walls.'

A hailstorm of bronze tipped arrows fled from the northern gate, raining a wave of death upon Valerik's men. Valerik shouted at his soldiers, 'Get those ladders to the walls! The rest of you form a testudo!' Valerik's units, not carrying ladders, used their large rectangular shields to create a shield wall. The legionaries grouped together in rectangular formations, raising their shields at their sides and over their heads to create an almost impenetrable defense against oncoming arrow fire.

Vindex and Viridox were burning through their stocks of arrows, trying to cause some damage. Only Viridox was precise enough to shoot through the small cracks in the shield wall. 'Here, take my arrows,' Vindex said, handing his ammunition to his brother in a hurry. 'They are better used with you.'

Viridox did not protest. He took the arrows and continued to fire down upon the Umbrians who had now reached the city wall. As the ladders went up, Valerik ordered his men out of the testudo. Breaking the shield wall instantaneously, a mass of Umbrian legionaries stared down at the brave axe-men and swordsmen of Trevonum. The Umbrian troops took out their javelins and fired a wave of spears into the clumped together Trevonum army. Spears rained down from the sky, killing many axe-men who had no shields to protect themselves from such a barrage.

With the Galicians startled and weakened, Valerik ordered the charge, and the soldiers ran through the front gate. The two sides ferociously collided. The clangs of swords and shields alike polluted the air as the battle began. Trevonum axe-men used both arms to swing down with their large hatchets at the Umbrian forces pushing through the gates. Some strikes were successful, while others were met by the large rectangular shields of the Umbrian legionaries. More and more Umbrians entered the gate, cutting through the brave Trevonum soldiers. The skill disparity grew quickly as axe-men with no shields or heavy armor quickly fell to the Umbrian blades. The Trevonum swordsman stood a better chance against Valerik's soldiers, but even they struggled to push back the well-trained legionaries from their city's entrance.

As the battle on the street continued, the Umbrians began the offensive on the walls. The legionaries climbed the ladders swiftly, hoping to seize the walls, thus ensnaring the Galicians within their own city. The legionaries raised twenty ladders in total. Ten on the right side of the gate where Megorath stood, and ten on the left where Vindex and Viridox were positioned. When the Umbrians made their way to the top of the wall, they drew their swords on the bowmen and, with no hesitation, cut them down, securing footings along the palisade.

The left side of the wall was no longer safe. Umbrian legionaries stepped over the deceased Galician bowman, slowly encroaching upon Vindex and Viridox, who were now completely without reinforcement. This was Viridox's first time in the front lines. He was grateful for the year spent training with his brother, as he felt he was a comfortable match for the Umbrian legionaries. With his sword and shield, he battled two Umbrians at a time as his brother fought next to him.

'Is this what you expected?' Vindex asked his brother, ducking under an incoming swing of a legionary's sword before pushing him off the outside portion of the wall.

Viridox was slow to reply as he was blocking the incoming swings of two Umbrian soldiers, one with his shield and the other with his blade. After parrying each attack, he swung to the left of the soldiers. Kicking one into another, he watched as they fell twenty feet onto the city streets. 'I thought it would be less stressful,' he replied, taking a swing at a soldier who had just come off the ladder.

'It has not become stressful yet, brother,' Vindex replied with a smile, making quick work of the Umbrians that stood between him and his brother. 'And I plan to be here with you when it does. I do not know how long our line can hold.'

The pair briefly looked down at the street and saw the Umbrian legionaries flooding the path, taking more ground with each passing second. As the fighting continued at the front gate, Dara planned her attack on the western wall. She could hear the battle even from so far away. Valerik had clearly made contact, so she ordered her men to push up on the walls where only two watchmen stood on the lookout.

Dara turned to her archers. 'Which two of you know you can take those men out silently on your first shot?' she asked as two came to the forefront, bows in hand.

'Good. You fire on three, understood?' Dara whispered to the archers.

'Orders understood,' the archers replied, lining up their shots.

'One … Two … Three!' Dara exclaimed.

The two Umbrian archers did as instructed, releasing their arrows in unison at the unsuspecting town watchman on the gates. The Galicians on the wall heard a brief whistle in the air before the Umbrian arrow struck them both. Dara and her men looked on as the soldiers fell off the wall, a trail of blood leaking out from each of their arrow wounds.

'Perfect!' Dara exclaimed with glee. 'You did a good job, men. Continue to not disappoint me and get those ladders to the walls. I want to join the fun.'

Dara's men rushed to the walls. Every passing second meant more and more Umbrian life lost on the frontline. The legionaries wanted to gain the city walls and implement a flank attack to ensure minimal Umbrian casualties. Dara smiled as the ladders went up. There were no Galicians in sight. *What a foolish people,* Dara thought to herself. *Only having two soldiers on guard. Pathetic barbarians.*

Eight legionaries climbed the ladders to ensure control of the western entrance. When the coast was clear, Dara, who was waiting at the closed gate, looked up at her troops and yelled, 'I'm waiting! How long does it take to open a door?'

'One moment, commander!' a terrified legionary screamed as he released the lever for the main gate.

The hinges popped, and the iron gate pushed back into the city street. Dara would soon join the battle. She reached to her side and unsheathed her sword. With a firm grasp on her weapon, she walked into the city, stepping over the corpses of the two watchmen who died before ever getting the chance to warn of Dara's presence.

Gods, they are more disgusting up close, Dara thought to herself as she stepped over the second body. *These two were lucky, though. Their deaths were peaceful by my standard. I'll be sure to make the next barbarians more gruesome.*

While Dara and her legions marched through the city streets, the fight on the frontline was turning into a complete blood bath.

Megorath had lost all of his men on the right side of the gate. He was battling alone when Viridox called for his brother's attention. 'Vindex! Megorath is alone. We need to help him!' he shouted as he blocked an incoming attack with his shield.

Vindex turned around briefly to see Viridox was telling the truth. Megorath was alone, and while fighting valiantly, he stood no chance against the growing numbers of Umbria's elite. Vindex grunted, thinking about the situation. *If I leave, my brother will be the one overrun. Despite being an oaf, I do not wish for Megorath to die, but I can't lose Viridox's life trying to save his.*

Vindex shouted back at his brother while swinging his sword at an Umbrina legionary. 'We have our own battle here. We have to hope he can handle it.'

Viridox looked betrayed. Sure, Megorath was an oppressive ruler and a buffoon, but did he really deserve to die at the hands of cold Umbrian iron? 'He will die, brother,' he said earnestly while continuing to fight.

'So will you if I leave,' Vindex sternly replied as he sliced down an Umbrian aiming to throw his javelin at Viridox.

'Then I will go. I know you can hold the line here on your own,' Viridox responded as he withdrew from the current front leaving Vindex alone to fight the onslaught.

'If things go south,' Vindex exclaimed as Viridox ran towards Megorath, 'remember the plan!'

Viridox bravely charged into battle, pushing over a soldier who had positioned himself at Megorath's side. 'I can do this without you!' Megorath exclaimed, protesting Viridox's aid.

'I can always go back if you want,' Viridox quipped as he ducked under the swing from an Umbrian's sword.

'Just focus and fight, boy!' Megorath yelled back while pushing an Umbrian off the wall.

Despite their combined strength, they were still losing ground. 'How many men did they bring?' Megorath angrily yelled, whilst grabbing a legionary by the chest plate before stabbing him in the side.

Viridox watched as five more legionaries climbed up the ladder onto the wall. He was tired and out of breath. 'We are so screwed,' he said while swinging his sword into the Umbrian line.

While things were looking bleak on the wall, they were still optimistic compared to what the battle on the streets offered. The muddy brown road had turned red from all the lives lost. The axe and swordsmen of Trevonum did not have the equipment to adequately battle elite legionaries. An Umbrian sword or javelin easily penetrated their light gear and armor and while their weapons could crack even the best shield, that simply was not enough when faced with the hoards of oncoming soldiers.

To make matters at the gate even worse, the mighty Valerik joined the battle. Megorath watched from the wall in horror as his men fell one by one, cut down by the Umbrian Emperor. Angered beyond reason, Megorath grabbed a javelin from a deceased Umbrian. He turned his back away from the fight on the wall and held the spear over his head, taking aim at the Umbrian Emperor.

'Take this, you bastard!' Megorath screamed, blinded to the legionaries next to him on the palisade.

Megorath swung his arm, but just before letting go of the pilum, he felt a piercing pain from his side. An Umbrian legionary had stabbed him in his right kidney only a second before he released the javelin at Valerik. Megorath fell to his knees, holding his side in shock. He was paralyzed, overcome by pain, unable to do anything but look up at the Umbrian assailant. The soldier pushed Megorath off the wall to clear a path to Viridox, who watched in horror, powerless to help.

'Brother!' Viridox exclaimed in a panic. 'I am in some trouble here!'

Vindex looked over to see Viridox pushed back to above the gate. He realized Megorath must have been killed and now needed to save his brother from meeting the same fate. The legionaries had stopped climbing the ladders on Vindex's post, so if he could defeat the last remaining soldiers, he could help his brother escape. Though tired and aching from the fighting, with one last effort he charged the six Umbrians ahead of him, pushing some off the wall while using others as human shields for quick incoming stabs.

'I am coming, brother!' Vindex screamed while disposing of the remaining Umbrians in his way.

With the screams of several men falling off the wall at once, Valerik briefly turned around on the battlefield to see the man who mourned for Kastis cutting through his elite legionaries as if they were new recruits.

'That's him,' Valerik whispered sinisterly. A big smile grew on his face as he returned to the frontline battling multiple Galicians at once. Three swordsmen from Trevonum attacked the Emperor in unison, believing they had the advantage. Valerik quickly countered with a quick slash of his own. Only a moment later did all three swordsmen fall on the muddy road bleeding from the neck. *There will be only one man who can challenge me here today,* Valerik thought to himself. *I just need to get to the wall.*

'Any time now, brother!' Viridox exclaimed again.

Vindex cut down the last soldier that stood on his side of the palisade. *Perfect,* he thought to himself. *Now I will just head over to Viridox and … oh my gods.*

Vindex saw nearly thirty Umbrians in front of Viridox. He was too tired to fight that many soldiers all at once. He needed a new plan to make for an easy escape. Vindex ran to his brother's side, frantically looking around the walls for something to help them flee. Out of the corner of his eye, he spotted a container filled with oil, which was used to ignite the cloth on fire arrows. *That's it!* he thought while engaging the Umbrian frontline.

'Fall back Viridox and slice open that barrel,' Vindex screamed as he and his brother stood alone, fighting a legion over the gate.

Viridox did not question the orders. He trusted Vindex with his life and withdrew at the first safe opportunity, leaving Vindex alone to deal with the frontline. With his Galdeshan sword, he sliced the barrel and let the oil soak over the wooden palisade. He then ran back to where Vindex was fighting before, standing amidst the corpses of the fallen Umbrian soldiers.

'It is done!' Viridox shouted, out of breath. He could barely hear himself over the sound of his racing heart.

With all of his strength, Vindex redirected the momentum of a legionary's attack to cause the soldier to fall down onto his knees. This caused the other legionaries to pause their advance as they needed a moment to safely maneuver around their toppled comrade. With this distraction, Vindex turned and ran to Viridox, grabbing a torch that rested on the outer wall and, after passing the oil barrel, threw it onto the greased wooden platform. The flames burst up immediately, cutting off the Umbrian legion in their tracts, giving Vindex and his brother time to escape.

Vindex could now clearly look at the state of the battle on the ground without worry of an incoming attack. 'Oh no,' he whispered, seeing how far the Umbrians had made it into the city. There were only a few hundred Trevonum soldiers left fighting. The rest were corpses. Vindex looked away from that battle, realizing it had been lost, and said to his brother, 'To the boat.'

Viridox turned around and began running down the wall to the southeast coast, where the boat was hidden. Vindex however paused for a moment, needing to catch his breath. As he breathed, hands on his knees, back bent over panting, an Umbrian soldier who had just climbed up the ladder took him by surprise. The legionary had been thrown off the wall earlier by Vindex and knew firsthand how dangerous this barbarian was. The legionary feared battling him with a blade. Instead, he tackled Vindex, sending both himself and the Norova native flying over the wall into the city below. Hearing his brother's scream, Viridox turned around to see Vindex falling off the twenty foot drop onto the street, which was riddled with Umbrians.

'Vindex!' he exclaimed, watching his brother fall to the street below. Muscle memory kicked in and Viridox grabbed his arrow pouch, hoping to find some leftover ammunition so he could give his brother some cover from above. Sadly, he had no arrows left to use. He looked away from the street to inspect his pouch. *There has to be some left,* Viridox panicky thought as he stared at the empty bag. *Oh, no,* he thought, looking back at the battle on the street. *Vindex, where did you go? I can't see you. Shit.*

With time of the essence, Viridox knew he had to trust that his brother would make his way to the boat. He then turned back towards the bay and continued running down the wall.

The battle that Vindex had fallen into was more precarious than the one fought on the wall. Not only had the Galician forces been reduced to only a few hundred, but Dara and her forces were now coming from the rear. Valerik, having heard someone yell out Vindex, looked back up at the wall where he presumed the Galician to be. He saw a man wearing the same chest plate running from the battlefield. Unable to escape the mosh pit of fighters he was trapped in, he signaled to Dara, who he saw fifty feet away behind the fighting.

'Dara! The man on the wall!' Valerik exclaimed from the battle-line. 'Stop him! He is who we are looking for. Don't let him escape. I will meet you when I can.' As he spoke, he was easily making his way through trooper after trooper that dared contest him in combat.

Dara looked up and saw the man running on the wall. 'I'm on it!' she exclaimed, separating herself from the legion to chase after Viridox.

Viridox's heart was racing. With every step he took, he felt like he wanted to collapse. Never had he been so strained for so long, and never had he had a legitimate fear of death. The only thing fueling him was adrenaline. A simple wish to get the boat ready, hoping his brother would follow behind him. Viridox slid down the last ladder on the wall, leading him to a city alley.

I don't know this road, he thought. *Where's the barn? Where's the barn? I know he said there was a barn by the coast. It has to be here.*

In a panic, unsure of his surroundings, Viridox ran out of the alley to the main road. Just as he exited the alley onto the main street, he ran into Dara. The two collided, causing both to fall into the muddy street. Dara, fresh and ready for battle, quickly got up out of the mud.

'I didn't take you for a coward,' Dara said as she took her battle stance, mud dripping down her face and hair.

Viridox was much slower to rise from the dirt. He began panting, trying to catch his breath. Dara could see even from a few paces back that the man was tired, as with each exhale a new fog formed from his breathing in the cold winter air. Eventually, he stood and took his own stance, saying, 'Lady, I think you have me confused with someone else.'

Dara did not answer Viridox. She was convinced that he was the son of Brunos that Valerik wanted. She charged Viridox, colliding her sword against Viridox's shield. After blocking the first attack, Viridox sloppily swung his sword at Dara, who easily blocked it with her own shield.

'I thought you were supposed to be an expert fighter,' Dara said condescendingly, disappointed at Viridox's technique.

'Again,' Viridox replied, struggling to breathe, 'I am pretty sure you've got the wrong guy.'

Dara was not willing to admit that she could have the wrong person. This man had the same armor as the one she followed from the wall. *I know it's you, Vindex, so stop playing dumb and answer for your crimes,* she thought to herself.

Viridox threw a blow trying to generate defense with an offensive strike. This backfired immediately as Dara blocked the blade with her own and spun Viridox's arm in such a manner that flipped the sword several feet behind him. Now, without a weapon, Viridox relied on his shield to block Dara's incoming strikes, which worked for a few attacks until she grabbed the shield with both her hands and slammed it into Viridox's head. Viridox's vision became blurry, but he felt Dara ripping his shield off his forearm.

She looked at the shield in her hand and spoke. 'This is rather well crafted for a barbarian.' She then looked to see where Viridox's sword had fallen and then threw the shield next to the blade. 'Too bad it is still rubbish compared to Umbrian forging.'

Viridox was dazed for a moment after Dara's attack. When his vision normalized, he saw the boot from Dara's foot coming to his chest. The kick connected and sent Viridox flying onto his back. He lay there on the muddy, rocky road looking up at Dara, who stood above him. 'Such a pity. I expected so much more from the mighty Vindex,' she said as she raised her sword over her head.

Viridox put his hand out over his face, trying to block the incoming swing. As Dara swung down, striking with an overhead thrust, Vindex jumped out from behind a building, blocking the blade with his own mere inches from Viridox's face. 'Brother!' Viridox exclaimed with tears of joy.

Dara did not believe what she had heard. *It must be some savage trick,* she thought to herself. She would soon realize her mistake when looking down at the blade protecting the Galician on the street. The silver and bronze colors were unmistakable. That was the sword Brunos had used in their duel many years ago. She then turned her head to see Vindex's face staring back at her with raging eyes.

Vindex in a fit of anger muttered threateningly, 'Leave my brother alone.' He swung his left hand, which held his shield as hard as he could, smashing Dara's face and knocking her helmet clean off. He watched as she fell down, blood running from a massive gash left by his shield on her face.

'I should kill you right now,' Vindex said with no hesitation. He then looked down the street to see the incoming legionaries. 'You got off lucky today. If you hurt my brother again, I promise I will end you.'

He turned back to Viridox, who was struggling to get to his feet. 'We need to get to the boat,' he blurted as he rushed to Viridox's side, helping him up.

The two picked up Viridox's sword and shield before making their way down the road to the barn. Once there, Vindex grabbed the boat from under the hay and started pushing it towards the water. Viridox grabbed some arrows that Vindex had left on the floor of the boat and started firing into the oncoming Umbrian legion. When in the water Vindex exclaimed, 'Quickly brother! We are leaving now!'

Viridox turned around, seeing his brother paddling out into the lake. Running down the slope, he jumped into the boat and began paddling with the spare paddle left under his seat. The Umbrian legionaries chased the brothers until they reached the bay themselves. A few soldiers attempted to reach the boat with their javelins, but the brothers were too far gone. The pair had escaped.

Not knowing the brothers had already slipped away, Valerik ran down the road following the tracks of the legion when he saw Dara out of the corner of his eye sitting in an alleyway, head tucked in between her knees, sobbing in pain. Valerik, without hesitation, stopped following the legionaries and ran over to his second in command.

'Dara!' he exclaimed nervously, 'What happened?'

Dara did not look up at Valerik instead, replying with her head still covered by her knees, 'They humiliated me!' she yelled in response, trying to compose herself despite being in physical and emotional pain.

Valerik took a knee in front of her, reaching his hand out as he placed his arm around her shoulder, comforting her. 'Look at me,' he said sincerely. 'Tell me what happened.'

Dara looked up and Valerik saw the gash on her face so fresh that it was still bleeding. It was a three-inch gash above her eye which extended through her brow. 'By the gods. This is my fault,' Valerik said, wracked with guilt.

He had warned Dara before the battle began not to engage with Vindex, but in the heat of the conflict, he sent her after the Galician alone because he was trapped on the frontline. He held her tightly, embracing her, happy that she was even still alive.

'This was not your fault Valerik,' Dara replied, trying to hold back her tears, 'I was stunned and, in that moment, the barbarian filth took me by surprise. Nothing more.'

Valerik responded, 'Tell me what happened. Is he still here?'

'No,' Dara replied, answering the question. 'He escaped on a boat with his brother.'

'A brother?' Valerik asked curiously. 'We were told nothing of a brother.'

'I know,' she replied. 'He is not the warrior that Vindex is. I had him beat on the ground easily when Vindex jumped me by surprise.' Dara had stopped crying, wiping the last tears from her face. 'We have to go after them,' she insisted, pushing Valerik off her and standing up from the gutter she was in.

'In time we will,' Valerik said. 'But first we need to get you medicine. We shall get you the medical attention you need and then we shall go after the two together.'

Dara nodded her head slightly. 'I can agree with that,' she said somberly as the pair left the alley and walked back to the town square together to find the city's doctor.

As they walked back to the city square, Valerik thought to himself about how lucky he was that Dara was still alive. He vowed never to place her directly against Vindex again. He could not risk losing his second in command. Dara, however, was not so grateful to be alive. She felt humiliated. Never had she lost in combat in such a humiliating manner. Angered, she vowed to never be bested again.

While the Umbrians were occupying the city and removing the dead bodies from the streets, Vindex and Viridox were still paddling away in the lake's waters. 'Just keep paddling, Viridox!' Vindex shouted.

'Nope, nope,' Viridox replied, taking his paddle out of the water and placing it back on the boat. 'I've done all I can. I can do no more. I am about to collapse. Surely, we can rest now, brother. I don't see them anywhere.'

'We can't assume they won't follow us, brother,' Vindex replied, having flashbacks of the night he and Viridox ran away on horseback from the burning town of Norova. 'We cannot rest until we get to safety. We have come too far to foolishly let ourselves be put back into danger.'

Viridox sighed in agreement. With no adrenaline left, Viridox used his sheer willpower to continue. He paddled with his brother until they reached the shore.

The two got out of the boat and with weak legs climbed up the shore looking for their horses.

'Where are they?' Viridox asked his brother, trying to find his horse.

'I am not sure,' Vindex responded panting. 'It was daytime still when I brought them out here.'

'Oh, great,' Viridox replied, exacerbated. 'You look. I'm just gonna sit down for a minute. Maybe catch my breath, maybe die of exhaustion, whatever comes first.' Viridox finished as he collapsed onto the forest floor.

'You fought too hard today to die from exhaustion now, Viridox,' Vindex proudly said as he looked for the horses.

'Thanks,' Viridox replied. 'I will let the gods know that when they come for me.'

Vindex smiled and continued the search for the horses alone. The forest was dense and full of wildlife. Dead leaves rustled as mice ran underneath hiding from the owls hooting in the trees. The Oak and birch trees were so congested together that their branches shielded the forest floor from the snow that had fallen on Trevonum. Viridox, staring up at the branches above him, called out to his brother.

'Have you found them yet?' he asked, hoping he could mount Alesia soon.

'I believe I have,' Vindex replied from afar. 'Get up and come.'

Viridox, hearing this news, got up slowly and walked to where his brother was. He had found the two horses. Vindex was already on Bucephalus when Viridox arrived. Viridox gave Alesia a big hug around the neck and placed his head on hers. 'It is good to see you,' Viridox said before mounting his horse.

'Are you ready?' Vindex asked his brother, looking behind to make sure he was on his horse.

'I am,' Viridox replied. 'Where are we going now?' he asked as his brother led him into the forest.

'To the last hope we have left,' Vindex replied, leading his brother through the darkness. 'To the city of Narbo Martius.'

CHAPTER 18

REST AND RECOVERY

Vindex and Viridox cautiously rode through the dense wood of the Numok Forest. Their horses could barely traverse the path and so they rode slowly one behind the other. They remained single file until they entered a very large meadow in the center of the forest. It stretched half a mile in length and width and was full of tall grass and wildflowers. Dense foliage surrounded the pasture on all sides. The path to Narbo Martius crossed through the meadow and entered the tree line on the other side.

Viridox saw this beautiful meadow as an opportunity to rest. He asked his brother, 'Can we please rest now, Vindex? I doubt they are following us. We have heard nothing and if we set up camp across the plain, we will be able to see them coming before they get to us.'

Vindex, weary in his own right, nodded gently. 'Okay. You've convinced me. We'll set up camp there.'

Vindex pointed to the bottom right side of the field from their position. They quickly rode over and unpacked their rucksacks from their horses. They situated themselves under a large oak tree and looked back at the other side of the field. The pasture was at least two hundred yards wide, which allowed great protection for Vindex and Viridox in case the Umbrians came chasing after them.

'You can sleep first, brother,' Vindex said, taking his sword out and placing it into his lap. 'I will take the first watch.'

Viridox was weary and sore, but he knew his brother must have been feeling everything he was and more. 'No,' he replied. 'You rest. I'll keep watch. I'm sure you need it more than me.'

Vindex was too tired to protest. He nodded and fell asleep on his rucksack almost immediately. He felt safe in his brother's hands. Viridox could hear his brother snoring only a few moments after lying down. He thought to himself, *How can he sleep so easily after what we just endured? My body is still shaking. As much as I want to rest, I don't know if I could sleep after all that's happened. Those poor soldiers. Poor Megorath. Even the Umbrians must have had families of their own.* Viridox felt his heart drop as he looked over at his brother. *Orla. What if the Umbrians did not keep their word? He would know. Should I wake him?* He took a moment to stare at his sleeping brother, hearing his snores grow louder. *No, that would not be right. Besides, I doubt he could even conjure the Maith in this state, anyway. I will ask him later to ensure she is safe. We should have brought her with us.*

Viridox continued to silently ramble to himself. Despite the silence of the peaceful forest, he could vividly hear the screams of men on both sides who laid down their lives in the battle. Haunted by what he had done and witnessed; he could not rest. Viridox watched the moon fly across the night sky as each hour became longer than the previous one.

So I guess this is war, Viridox thought to himself. *So much guilt, and so much blood. I never want to fight on the frontline ever again.* A loud snore from Vindex startled Viridox, causing him to look at his brother, who cozily slept in his rucksack. *I can't do that, though. I made a promise to him and to myself. We need to avenge our father, but after that, I will personally throw my blade at the bottom of Loch Connacht.*

Viridox thought to himself in silence for a few more hours before hearing a loud scream. He looked over at his brother and saw that he was sweating and now sitting up in his rucksack.

'Another nightmare?' Viridox asked.

'Yes. Not a very pleasant one.'

'Nightmares never are.'

'At least you can sleep now, Viridox. I have had my fill,' Vindex said as he sat up to take watch.

Viridox laid down and rested his head on his rucksack. He looked up at the snow still falling so gently in the night sky he asked his brother, 'Can you do me a favor?'

'Of course.'

'Can you find Orla with the Maith? I need to know if she is alright. I am worried.'

'I will do my best,' Vindex replied sincerely. 'Now get some rest.'

'Thank you, brother.'

He then turned to his side and eventually fell into a reluctant slumber. With his brother asleep and no sign of any threat, Vindex drew the Galdeshan symbol from Cato's cave in the snow to strengthen his bond with the Maith. *Surely the Umbrians would be here by now if they were pursuing us,* Vindex thought as he knelt at the center of the symbol.

Vindex cleared his mind, determined to help his brother. He meditated for a few hours until the break of dawn. When he saw the rising sun, Vindex stopped meditating. He then packed up his rucksack and placed it on Bucephalus. The birds and the forest creatures were now awake, too. One eager morning squirrel ran across the oak tree above Viridox's rucksack and dropped a nut on top of his forehead.

'Ow,' Viridox groaned, opening his eyes unsure about what had hit him.

Vindex heard Viridox's voice and said, 'Time to get up. Mount Alesia. We have a city to go to.'

Viridox was still tired and sore, but only had one thing on his mind. He sat up and asked, 'What about Orla? Did you see her?'

Vindex, now on Bucephalus, looked at his brother and replied, 'She is safe. Valerik was a man of his word. No harm came to her or any of our troops who stayed in the tavern. Now come, we must get a move on if we want to reach Narbo Martius by sundown.'

Viridox did not know what to say. He trusted his brother, but because of his dismissive nature of the topic, he was not sure if he had been telling the truth. As he hopped on Alesia, he asked, 'Are you sure you saw her specifically?'

As the two rode, Vindex replied, 'Don't you trust me?'

'I do Vindex,' Viridox replied, 'Always, but …'

'I saw her in the tavern. She is safe, Viridox. I wouldn't lie to you,' Vindex replied, leading his brother back into the forest.

Viridox just nodded his head and internalized his own relief that the love of his life was safe and sound. The only thing that was left to do now was find allies in Narbo Martius. If they could gain some powerful new friends, there was hope of taking back Trevonum from the Umbrian Empire.

The two brothers traveled all day and only reached Narbo Martius as the sun set. Greeted by two friendly watchmen at the gate, Vindex said, 'Greetings. My name is Vindex of Norova. Son of Brunos. This is my brother Viridox. We seek an audience with your leader.'

The two soldiers at the gates looked at each other and asked in unison, 'Are you sure?'

'Why would I not be?' Vindex asked, trying to probe for information.

One guard replied, 'In order to speak with our chieftain, the two of you will need to duel?'

'Each other?' Viridox asked, standing behind his brother.

'No, the chieftain. If you don't win, however, you will not be granted an audience to speak. And based on the look of you two, I don't think you would stand a chance. At least not now,' Emiscor the watchman spoke as he looked at the two men in front of him, covered in dirt and dried blood from the battle of Trevonum. 'Is that your blood?' he asked, concerned about their health.

Vindex and Viridox looked at each other, inspecting their wounds. 'Maybe we should clean up a bit before meeting their leader,' Viridox suggested to his brother, recognizing how awful they looked. Vindex ignored his brother and wanted to probe for further information about the city's ruler.

'How strong is your chieftain?' Vindex asked, looking up at Emiscor on the city wall.

'Hasn't lost a battle to date,' he replied confidently.

Vindex and his brother looked at each other, impressed with the claim of the watchman, who seemed sincere. Emiscor was not boasting. He merely answered factually, trying to warn the two travelers about what they faced. 'In that case,' Vindex answered, 'maybe we could rest tonight and then have the duel in the morning.'

'If that is what you wish, I will arrange it,' the watchmen replied, inviting the brothers into the city. 'There is an inn down the way where you can find accommodations. Get a hot meal and have lots of rest. You will need it.'

'Thank you,' the brothers said, grateful for the hospitality.

'I will greet you in the morning and bring you to the arena where your duel will commence. Until then, have a good evening,' the watchmen replied before walking toward the chieftain's home.

Viridox looked at his brother as they walked down the street. 'What's another battle?' he said sarcastically as they made their way to the inn where they would bathe and rest.

Only a block down the road, the two brothers immediately noticed a difference between the architecture of this city and that of Trevonum. Narbo Martius was shockingly larger than Trevonum, but it was not just the size which impressed them. The roads were made of assorted cobblestone instead of dirt and mud. The buildings used a combination of wood and marble, employing complex engineering the likes of which Vindex had never seen.

'This is nothing like how our father described Narbo Martius,' Viridox said as they approached the door to the inn.

'I know. I wonder what happened here?' Vindex pondered as the two made their way inside the inn.

The inn was a beige stucco building with a blue clay tile roof. At a whopping three stories in height, it was not even the largest building on the street. Vindex and Viridox opened their mouths in awe as they entered. As they opened the birch door, the pair noted how detailed the interior of the inn was, especially when compared to its Trevonum counterpart. The floors were made of decorated smooth stone, all intricately placed tile by tile. Along the walls, freshly sanded wooden beams stood strong, supporting the weight of the wooden roof above. Vindex and Viridox walked past the set-up tables and benches to the counter against the back wall. There they received a hot meal and were told what room they could stay in. After dining, the pair walked up the stairs to their room on the second floor.

Vindex and Viridox were stunned as they opened the door to their room. The size of their quarters was more than double the size of the inn in Trevonum. On top of the standard essentials such as beds, trunks and linens, this room also had its own private bath. A large wooden trough sat in the room's corner, filled with clean water.

'I get the first bath,' Viridox quickly said before his brother had a chance to claim it for himself.

'Very well,' Vindex replied. 'You bathe and I'll nap. Let me know when you are done.'

The pair freshened up, relaxed, and had two hot meals before calling it an early night. They did not know what challenge they would face in the morning. For Vindex, he was getting excited. The city's size and amicable people gave him hope he would find a large force here that he could use to battle Valerik. As for Viridox, he too was excited. Not for battle, but because he had a comfortable bed to sleep in once more.

CHAPTER 19

A FEARLESS LEADER

It was a bright and warm day when Vindex and Viridox woke up. The small amounts of snow that had settled on the land started to melt as the sun shined down with no cloud to stop its heat. The two brothers were surprised but pleased to have such a warm day after all the chilly nights they had endured.

'Do you think you are ready for today?' Vindex asked his brother.

'Me?' Viridox questioned. 'You mean you. You are the swordsman here, not me.'

'What happened to not hiding behind my shield forever?' Vindex asked as the two got dressed in their armor.

'It almost got me killed!' Viridox exclaimed. 'The front line is something I hope to never endure again.'

Vindex looked at Viridox with a disappointed look. 'How do you expect to beat Valerik with that attitude?'

'By your side or from a distance with my bow,' Viridox replied, grabbing his bow and placing it on his back.

'And I suppose you'll do the same when we take back Trevonum? What will Orla think?' Vindex continued in a slightly disappointed tone.

'I think she'll be happy I'm alive,' Viridox mumbled to himself as he put on his helmet, fully ready for the duel in the event he needed to fight.

'Brother, you don't give yourself enough credit. I am sure this duel will be with wooden blades like we used in Trevonum. You can do this,' Vindex said, trying to boost Viridox's confidence.

'We shall see when we get there,' Viridox replied as he held the door open for Vindex. 'Now let's go.'

The two met up with the watchman Emiscor from the day before outside the inn. 'Are you sure you wish to do this?' the watchmen asked, providing one last chance to back down to the challenge that lay ahead.

'Of course,' Vindex replied for the pair. He leaned over and pulled his brother in by the shoulder. 'And he will be the one fighting.'

'Brother,' Viridox anxiously protested.

The watchman looked at the brothers, unamused. 'I informed our leader of your arrival. I was instructed to inform you that each of you would be fighting. Not together, though. Individual duels.'

Vindex, completely content with hearing this announcement, turned to his brother and said, 'See Viridox, you can't get out of this now even if you want to.'

Viridox looked up at the sky and with great reluctance replied, 'Fine. I will go first.'

'Excellent,' Emiscor replied. 'Now let me take you to our theatre.'

'The theatre?' Vindex questioned as the three men walked down the stone slabbed road.

'Our leader requests the theatre for all the duels. It is free entertainment for the public,' Emiscor answered as the two brothers continued to follow his lead.

'Who is this leader of which you keep mentioning?' Vindex asked. 'When I was younger, my father told me, a man named Keir ran Narbo Martius. But he also mentioned this being a much smaller settlement than the one I see before me.'

The watchman turned back to face Vindex. 'That was a very long time ago,' he replied. 'Keir has not been our leader for at least a decade, maybe more. Our new chieftain dedicated night and day to our town, and what you see before you is the result of such labor.'

'Sounds like a great man,' Viridox chimed in.

'Agreed,' Vindex replied. 'How much farther until we meet the man face to face?'

Emiscor turned his head back straight, looking only at the road ahead. He smiled and replied, 'You two have no idea what you're getting yourselves into.'

The three men continued down the road for some time until they arrived at the theatre. It was in the shape of a semicircle with wooden posts supporting bleachers where nearly a thousand citizens of Narbo Martius sat in eager anticipation for the duel they had been promised. Instead of bringing Vindex and Viridox through the main gate leading to the stands, he brought them to the flat backside of the theatre. They entered one of two doors of the large wooden wall that made up the back half of the stadium. As they entered, they saw the staging area for what would typically hold plays and dramas, not duels. That being said, there was an assortment of wooden weapons provided for the two brothers. They merely had to choose what they wanted to duel with.

'What do you think of these?' Viridox asked as he picked up a medium-sized blade and a round wooden shield.

'Not bad, but I prefer the classics,' Vindex replied as he picked up a long blunt wooden spear with no dagger on either end.

'Are you two satisfied with your selection of armament?' Emiscor asked the two men.

Vindex and Viridox nodded at Emiscor, showing their selections were final. They were ready to begin the duel with the city's chieftain.

'Very well. Follow me,' the man replied, leading the two brothers to the stage.

Vindex and Viridox could hear the crowd cheering as the chieftain of Narbo Martius kept the crowd entertained with boasts of glory. The two came out from backstage to a waiting area separated from the main stage by a waist high wooden gate. As they entered the fenced off portion of the arena, they looked out at the crowd who booed at them for their arrival.

'Do you think a thousand people can be wrong?' Viridox quipped, unsettled that he was about to fight in front of so many people.

Vindex looked out at the crowd and replied, 'Just remember what I taught you in our sparring sessions. You will be fine.'

Just then, they heard a woman speak from center stage in a brash and cocky manner. 'Is this really my opposition?' She turned to the crowd and continued, 'Maybe I should let them fight me together just to even the odds.'

Vindex and Viridox looked over to the chieftain standing in the center stage. She stood with confidence, wielding two identical wooden swords while carrying a silver blade on her waist. Her hair was brown, and she had bright blue eyes. She was tall and athletic. Vindex knew just from her mannerisms that she was, in fact, a warrior, unlike the previous chieftain he had dealt with.

After hearing their leader's words, the stands changed from boos to thunderous applause, causing the watchman to talk to himself softly from behind the wooden gate backstage, 'I hope she goes easy on them. Just once I would like to see our challengers not be completely humiliated.'

The chieftain turned to face the two brothers in the pen but did not address them. Instead, she screamed past the two to the watchman who had brought them here. 'Emiscor! Are these seriously the two warriors you spoke of last night?'

'They seek an audience with you, Iodona!' the watchman yelled back, elevating his voice over the cheering crowd. 'I told them that this was unwise.'

The chieftain smiled, pointed to the two brothers and said, 'Unwise indeed. Now which one of you will be my first challenger?'

Viridox panicked. Overwhelmed by the environment and the imposing lady in front of him, he grabbed Vindex's arm and raised it high. 'Right here, your lordship,' he said nervously. 'He's the one, not me.'

Vindex looked over at his brother with expressive sarcasm. He then replied dryly, 'You either fight her or you fight me. And I won't hold back.'

Viridox slowly dropped his brother's arm. 'There has been a change of plans!' he announced wittily. 'You will be fighting me, after all.'

The chieftain chuckled slightly. 'I hope your fighting is as good as your humor,' she said as she waved her hand, calling him to her.

Viridox took a breath. 'I can assure you it's not,' he said to himself. Despite being insecure and nervous, he opened the gate and walked out onto the sandy stage. His only reassurance was the confidence his brother had in him. He just wished he felt the same way.

The two approached each other until there were only three paces between them. Viridox was about to ask if she was ready to begin when she suddenly charged at the Norova native. With both of her hands held behind her, she dashed forward and swung her identical wooden swords up on either side of Viridox, who was not ready for the engagement. He narrowly blocked each strike with his own sword and shield. With the thud of the wood, Iodona struck again, this time with an overhead swing with her right sword. Viridox, needing space, ducked and rolled to his right, attempting to gain some distance.

Vindex looked on from the pen with wide eyes, very intrigued by the display he was watching. He leaned against the fence post and held his chin in one hand. He had little faith left in his brother's ability to win this battle, but he did not try to stop it. Vindex believed this duel was good practice for his younger sibling, who was just now getting back on his feet after rolling away from Iodona's swing.

'Do you think you could use one less sword?' Viridox said, panting. 'It would give me a better chance.'

A small smile grew on Iodona's face, but she would not stop the battle for the pleasantries of passing conversation and quips. Instead of speaking, she replied with action. She quickly darted over to Viridox, who stood behind his shield. Viridox, feeling safe with the shield in front, threw a swing of his blade, striking downward on Iodona. The chieftain blocked the sword with her two swords, forming a cross with her blades. With one push back in retaliation, the force was too great for Viridox to bear, and his sword went flying from his hand. Without a weapon, he panicked and attempted to strike Iodona with his shield. He punched his left arm forward in a manner that led with the wooden shield, but his attack did not connect. The chieftain expected his strike and ducked underneath the shield. Still in the motion of his swing, Viridox looked down to see Iodona, who was ready to strike. She took her elbow and jabbed it into Viridox's unguarded abdomen. Before he could react, he faced the flat end of the chieftain's blade as she swung it up, slamming it into the front of his face.

This was enough to knock Viridox on the ground. The crowd went wild, cheering in admiration for their leader as she stood over Viridox with her left sword pointed by her side and her right pointed forward at Viridox's head. The duel had an obvious winner. Worried for his brother's safety, Vindex screamed from the sidelines, 'That's enough!'

Iodona put her sword down and looked over at Vindex, who was now entering the arena. As Vindex slowly approached, she sheathed her blunt blade and extended her arm to Viridox, who remained on the ground.

'A battle well fought,' Iodona remarked as Viridox took hold of her arm, accepting her assistance back up.

Viridox nodded and positively remarked, 'You're about to have a much harder one now. Good luck.'

The two turned to Vindex, who was nearly in the middle of the arena now. He spun his staff around before stabbing it into the sand, causing it to extend upright without his aid.

'Is that so?' Iodona asked, excited for a real challenge as she turned to face Vindex.

As the two warriors closed the distance between them, Viridox scurried off back to the sidelines to watch the ensuing duel.

'When I win, I get my audience with you. Is that correct?' Vindex spoke clearly.

'Do not get ahead of yourself,' Iodona replied. 'Focus on this battle first. Then we will see if I will hear your plea.'

Vindex nodded in agreement. He picked up his staff from the sand. Boasting, Vindex spun the staff around his side and back before eventually taking his stance, holding the wooden rod horizontally in front of him. Iodona too took her stance. She held both swords by her side and looked as if she was ready to pounce forward. The true duel was about to begin.

VINDEX'S POWER

Iodona could tell that this challenger would be no ordinary opponent. *He is clearly well trained,* Iodona thought as she took her battle stance. *Let's see if I can bait him into attacking first.*

The two circled around each other as the arena grew quiet. Those in the audience leaned in, literally on the edge of their seats as they waited to see who would take the first strike. The two teased each other and the crowd with several fake jabs, trying to take the other off guard, but neither bit. Vindex believed he saw a weakness in the chieftain's defenses and took the first strike of the duel. He took his spear and swung it horizontally, hoping to hit Iodona's side.

Just what I wanted, Iodona thought while ducking under Vindex's swing. From a squat, she pushed off her feet and closed the distance that Vindex had created with his six-foot-long staff.

Vindex watched as Iodona closed the significant gap between them and immediately paced backward, bringing his spear in to create a defensive position. This defense was not enough to deter Iodona from her attack. With each hand, she took her swords and flew both one after the other towards her challenger's sides. Vindex, startled at the ferocity and speed of Iodona's attacks, quickly tried to parry each blow with both ends of his staff.

It was now clear Vindex was not dealing with any ordinary opponent. He struggled to keep his ground as Iodona forced him back three feet with each swing of a blade. This continued until Vindex was up against the stone and wooden wall of the arena. Vindex had his back against the wall. The fight appeared to be over, since with no place to run, Vindex could not use his spear in such a confined space. The crowd erupted in applause and screams, cheering on their chieftain.

Bystanders in the streets outside the theatre could hear the people's chants clearly. 'Iodona, tiarna! Iodona, tiarna! Iodona, tiarna!'

Vindex grunted and thought, *They may call her lord now, but wait until I break free. I will not go down so easily.*

Iodona smiled, overjoyed at what should have been another victory. 'This duel ends now. I guess you won't get that audience after all,' she spoke while swinging her left sword towards Vindex's exposed neck.

'It isn't over yet!' Vindex exclaimed, pushing his spear against Iodona's incoming sword. The force of the deflection overpowered the chieftain, causing the wooden blade to be pushed away.

Vindex kept the momentum from his strike and spun his spear counterclockwise, positioning his spear perpendicular to the sand floor. He then quickly slammed the staff into the sand and applied all his strength to jump up into the air as he held the staff from the top. Mid-jump, Vindex then pushed off the back wall, causing him to flip over Iodona's head. While landing, Vindex yanked on the spear, still in hand, to pull it out of the arena floor.

A hush fell over the crowd, and the chanting ceased. They had never seen such a powerful display of strength before. 'How …' Emiscor mumbled to himself in disbelief at what he just witnessed. Viridox looked over to see the watchman shaking in his boots.

'What a showoff,' Viridox said while leaning in on the fence post to get a better view of the fight.

Even Iodona could not believe what she had witnessed. *He just got lucky,* she thought, *Get your head back in the fight.* She turned around quickly to see the Norova native resuming his battle stance with a cheeky grin on his face.

'It's your move,' Vindex scoffed sarcastically, while gesturing Iodona to take a swing at him with his free hand.

'You dare!' Iodona exclaimed in anger.

'I do dare,' Vindex replied sarcastically, having fun with what was his most challenging opponent to date.

Iodona took a deep breath, trying to compose herself. She charged at Vindex, who attempted to trip the chieftain by taking out her legs with his staff but was unsuccessful as Iodona jumped over the swing. The strike failed and Vindex saw anger in Iodona's eyes. He panicked, realizing he was not actually in control of this duel. With no time to bring the staff in to defend him, Iodona struck Vindex on his left side with her sword. Wincing in pain from the blunt blade that just slammed into his ribcage, Vindex pulled back on his spear, attempting to land a blow on Iodona from behind as she now stood within striking range. Iodona knew this was Vindex's plan. She took both swords and forcefully swung down on the end of the staff the Vindex held, causing him to drop it, as his one arm was not comparable to the strength of her full strike. Vindex was now completely defenseless without his staff and, seeing this, Iodona calmed down.

'Do you surrender?' she asked, pointing her blade at Vindex.

Vindex looked at her and then at his staff, which was behind her. He shrugged his shoulders and responded, 'Not a chance. Things are just getting exciting. Why would I stop now?'

Iodona squinted her eyes and lowered her brow. She slowly walked toward Vindex, who was ever so slowly trying to get around her to reach his staff.

'You're not getting your weapon back,' Iodona spoke as she continued to cut off Vindex's angle around her.

'Let's agree to disagree,' Vindex replied cockily, which aggravated Iodona greatly.

This irritation led to another charge on behalf of Iodona. She frantically swung her swords in every direction, attempting to land a blow on Vindex. She hoped one of these blows would be enough to end the match. Vindex dodged some strikes and winced in pain from the contact of others. He was biding his time, waiting for an opportunity to get his weapon back.

'Just give up!' Iodona screamed, swinging a diagonal blow with her left blade. She was directly in front of Vindex, which made it hard to go around her, but after dodging this strike, Vindex saw an opportunity.

Iodona swung with her right arm. Vindex parried the attack by lunging at her grabbing her forearm with his hand. Then with his free left hand he pushed down on Iodona's shoulder, which combined with her momentum from the previous swing, made her stumble onto her knees. Now face down, looking at the arena ground, Iodona felt something hit her back as Vindex let go of her right arm. It was his foot. Vindex used her like a stool and jumped off her back over to the side of the arena which held his weapon. Irate that she let this happen, Iodona turned her head to see Vindex touch down on the arena floor from his leap. She immediately stood up and chased him. Vindex was only a few meters ahead as they ran to the staff. If Iodona could not beat the son of Brunos in the leg race, the duel was back on.

The crowd was mesmerized by the performance of each Galician warrior. Never had they seen such a spectacle in the great arena of Narbo Martius and never had they seen anyone stand up to Iodona like this. The fight was not over, though, and Vindex knew this very well. He heard Iodona right behind him and leaped out to grab the spear first. Sand flew from the arena floor as Vindex reached out, grasping his staff in hand. Quickly after reuniting with his weapon, he rolled onto his back to see Iodona in the air with her swords drawn over her head. She was descending onto Vindex with full force. There was no more holding back from either party. She struck down with both blades on Vindex's wooden spear and a loud crack was heard throughout the arena. Someone's wood was surely soon to break. The two warriors were too powerful for training weapons.

Vindex knew how to use Iodona's strike against her. When she collided with his spear, Vindex raised his leg, and pressed his foot on

Iodona's abdomen. He pushed off with his staff and his foot, causing the chieftain to go flying overhead. Crashing down north of Vindex in the arena, Iodona was slow to rise from the sand. Vindex, now exhausted from this ferocious battle, also struggled to stand up. Vindex used his staff like a cane and pushed off the ground to stand and face the chieftain. Sand falling out of both soldier's garments, the pair paused their fight for a moment as they caught their breath. The crowd in the arena was screaming.

'Iodona, tiarna! Iodona, tiarna! Iodona, tiarna!' continued to be chanted all throughout the arena. The loyal citizens of Narbo Martius had not given up on their leader.

Emiscor and Viridox continued to look on with amazement from behind the stage. 'Who the hell is this guy?' Emiscor asked, astonished by the battle he saw unfolding.

Viridox didn't take his eyes off the arena for a moment but replied to Emiscor's question. 'He's my brother,' he said proudly.

'We should do this more, you and me,' Vindex said, huffing after every other word. 'I'm having a lot of fun.'

Oddly, Iodona did, in fact, feel the same way. 'I must say, I didn't expect this much of a challenge out of you. I hope you know, though, just because this is a good battle, I won't just give you an audience with me. If you wish to discuss a political matter, you will have to defeat me.'

'I wasn't expecting any charity,' Vindex replied with a smile, taking his battle stance once more. 'I say it's about time we end this.'

Iodona grinned. 'I couldn't agree more.'

The two charged at each other once again, this time with a resolve to end the battle. There was no holding back. Both parties used what strength they had left to gain the upper hand. It would be Iodona who would find the first fault. Vindex's footing became sloppy as the fight progressed. Iodona went to strike Vindex's chest with her two blades, hoping the impact would be enough to win her the duel. As the wooden swords grew close to his chest, Vindex dropped onto one knee to dodge the attack. He knew he only had a fraction of a second to react. Vindex moved quickly. He took his staff and broke it over his knee. Vindex moved his right hand into the interior portion of the divided staff and used all his strength to push out and jab Iodona in the abdomen. As Iodona stumbled back from the blow, Vindex knew it was time to finish this duel. He grabbed his left hand, which held the other half of his spear, and swung the staff like a baton at Iodona's neck. A loud crack was heard in the arena, and Iodona sprawled on the ground in pain. Vindex rose from his knee. He had won the duel.

The crowd grew silent as they watched their leader lay on her back in the sand. Emiscor could not believe his eyes.

'Did he just win?' Emiscor asked, utterly shocked, gripping the fence post with both hands.

Viridox smiled. 'Yes, he did,' he said happily, seeing his brother relish in a hard earned victory.

Iodona groaned loudly as she sat up on the sand floor. She looked up at Vindex, who stood above her. She had too much pride to protest her loss and instead she accepted it graciously.

'I may have a temper, but I know when I am beaten,' Iodona said sincerely, staring up at Vindex who was reaching out with his hand, offering to help Iodona to her feet. 'I have not lost a duel since I was a child. This is very new to me.'

'It was a good duel. It was an honor to fight you,' Vindex replied truthfully as he helped lift the chieftain up from the ground.

With Iodona back on her feet, the crowd stood and cheered. Despite losing the match, they still had a great admiration for their leader and were proud that she fought so valiantly. During the applause, Emiscor and Viridox made their way into the arena center.

'Iodona!' Emiscor shouted in a panic. 'Are you alright?'

'I am fine, brother. A little humiliated, but besides that, fine,' Iodona replied, hugging Emiscor as he went to embrace her.

'You two are siblings?' Viridox asked. 'Why did you not tell us?'

Emiscor finished his embrace with his older sister. 'I didn't think it mattered,' he replied.

'The only thing that matters now is learning who just defeated me in my own city,' Iodona interrupted, turning her focus to Vindex. She pointed at his chest and asked. 'Who are you?'

'My name is Vindex,' he replied, 'Son of Brunos, last of the Galdeshans. There is something very important that I wish to discuss with you.'

'Ha!' Iodona laughed. 'I am sorry. You are a powerful warrior, but I will not have an audience with a crazy man. The Galdeshans are just myths. You may stay inside my city's walls and if you ever want to duel again, please let me know. As for business, though, I have more important things to attend to than dealing with myths.'

She turned to her brother and headed for the theatre's exit. Viridox looked over at Vindex in worry. He thought they had just lost their opportunity to get the help they needed. Vindex was not as concerned. He had a way to prove to her he was telling the truth.

'Wait!' Vindex exclaimed, chasing after the two. 'I have a way to prove my claims.'

Iodona and Emiscor turned around. Iodona walked back in front of Vindex and asked, 'How can you possibly prove you're a Galdeshan?'

Vindex looked down at Iodona's belt. It had but one sword on it, unlike the two she had used in their duel. 'Give me your sword,' Vindex said confidently.

Emiscor looked over at his sister and said, 'Don't listen to this madness. We must be going. We have real business to attend to.'

Her brother's words did not sway Iodona. Her curiosity piqued, and she wanted to hear out Vindex's claims.

'Let's not be too hasty, brother,' Iodona spoke. 'I will listen to you, Vindex, but make it quick. Come back stage and I will hand it over.'

The four Galicians stepped off the theatre floor and went to the privacy of the backstage. She took the sword out of her sheath. It was a shimmering silver blade with two studded sapphires at the top of a silver handle. Iodona handed it gently over to Vindex, who inspected it in his hands.

'Why don't you use two blades in battle like you did in our duel?' Vindex politely asked.

'Because no blacksmith has been able to give me a proper replica,' Iodona replied. 'This sword has been in my family for years. Each craftsman who has tried to replicate the blade has failed.'

'Perhaps I can help with that,' Vindex spoke confidently.

Even Viridox was shocked by his brother's assurance. *Has he finally connected to the Maith?* Viridox thought to himself as they all huddled around Vindex backstage.

Vindex breathed deeply as he tried to recall Cato's teachings. He had created one item before, a ring for his brother's fiance. This sword, however, would be much more difficult. Not only did he not have Cato advising him, he also did not have the luxury of time like he did when constructing his brother's ring. He needed to prove to the chieftain of this city that he was, in fact, a Galdeshan. If he could not, Vindex would be left with no ally against Valerik, and the entire Galician civilization would be conquered.

Vindex closed his eyes. He shut out the world around him and found peace with the spirits of the Maith. Now sensing the fairies with him, Vindex used all his focus and strength, calling on the spirit's power to pull the argon from the air into the exact shape of Iodona's blade. When in place, he then focused the energy given to him by the fairies to change the properties of the gas to that of solid silver with two sapphire jewels. Vindex now opened his eyes. He looked down at his right hand to see a bright lime colored light. As the light died down, it was clear to all what Vindex had done.

'That's not possible,' Emiscor said, stunned, stammering over his words. 'The Galdeshans, they're just myths.'

Iodona reached out and took the blade from Vindex. She swung the swords around in unison to find that it was an exact replica in weight, image, and grip. She smiled and nodded her head. 'You have been granted your audience, Vindex. Be at the city center tomorrow. I will meet you outside the main hall. We will talk then. I hope you know that I have several questions for you as well.'

'Understood,' Vindex replied as he reached out his hand, looking to commemorate the deal.

Iodona accepted the gesture, and the pair grabbed each other's forearm. After the handshake, she and her brother turned back and departed from the arena.

'The Galdeshans are just myths,' Emiscor said to Iodona as they walked out of the arena.

'I know,' Iodona replied, holding up her new sword, 'But how else can you explain this?'

'I just wonder what other legends are true now,' Emiscor responded, reluctantly accepting that Vindex was telling the truth.

'As do I. And hopefully we shall have those answers tomorrow. But for now, like you said, we have work to do,' Iodona spoke as the two walked down the cobbled road back to the grand hall.

This left Viridox and his brother alone in the backstage of the arena. Vindex walked back to the main stage and sat down in the sand, exhausted from both the fight and the creation of the sword for Iodona.

'Are you alright, brother?' Viridox asked, walking over to his brother.

'Yes, yes, I'll be fine,' Vindex replied. 'Just a little winded is all.'

Viridox took a seat next to him in the arena and looked out at the now empty seats. 'I can imagine. That was quite the fight. My body is sore just from watching,' Viridox said, attempting to humor his brother.

'That and from getting your butt kicked, too,' Vindex quipped with a smile.

'Yeah, that too,' Viridox said shamefully.

'I am only kidding, brother. You fought well. Iodona is a very dangerous opponent. There were times I wasn't even sure if I could win,' Vindex responded honestly, realizing he made his brother upset.

'I suppose you're right,' Viridox replied while running his hand through the sand of the arena.

There was a long pause as the two just sat there relaxing in the empty arena. It had been sometime since they had a chance to just unwind.

'So now what?' Viridox asked Vindex, not sure on what to do next.

Vindex thought for a moment. 'Do you reckon this city has a tavern?' Vindex asked, titling his head to his brother.

'I reckon we should find out,' Viridox replied, shooting up from the arena floor, helping his brother get to his feet.

Vindex let out a loud groan and grabbed his right arm in pain. 'Are you okay?' Viridox asked, concerned.

'Yeah, just a little sore still,' Vindex replied, strolling with his brother out of the arena.

'Oh, you know what's great for muscle pains?' Viridox said as he placed Vindex's arm over his shoulder to help his gait.

'No, I can't say I do,' Vindex replied. 'What is it?'

'Beer,' Viridox answered in a serious tone.

'Oh, is that right?' Vindex replied. 'And where did you hear that?'

'At the tavern in Trevonum,' Viridox replied deadpan.

'Of course you did. Well, no harm can come from it, anyway. We might as well see,' Vindex said as they made their way out of the arena.

The two brothers spent the rest of the day drinking in the tavern and relaxing in their room at the inn. They knew that tomorrow would bring a plethora of new challenges, so they enjoyed the day for what it was, and when it was over, they went to bed soundly.

DECIDING FATES

The moon's light was dimly seen through the thick clouds of the winter's night. Valerik walked down the muddy road to the hospital at Trevonum, relying on nothing but torches on posts for light. He pushed open the raggedy orange cloth that sealed the wooden building from the street, and approached the druid doctor, who was standing in the center of the room.

'How is she?' Valerik asked earnestly.

'So far, she is okay,' the druid replied nervously. 'We will still need to watch her for a few more days to make sure there is no infection.'

'You will take me to her now,' Valerik said demandingly, towering over the old, withered man who was caring for Dara.

The druid doctor shook in his leather boots. Sweat ran from his old, wrinkled face. A chill ran down his hunched back and with a wobbly gait, he quickly guided Valerik into the back of the hospital. Valerik looked at Dara, who was resting on a hay mattress.

Valerik placed his hand on the druid's shoulder and said, 'Leave us.'

The old man quickly rushed out of the room thankful to be sent away.

Valerik approached the side of Dara's bed and knelt down. She was lying flat; her face half covered in a cloth rag soaked in castor oil. Dara's left eye was closed as she was resting. Valerik sat down in a chair next to her and waited.

After a few hours, Dara awoke from her slumber to see Emperor Valerik sitting at the foot of her bed. She quickly looked away and let out a scornful, 'I am fine. You do not have to keep checking in on me.'

'You act as if it is a burden.'

Dara sat up in the bed and placed her feet on the ground. 'I shouldn't be here wearing an oily rag! I should be commanding a garrison marching down to wherever that bastard scurried off to!' she shouted as she tried to unwrap her bandage.

Valerik got up and took hold of Dara's hands, trying to stop her from dismantling her dressing. 'Leave that on,' Valerik spoke, resetting the half removed bandage. 'The doctor said you'll need to wear it for some time.'

Dara screamed at Valerik, 'You trust this druid! He is no doctor! He is nothing but a filthy barbarian! We are Umbrians! Have you no shame?'

Valerik stepped back from Dara and sat on a stool next to the bed. He looked at his long-time companion and said, 'I have no shame, Dara. Especially when it comes to your safety. I believe that even the simple farmer can teach the most prudent scholar something new. So I see no reason to believe these Galicians can't teach us as well. I am sure the oil the druid has given you is helping your wound.'

'A better man would not say such foolishness.'

Valerik quickly interjected in an imposing tone. 'There are no better men than me. I know what's best. Just like I know, it is best to trust this druid with your care. He knows more than you or me about healing. So, you will stay here until you are recovered. That is an order.'

'Fine,' Dara snarled. She returned to her bed and calmly spoke. 'But I have one demand. The minute I am released from this mud pit, we hunt for Vindex.'

Valerik sighed. He looked at his second in command and bluntly replied, 'You will not be fighting him again, Dara.'

Dara shot out of bed and stood next to her commander in the dark hospital room. 'And why is that?' she retorted while gritting her teeth.

'Because you are not strong enough, Dara. He could have killed you in your last meeting. There is too much at stake now to have you needlessly risk your life. You are my second in command. If anything happened to me, you would need to run the Empire. I am more than capable of dealing with this threat alone.'

'After all these years, you question my strength? I was merely taken by surprise in that fight, nothing more. Had I been more aware, both brothers would be dead.'

'Is that so?' Valerik spoke. 'I can't lose you like we lost Agis. You are too integral to the Empire and my future plans.'

Dara stood still, unwavering. She took her hand and held it over her bandages. 'I know I can fight them. If not alone, at the least by your side. Let me get my revenge.'

Valerik let out a small smile and replied, 'You have convinced me. After you have healed, you may rejoin the campaign. I sent scouts out to see where the two brothers may have gone the morning after our victory. I suspect they traveled directly to the city of Narbo Martius south of here through the forest, but I will wait on making any firm strategies until our scouts come back.'

Dara's eyes gleamed with excitement. She had not healed yet, but was still eager to pursue the enemy. She quickly blurted out, 'Let me help you make the plan. I need to have some say in how we take down this savage. I will give him a slow and painful death for how he humiliated me.'

Valerik put his hand on Dara's shoulder and said, 'Very well. I will let you help, but go back to bed and rest. You can worry about the war after you have healed. You are in no state to fight anyone right now.'

'I suppose you are right,' Dara replied as she slowly got back into the hospital mattress.

'I always am,' Valerik confidently replied.

Before the pair could continue talking, an Umbrian lieutenant came through the door. 'I am sorry to interrupt your meeting, sir,' the soldier reported, 'But you asked me to inform you the moment the scouts had returned, and they are here now.'

Valerik nodded and replied, 'Tell them I will be right there. I am eager to hear their report.'

'Yes, sir,' the soldier replied before exiting the room.

'Make sure they spare no detail,' Dara spoke. 'I want to know everything that bastard Vindex has done since he fled like a coward.'

'Of course. We will be more prepared this time. He won't be able to escape us,' Valerik replied before exiting the room.

Dara, now alone in the cold dark room, thought to herself. *That barbarian better pray Valerik finds him on the battlefield before I do, for I do not have a quick death planned. Murder is not enough. He must be tortured. He and his pathetic runt of a brother.*

Valerik left the hospital and made his way down the muddy streets. He looked around at the Galician people, who all leered at him in disgust. *What an ungrateful people, he thought. I could have had their homes destroyed and fields salted. Instead, I offered them a home in the Umbrian Empire, and this is how they repay me. No matter, they will, in time, succumb to the Umbrian ways. Until then, the only thing that matters is ending this Galician threat by killing the sons of Brunos.*

Valerik continued down the road to the main gate, passing Umbrian legionaries patrolling the streets. On his journey, he walked by one Galician woman who seemed to be studying the Umbrian patrols. Before Valerik could confront the woman, he heard his name being called by the scout regiment.

'Emperor Valerik!' the scout commander exclaimed over the bustling city street.

Valerik quickly turned his attention away from the woman and addressed the scout. 'What is your report?' he asked impatiently.

The scout commander replied, 'Based on all the information we could muster, we believe he went to Narbo Martius. We left one of our members behind on the outskirts of the city to continue to monitor his whereabouts.'

Valerik nodded, pleased that his own suspicions had been verified. 'Is there anything else you wish to report?' he asked, trying to get as much information as he could before making a plan of attack.

'Actually, yes,' the scout replied. 'The city of Narbo Martius is nothing like what our previous information had said. It appears that it is much larger than Trevonum.'

'Impossible,' Valerik replied, shocked. 'Trevonum was supposed to be the capital of the Galician world.'

'Apparently not,' the scout said. 'Estimating their forces based on the city walls, I would say you will need an army of at least eight thousand men to take the settlement.'

Valerik thought to himself for a moment. After the Battle of Trevonum, he only had about five thousand men, which he could dedicate to an invasion. The remaining force would need to garrison the city. 'The forest that you traveled through. How many men do you think could pass there with me?' he asked the scout.

'Maybe fifteen hundred, if you are lucky. It is extremely dense terrain except for one open pasture in the heart of the woodland.'

Valerik nodded, listening to the report. He then asked one more time, 'Is there anything else I should know?'

'No sir. That is all,' the scout confidently replied, satisfied with giving a full report.

'In that case, you are dismissed. Send one of your men to go back to accompany the scout still in the woods. The rest of your men may do as they wish,' Valerik replied as he walked away without waiting to hear the scouts reply.

He made his way quickly to his tent, which he set up inside the town square. He took a seat at his desk and looked at maps of the region. Valerik examined the surrounding terrain on the documents in front of him and postulated possible attack strategies for conquering Narbo Martius. With every strategy he planned, there was only one consistent factor in it. Vindex must die.

Valerik was so consumed with his thoughts that he forgot about the promise he made to Dara about creating a battle strategy together. By nightfall, he had broken his promise. The plan to defeat the Galicians once and for all was ready.

CHAPTER 22

THE AUDIENCE WITH IODONA

The next morning, Viridox and his brother woke up well after sunrise.

'Too loud!' Viridox grumbled as a crowing rooster awoke him.

Vindex quickly got up woozy. His head pounded and his eyes shunned the light. 'What are you screaming for, Viridox? I have a headache.'

'So do I!' Viridox moaned back. 'That's why I am screaming. It hurts!'

The two brothers sat up on the side of their beds, feeling nauseated and sick to their stomachs. Vindex remembered they had a meeting with Iodona and thought to himself, *We're late. That is not good.* He promptly began getting dressed, ignoring his discomfort.

'How much did we have to drink last night?' Viridox asked as he collapsed back down on his bed.

'Too much,' Vindex said while holding his head in his hands. 'Now get changed. We have a meeting to go to.'

'By the gods,' Viridox retorted as he rolled off his bed onto the floor. 'I forgot the meeting was this morning.'

Viridox quickly threw on his clothes. The pair hurried out of the inn and headed for the town hall, where they had planned to meet Iodona and Emiscor. As they left the building, the bright sun irritated the two brothers, and they held their hands above their eyes, trying to diminish some of the light. The rather short walk to the meeting spot seemed like an eternity for the pair, as they were subjected to a noisy trade market and the sounds of wagons clicking their wooden wheels against the cobblestone street. Eventually, they reached their destination, where Iodona and Emiscor were waiting outside.

'We are here,' Vindex said, still shielding his eyes from the sun. 'Is there a quiet, maybe even dimly lit, place we can meet inside?' he asked as Emiscor and Iodona looked on at them judgingly.

'Are you two hungover?' Iodona asked, bluntly shaming the two brothers.

'Don't blame us,' Viridox said. 'If anyone should be at fault, it's you. Your tavern is too comfortable. How could you expect anyone to show restraint?'

'Absolutely unbelievable,' Iodona said with an exasperated look on her face. 'Get inside now,' she barked. 'We will be meeting in the room in the back-right corner.'

'Thank you,' Vindex said graciously, understanding that he and his brother were being unprofessional.

When entering the building, the two brothers made their way to the meeting room. Iodona turned to Emiscor and said, 'I really can't believe this.'

'Nor can I,' Emiscor responded, 'But we do need answers from them.'

'I know. Go make them each a cup of tea. Hopefully, we can wake them up a bit more,' Iodona replied as the siblings entered the meeting hall.

Emiscor went to brew a pot of water while Iodona went into the meeting room where Vindex and his brother had already become situated. When Iodona entered, she saw Viridox lying on one of the wooden benches that was built into the wall, and Vindex sitting at the table looking at the papers Iodona kept at her desk.

'Iodona, I have a few questions for you,' Vindex said as he saw her entering the chamber.

'If it's all the same,' Iodona replied, 'I would like to ask mine first. Starting with, who are you really?'

'My name is Vindex,' he replied, finally waking up, 'I am not a liar. I am the son of Brunos of Norova.'

'I don't mean to be rude, but if you are simply the son of Brunos, a Galician chieftain, how did you make my second sword?' Iodona replied, taking the blade that Vindex created from her side and placing it on the table.

'I am part Galdeshan as well,' Vindex replied.

Before he could continue his statement, Iodona jumped in, pressing for more information. 'And is your brother? Can he do this as well?'

'No. He cannot. We share a mother, but apparently not a father,' Vindex said honestly.

'But you called yourself the son of Brunos,' Iodona replied, trying to cross-examine his testimony.

'Because I am,' Vindex retorted testily, now beginning to become agitated. 'He is the only father I ever knew. No one ever mentioned another father when I was young. It was only a few years ago where I found out I was part Galdeshan.'

Iodona took a seat across the table, looking at Vindex. 'How did you find out?' she asked with a tad more empathy in her voice, realizing her question had upset the man.

Before Vindex had time to answer, Emiscor arrived with the tea. He opened the wooden door and handed a hot cup to Vindex at the table, who graciously thanked him. He then walked over to Viridox, who sat up on the bench in order to drink the beverage. After delivering the drinks, Emiscor took a seat at the right side of Vindex at the table so that he too faced Iodona.

Vindex took a sip of his tea before answering. 'It's a long story,' he eventually said. 'One that we really don't have time for.'

Confused by what was being discussed, Emiscor opened his mouth, trying to ask what he had missed. Before he could speak, Iodona quickly asked Vindex, 'What other myths are true?'

'All I know for sure is that the Maith and the Olc exist. Besides that, I don't know,' Vindex replied, taking another sip of his drink.

'The Olc?' both Emiscor and Iodona replied, confused, never having heard of that legend before.

'It doesn't really matter,' Vindex said, slamming his drink down on the table. 'I battled for this audience to ask you questions. Not to be interrogated myself.'

Iodona looked shocked. 'Very well,' she said calmly, 'Ask away. It's just not every day a magical wanderer comes to my city seeking refuge. But you are correct, I will hear your concerns. What do you want to discuss?'

'I need an army,' Vindex demanded, giving no context as to his intentions.

Emiscor and Iodona's eyes opened, and they leaned forward, making sure they had heard Vindex correctly. 'An army for what?' Iodona asked. 'That is one big ask.'

'An army to kill Valerik,' Vindex said seriously, staring down at his tea.

Iodona and Emiscor looked at each other, hoping that either would have heard of the man Vindex named. It became clear neither had, so Iodona asked. 'Why do you need an army to kill one man?'

'Because that one man has an army of his own,' Vindex replied. 'He is an Umbrian general who turned their republic into an empire. His Empire. He marched through the Western Tribes like we were made of butter. Trevonum has fallen. Narbo Martius is the capital of the southern tribes, correct? Without this city, Istras and Gabala would fall too. So really, we are now the last line of defense for the Galician world. Now you don't have to listen to me, Megorath surely didn't, but if you value your city and our people, you will give me the resources I need.'

'You know Megorath?' Iodona asked, appearing to have ignored the rest of what Vindex had said.

'I knew him, yes. He fell fighting nobly on the walls of Trevonum,' Vindex answered, confused why that was the detail she fixated on.

'This could be your chance, sister,' Emiscor said, excited to hear that Megorath was sleeping with the ancestors.

Vindex, now more confused than ever, interjected, 'What are you talking about? What chance? There is nothing left north of here besides an Umbrian army and Emperor who are both trying to destroy our people!'

Iodona looked at her brother, disappointed that he had said anything, but after a brief glare, she answered Vindex's question. 'I have long possessed the ambition to reunite the Galician Tribes. I want to do for them what I was able to do for Narbo Martius,' Iodona said openly.

'If that's the case, why didn't you speak to Megorath about reunification?' Vindex asked.

'You said you knew him. So, you should already know,' Iodona spoke, 'He would hear nothing of it. And war was never something I would contemplate, as I would never want to go to blows with my fellow brothers and sisters. But now you say they are under Umbrian occupation.'

'That is correct. By the Emperor himself Valerik,' Vindex replied, placing both his elbows down on the table, leaning inward to face Iodona. 'So, shall I assume we have a deal?' he asked as he stared down the chieftain.

'That depends on your intentions,' Iodona tactfully replied. 'You know I want to rule these people. What do you want?'

'I want to see Valerik meet his demise at the end of my blade,' Vindex said bluntly.

'But to what end? Do you want to lead the people we free?' Iodona asked, trying to grasp what more Vindex wanted.

Vindex simply replied, 'My leading begins and ends on a battlefield. I don't want to be an emperor or a chieftain. That's not my business. I have told you what my goal is. Now I must know, will you help me?'

Iodona didn't know how to respond. Before making any commitments, she asked, 'If Valerik dies, what will you do?'

'I have a promise to keep with an old friend. After Valerik dies, you most likely won't see me again,' Vindex answered honestly after a brief pause.

Iodona remained skeptical, and Viridox could see it in her expression from across the room. He stood up from the bench on the wall and walked behind Emiscor and Vindex. He addressed Iodona directly, 'Valerik is the man who murdered our father. He burnt our home and spared only my brother. I would not be here today if it were not for him.' He placed his arm on Vindex's shoulder. 'It's a simple matter of revenge. There is no other meaning or purpose.'

Iodona now understood what had motivated the warrior in front of her. She then asked Viridox, 'And what of you? Where will you go when we kill Valerik?'

Vindex smiled seeing that Iodona was going to help them, but he did not speak, wondering what his brother's answer would be.

'When it's all said and done, I plan to go back to Trevonum and be with my beloved. Maybe buy a farm, live off the land, raise a family. What more could I ask for?' Viridox replied.

Iodona was glad to hear there would be no competition for power if she reclaimed Trevonum. She smiled and spoke, 'Then I think we are in agreement. Together we will lead an army against Valerik.'

Vindex was very pleased. 'There is something else you should know,' he said. 'I can use the Maith to tell you exactly what we will be up against.'

'So, you are a spy and a warrior?' Iodona replied, not understanding the Maith's abilities.

'In a sense,' Vindex said. 'You will see in due time. Until then, it may be best to start preparing your forces. We will need skill and numbers to defeat the Umbrian legionaries. They are a considerable threat even without their general.'

'Very well,' Iodona spoke. 'Emiscor, prepare the men in the barracks. Have them commence training drills immediately. I am going to stay here and learn what Vindex has to teach me about the Maith.'

'It will be done,' Emiscor said, standing up from the table. He moved around Viridox and made his way to the exit.

'The long story you mentioned before, I would like to hear it now,' Iodona said to Vindex.

Vindex happily obliged. As Viridox sat beside him, the two shared every detail of their life since the burning of their home. They sensed something good in Iodona and felt she could be trusted. Vindex revealed the secrets of the Maith and where Cato, the last true Galdeshan, lived. Despite only just meeting this chieftain, the two brothers sensed a blossoming friendship with the proud warrior leader of Narbo Martius.

As the three finished discussing the past, Vindex turned to the future. He broke from the group and headed back to the inn. Vindex hoped he could conjure the Maith, to see what Valerik's plans were. Vindex thought to himself before meditating. *No matter what Valerik is planning, we will be ready. He will not overcome this new alliance. Father, I am so close to avenging you. The time for retribution will soon be here.*

WANDERING IN THE MAITH

Vindex left the meeting with Iodona more determined than ever before. He knew there would be a fierce battle approaching, but he believed Galicia would prevail and that Valerik would meet his end. Vindex wandered the streets, clearing his head before returning to the inn. His skills with the Maith had improved, but he would still need to clear his mind if he wanted to spy on Valerik. After some time walking along the cobblestone streets, Vindex decided it was best to return to the inn and begin his meditation. He did not want to waste more time.

Vindex arrived at the inn and walked up the stairs to his room. He sat directly in the center of the wooden floor. He tried to clear his mind before conjuring the Maith's power, but despite his best effort, his thoughts still lingered on revenge. Despite this lack of focus, he felt the fairies' presence. The spirits felt different from usual, but Vindex did not fight this unfamiliar sensation and instead welcomed the fairies, giving them control until he felt united with them. Upon opening his eyes, he found himself in a place he did not know. It was a black void that contained only sparsely spaced, pale violet circles of light that seemed to float in all directions around him.

'What is this place?' Vindex asked to no avail as there was no reply.

'Hello?' he said, now standing up, only to realize he felt nothing solid underneath his feet. He was in a void, and although this place appeared barren, he had never felt a stronger connection to the spirits.

Vindex explored this void, curious to see what secrets this place held. There was nothing underneath him, yet he could walk as if on solid ground. Vindex felt as if he was being pulled in a certain direction. He could not explain it, but it was as if something or someone was calling to him. He followed this force until he found himself at a bright ball of pale violet light.

Vindex tried to communicate with the orb, asking, 'Are you a spirit?' but there was no answer.

What is this place? Vindex questioned, thinking to himself as he tried to reach out and touch the floating orb of light.

Vindex's hand slowly approached the flying orb, but right when he was about to grab the spirit, the orb flew away, terrified of Vindex.

'I won't hurt you, little fairy. I just want to know where I am,' Vindex calmly replied as he slowly inched his way to the violet ball.

He tried again to grab the spirit, but just like the last time, the orb moved before he could touch the light. *Okay,* Vindex thought to himself. *I won't do it slow next time. One quick grab and I will figure out where I am.*

Vindex cautiously approached the spirit for a third time. With his arms already extended, ready to grab the orb, Vindex positioned himself within arm's reach of the fairy. Without talking or any hesitation, Vindex threw both of his arms forward, grabbing the spirit in his hands.

'Aha!' Vindex spoke, holding the orb in his hands pulling it closer to his chest. 'Now tell me where I am, please. You have nowhere to run now.'

The fairy did not speak. Unable to move, the spirit emitted a brighter light, releasing energy. Vindex could feel this power traversing through his arms and up his body. Eventually, the power reached Vindex's skull and for a moment he felt transported from his body. He saw a bright white flash and felt a fire on his body hotter than anything he had experienced before, including the night when Norova was burned to the ground.

He heard a very familiar voice yell, 'No!' while he heard a stranger's voice yell, 'You fool!' Suddenly the warmth surrounding Vindex faded and he felt cold and wet. The white light had subsided too and was replaced with cloudy darkness. He felt waves of pressure throwing him about for what felt like hours until he eventually was set free on a coastal beach. Vindex saw an area unfamiliar to him. The shore seemed barren and there were no ports or boats in sight. The shore was also very small, as if he was on some tiny island. He looked up the hill from the beach and saw a hare run out from behind a hazel tree, which stood alone in an empty grass field. Behind the field was a dark cave built into a small mound on the island. The rabbit stared at Vindex, who remained on the beach. He then heard the same stranger's voice speak once more. 'You should not be here yet.'

'Who are you?' Vindex exclaimed. 'What is this place?'

There was no answer. The hare that stared at Vindex suddenly dashed away behind the tall hazel tree. Suddenly Vindex felt a wave hit him from behind, causing him to fall face first onto the sandy beach. When opening his eyes once more, he saw the sand had gone and the hardwood floor of the inn in Narbo Martius was underneath him. He stood up and dashed to a window in the inn. Vindex looked out and exhaled a sigh of relief, seeing countless Galician citizens walking about the city streets.

What was that place? Vindex thought to himself, catching his breath after such an adventure. *And who were the voices I heard in the visions? Was one of them Cato?*

Vindex realized his mentor would be the best person to turn to in order to get answers about the mystical experience he had just endured. He knelt down once more on the hard floor of the inn and began thinking about nothing but Cato and the Galdeshan peaks.

'Why isn't this unexpected?' Cato spoke in a friendly manner, seeing his pupil appear from nowhere on the adjacent side of his encampment. 'To what do I owe the pleasure?' he asked knowing Vindex clearly needed something from him.

'I need your help,' Vindex said bluntly.

'First time you've ever told me that,' Cato replied with a smile. 'Very well, take a seat.'

Vindex sat on the bench facing in at the campfire. He looked at Cato, who was still brewing his concoction, 'Well, before I say what I need, I just wanted to say our practice paid off. I was able to make Orla's wedding ring and a sword by using the Maith.'

Cato's face lit up. 'Really?' he replied, shocked, 'I will be honest. I did not know if you were going to pull it off.'

'Neither did I, if I am being truthful.'

Before Vindex could speak once more, Cato quickly asked, 'Then what brings you here? It would seem that you have things sorted out, considering your power has improved greatly.'

'Improved, yes, but not nearly mastered. I need to communicate with the spirits, as you do. I need to know information only they would know.'

Cato mumbled to himself, pausing his brewing. He held his hand to his chin and replied, 'That is one of the ultimate skills of the Maith Vindex. I am not sure if you are ready.'

'I think I am ready, Cato,' Vindex replied confidently. 'I think I am close as it is. Before coming here, I was in what I think to be the spirit domain. It was a black void with pale violet light. The fairies gave me visions and I think they were trying to communicate with me. In fact, I think I heard your voice in one of them.'

'What did you just say?' Cato replied mildly angrily as he dropped his potion onto the ground.

'I was meditating earlier, and I felt the fairies, just as you taught me. They pulled me into a black void. Why, what's wrong?' Vindex replied defensively, as he saw concern come across the old man's face.

'What were you thinking about before meditating?' Cato asked, slowly delivering each word with a heavy weight and bold emphasis.

Vindex felt on edge. He was almost scared seeing his mentor so concerned. Not thinking clearly, he blurted out, 'I was thinking about defeating Valerik! We made an alliance that will surely beat him. I just need to get more information on him before we make our next move.'

'Destruction of course,' Cato scolded. 'Of course, you couldn't learn to let things be and embrace the Maith around you.'

'I just did!' Vindex yelled in response to Cato's ridicule. 'What is your problem? You knew I wanted to kill Valerik before I came back to finish my training. We had a deal.'

'Yes, we did,' Cato scolded. 'You were to complete your training in the Maith, not the Olc! Where you went to is the realm of the Olc, and you let yourself be pulled there because of your own fixation upon a fruitless revenge.'

Vindex ignored what Cato said about the Olc, and in a simmering rage responded slowly, 'He killed my father.'

Cato looked back at him and stood up from where he sat and replied in a serious tone, 'He wasn't your father, Vindex. Which in of itself deeply concerns me. There is a much greater threat out there that, if not discovered, could mean an end to not just Galicia, but the entire world. You have to let the past go, Vindex. Killing Valerik won't bring Brunos back.'

Vindex could not control his emotions. In a fit of rage, he got up and took a swing at the old man's head. The blow passed right through the old man, however, as Vindex was merely an apparition.

After the failed punch, Vindex calmed himself as best he could and said, 'Tell me what I want to know, and I'll be on my way.'

Cato looked at his pupil. He had hoped for an apology, but got an order as if he was a soldier under his command. 'No,' Cato said without a second word, now picking up the potion he had dropped.

Vindex was at an impasse. He needed the information to create a new plan, but he did not want to apologize to Cato, as he now understood that the old man had not told him everything about himself or the Maith. After a moment, he tried to think clearly about how he should proceed, and then he spoke again. 'I didn't know it was the Olc

Cato. I had no idea where I was, which is why I came here. I wanted you to tell me about the visions I saw. There was a hot fire and …'

Cato harshly interjected, cutting Vindex off in the middle of his sentence. 'It doesn't matter that you did not know,' Cato replied with fear in his voice. 'You were there. Your judgment is clouded.'

'What about the visions I saw?' Vindex quickly asked, wanting Cato to address what he saw in that other world.

Cato looked worried. His eyes were focused on his potion, refusing to meet Vindex's gaze. He replied softly, 'They were nothing. A mere hallucination of the Olc. I cannot help you until you fix your clouded mind.'

'You know the only way that I can fix that.'

'I suppose I do,' Cato said, standing back up once again. 'If I give you the information that you need to know, you have to promise me one thing.'

Vindex was still slightly angry, but was willing to make a bargain. He had a respect for his mentor that would make him uphold any agreement the pair made. 'What is the promise?' Vindex asked calmly.

'You cannot use the Maith or the Olc again until you kill Valerik and return to me for proper training,' Cato said, knowing that the only way to prevent Vindex from using the Olc would be a complete prevention of his Galdeshan power.

Vindex, without hesitation, replied, 'I accept.'

Cato was stunned at how fast Vindex had responded. 'You're really nothing like …' Cato mumbled to himself before silencing his own words. 'Very well,' Cato continued. 'Valerik is waiting for his second in command, Dara, to heal. When she is healthy, he will send out two armies, one led by him through the Numok Forest and the other led by Dara over the Cruach Mountains. The latter will be the main army, about four thousand strong, while Valerik's will only be one thousand at most. There are two scouts in the Numok Forest, as is, and the expected departure for the Umbrians is in exactly three months from now. You don't need to know anything else.'

Vindex looked at his mentor and sincerely replied, 'Thank you Cato.'

A simple omission of the Maith until he returned to train meant nothing to Vindex so long as he could bring the man who killed his father to justice.

'You are welcome. Just do not forget our agreement,' Cato said, hoping Vindex would keep his word.

Vindex nodded his head in acknowledgement of the terms he had agreed to. He had all the information he needed to bring down Valerik. The Maith was now the last thing on his mind. The moment he had been waiting for his entire life was almost upon him.

'Very well,' Cato said. 'The next time I see you, it will be here, but in person.'

'That sounds like a plan to me,' Vindex said with a small smile, letting go of his anger.

Cato smiled back and watched him fade into nothing as Vindex's spirit returned to his body in Narbo Martius. Cato walked over to the cliff's edge. *I hope I am doing the right thing. One slight error and everything I have guarded here will be for nothing. Vindex must return to complete his training,* he thought to himself, while staring out into the valley.

As Cato brooded on his mountain, Vindex arose from his meditation. With immense ambition, he ran out of the inn to find his brother and Iodona. He needed to tell them what he had learned. The final battle was coming, and they all needed to prepare. He would not let another opportunity to kill Valerik slip away because of improper planning. He ran down the street, knocking over anyone in his way with no regard for others. Vindex only had one thing on his mind. *I am about to have my revenge. Finally, it will all be over.*

CHAPTER 24

ORGANIZING THE TROOPS

'Is that everything?' Iodona asked bluntly after hearing Vindex's report.

'That is all I know,' Vindex replied, leaning back from the commander's desk in her quarters. As he sat down, he saw a troubled look on Iodona's face.

'What's wrong?' he asked.

'You said that Valerik will have about five thousand troops at his disposal, correct?' Iodona asked, clenching her fist in anger.

'Yes, I did,' Vindex replied in a panic. 'Tell me you have as many. This city was supposed to be a militaristic society. How can you not have an army of comparable size?'

Iodona widened her eyes and let out a hefty sigh before responding, 'It was when Keir was in charge,' Iodona mumbled. 'Hasn't been that way for a long time.'

Iodona's eyes glazed over as if she was lost in thought. Her brother, Emiscor, snapped her out of it.

'Sister!' he exclaimed. 'This is not the time for that. We need a plan.'

'Right,' Iodona replied, reorienting herself to the present moment. 'As of now, we only have about thirty-five hundred soldiers, but I suppose we can recruit more. Maybe we can even enlist citizens from Gabala and Istras.'

'No,' Vindex replied defiantly.

Shocked at the Galdeshan's reply, Iodona looked away from her brother to face Vindex in the eye. 'Why not?' she asked, 'This is the only way we will stand a chance. We are heavily outnumbered otherwise.'

'If you bring new enlisted novice soldiers into this, every one of them will lose their life. I fought these soldiers before. We are going to face the best of the best Umbria has to offer, and I will not sit idle and see us throw away Galician lives like lambs to the slaughter, just to shield ourselves,' Vindex replied bluntly, staring back into Iodona's eyes, showing her he would not budge.

'Then what do you suggest we do, Vindex?' Iodona asked. 'After all, you are the one with the experience.'

Vindex paused, thinking about all the viable options they had at combating Valerik. After a short while, he looked at Emiscor and said, 'Go find Viridox for me. Iodona and I will plan this. I want you two here when we are done.'

Emiscor looked over at his sister, waiting to see what she would say before taking orders from this outsider. Iodona nodded in agreement with Vindex's orders and with that approval, Emiscor quickly left the room in search of Viridox.

Vindex watched as Emiscor left and then turned to Iodona with a smile, saying, 'Take out your maps. We have a plan to make.'

Iodona promptly retrieved and shared the maps of the surrounding area. The two then sat down next to one another, bouncing plans off each other for a few hours while Emiscor searched all over the city for Vindex's younger brother.

Finally, after over two hours of searching, Emiscor found Viridox sitting in one of the town's public parks, staring at a marble fountain.

'Viridox!' he exclaimed, running over to him, 'Your brother and my sister have requested your audience at the main compound.'

Viridox's head looked behind him to see Emiscor quickly approaching. 'Is it urgent?' he asked in a morose tone.

The inflection of Viridox's voice told Emiscor that something was eating at the man. Emiscor replied, 'Yes, but it can wait a moment. What is wrong?'

Viridox quickly stood up and, in a tone masking sadness, replied, 'Nothing at all. It is probably best that we get going.'

Emiscor put his hand out to block the man from passing. 'We are not going back till you tell me what it is.'

Viridox respected Emiscor's wishes, inwardly thanking him for the release of his emotion. He sat back on the bench and gestured to Emiscor to sit with him. 'I just feel overwhelmed I suppose,' Viridox replied, staring straight ahead.

'I understand that feeling myself,' Emiscor said, sitting next to Viridox on the bench.

'Do you?' Viridox replied sincerely, not to be condescending to the Narbo Martius native. He continued, 'The love of my life is captured in a city the Umbrians just conquered, and I know I will need to fight to get her back, but I do not know if I have the strength. Vindex is probably calling for me because he has a plan to counterattack the Umbrians. Is that correct? I'll presume it is, and in that case, I don't know if I can keep fighting. Last time we faced Valerik's army I would have, no, I should have, died. Vindex saved me and we escaped together.' Viridox looked over at Emiscor, who was also staring ahead, facing the fountain. 'I am sorry. I shouldn't have bothered you with these issues,' Viridox said, looking down at his feet.

Not expecting any reply, Viridox was stunned to hear Emiscor's voice. He muttered. 'I understand and I know what it is like to be the sibling of a true warrior while you cower on the battlefield hoping that your life is not the next one lost. I'll be honest with you Viridox, that feeling, that sense of dread, it never goes away. When we were younger, Iodona and I fought in many battles together and she always protected me. There will never be enough words to thank her for what she has done.'

Viridox's eyes opened wider as he turned his head to Emiscor, who stared forward. He was hoping for words of encouragement, not his bleak take on reality. 'Do you mean …' Viridox said before being cut off.

'That this feeling will never go away, yes I do,' Emiscor said, interrupting Viridox. 'But that is not to say it isn't a good thing. No man wants to kill another, and no man wants to die at the end of a blade. I imagine all soldiers think this way. I could be wrong, but I can see that you feel as I do. Your guilt, your fear, and your own cowardice are tools to drive you further. Recognize them and don't accept that they will be the traits that define you. Push past them and fight.'

Viridox nodded his head. 'You are right,' he said confidently, standing up. 'Now let us see what battle Iodona and Vindex have in store for us.'

Emiscor stood with him and replied, 'After you.'

The two made their way back to the compound. It had been well over two hours since Emiscor had left and by this time Vindex and Iodona had made their plan of attack.

'That just might work,' Iodona said, satisfied, as Emiscor and Viridox opened the door to her planning room.

'Brother, you are back!' Iodona and Vindex both exclaimed in unexpected unison, seeing their siblings return.

'What is the plan so far?' Viridox asked, making his way to the war table, saving the pleasantries for later.

Vindex smiled, happy with his brother's resolve. 'Let me show you both,' he said confidently.

The two commanders shared the plan with Emiscor and Viridox step by step, asking them for their feedback as they went along. By the time the two got to the end of their strategy, Emiscor seemed visibly worried.

'This is one big gamble,' he said, unsure about their plan of attack.

'I know it is,' Vindex replied with honesty and complete transparency, knowing full well that the plan could backfire. 'But it is the only strategy that even comes close to winning.'

Emiscor mumbled to himself under his breath, 'Damn it. I guess we have no other choice then.'

Vindex noted Emiscor's reluctance to the plan and turned to his younger brother and asked, 'And what of you Viridox? Are you with me?'

'Always,' Viridox replied stoically, showing his devotion to the plan.

'Good, in that case, all that's left is training the troops until the day comes,' Vindex replied.

'I shall inform my men and women. I will also let them know that starting today, they are to take orders from you two as well,' Iodona replied. 'Now let's get ready to reclaim our land!'

The four cheered before leaving the planning room to inform the soldiers of their new training regimens. Emiscor stayed back as Vindex, Iodona, and Viridox left the room. He stared at the maps and couldn't help but feel that this plan was nothing more than disguised suicide. After hearing his sister call his name, he left the room and slowly joined his new comrades in the street.

While the Galicians began their drills with Vindex and Iodona to bolster their strength, the Umbrian army was hard at work as well. Valerik, enraged by what Vindex had done to Dara, demonstrated a passion he had not shown since his first days as a foot soldier. He wanted a swift, decisive, and brutal victory over Vindex and Galicia, and he would stop at nothing to make this happen.

'You have two months, men!' Valerik barked at his Umbrian legion, who were practicing their sword fighting with wooden swords and spears in a training field. 'Two months until we invade Narbo Martius and finish off the rest of Galicia! This land will be Umbrian and those who defy us will meet their ancestors by our blades and spears!'

Orla was walking by the training grounds when she heard Emperor Valerik. She reminisced about the days before meeting Viridox, where the largest threat she faced was Megorath. She saw how capable these soldiers were and how powerful their Emperor was, and feared there would never be a free Galicia ever again. After briefly reflecting on her own situation, she became worried sick about Viridox. She shed a tear for her love as she quickly scurried past the barracks. Viridox's body had not been found after the battle, nor was his brother's, which gave her hope that she may someday see her true love again. She could hear Valerik's booming voice long after she had passed the barracks. She placed her hands over her stomach and jogged down the muddy road trying to escape what she was hearing. Powerless and trapped within the city limits, there was no way she could help Viridox even if she knew where he was. She could only hope that he would live to fight another day.

'You will not surrender! You will not fall! You will not lose!' Valerik continued to scream as he drilled his elite legionaries. 'I want you at your best! I will not accept failure! Do you understand?'

'Sir yes sir!' his legions replied in unison.

'If that is so, how come you look so sloppy!' Valerik exclaimed, absolutely irate. He ran over to one particular soldier who was showing poor form and kicked out his knee, bringing him to the ground.

He stared down at the legionary with a scowl and continued, 'We are not up against any standard opponent. We face a man named Vindex. You should fear him as if you had to face me on the battlefield. There is no room for error, no room for a mistake. There will be no second chances! You need to be perfect! Am I clear?'

'Sir, yes sir!' the legionaries replied in unison, louder than before.

Before Valerik could continue drilling the men, he saw Dara enter the barracks with her head still wrapped in bandages. He rushed over to her and softly said, 'What are you doing up? We both know that you need to be resting.'

'It is a little hard to rest with all the screaming,' she replied with a smile. 'Plus, I enjoy watching you drill the men. It comforts me.'

'Well, frankly, I do not care if you find comfort in training. You are still wounded. Rest now.'

'How can I rest when we still haven't planned our attack? The men are training sure, but we need to figure out our strategy if we intend to win.'

Valerik's face grew pale. 'About that,' he said. 'The plans have been completed. I need to debrief you on our strategy. We can do that inside now if you would like.'

Dara was crushed. She spun around and went back inside the barracks. Valerik immediately followed.

'Don't be like that,' Valerik said, trying to calm his second in command down.

'You clearly don't respect me,' Dara said sternly, refusing to face her commander.

'When the scouts returned you were still resting. I could not help but plan the invasion. Besides, I am counting on you for the most pivotal role,' Valerik replied sincerely.

Dara turned around. 'That is hardly an apology, but I accept the responsibility of being the key piece to destroying these barbarian savages. What do I need to do?'

'We will have a split attack,' Valerik began. 'I will divide the legion into two parts. I will take almost one thousand infantry men down the Numok Forest and lay siege to the city from the main gate. I need you and your army to cross the Cruach Mountains and march down from the West. With any luck, I will be able to coax the barbarians into attacking my smaller force outside the city and you and your men, four thousand strong, will breach the city walls and encircle the barbarian horde.'

'That is suicide. You are strong, but you cannot face the city's militia with one thousand men. You will be wiped out,' Dara protested. 'This is why I should have been consulted on the plan. It is too big of a gamble.'

'Not necessarily,' Valerik confidently replied. 'You and your men will bring artillery with you. You can set them up on the city's walls and fire at their forces from behind. In the confusion, I can reroute my men past the enemy to the city gates or back into the forest, depending on what option seems more viable at the time.'

'I see. And if I fail, and I am unable to make my way into the city. What then? Even if I came from behind the enemy on the flatland, they would most likely outnumber us based on the size of the settlement. We could lose,' Dara replied, trying to see what contingencies her general had planned.

'Dara, these soldiers are Umbria's elite. The enemy could be triple our size and we would still have the advantage. However, if things turn in the enemy's favor, I will have Genitor to get me out of the mess. I will simply order a tactical retreat, and nothing will be lost but our pride. The woods are so thick that any pursuing barbarian force would need to split up, at which point they are no longer a threat,' Valerik confidently replied.

Dara looked reassured. 'It would appear you have thought of everything then,' she said, eager to help her Emperor in the last assault against the Galician tribes.

'I always do,' Valerik replied, putting his hand on her shoulder. 'Now, get some rest. This plan depends on your ability to lead the main battalion. I am entrusting this to you.'

Dara looked into the eyes of her leader. He had all the faith in the world that she would accomplish this mission. She was not ready to disappoint him. 'I won't let you down,' she said sincerely.

'I know. You never have before,' Valerik replied, taking his hand off her shoulder. 'Now, go get your rest. I have drills to run.'

Dara watched as Valerik returned to the men. She admired his commitment and ferocity in his training instruction. As she rested, watching the drills take place, she felt pleased, knowing that she would use these men to conquer and kill the rest of the barbarian world.

For two months, both factions trained day in and out to prepare for the battle that would decide the fates of every Galician. At the head of each army, there were two people using their soldiers as means to obtain personal vengeance on one another. The soldiers trained daily being told to lay down their lives for their nation with no knowledge of their leaders' own personal vendettas. Valerik's obsession with Vindex slowly manifested itself with each passing day. By the time Dara had fully healed, he was thinking more of watching the light of Vindex's eyes fade more than bringing the Umbrian way of life to the southern Galician tribes. Eventually, Dara's scar above her eye, which extended through her brow, had fully healed. There was no risk of infection and her sight was unimpaired. It seemed as if it was time to implement Valerik's plan.

When the day to deploy finally arrived, Dara and Valerik equipped their gear and marched out of Trevonum, at the head of their respective armies. They shared a sincere goodbye before vowing to see one another in the city square of Narbo Martius. Both generals were on horseback and positioned themselves at the front of their men as they set off on their separate paths to the last major city of the Galician world. As the Umbrian legionaries marched through the muddy roads of Trevonum, Orla watched helplessly, thinking about the insurmountable odds Viridox would face if he were still alive. After the legionaries vacated the city, she made her way to the temple to pray for Viridox's safe return.

THE FINAL BATTLE

The day for Vindex and Iodona to march into battle had finally arrived. Iodona and Emiscor brought twenty-five hundred armed soldiers to the town plaza, leaving just one thousand town watch to defend the city in the event Vindex and Iodona were defeated by Valerik. Each soldier stood shoulder to shoulder, facing straight ahead at a wooden stage. Horses waited in the adjacent streets for the soldiers, each packed with provisions and weapons for their journey. The citizens of Narbo Martius looked out their windows and gathered around the plaza to watch this historic moment. Vindex took the stage with Viridox to his right and Iodona to his left. Each soldier knew Vindex was in command and the crowd grew silent when they saw the Galdeshan ready to speak.

Vindex stepped forward so that his feet were touching the very end of the stage and looked out at the troops he would lead into battle. The crowd hushed. He began, 'Nearly seven years ago, a man named Valerik came to my hometown of Norova. He and his Umbrian cohort burnt it to the ground. My brother and I are the only survivors of the carnage. I vowed that day to avenge my father and my people, but that is not why we fight today. Today we fight for all of Galicia! If we fail, if we falter, Valerik and the Umbrians will take every last bit of Galician land for their own. It will be the end of not only you and I, but of all those who we love dearly. Everyone who inhabits this land will be subjugated to their whims. Do not let this happen! Losing is not a luxury we can afford! You will be divided into two divisions.'

Vindex took a pause looking out at his soldiers. 'Listen carefully so you know your assignments. I will take the cavalry from the third and seventh regiments to the Numok Forest. We will lay an ambush for Valerik and his men there. The remaining squadrons will go with Iodona, your chieftain. You will travel to the Cruach Mountains and engage with the enemy's primary force. I will leave the specifics of your battle up to your commander, but no matter what strategy is taken, no matter what casualties we sustain; remember that if we lose, we lose it all. Take a look around you now. This is the cost of failure. Your homes, your families, and your futures. Give me everything you have! Fight till your last breath and I promise you we will win! We will protect our lands! We have no other choice! Now who's with me!'

Vindex raised his sword into the sky in front of the soldiers. After a moment of silence, he saw the results he wanted. Every soldier which Iodona had provided lifted their swords tall into the air following the lead of their general. They followed with a tremendous, inspired shout that sent chills through Vindex's body.

'Very well then! Ladies and gentlemen, advance!' Vindex yelled as loud as he could. He and his brother rushed off the stage and mounted Bucephalus and Alesia, and led their soldiers in the third and seventh division through the streets of Narbo Martius.

Iodona watched as the two divisions marched through the streets on horseback. She looked back at the rest of the men and women she would lead, and yelled, 'What are you still doing standing here? Follow them and meet me outside the wall!'

'Yes, ma'am!' the soldiers screamed out. The infantry marched down the city streets as the remaining cavalry soldiers mounted their horses. They would wait for their chieftain just outside the city's main gate.

Emiscor looked up at his sister, who had yet to leave the stage. *This plan might be suicide, but I have to fight too. I just know she will need me in this battle,* he thought as he quickly made his way to his horse.

Iodona stepped down from the stage and saw her brother running to his horse. *He better not be doing what I think he is.*

Emiscor mounted his horse before hearing his sister call out. 'Emiscor, wait!' Iodona exclaimed. 'You are not coming to the battle.'

Emiscor turned to face his sister. 'Iodona, I have to come with you. This is my home, as it is yours. I can't sit idly and hide behind your shield forever.'

'I understand how you feel, but I need someone here with the garrison in case Vindex and I fail. You need to be our last stand,' Iodona explained.

'Then leave Odella here to command the garrison. She can be the last line of defense.'

'I know she can,' Iodona replied. 'But she is far too capable to leave behind. She is my captain. I need a warrior like her on the battlefield. You must be the last line of defense. There is no other choice. Stay here and command the town watch. That is an order.'

Emiscor took a deep breath and remembered what he had told Viridox only days before. The journey Vindex and Iodona were about to undertake terrified him, and yet he fought through his own fear. He stared at his sister with a rare look of defiance and said, 'I am going with you, Iodona. We need every soldier we can get. If our troops are ready to sacrifice their lives, so can I. I can live with that possibility.'

Iodona was shocked to see her brother disobey orders. More than that, though, she was taken aback by his courage. Emiscor held his head high, feeling the wind in his hair from atop his horse. Iodona stared at him and said with deep concern and fear, 'Just don't die on me.'

Emiscor said with a smile, looking down on his sister from his horse, 'I don't see that happening when I have my chieftain looking out for me. But please don't worry, I will be fine.'

Iodona smiled back and replied, 'You know I won't always be able to look out for you, brother, but given the circumstances, I think I could do it one more time.'

She then ran to her horse's pen and mounted her steed. She kicked the horse and joined her regiments who were falling in ranks outside the city walls. When outside, she pulled in front of her soldiers and yelled, 'With me!'

The regiments then followed her as she moved fast to the west, hoping to reach the Cruach Ruins before the Umbrians had passed through the mountain range. Their destination was an ancient and ruined city at the foot of the Cruach Mountains. A well timed ambush in this abandoned city could tip the balance on the battlefield despite Dara's superiority in numbers.

Iodona and her troops marched fast through the open plains. Her determination grew with every stride of her horse. She had not led an army in nearly three years, but this did not concern her as she knew failure was not an option. She looked down at her belt and made sure she had both her original blade and the one Vindex had made. After examining the latter sword, she became slightly worried, not for herself, but for Vindex. He had only brought six hundred men to face Valerik's thousand. Putting those thoughts away, she continued to ride. Worrying was a luxury she could not afford. She needed to hope that Vindex knew what he was doing.

Iodona was not the only one having doubts about Vindex's likelihood of success. As Vindex's army marched, his brother rode next to him and asked, 'Vindex, why are we all mounted on horseback? I understand the need to get to the forest quickly, but once we're there, the horses will become useless. The trees are too dense to properly use our mounted troops.'

Vindex did not look at his brother. He stared straight ahead and gave Bucephalus a squeeze with his heels to speed up. After a pause, Vindex turned his head to his right, seeing that Viridox and Alesia were still next to him, keeping the new pace. He finally answered in a serious tone, 'Do you trust me?'

'I never stopped,' Viridox replied instantly.

'Then you will need to do exactly as I say. We have no room for error,' Vindex replied sternly.

'I know that,' Viridox replied. 'I will do whatever you need me to. I promise.'

Vindex turned his head back forward. He only replied, 'Good. I will tell you when we get there.'

Viridox slowed Alesia, letting Vindex take the lead once more. *He seems a little different,* Viridox thought to himself. *Perhaps he too is nervous about our odds or maybe he is nervous about matching Valerik in single combat. I wish I knew what he was planning, but for now, I will just have to trust him. He has never let me down before. He won't start now.*

The men and women traveled without stopping, riding fast through the open green plains of south Galicia. After many long hours, the army reached their destination.

'We're here,' Viridox said nervously, looking at the edge to the Numok Forest.

'Indeed, we are,' Vindex replied, staring up at the sky. The sun would set soon and Vindex wanted to get moving quickly to lay his ambush.

'So, what is your plan?' Viridox asked, hoping to get some direction before advancing.

Vindex looked over at Viridox and then turned Bucephalus around to face his troops. He reared back on his horse and confidently announced, 'Listen up! These will be your final orders from me until after we win the battle, so pay close attention. I am dividing the seventh regiment in half. The first group will join me and the third regiment inside the depths of the Numok Forest. We will set up an ambush in the woods on the edge of the meadow. This is where Valerik will re-enter the forest in order to get to Narbo Martius. We know the enemy must pass this way and it is an ideal place to strike as it allows my brother time to ambush the Umbrians from the rear. The soldiers following him will stay on their horses and attack the enemy from behind. Virdox's mounted men will discharge their arrows into the surprised enemy charging into their ranks. Whoever is with me, it is important to understand that we cannot flee. We cannot waiver. We must hold the line! This plan only works if we keep the Umbrians from entering too deep into the forest. If we fail, the enemy can push into the forest from the plain to protect themselves from our horse archers. The only chance of victory is to plant ourselves as if we were one of the trees in the forest and give enough time for Viridox and his men to successfully surprise our foe. I will not lie, many of us will fall, but this is the sacrifice we make to protect Galicia! This is the sacrifice we make to keep our people free from these oppressors! This is the sacrifice we make to avenge those who have fallen before us! Now all of you who stand with me dismount your horses and move out!'

Viridox's heart sank after hearing Vindex's plan. It was all resting on him. The entire Galician world came down to whether he could successfully carry out his brother's orders. Exceedingly worried and almost in a panic, he called out for Vindex, who was still on Bucephalus, waiting by the edge of the forest. 'Brother,' he spoke timidly, 'I don't see how this plan is going to work. You are only taking three hundred of the men into the woods.'

Vindex turned around to face his brother. 'In order for this plan to work, I need at least three hundred archers ready to flank Valerik's men. Otherwise, this would be nothing but suicide, even with all six hundred of us in the forest. We are no match in hand to hand combat with their legionaries. We need half the men to surprise the Umbrians from behind.'

Viridox's heart raced. He was not sure if he could successfully carry out the orders. 'You should lead the cavalry charge, then,' he blurted out quickly, looking down at the ground from his horse instead of making eye contact with his brother. 'If it is so important, then you need to be the one to carry it out.'

Vindex dismissed that thought and instantly replied, 'No. Without me, the front line would collapse. Both of us need to play our part in order to seize victory this day. Iodona and I prepared for this attack, analyzing every advantage we had. We combined my insight gathered from Cato and the Maith and her knowledge of the land to create our best chance to win. I promise this plan will work, but you must carry out all my orders exactly as intended. This forest is surrounded by water on either side. I need you to use the coastline to advance your men. Run along the east shore until you see a large, almost mountainous rock protruding from the sand. According to what I have seen with the Maith, there will be only one large enough that it reaches all the way to the shoreline. Line your men up there in a single file line. When you hear the battle begin, lead your troops thirty yards ahead. There, you will find a small narrow path just wide enough for one horse to fit through at a time. It will take you through the woods to the opposite side of the plain. Do not open fire until all your men have left the woods and have mustered on the field.'

Viridox looked up slightly, but still avoided eye contact with his brother. He asked Vindex, 'Why not have my men waiting on the edge of the forest waiting to charge? The small path will only delay our ability to respond. If it is so imperative that I make the attack, shouldn't I march through the Numok Forest just as the battle begins?'

'We cannot risk you being seen,' Vindex replied bluntly. 'We also need time to engage all of Valerik's forces. Until he knows his rear is secure, it is unlikely that he will engage all his troops, but if time passes and he sees no threat from the rear, he should engage all of his legions against our soldiers. By that time, you will have come out and it will be too late for him to disengage. He will be surrounded on all sides, and we will finally get the bastard.'

Viridox could hear the confidence in his brother's voice. He truly believed the Galicians could win. Viridox then looked into Vindex's eyes to see nothing but unbridled determination. Taken aback by how certain his brother was in the strategy, Viridox opened his mouth to speak, but he was cut off.

'I trust you Viridox,' Vindex said. 'You can do this.'

A surge of confidence overcame the younger brother as he nodded his head, understanding what he had to do. 'I will see you on the other side,' Viridox replied before turning around to lead his men down the coast.

Vindex turned to face his men once more. The last of them had finally entered the forest, and with that, he followed them riding Bucephalus slowly, as to avoid all the branches protruding out, blocking his path. When they finally arrived at the large clearing in the woods, it was late afternoon, and they could hear the Umbrian legionaries approaching from the other side of the forest. They set up in their positions and waited for the inevitable.

Vindex was not the only one who had to prepare for an ambush. Iodona also had a battle to prepare for and a trap to set. The march Iodona took was much longer than Vindex's and his battle was already over before Iodona had even arrived at her destination. Iodona could not afford to worry about his battle. She had to focus on her own fight and hope that Vindex was successful in protecting Narbo Martius from Valerik.

Iodona was steadfast and determined when she arrived at the Cruach ruins. She knew what had to happen. The ruins were of a massive stone city resembling that of a castle town. Two large, withered stone towers faced the Cruach Mountains, with a small archway between the walls. This was the only way to pass through the ruined city as the walls and natural terrain prevented anyone from traversing around the settlement to the other side. No one knew for sure when this city was built or what happened to its people. The Galician people were suspicious of this place as it was shrouded in myth and mystery just as the Maith was, but Iodona had no choice but to press on. She could not let superstition deter her from laying her ambush.

Iodona stared at the half-destroyed stone city at the foot of the Cruach Mountains and turned to her Captain, Odella, and said, 'I want troops inside the homes facing the archway and missiles on top of the remaining walls.'

'Where will you go?' Captain Odella replied.

Iodona paused for a moment. 'I think I'll hide at the bottom of the staircase in the tower leading to the upper walls. My brother will join me there. And what of you?'

She looked back at Iodona and said, 'If you and Emiscor take the one on the left, I will man the one on the right. That way, the Umbrians won't be able to get to our archers on the wall.'

'Good plan. Tell the troops and let's get our ambush set. While you coordinate that, I am going to scout ahead and locate the enemy,' Iodona replied before trying to run off ahead on her horse Marengo.

'I'm going with you,' Emiscor insisted before Iodona could get too far ahead. He had been riding next to Odella and his sister while they were discussing the strategy.

'Very well, scout ahead with me, brother. Odella, I leave the rest to you,' Iodona ordered as she and Emiscor rode ahead to scout the nearby terrain.

Captain Odella looked back at the troops and said, 'Alright you heard her. I want archers on that wall, and infantry in the towers and hidden in the ruined homes. Leave your horses here away from the city and let's move!'

Iodona's troops marched up the incline to enter the abandoned city, leaving their horses well out of sight to ensure that Dara and her men would not see them when they entered the decaying outer walls. Meanwhile, it did not take long for Iodona to find the enemy. She rode to the bottom of the mountain range and there in the distance, just below the snow line, she saw hundreds of Umbrians descending the mountain. Fearful of being spotted, Iodona quickly turned around and ran back with Emiscor to inform her soldiers this battle would begin before the next sunrise. Iodona waited with her men, hoping that Vindex had done his job in defeating Valerik. Otherwise, all would be for nothing.

Vindex and Valerik's battle had already ended days before. The sun was setting on the day of battle as Valerik on horseback marched with his legionaries through the Numok Forest. They emerged into the meadow from the woods on the northern side of the Numok Forest. Slowly the Umbrians marched across the grass until they approached the trail into the southern portion of the woods where Vindex was waiting.

'Move, men!' Valerik exclaimed. 'I want to be through the other half of the woods before nightfall. We will set up camp after we have left the forest and wait for Dara's forces.'

Vindex's rage boiled. The last time he had seen Valerik there was a battlefield separating them. This time, Vindex would do everything in his power to bring an end to Valerik's life.

The Umbrian force reached the other side of the plain. Valerik looked at the sky and knew he had to hurry if he was going to traverse the remaining forest before nightfall. He dismounted Genitor, leaving his horse in the plains. The path was too small to lead by horse, so Valerik entrusted his soldiers in the rear to bring Genitor through the forest after all his legionaries had entered.

Valerik spoke. 'Form a column formation. We will be traversing thick foliage. Just move slowly and keep marching south.'

This is perfect, Vindex thought as he watched the Umbrians break up into small groups to march single file through the dense wood. Vindex's troops now had the advantage. The Umbrian army continued to march without any suspicion of the Galician soldiers which surrounded them. After nearly fifty of Valerik's men entered the woods, Vindex called for the ambush. The Galicians saw the hand signal from their commander and aimed their spears at the Umbrian invaders.

Something isn't right, Valerik thought. *Why do I feel like I am being watched?* Just as Valerik finished his thought, he spotted something out of the corner of his eye moving quickly behind a tree. He turned his head to face where the movement came from and saw a spiraling javelin headed towards the soldier in front of him.

'Move!' Valerik exclaimed, pushing the legionary in front of him out of the way from the incoming attack. The javelin missed the legionary but struck a tree, cracking the bark open. The sound was heard throughout the forest and crows began to take flight as if they sensed what was coming next.

'It's an ambush!' Valerik screamed, alerting his men. 'Soldiers, brace yourselves!'

Before the Umbrian legion could react, another volley of spears had been thrown. Valerik felt blood on the back of his neck. He turned his head and saw one of his legionaries impaled, spewing blood from his neck. *They'll keep picking us off one by one if we do not attack. I need to break formation and spread our troops out to take the forest,* Valerik thought.

Vindex smiled. His plan was working. 'Keep firing!' he yelled. 'We have them now!'

Valerik looked behind him. There were no attackers from the rear side of the plains. He thought, *I can't believe these barbarians laid an ambush. How could they know? I can't retreat to the plains. If I do, they will continue to pick us off from the tree line. I have to flush them out now. That is our only chance!*

'All Legionary Cohorts! Disperse in the woods and spread out! Find all the attackers and end this ambush!' Valerik exclaimed.

'This is it!' Vindex exclaimed. 'The battle for Galicia is here! Do not let them advance! You know what is at stake!'

Umbrian soldiers gripped their swords, looking left and right, wondering where the enemy would strike from. Meanwhile, the Galician forces moved to encircle the enemy. If Vindex's plan was to work, the Umbrians could not advance any farther into the forest.

'For Galicia!' Vindex screamed as he charged into battle. He swiftly appeared behind a tree and impaled one of the Umbrians that had entered too deep into the forest in his stomach. The legionary fell and caught the attention of the Umbrians near Vindex. When they turned to face the Galdeshan, the soldiers from Narbo Martius made their move. They charged in at the Umbrian legionaries with all their might. The sounds of swords clashing with shields echoed through the forest and as many trees were struck as soldiers.

Viridox, in position on the beach, could hear the roaring screams of the two factions battling. He looked at the sky and saw hundreds of birds scattering. He knew the time had come. Viridox turned to his men and proclaimed, 'The battle for Galicia has started! It's time to move out!'

Alesia reared, and Viridox squeezed tight in the saddle. When all her hooves were planted back on the ground, she sprinted down the coastline, kicking up the sand and the ocean water as she ran. Three hundred horse archers followed, all kicking up sand as they ran single file, following their leader into battle.

While Viridox and his soldiers were fast approaching, Vindex and his troops battled hard in the forest, trying to push the Umbrians back to the plains. They had one goal: to not let Umbria advance any farther. They needed to keep the legionaries enclosed in order to optimize Viridox's strike. Initially, the battle was evenly matched. The sneak attack had worked, but as more time went on, more legionaries entered the forest from the plain. With more Umbrians in the woods than Galicians, Vindex's forces began to dwindle. It did not matter that the terrain was hiding them anymore. Each Umbrian slain exposed the Galician's position. The Umbrians were relentless, using their fallen comrades to exploit Vindex's one advantage.

'Keep fighting!' Vindex shouted out, cutting down another Umbrian soldier on the forest trail. 'We can't let them advance any farther!'

Vindex continued his brutal assault on the Umbrian invaders. One by one, the Galdeshan pounced on his enemies. The thick foliage acted as an extra defense for Vindex, who used the trees to block incoming sword strikes before parrying fatal blows. Vindex rushed to the middle of the forest path, where most of the Umbrians were. He knew this would leave him more exposed to the enemy, but he needed to slow down the Umbrians from reaching his soldiers.

Hurry up Viridox, Vindex thought to himself as he ducked under an incoming swing from an Umbrian legionary.

'Die you scum!' an Umbrian legionary exclaimed, aiming to strike Vindex from behind.

Before Vindex could turn around, he felt a small push against his back. The legionary had stabbed Vindex, but Cato's armor protected him against the weak blade.

'How …' the legionary mumbled before coming face to face with Vindex, who turned around, ready to strike. As Vindex raised his hand to swing down on the soldier, the legionary let out one last cry before being slain. 'Emperor Valerik, help us!'

Valerik heard this scream from the other side of the battlefield. He looked over through the woods and saw a Galician soldier on the main trail leading to Narbo Martius. Valerik's eyes widened as he realized the soldier was wearing the same armor as the one from Trevonum whom he ordered Dara to assault. *It's him,* Valerik thought as he turned his attention to Vindex.

Valerik slowly made his way through the dense terrain with little regard for his safety or for his own men. He watched both Galicians and Umbrians fall in droves and would not interfere in their skirmishes. He was determined to make his way to the dirt path where Vindex was fighting. Those who challenged the Emperor, though, quickly met their end by his blade.

One brave Galician woman hid behind a tree, waiting for Valerik to pass by for a surprise attack. Her name was Cróga. She was a woman in her mid-twenties. She was a widow and made a living in the local fishery before joining the town watch to support her child after her husband's death. When she heard of Vindex and this Umbrian threat, she volunteered to join his party. Cróga believed the best way to end this assault would be to kill the Emperor.

Cróga imagined what she was fighting for; her child, her home, and her country. She gripped her sword and quickly lept out from behind her tree and thrust her blade towards the Umbrian Emperor's head. While the attack was fast, Valerik's reactions were faster. He gently leaned his head back and dodged the attack, watching the sword pass within inches of his head. Valerik then grabbed the woman's wrist, crushing it. Cróga dropped the sword and Valerik pulled her body close to his. He grabbed her hair and pointed her head at Vindex, who was still battling on the dirt trail. Nine Umbrian bodies laid behind the Galician commander.

Valerik spoke. 'When you meet your gods, tell them the person who killed you was him, not me. It did not have to be this way.' He then took his blade and sliced the woman's throat, kicking her body down before continuing his march towards Vindex.

Cróga fell to the ground, grabbing her fatal wound. She watched the Emperor advance towards Vindex as if nothing ever happened. She looked around the woods and saw nothing but hundreds of Umbrian and Galician bodies scattered at every tree and bush. Cróga tried to stand, but fell once more. Her vision was blurring and she knew she was dying. She prayed for Galicia's victory and that someone would see her last message. She used her finger to write a message in the dirt before passing away. It read *To my child, Laoch. I love you.*

The Umbrian forces now had control of the battle. The Galician army had held the invaders from advancing farther into the forest, but they were losing numbers rapidly and without reinforcements, defeat was inevitable. Vindex looked ahead down the trail at the hundreds of soldiers who had not yet entered the woods.

Where are you, brother? Vindex thought, panting and out of breath. Vindex did not know for how much longer he and his soldiers could keep fighting. They would all fight to the last breath, but at this rate, it looked like an Umbrian victory was all but guaranteed.

Suddenly, the Umbrian legionaries on the dirt trail halted in their tracks and refused to approach Vindex. *Are they too scared to approach me?* Vindex thought. *After all, I did kill dozens of their comrades. No, that can't be it. What is happening?*

While Vindex was questioning why the enemy had stopped, he saw what would turn the tides of this battle. Viridox swiftly emerged on the other side of the plains, followed by his unit of horse archers.

One by one, the Galician reinforcements entered the field and quietly approached the Umbrians from behind.

Vindex screamed out to his troops scattered in the forest one last time. He looked high in the sky and pointed his blade upwards as he shouted, 'This is it, men! Hold the line! If you give up now, it was all for nothing. Keep these brutes from pushing forward and show them the true strength of Galicia!'

A tremendous roar came from the remaining Galician troops. The forest erupted with chanting, and Vindex could see Umbrian legionaries being pushed back to the plains. Vindex gripped his sword tighter than ever, invigorated from the knowledge the battle would soon be over. 'Why don't you attack me!' he shouted at the Umbrian legionaries staring at him on the dirt trail.

Vindex then felt something push against his leg. He looked down and saw a body of a slain Galician man with blood leading up a small dirt mound to Vindex's left side. On top of the hill was the mighty Valerik, his sword dripping with fresh blood.

'Vindex I presume,' Valerik spoke coldly, looking down on his foe.

'Valerik …' Vindex said with a snarl. His throat was tightening and his legs trembled.

'You have caused quite the commotion, Vindex,' Valerik said. 'You have started a war, killed my close friend, and left my most trusted companion with a nasty scar. This pointless revenge quest of yours ends now. It was truly a shame what happened to Brunos. You have my condolences for that, but I cannot allow you to live after all you have done. I hope you are ready to see your father again.'

Valerik took his battle stance while Vindex gritted his teeth. 'You self-righteous bastard,' he mumbled.

Vindex took his stance, ready to avenge his father and thought, *By my father's blade, you will die today.* The two most skilled warriors in all of Talamh were about to clash.

Before the two leaders could come to blows with each other, two of the Umbrian legionaries on the dirt trail in the woods collapsed face first. Two well-placed arrows protruded from each soldier's nape. Valerik looked to where the arrows came from and saw a force of three hundred horse archers barreling towards the edge of the woods.

Viridox led the charge. His face was serious and weathered. His bow drawn in his hand, he was picking his targets carefully, aiming for the most exposed Umbrian soldiers. 'Soldiers!' he yelled. 'This is where the battle ends! Keep firing upon the enemy until there are none left! For Galicia!'

Valerik scanned the battlefield and saw more and more Umbrian legionaries being picked off from the rear. He looked down at Vindex and saw the Galician smiling.

'This battle was over before it even began,' Vindex said proudly. 'Now prepare to die!' Vindex pushed forward, running towards Valerik's position.

Valerik only had a split second to think. He did not know the full extent of the enemy's numbers still in the forest and, with his flank exposed, he only had one choice. He opened his mouth and screamed at the top of his lungs, 'Fall back! Fall back! All units disengage! I repeat disengage!'

Vindex halted in his tracks when he heard the retreat order. He looked over to see the Umbrian legionaries cutting off their battles and retreating. Some ran to the meadow while others disappeared further into the woods. He then looked back at Valerik, who stood staring at Vindex with disgust.

'Until next time, Vindex. Until next time,' Valerik spoke before retreating with the rest of his men.

'No!' Vindex exclaimed, running up the hill where Valerik had stood. By the time he got to the top of the mound, it was too late. The Emperor was too far away to catch.

Valerik thought to himself as he ran back to Genitor. *How did they know I was coming? Could there have been a spy? Surely not. The only one who knew of our departure date was Dara. There would not be enough time for Vindex to have coordinated this attack. He also knew when I had first ordered Agis to siege Trevonum. Something strange is at play here and I intend to figure out what it is.*

Viridox and his soldiers continued to shoot down any retreating Umbrian they saw. 'Do not let up!' Viridox exclaimed. 'Keep firing until you run out of arrows!'

Valerik, ever aware of his surroundings, blocked countless arrows with his shield while running back to his horse. He mounted Genitor and began riding along the edge of the woods to avoid being ensnared by Viridox's forces.

Vindex looked at the fleeing Umbrians and yelled at his soldiers, 'The time is now! Charge!'

'You heard him, men!' Viridox exclaimed. 'Advance!'

The remaining Galician forces emerged from the forest, charging at the enemy, who were retreating in all directions. Many Umbrians were struck down as they tried to flee, but nearly four hundred managed to escape. Vindex burst out of the woods. His soldiers had collapsed from exhaustion. They thought the battle had been won and pockets of men and women were lying prostrate all over the grass. They had stopped chasing the enemy. Vindex realized his soldiers could not pursue the Umbrians, but he only really cared about one man – Valerik.

Vindex spotted Valerik riding his horse across the plain. 'Viridox!' he exclaimed. 'Shoot his horse! Do it now! We cannot let him escape into the woods!'

Viridox drew his bow and fired a perfectly placed shot. It was well on pace to collide with Genitor's head, however Valerik sliced the arrow out of midair with his blade as he fled. Vindex growled, angered that Valerik could block such an attack. Vindex pursed his lips and whistled, calling for Bucephalus, who was left on the outskirts of the forest on the side of the Galician infantry. The steed quickly came running to his side. Vindex promptly hopped on his horse and chased Valerik who had already entered the forest on the side closest to Trevonum.

'Brother, wait!' Viridox exclaimed urgently, trying to get his brother's attention before he ran off chasing after Valerik.

Vindex angrily retorted at his brother, saying, 'What could possibly be more important than chasing after Valerik! He is getting away!'

He then turned around to see what his younger brother already understood. Only about forty of the initial three hundred infantrymen and women survived the battle. The cavalry unit that Viridox had commanded, after seeing the Umbrians retreat, turned their attention to their fallen comrades. Tears were flowing through the eyes of every remaining Galician soldier. Vindex's army was composed of families, not just friends. Brothers and sisters, fathers and sons, all fought beside each other in the ranks. The bloodshed had been extreme and there were few uninjured survivors.

'I see,' Vindex replied calmly. He understood. In that moment, supporting his surviving troops, aiding the injured, and grieving with the families of the fallen was more important than his own personal revenge. He turned back to the tree line once more to find that Valerik had already escaped into the forest. The battle was over, but that did not mean the suffering had stopped. The two brothers got off their horses and made their way to the brave soldiers of Narbo Martius. Vindex felt incredible guilt for the pyrrhic victory he had led. Vindex and Viridox stood there in silence as they watched their soldiers go through the battleground, hoping to find their loved ones still alive.

Vindex had his victory, but Narbo Martius would not be safe unless Iodona won her battle against Dara. Many miles away, Dara was leading her men through the Cruach Mountains from the lead column, eager to engage in any conflict that may arise. The sun had finally set by the time her forces had come down the mountainside. She faced the dilapidated and abandoned city in front of her and put her hand up in a fist, signaling to her men it was time to stop marching.

'What is it, my lady?' one legionary captain asked her. 'Are we setting up camp here for the night?'

'No,' Dara replied with a suspicious tone of voice. She got off her horse and looked at the terrain in the bright moonlight. The full moon and stars lit up the land, as there was not a single cloud in the sky.

'Is something wrong, general?' the legionary captain asked curiously.

'I have a bad feeling about this, captain. That town there, there is no way around it. Our only option is to go through it. Is that correct?' Dara spoke rather calmly, contemplating her next move.

'Yes, my lady,' the captain responded, 'But the maps that we stole from the Trevonum war camp show this city has been abandoned for more than a hundred years.'

Dara looked to her side to see the legionary captain standing next to her. She spoke methodically, 'If that is true, how come we spotted two horses running around the settlement when we were still on the snowcaps? Never trust a savage, Captain. Bring the onagers to my position. I want to send a few fireballs into the ruin before going in myself.'

The soldier wasn't sure why Dara believed that the enemy may set an ambush in the abandoned city, but he would not disobey his commander's orders. He got the onagers to a firing distance of a hundred and thirty yards before loading in the seventy-pound stone balls each wrapped in cloth into the firing compartment. Next, he poured oil over the balls so they could be lit before firing. The Umbrians waited for Dara's command.

'We are ready for your order, commander,' the captain informed Dara, who had not moved from her spot. He noticed a sinister smile grow on her face as he awaited her orders.

'Something is wrong,' Emiscor said to his sister nervously as they waited inside the western stone spire at the gates of the city walls.

'I know,' Iodona replied. 'They should have been here by now. We can't risk exposing our position. We just need to stay vigilant.'

Emiscor nodded in agreement. With weapons drawn, Iodona and her troops waited for the Umbrian forces to enter the ruined city. Immediately after the pair had finished talking, there was a sharp, loud snapping sound from outside the city. It sounded as if wood was banging against a metal base with tremendous force.

'What was that?' asked Iodona.

Before anyone had a chance to reply, there was a ferocious bang against the tower's stone walls and dust and debris filled the air of the already unsteady building.

'What just happened?' Emiscor quickly asked in a panic.

Before Iodona could answer, there was another crash at the wall and a thud from the city street. Iodona looked out to see a stone ball wrapped in cloth on fire in the middle of the overgrown cobblestone road.

'We're under attack,' she said to Emiscor and the infantry soldiers with them, 'How did she know we were here?'

'Not important,' Emiscor replied quickly, as they all braced for another barrage. 'What is important is that we act quickly. Orders sister. We need them now!' he exclaimed.

Iodona froze for a moment, trying to decide the best course of action. Another volley came and hit the tower once more, as well as the surrounding buildings inside the city where her men were hiding. She then looked at the soldiers around her and said, 'There is no way Dara knows we are here. This is a precautionary barrage. Do not break formation. Brother, run and advise the archers to maintain cover. We cannot have the Umbrians see us and lose our element of surprise.'

'On it!' Emiscor exclaimed back as he ran up the stone spiral staircase which led to the top of the walls.

When he made it to the top, he looked down the staircase spiral to see his sister looking up at him. As he was about to step out onto the stone walls, he felt the tower shake once more. It had been hit one too many times by the stone balls that Dara had been firing. The aged and decrepit infrastructure could not hold any longer and in a split second, Emiscor watched as the tower collapsed around him. He instantly jumped through the door and onto the wall before the stairs fell from underneath him. He looked behind him to watch as the tower crumbled into a pile of stone and dust.

Emiscor instinctively screamed as loud as he could, 'Sister!' he listened carefully but there was no reply. Emiscor, fearing the worst, ran past the archers that he was supposed to order to remain hidden in order to get to the other tower, which had not yet collapsed.

Emiscor's scream was so loud, however, that the Umbrians took note. Dara watched as she saw a figure run over the walls, away from the collapsed tower.

'See captain,' she spoke, 'This is why we don't trust barbarian filth. Send in the cavalry. I want a brief fight.'

'Yes, my lady,' the captain replied as he ordered the cavalry into battle formation. Meanwhile, Emiscor had made it halfway down the adjacent tower when he ran into Odella.

'What is happening out there?' Odella asked Emiscor, who was pushing past her soldiers.

'Dara knew we were here. I don't know how. She is raining artillery down upon us and our tower just collapsed. Iodona was still inside. I need to help her. Without her, this fight may as well be over.'

Odella, seeing how the situation had gotten out of hand, ordered her men to vacate the tower and to guard the entrance to the city. The element of surprise had been lost. Odella and Emiscor looked out through the archway and saw the Umbrian calvary advancing. There was still time to fortify the city gate before the Umbrians arrived. They ran to the gate to rally the troops.

Odella, taking command because of Iodona's absence, yelled, 'The ambush has been lost! We need defensive positioning around the gate! I want spears in the first row! We need to slow down their cavalry. Archers stay on the walls and open fire now! The battle has started!'

With Odella's words, the soldiers that originally were hiding in the city buildings ran out onto the streets to fortify the position around the gate. As the troops fell into battle lines, it was abundantly clear Dara's artillery strike did not just affect Iodona and her small battalion. There were nearly a hundred soldiers missing. Iodona's troops never wavered.

They knew what was at stake in this fight and they quickly maneuvered around the debris left by the fireballs.

Emiscor and Odella were trying to move the rubble that had landed in the doorway of Iodona's tower while their soldiers were preparing for the cavalry charge. As they threw away the smaller pieces of rubble, they opened up a small opening in the debris pile.

Emiscor screamed in, 'Sister, are you there?'

Iodona heard Emiscor's voice and woke up. She had been hit in the head with a falling stone, knocking her unconscious.

'Brother, is that you?' she asked as she struggled to remember what had transpired. 'Where are my men? Where am I?' she frantically asked as she stood in the demolished tower.

Emiscor was elated. His sister was alive. 'Thank the gods!' he exclaimed. 'We need to get you out of there. The battle has started.'

Battle? Iodona thought to herself. Suddenly, a loud clash was heard. It was the Umbrian cavalry engaging with the Galician spearmen at the city entrance. The sound of combat triggered Iodona's memory. She remembered exactly what had happened.

Iodona examined the rubble blocking her path. She tried to move the granite blocks, but they were too heavy and were wedged in place. She moved her head to the small opening and said, 'You need to get me out of here.'

'Working on it,' Emiscor replied as he whistled as loud as he could. He was hoping his horse could hear him over the battle that raged on next to them.

'Why are you whistling?' Odella asked as she kept trying to move the larger stone bricks from the doorway.

'I'm calling my horse. There is no way we can lift this rubble, but with some rope and my horse …' Emiscor said.

'You'll break me free,' Iodona chimed in. 'Odella, I need you on the front lines. Slow the enemy down until I am out of this rubble.'

'Understood commander,' Odella responded as she drew her sword from her sheath and ran into the fray.

'Is there anyone else in there with you, sister?' Emiscor asked, hoping that some of her soldiers survived the collapse as well.

'It is very dark, but I don't think so,' Iodona replied as she surveyed the ground floor around her. The bodies of her fellow Galicians were lifeless, crushed by the giant stone debris.

'Well, at least you made it,' Emiscor said, looking around for his horse.

The battle at the gate became intense. Horses and riders fell to the Galician's spears as they tried to advance their position inside the city. When a Galician spearman fell, the archers on the walls quickly took down the advancing Umbrian. Victory over the calvary seemed inevitable, but the Umbrian infantry had yet to arrive. Galician soldiers looked on as thousands of legionaries marched heading for the gateway.

'Hold the line!' Odella yelled as she blocked an incoming swing of a cavalry spear. 'Remember what we are fighting for!'

This proved to invigorate the soldiers as they tightened their formations, causing the Umbrians to amass into a chokehold. The remaining cavalry units had no room to operate and retreated before the infantry could engage to support the ranks. As the few horses fled, one unfortunate soldier had the misfortune of running past Dara and the legionary captain that were dismounted and watching the fight.

'You there!' Dara exclaimed. 'Where do you think you're going?'

The soldier, terrified and exhausted, quickly replied, 'The Galician's created a spear wall. We had no chance. We will reengage when the infantry pushes past their chokehold, but for now, it's suicide for us to go back in.'

'Suicide?' Dara asked quietly to herself while staring ahead at the battle, not looking at the soldier at all. After a few moments of silence, she looked at her captain on the right and asked politely, 'May I have your spear?'

'Of course, my lady,' the legionary captain replied.

Dara took the spear, inspected the tip, and swiftly threw it into the cavalry soldier's chest, causing him to fall off the horse.

She then mounted the horse of the fallen Umbrian and turned to her captain saying, 'Well captain, it looks like it's time for a bloodbath. Wouldn't you agree?'

The legionary captain was startled and quickly mustered, 'Yes, commander, I do.'

'Good,' Dara said cheerily. 'I will see you inside the city.' She then set off to the battle.

The Umbrian legion had made its way to the front lines by the time Dara arrived to join the melee. The Umbrian infantry also was having trouble pushing through the Galician lines at the gate. Each time the Umbrian surged against the Galician lines, the Galicians were able to push the Umbrians back. However, the sheer numbers of the Umbrian infantry were taking its toll.

Meanwhile, the Galician commander had yet to be freed. Emiscor focused on the rubble in front of him. He saw the tower had fallen into the doorway leaving behind a pile of stone in the general form of a pyramid. If he could remove some of the blocks from the top there was a good chance that Iodona could crawl through. Emiscor grabbed a spear and climbed to the top of the pile. He used it to pry some of the smaller rubble from the pile while Iodona did the same from the inside. They were able to create small openings but there was one large granite block that could not be moved. Emiscor knew that if the large granite stone could be moved Iodona could escape. He ran back to his horse and retrieved a rope. Maybe his horse could pull the granite down the slope if only he could tie it into a net. They needed more time, something the Galicians did not have.

Several times Emiscor passed the rope through the small openings to Iodona who returned the rope until a makeshift net was nearing completion.

'We're almost there,' Emiscor said. 'Just a few more loops. Make sure it is completely secure.' He passed the rope yet again to Iodona, who passed it back underneath the stone through a different, smaller opening.

'We need to hurry,' she spoke. 'Odella and our forces are strong, but I do not know how much longer they'll be able to hold their position.'

'I know I know,' Emiscor said as he grabbed the rope back from his sister. 'You are almost free, and the line is intact. You will be back in action before you know it.'

Dara entered the battle just as Emiscor finished tying the knot. She rode her horse ferociously, trampling over any of her own men who got in her way. Upon getting to the front lines, she removed her feet from the stirrups and squatted carefully on the back of the borrowed horse. She jumped up from her squatting position and soared over the first three lines of soldiers, landing on an unsuspecting swordsman in the rear of the Galician lines, while the horse was impaled on Galician spears.

She immediately impaled the disoriented swordsman. She then spread terror as she sliced and cut the soldiers directly around her with ferocious strikes. The surrounding Galicians were no match for her blood thirst. She cut exposed lower legs, stabbed swordsmen in the back and slit throats, all while blocking any counter attacks the Galician soldiers offered. Dara drew the attention of every soldier on the battlefield, including Emiscor and Odella.

This distraction gave the Umbrian legionaries the perfect opportunity to push through the distracted Galician spearmen. Emiscor looked on as the Umbrian legionaries slowly made their way through the bottleneck at the gate. *Things are getting bad,* Emiscor thought to himself. *I need to act fast.*

Iodona would need to be freed if the battle was going to be won. Emiscor ran down the rubble pile and placed the lasso he created over the head of his horse. While doing so, though, he unintentionally piqued Dara's interests. She saw Emiscor and his efforts to free the rubble from the tower and wanted to know why. Dara saw her legionaries pushing through the Galician lines and believing that the Umbrian soldiers would be fine without her support; she made her way towards Emiscor's position. One by one, Galician soldiers would get in her way, striking with their blades and axes, and one by one, they would fall by Dara's wicked hand.

Emiscor saw this advance and panicked. He yelled nervously, 'Odella! I need some help!'

He slapped his horse trying to get it to move the granite block. Odella turned to see the situation. Emiscor was pulling on the rope with his steed, trying to move the rubble, while Dara inched closer and closer to him with every passing second. Odella disengaged from her fight and returned to Emiscor's side. Their line was still holding and without Dara decimating the back rows, they stood strong, halting the Umbrians' progress into the city.

'I'm here,' Odella said as she stood in between Emiscor and Dara. 'Just get Iodona free quickly.'

'We're trying!' Emiscor said as he pulled on the rope along with his horse.

'You two look like you're doing something really important,' Dara said menacingly as she cut down the final swordsman that stood in her path to Odella and Emiscor. 'It would be a shame if someone stopped it now, wouldn't it?'

Odella dug her feet into the dirt ground and took her battle stance. She had seen what this Umbrian could do, and she knew she was no match, but she stood ready to die if it bought enough time for her commander to break free. Iodona was the only chance they had to stop this monster and Odella knew it.

Dara charged Odella, causing her to fall back four paces just to keep out of the reach of the Umbrian's swings. Odella regained her footing and pushed forward with her shield, which she used to block an overhead blow from Dara. She then took her sword and thrust it towards Dara's chest. Dara easily blocked it with her long shield and laughed at her opposition.

'You'll have to do better than that,' Dara scoffed. 'That said, you are doing better than all those guys over there.' She gestured to the long row of bloodied, dead, and dying soldiers.

Odella grunted and took a few steps backward, trying to gain some distance between her and the Umbrian sociopath.

'Aw, you're trying to gain distance,' Dara commented. 'How precious. It is a shame it won't do you any good.'

The Umbrian then went back on the offensive, striking between the gaps in Odella's armor. Dara cut each side of her shoulders, cutting open the green tunic Odella wore under her iron armor. The inside of her wrists and the top of her thighs were also targets for Dara's assault. The Umbrian had already won the fight. She was just torturing her victim. Odella fell to her knees, arms dangling at either side. The sword and shield fell from her hand. The pain was simply too great.

'How sad. I was hoping for more of a challenge,' Dara said, purposefully making her face into a frown.

Emiscor looked at the tower and saw the block beginning to move. He knew his horse could finish the job without him pulling, so he drew his sword and shield and rushed over to Odella.

Dara was so focused on the satisfaction of the kill that she failed to notice Emiscor. Just as she raised her blade to strike off Odella's head, she heard Emiscor yelling, 'No!'

She turned to the right and saw Emiscor charging at her. Quickly, she kicked Odella's body to the ground and moved her position to face the Galician.

'Maybe you'll be more fun?' Dara said mockingly with wide eyes and an evil grin.

Emiscor had no time for her games. He swung his blade down with all his might, only to be blocked by the Umbrian's shield. Dara then pushed with her shield forward until she had backed Emiscor up to the tower wall where he was trying to free Iodona. Pinned and with nowhere to go, Emiscor hid behind his shield as Dara threw a fury of strikes towards the Galician. Emiscor blocked and dodged most of Dara's strikes, but with no way out, he lifted his foot and stomped it down on Dara's left knee. He used this brief lapse to escape from against the wall. He positioned himself between Dara and his horse.

Dara, now angrier than ever after being hurt by a simple barbarian, said, 'You are going to regret that.'

She then extended her sword to her right side and held her shield so that it was blocking her chest. While she did this, she sneakily grabbed the dagger she kept in her belt and charged at Emiscor. As she attacked, she feinted to make it look like she was going for a side swing with her sword. Emiscor calculated her attack and blocked the strike with his shield. Right as that sword clashed with his shield, a loud sound was heard to the side of them. Emiscor's horse had finally pulled out the large stone and it crashed down the slope of the stone rubble, creating a shroud of dust in the air. This distraction was the perfect time for Dara's sneak attack. She tilted her shield away from her body, exposing the dagger she held in her left hand. She then thrust the dagger into Emiscor's side, piercing through his armor.

Emiscor let out a gasp, as if all the air had been taken from his lungs. The battlefield seemed to slow down for Emiscor and he could hear everything very clearly. He saw Iodona release herself and stand tall on top of the debris pile from the collapsed tower, and could hear Odella struggle for her last breath. He saw his fellow Galicians pushing the Umbrians back from the gate and he knew all would be okay.

Dara smiled with an evil grin as she pulled the dagger out of Emiscor's side. Emiscor collapsed to the ground immediately. She then turned her attention to Iodona, who had both of her swords already drawn.

'So, you are who they were trying to free?' Dara said smugly. 'I hope it was worth it because it cost them their lives.'

Iodona was enraged. She saw her brother and could tell he was still breathing. Her only mission now was to end this fight quickly so she could tend to her brother's wounds. She slid down the rock pile in one smooth motion. 'You are going to pay for that, you bitch,' Iodona said angrily behind clenched teeth.

'We'll see,' Dara replied as she wiped the fresh blood from her dagger and put it back into her belt. The Umbrian leader then charged Iodona, who was steadfastly waiting for the assault.

Iodona knew she could not let her emotions consume her, as maintaining clear thinking on the battlefield is the difference between life or death. She needed to stay calm and trust her skill if she was going to win. She carefully blocked each swing of Dara's blade with her own and used the second sword gifted by Vindex to launch a counterattack. This measure initially failed, as Dara just grew more aggressive and took her long shield and smashed it into Iodona's face, stunning her. All Iodona could do was to hold her swords parallel to one another defensively to block any new strike that Dara may throw.

Dara laughed as she saw Iodona fall back into a defensive position. She spoke, 'I am the second strongest soldier in all of Umbria. What makes you think you can defeat me? You should just tell your troops to give up and surrender. If you do, I might consider taking prisoners.'

Iodona looked over her shoulder to see the development on the battlefield. While progress seemed slow, the Galicians were winning because the narrow opening at the gate prevented the Umbrians from taking advantage of their numbers. Iodona turned back to Dara and replied as she slowly walked in circles around her opponent, 'There will be no prisoners. You and your soldiers will meet your end in this very ruin.'

Dara's eyes darted in anger. 'You will die for your insolence.'

Dara took her sword and pointed it perpendicular to her long shield. She then charged at Iodona, but this time, Iodona was ready. Iodona spun past Dara's left and pushed the Umbrian, which redirected her momentum into the adjacent stone wall. After Dara collided with the wall, Iodona took her two blades and struck. Dara, who had lost her balance and was down on one knee, faced Iodona with her shield held high. Despite the unfair advantage, Dara was able to block the vicious blows thrown by Iodona. Suddenly, by instinct alone, Dara realized Iodona had again moved and was ready to strike her from behind.

Iodona stabbed her sword at the back of the Umbrian's neck. She wanted to finish this right now, but with a surprising amount of agility, Dara took her left hand, which held her shield, and slammed it against Iodona's arm, snapping it against the stone wall. Iodona screeched out in agony. Not willing to be beaten after all she had suffered, Iodona worked through the pain of her broken arm and used her free sword to stab through Dara's exposed forearm just below the elbow joint. Now Dara screamed in pain as the two soldiers fell over onto the ground.

'You bitch!' Dara shouted, looking at the blood run out of the gash on her arm. Still on her knees, she looked onward, seeing her soldiers getting pushed back by the Galician force. The defensive line at the gate had not broken. The battle was a stalemate.

Iodona slowly got up, using the wall as a support. Holding her sword in her left, and only functional arm, she walked over to her enemy, who had also struggled to her feet. She stared at Dara in the eyes with a rage Dara had never seen before. Iodona spoke mercilessly, saying, 'This is for my brother.'

Dara looked back at Iodona, who was about to take a final swing. Dara was bleeding profusely now and was quickly becoming too weak to fight. She needed to quickly take action. She dove away from Iodona's blow and rolled to gain space. At the same moment, Dara picked up a small rock from the rubble and threw it at Iodona with her uninjured arm. Iodona was hit in the forehead and was temporarily stunned.

The Umbrian leader realized she could not continue the fight in her present condition and took the opportunity to make a hasty retreat. She quickly got up, grabbed her sword, and ran back to the front lines where her soldiers were still fighting. The Umbrian infantry saw Dara approaching the battle line and massed on the right side to push the enemy back from Dara's escape route. The legionaries then formed a shield wall on the right side of the line in order to push the enemy back to protect the injured Dara's withdrawal. Once safely within the Umbrian ranks, Dara ordered a retreat. Slowly, the Umbrian soldiers disengaged, and the Galicians cheered in their victory.

Iodona had watched Dara's escape and the retreat of the Umbrians. Her arm throbbed in pain and she could not move it, but she was more concerned with Emiscor. He was still alive, but barely breathing. Iodona knelt down beside him and called out his name over and over.

Eventually Emiscor's eyes opened. He saw his sister at his side. He smiled, knowing that she had made it out of the tower alive. 'Did we win?' he asked quietly, his voice wheezing with each word.

'Yes, we did. We did,' Iodona replied with tears coming through her eyes. 'Now we're going to get you back home and fix you up. You'll make it, brother. Just hold on.'

'Its funny,' Emiscor said, coughing after each deep breath. 'This is the first time I saved you. I have to say it feels pretty nice.'

Iodona cracked a small smile as tears continued to run down her face. She replied, 'You can hold it over my head for the rest of our lives, brother. We just need to get back home. You are going to be fine.'

'We both know I'm not going to make it,' Emiscor said through his wheezing breaths. He lifted his arm to hold Iodona's hand. 'I love you, big sister,' Emiscor said before his eyes closed once more.

His hand went limp in Iodona's and the soldiers that surrounded them watched as their chieftain's brother died in her arms. The losses were many, but none were more personal than this. She mourned at his side for the next few hours while the remaining soldiers tended to the rest of the fallen and wounded. Eventually, Iodona stood up, ready to receive care for her own wounds. She asked that his body be brought back to Narbo Martius so that he could receive a proper burial. The soldiers obliged.

Iodona went back to a temporary infirmary tent that the Galicians had established after the battle. She was given a makeshift splint for her broken arm. It was only sticks tied with rope, attempting to keep it fixed in one position. Iodona was deep in her own thoughts when she heard a familiar voice.

It was the voice of her Captain Odella. She spoke with great concern in her voice. 'Chieftain, are you alright?'

Iodona looked to her side to see Odella wrapped in cloth and bandages almost all over. 'Yes,' she answered after a brief pause. 'I am still processing what happened.'

Odella understood what she was referring to. 'He saved my life, you know,' the captain said softly with deep respect for Iodona's brother.

Iodona did not take her gaze away from the fire that was inside the infirmary tent. 'I know. He saved mine, too. I just want to go home,' she replied somberly.

'We have a home to go back to because of him,' the captain continued. 'He will be remembered as a hero.'

Iodona's tone swiftly changed. She became passionately angered. 'I will make sure his sacrifice was not for nothing. Tomorrow morning, we go back to Narbo Martius. We will meet back up with Vindex and the others and take this campaign right to Trevonum. Dara is going to pay for what she did here.'

Captain Odella nodded in agreement. She was also angry with Dara after the way she had been tortured. The two stayed up a little while longer before falling asleep. They needed rest for the journey home the next day.

While Iodona was victorious in her battle, it came at a tremendous cost. Nearly a third of Iodona's troops lost their lives or were severely injured, with many finding their final resting place in the abandoned city. The magnitude of loss did not differ from what Vindex had experienced during his battle. Vindex and Viridox buried their fallen heroes in individual graves in the plain surrounding the battlefield. What once was a beautiful and peaceful meadow had become a cemetery with graves for the fallen soldiers each marked by branches taken from nearby trees. The pair walked back to the campsite, where they found the three-hundred and sixty remaining soldiers sitting around their campfires. Vindex felt their loss. He gathered them for the last speech of the campaign.

'Ladies and gentlemen,' he softly spoke, 'Today we lost many good men and women. They all died fighting for the belief that burns within us, the need for freedom. I know many of them were your friends and family, and trust me, I know what it is like to have those taken away from you, but this is no time to give up the fight. Mourn the dead, respect the dead, but do not give up the fight for those who died fighting for the cause. Soon we will march to Trevonum to avenge the fallen. We will avenge those who gave the ultimate sacrifice in the name of freedom. I won't talk anymore. Just promise me you will not give up the fight. Not for me, but for them.' He gestured towards the new graveyard before stepping away from the soldiers.

'Brother,' Viridox spoke softly, 'I don't know if I am saying this because of what has happened today, but do you think …'

Vindex cut off his brother as they both looked at the trail that led to Trevonum. 'Orla is fine Viridox. I swear. She has not shared the same fate as our fallen comrades.'

'Okay,' Viridox said, reassured, 'It's just … that monster is terrifying. Almost a quarter of our fallen were from him alone.'

'All the more reason we need to hunt him down,' Vindex stated bluntly, staring off into the dark tree line. 'We will free Orla and all of Trevonum and get justice for the dead. It's not just for us anymore. It's also for them.' He turned around to see the pain in his remaining soldiers' faces.

'So, what do we do now?' Viridox asked, looking for direction.

Vindex looked into his brother's eyes and simply replied, 'For now, get your rest, brother. I will tell you the plan tomorrow.'

As Viridox returned to his cot and slept, Vindex stared out at the army he led. He turned to the graves and saw nearly as many gravestones as the remaining soldiers. Vindex took these deaths personally, and his hatred for Valerik only grew greater. *They would still be here if it was not for that monster,* Vindex thought to himself. He stayed up all night plotting their next move. He wanted to end this needless bloodshed. The war needed to end, Valerik needed to die, and Vindex knew exactly how he was going to do both.

The Sons of Brunos Will Return.